A MEDITATION ON MURDER

A
MEDITATION
ON MURDER

A Helen Thorpe Mystery

BOOK 2

SUSAN JUBY

HarperCollins*Publishers*Ltd

A Meditation on Murder
Copyright © 2024 by Susan Juby.
All rights reserved.

Published by HarperCollins Publishers Ltd

First edition

Excerpt of Dhammapada on p. 144 translated by Andrew Olendzki.
Published with permission of the translator.

The excerpts from the Dhammapada on p. VII and p. 130,
translated by Bhikkhu Sujato, were sourced from https://suttacentral.net.

HarperCollins books may be purchased for educational, business or
sales promotional use through our Special Markets Department.

HarperCollins Publishers Ltd
Bay Adelaide Centre, East Tower
22 Adelaide Street West, 41st Floor
Toronto, Ontario, Canada
M5H 4E3

www.harpercollins.ca

Library and Archives Canada Cataloguing in Publication
Title: A meditation on murder : a novel / by Susan Juby.
Names: Juby, Susan, 1969- author.
Description: Series statement: A Helen Thorpe mystery ; book 2
Identifiers: Canadiana (print) 20230485510 | Canadiana (ebook) 20230485529
ISBN 9781443469524 (softcover) | ISBN 9781443469531 (ebook)
Classification: LCC PS8569.U324 M33 2024 | DDC C813/.6—dc23

Printed and bound in the United States of America
23 24 25 26 27 LBC 5 4 3 2 1

For my mother, Wendy

Painful is birth again and again. I've seen you, house-builder!
You won't build a house again! Your rafters are all broken, your roof-peak
is demolished. My mind, set on demolition, has reached the end of craving.
—Dhammapada, 146–156, translated by Bhikkhu Sujato

He who once was heedless, but turned to heedfulness,
lights up the world like the moon freed from clouds.
—Dhammapada, 172, translated by Bhikkhu Sujato

If the call comes, he can buttle with the best of them.
—*Stiff Upper Lip, Jeeves*, P.G. Wodehouse

PROLOGUE
ANTIGUA AND BARBUDA

It could not have worked out any better. Not for her, obviously. Things could have worked out considerably better for Trudee Burnett, personal assistant to Cartier Hightower.

The accident was intentional, but no one could have predicted the cartoonish chain of events that befell Trudee out there on the blue Caribbean water.

Kitesurfing is dangerous, but usually people sustain only modest injuries. They get dragged by their kites onto shore and torn up by bushes. They break their legs on driftwood. They crash when the wind gets gusty and unpredictable, or they end up getting dragged in and out of the water like tea bags being endlessly dunked when their kites go into a death loop. They don't usually die.

Any sport that involves being towed on a board while attached to a massive, partly inflated kite is going to involve an element of danger. Any sport that allows big air riders to jump high enough to clear a ten-storey building and downwinders to reach top speeds of over a hundred kilometres an hour is going to involve a degree of mayhem. People sustain bruises and abrasions. Sometimes they break bones. When things go really bad, people drown. Accidents aren't as common as they used to be, but they make for popular viewing on the internet. As a category, kitesurfing wipeouts can't compare with deadly car crashes or gruesome football injuries, but they get decent numbers on YouTube.

The Epic Kitesurf Crash Compilation got 1.2 million views. Worst

Kitesurf Accident Ever? 1.7 million views. Kiteboard Horror Costa Rica: 1.4 million. Kitemare! cracked 1.9 million views.

As luck would have it, Trudee's crash crushed them all.

Part of the attraction was the hours of video that had preceded it, every minute of which seemed designed to make the watchers at home jealous. The footage was taken on a one-week cruise on a ninety-five-foot luxury catamaran, outfitted with air conditioning, a captain, and a hot tub. They were all so beautiful and they lived the way other people only dream of. On the first day, they filmed their stops at various beaches and islands. Fans on the internet watched them diving and swimming, drinking and dancing, and partying with other wealthy, attractive people. Trudee, who was a little older and not so beautiful, stayed in the background, helping, helping, and helping. She was good at that. But on the second day, the wind finally cooperated, and Trudee was able to give them the kitesurfing lessons she'd promised, and boom. There it was. The perfect opportunity.

None of them had wanted to scuba dive, and try as one might, it was impossible to booby-trap a snorkel and swim fins. But messing with a kitesurfing set-up was easy. All that was required was jamming some sand in Trudee's harness release and using a nail file to saw partway through one of her kite's back lines, so it would break at a critical juncture, also known as a belt-and-suspenders approach to creating a wipeout.

If things went wrong and she got a little injured: fantastic. If not, there would be other opportunities.

Trudee never thought to double-check her gear, which was old and not well-maintained, because she was so excited about having her big moment in the spotlight. The others might be better-looking, funnier, and far, far more popular, but *she* was the only one who knew how to kitesurf. After they filmed themselves trying to get up, she was going to have her chance to show them how it was done.

All that had come to pass. The others had not had much success, in spite of her coaching. Then she'd put on an impressive performance while her new boss, Cartier Hightower, who was worth more than the gross domestic product of Antigua and Barbuda, filmed her. Trudee had sliced through the impossibly shining waters under the blazing tropical sun, doing things that looked, to the uninitiated, impossible. She performed tricks and jumps and, when the wind picked up, hung for a few seconds like someone for whom the rules of gravity were only a rumour. A person didn't have to be a contender for the Red Bull King of the Air competition to look impressive hanging from a kiteboard. Nor did you have to reach the elite level of the sport to have a wipeout for the ages.

The area around them was crowded with other boats, all of which had released their own windsurfers and kitesurfers onto the water. They swooped around the shallow bay on their boards, towed by their straining kites, and for the first part of her run, good old backstage Trudee, with her short, muscled legs and heavy jaw, was undeniably the star, at least until the line finally broke and the cascade of increasingly serious misfortunes began.

Was there any regret about what happened to her? A sharp sliver of guilt? Absolutely not. Trudee had proven herself an untrustworthy bitch who had the potential to ruin everything. She didn't have what it took to keep the secret for both of their sakes. Trudee was a problem and she needed to be taken out of the picture, at least for a little while.

A broken arm or leg would have removed her from the scene long enough to get through the rest of the plan. After all, influencing waits for no one. But, as anyone with access to a computer could tell you, instead of sustaining a break or two, Trudee had become the star of one of the most popular videos the sport of kitesurfing had ever produced. In death, poor, sad, striving Trudee got more attention, more fame, than she'd ever bargained for. She'd been removed from the scene for good. That turned out to be the ideal outcome. The lesson was to always aim higher. Always drive harder to the goal.

VANCOUVER

CHAPTER 1

Helen was closing the retreat for her employers, Mr. and Dr. Levine, their greyhound rehabilitation consultant, Dr. Levine's hairstylist, and their best friend from up the road, Mrs. Shelton III, who had the distinction of being the mother of the second-richest man in the world. The odd assemblage of people sat in front of Helen on their brightly coloured meditation cushions, except for Mrs. Shelton, who sat in a richly upholstered Bergère chair she'd had her driver bring from home.

"I invite you to take the blessings of your practice deep into your bones and then out into the world as you gradually reintegrate," said Helen. Then she rang the silver bell three times.

The five yogis let out long sighs and relaxed their postures.

"Amen," said the greyhound expert, who was Southern and couldn't stop talking for longer than forty minutes at a time. Her garrulousness didn't seem to bother the others. Mr. and Dr. Levine were people of unusually deep equilibrium, and the others, Helen suspected, were too busy thinking their own thoughts to notice or care what the dog trainer said.

The retreat took place at the Levines' home in West Vancouver. The meditation sessions were held inside the hall built by master craftspeople from Japan, hired by the Levines at great expense.

The Levines also had khutis constructed for each participant. The living and sleeping area in each charming little building contained a single bed and one chair. In the back was a small but exquisitely equipped bathroom containing a toilet, bidet, custom-designed concrete sink, Japanese

7

bathtub, and rainforest shower system with all spray types to simulate different sorts of jungle precipitation. It all had a vaguely Zen whiff about it, although the style of Buddhism the Levines practised was Theravada in the Burmese tradition.

All the guests enjoyed their accommodations, except for Mrs. Shelton, who'd taken one look at the khutis and said no thank you. Her driver and security guard escorted her home each evening so she could sleep in her own bed.

"I'll sleep in the second master bedroom," she'd told Helen, with zero self-consciousness. "Like some sort of renunciate."

Helen, who was the Levines' butler and a former Buddhist nun, loved that Mrs. Shelton was not one for pretending to be some sort of ascetic.

Helping her employers with their spiritual journey was just a sideline for Helen. Her full-time job was taking care of everything else for them. She made sure their various homes and estates ran smoothly and were fully and competently staffed. Helen travelled with her employers and handled all their social engagements and day-to-day needs. She used a combination of elite-level organization skills, love, and firm boundaries to keep all the irritations of everyday life at bay for Bunny and Benedict Levine.

Even though Helen was a highly trained butler and former monastic, the retreat had proven challenging. Helen had arranged for a number of high-profile teachers to Zoom in to give dhamma talks and conduct interviews, and their busy schedules had been tricky to coordinate. Then there were the complex personal requirements of the attendees. For instance, Dr. Levine's hairdresser, London, had a lot of highly specific dietary peculiarities and had diagnosed herself with a serious autoimmune condition on the basis of her fingernails.

"Ridges, Helen," London had said, when Helen asked whether she had any food allergies. "I think it's quite serious and a sign of deeper underlying issues."

Nail ridges, Helen thought, were more likely a sign that London was now in her forties. As a result of the nail situation, London had decided she could only eat meat, salmon, and berries, "like a bear." This was an issue because Buddhist retreatants usually take the five precepts when they go on retreat. The first of these precepts is to abstain from killing and at least refrain from harming other living beings.

"What should I do?" asked London when informed of the proscription. "My immune system simply cannot take another change."

"Well, you could not take the first precept," said Helen. She knew other participants were likely to have trouble with some of the precepts as well. For instance, the greyhound specialist was going to have a hard time abstaining from wrong speech, which was number four on the list of taboo activities. "Or we could find a way to meet your protein requirements without killing anything," she added.

"What about," said London in a conspiratorial tone, "if it was already dead before the retreat started and then I ate it?"

London's all-meat diet hadn't adversely affected her exuberant good looks. Skilfully braided hair cascaded down her back, and her green eyes glittered in a classically beautiful face. Aside from the nail ridges, she was a genetically blessed example of well-tended humanity, and she knew how to help Dr. Levine, a retired cardiac surgeon, reach the heights of her own aesthetic possibilities.

Instead of serving London beef and chicken and fish at every meal, Helen had the household chef, who, bless him, had not wanted to attend the retreat, prepare the stylist a nearly carbohydrate-free, protein-packed, but meat-free menu. London whispered to Helen many times, in violation of her vow of silence, how outstanding it was.

"Oh, bless your heart. This is just delicious. I think my nails are growing in smoothly. Oops. Sorry." Then London would make a key-turning motion at her lips, throw the key away, and glide off smoothly to do some languorous walking meditation.

While leading the yogis in walking and sitting meditations throughout the day, Helen was still receiving and responding to the endless stream of invitations, including one from a former U.S. vice president. The designer who would be outfitting Dr. Levine in couture for the season was in constant touch to set up the fitting schedules in Paris. The apartment the Levines were having renovated in New York was nearly ready for a walk-through, but there were questions about when the custom furniture would be ready. Triffon Whyte, famous for her Beatrix Potter–hued pastel sofas and chairs, was designing everything and was behind schedule.

Helen had wanted to gradually transition her employers out of the retreat and into the luxurious demands of their lives, but they'd insisted on scheduling a luncheon on the same day the retreat ended.

She would have preferred the Levines to have at least two days to process their insights and gradually reintegrate, but Dr. and Mr. Levine had invited Archie Hightower and his daughter many months before and they didn't want to reschedule.

Putting on a lunch for four adults was hardly a test of Helen's butlering abilities or Chef's culinary prowess, and everything was ready, but it was taking place too close to the retreat for Helen's liking. Shielding clients from harshness and inconvenience was the goal of every good butler, particularly those who also supported their employers' meditation practice.

Helen felt deep, abiding joy that she could use her skills as a former monastic and her abilities as a highly trained domestic professional in her care of the Levines and their friends. They adored her and she adored them, and she had enjoyed almost every minute of the two and a half years she'd spent with them.

By eleven thirty that morning, all the retreatants had gone and the Levines had retired to their rooms to dress for lunch. Helen carefully put the finishing touches on the table. The guests were due at noon. Helen had been informed that Mr. Hightower had "traditional tastes" in food, that the menu should not be too "refined," and that it should definitely include meat. Dr. Levine had not been able to provide any insights into Mr. Hightower's daughter's preferences other than to say that Cartier was a "delightfully girly girl." Helen, who was not and never had been a particularly girly girl, wasn't sure what that meant.

Helen and Chef had come up with a menu that started with a selection of crispy vegetables and small breads to dip in Chef's signature bagna cauda, followed by Spanish tortilla pie and roast chicken, a wild rice medley, a green salad with mint, olives, and pomegranate seeds, and a lemony pasta salad. Something for everyone, thought Helen. The Levines would not drink alcohol so soon after their retreat, but Helen had chosen a bottle of Dolcetto for Mr. Hightower, and Chef had conjured up a beautiful basil-and-cucumber-infused non-alcoholic drink and another one made with watermelon and strawberry for the Levines.

There was some discussion about the propriety of serving meat so soon after the retreat, but they decided to offer their guest what he seemed to require.

"Can we serve him a chicken that has died of natural causes?" asked Dr. Levine.

"We might have to delay the engagement, in that case. Our rescue chickens are remarkably long-lived, my love," said her husband.

The Levines were the anonymous benefactors of a farm animal sanctuary in the Fraser Valley that looked after chickens and cows and pigs and a variety of other creatures who'd had the good fortune to escape the agricultural industrial complex.

Helen was a life-long vegetarian, but even she hoped they wouldn't decide to serve a bird that had been partly eaten by a fox or run over by a tractor, and she was relieved when Chef had sourced one apparently so high-strung that it had died of fright during a thunderstorm. The rest of the details about its demise were sparse, but Helen felt confident it would be suitable for consumption.

The table was decorated entirely in cream and pink in honour of Ms. Cartier Hightower's alleged girly-girlness. Pale-pink stocks and white peonies ran the length of the table in small vases. The dinnerware was also pink and white, and the linen napkins were large and white, with the faintest pink pinstriping. The colour palette looked extremely appealing against the large Monet painting that hung behind the dining table.

Helen gazed over the table and was aware of her own intense feeling of pleasure at its beauty. She savoured the sensation but didn't cling to it.

Then, in her earpiece, she heard the voice of one of the security guards. "Hightowers have arrived."

"Thank you, Abbie."

Helen went outside to greet them and was surprised to see two cars approaching. One was a Mercedes sport utility vehicle. The other, a white Bentley. They rolled to a stop and Helen and the Levines' driver, Terry, waited with their hands behind their backs.

Terry was a wiry woman who used to drive race cars and now jumped show horses when she wasn't valeting or driving for the Levines. She approached the black Mercedes. A squat, balding man got out, shoved his keys at her, and headed for the other vehicle, ignoring Helen, who stood ready to greet him.

She'd just had time to register his poor manners when the driver of the Bentley struggled out of the front seat. He was a heavy-set man wearing a tight black uniform decorated, bizarrely, with dangly gold epaulettes, which made him look like a dictator from a small, broke country. Everything from his peaked driver's hat to his jacket seemed to be too small, and he was red-faced and unhappy in the way that suggested chronic breathing problems. He opened the back door of the Bentley and a young woman got out. Staggered out might be the better description. This must be Cartier Hightower. She had on a skin-tight bronze lamé dress and a head covering that made her look like an ancient Egyptian queen who had for some reason decided to wear a half-stuffed pheasant on her head. The girl's face was made up very dramatically, with the kind of extreme contouring that looked best on a phone screen and eyes that were accentuated with wild swoops of eyeliner. Her eyelashes were tremendous, even in the era of bizarrely long eyelash extensions. One of them had gotten tangled up in the headpiece, which had been knocked askew when she got out of the car. The dress was covered in a pattern of what looked like Egyptian symbols and decorated with random lengths of gold chain.

"Goddammit, Cartier," barked the short man, who must be the girl's father, Archie Hightower. "I told you to wear something proper."

The girl tottered in towering sandals with straps that wound all the way up to her knees, and tried to straighten her head covering. "Ha ha!"

cried his daughter, apparently delighted by her own predicament. "I'm stuck. Dad! Get a photo! I'm like seriously stuck!" She laughed uproariously as she wove around in circles, clutching at the feathered blob on her head.

"Cartier! Are. You. Listening?" yelled her father. "And no. I am not taking a photo of this for your social media. There's more than enough of you on the internet already."

Cartier was now screaming with laughter in a way that was somewhere between charming and deranged as she attempted to get the edifice on her head straightened out. She said several things that Helen couldn't hear because she was speaking into the mat of feathers that had somehow fallen over the front of her face—something about having taken part in a "Cher-athon" and more requests for someone to capture her plight on video.

"Should I take a picture for her?" Terry whispered to Helen.

Helen glanced at Cartier's father's thunderous expression and shook her head.

The girl looked as though she'd just come from a Halloween party, even though it was early June. In fact, she had the appearance of someone who'd been partying non-stop since the previous October.

"You!" Archie Hightower turned to his daughter's driver, who was being strangled to death by his dictator suit. "I told *you* to make sure she looked normal for this thing."

"Sorry, sir," said the driver. "I wasn't sure how to . . ." He didn't finish but instead looked at the unsteady young woman, who had now apparently caught her hair on one of the dozens of bracelets arrayed all the way up her arm and was struggling to free her arm from her head. "Do that," he concluded.

"I should dock your goddamned pay for this," said Hightower, staring at his daughter, who was bent in half and contorting herself into impossible positions in order to pull her arm loose. She was sobbing with laughter, and Helen found herself torn between joining in and worrying that the girl was going to do herself permanent damage.

Helen was about to go to Cartier's assistance when a sudden change in the driver's attitude put her on the alert that there was another crisis unfolding in the driveway besides the girl literally contorted by fashion.

The driver had stood up to his full height and was glaring at his employer. "Eat shit, guy," he said in a barely contained growl.

Archie Hightower, Helen, and Terry all stared, aghast. Even Cartier Hightower peeked at him from under her arm and stopped laughing.

"You can take this miserable job and blow it straight out your ass. I've got better offers. Employment Insurance, for instance. Welfare. Starvation. Any of them would be better than working for you."

And with that, he started to stomp down the driveway.

"I *paid* for that uniform you, you . . . *driver*," spat Archie Hightower, whose face was scarlet. He seemed to be having trouble knowing where to put all his rage.

The driver jerked around and glared at Hightower. Then with great difficulty and much grunting, he managed to struggle out of the dictator jacket. He let it drop to the ground. Then, alarmingly, he undid the top button of his too-small pants, unzipped them, and shoved them down to his ankles. When he couldn't get his pants off over his shoes, he sat down heavily on the driveway, pulled off his shiny black shoes, and finished removing the pants. He got back to his feet and stood, panting, in his rather jaunty black boxer briefs decorated with a bright-green monstera leaf motif. Then, to Helen's horror, he removed his dress shirt, with the effortful look of someone trying to get out of a wetsuit. The shirt, too, was dropped on the driveway, leaving his substantial torso clad only in a plain, white undershirt. And with a final flourish, he yanked off his driver's hat and hurled it toward Hightower, who stepped back, seemingly afraid to be touched by a garment worn by a "driver." The driver, looking a hundred pounds lighter, or at least emotionally unbound, rubbed at the deep lines the cap had cut in his forehead.

"The gaunch are mine. Same with the undershirt and shoes. The rest of it, you can shove wherever you can fit 'em." The driver bent over to pick up his leather shoes. "Okay, asshole?"

And with those final words, the former driver strode down the driveway, pantless and holding his loafers. He seemed, Helen thought, happy.

Helen slowly and deliberately took two steps away and held a hand over her mouth as she whispered into her earpiece. "Abbie. The driver is coming back through. Without his pants. Could you please arrange a ride for him? If we have a blanket, perhaps offer it to him?"

"What?" came Abbie's reply. But Helen didn't have time to explain. She needed to help Cartier get untangled, and get these guests into the house and settled before things got even more unseemly.

CHAPTER 2

When Helen was training at the North American Butler Academy, she'd learned that some of the super-rich did not consider the people who worked for them as equals. Indeed, some did not consider those in their employ as even fully human. She'd always felt grateful that the Levines, who were unfathomably wealthy, were also extremely kind and democratic to their core. They were people who acknowledged their privilege, enjoyed it immensely, and shared it widely. They were more likely to socialize with regular working people than other members of their rarified socio-economic class.

Helen had helped them to host multiple celebrations for staff and their families and for A-to-Z-level celebrities, as well as for a few guests of extreme means. Members of that last group were often alarmed at having to socialize with working people, but the Levines were the kind of rich people who set the agenda for everyone else.

The super-rich who took part reluctantly at these occasions frequently wore expressions like they had stepped in dog shit two seconds before getting onstage to accept their Academy Award. Their faces maintained rigid expressions for the duration of the events filled with housekeepers, cooks, dog trainers, staff from the local grocery store, and the guy who installed the floors, as well as financial advisors, doctors, artists, and Buddhist friends.

Sometimes the super-rich huddled together at such events, whispering to each other things like: "They really have the most unusual social circle, don't they?" and "Oh for god's sake, is that the *greenskeeper* from the golf course?" in tones that suggested a greenskeeper should never, under any circumstances, be allowed off the golf course.

"It's fine to be eccentric, but there are ways to go about it!" a certain kind of wealthy guest would hiss at the sight of some person they had in the past assiduously ignored as being beneath them.

Mr. Archie Hightower at first seemed to be that sort of person, but where the Levines' rich friends usually ignored staff and those of lower social standing, he chose to be actively abusive to everyone except for his hosts.

Helen escorted the father and daughter to a sitting room, where Dr. Levine waited. Hightower kissed Dr. Levine's long, sensitive hand, but even his attempts to be gallant came across as abrupt.

"Hello," he grunted. "Hello. It's, uh, nice to see you, Bunny."

Dr. Levine, an elegant Black woman who had retired from a career as a celebrated heart surgeon at age fifty-five, kissed his cheeks in the European way.

"Archibald," she said. "I'm so pleased you could join us."

Cartier smiled down at her phone.

"Cart!" said her father. "Bunny is speaking to you!"

"Oh, sorry," said Cartier Hightower. "Hello, Mrs. Levine. It's nice to see you." Her eyes kept drifting down to her phone, a fact that was lost on no one.

"CARTIER! TURN OFF YOUR PHONE!" yelled her father. "Jesus. I'm sorry, Bunny. I don't know what to do with—"

"I hear yelling!" said Benedict Levine, striding into the sumptuous sitting room. "That tells me my friend and colleague Archie is in the house!"

Bunny Levine, who currently wore her hair very short, smiled beatifically at her husband, who was six inches shorter than she was.

Unlike his wife, Benedict Levine was not instantly imposing for his good looks or his elegance. But he had the sheen of a man who is well tended and well loved. He had marvellous thick white hair, and he wore socks with his sandals, a sure sign that he was coasting along in the same post-retreat metta-filled bliss as his wife.

"Benny," said Archibald Hightower. "How are you?"

"I am well. And how is my beautiful girl?" Mr. Levine asked, turning to Cartier, who finally looked up from her phone. "Uncle Benny," she said, and for the first time, the girl seemed fully present.

"You look ravishing. Doesn't she, darling?" said Benedict Levine.

"Absolutely," said Bunny.

"She looks like she belongs in a Vegas revue," said her father. "Or walking the strip."

Cartier giggled as though he'd said something funny.

At Dr. Levine's signal, Helen invited everyone to the dining room. Helen was about to show Archie Hightower to his seat, but he shoved past her and heaved himself into it without a word, bent on pretending she didn't exist. His daughter ignored Helen not out of malice, but because her attention was again on her phone screen, which she stared at with an intensity that made her look like an advertisement for the dangers of cellphone addiction.

Dr. Levine raised and lowered her eyebrows at each new example of bad manners from the guests, but she remained gracious.

"Cartier, for Christ's sake, put the phone away during lunch. It's bloody rude to use it at the table," said Archibald Hightower.

The girl pulled her attention away from the phone screen with some difficulty, as though her eyes were attached to it with fishing line. She put it in her lap, so she could sneak glances at it.

"Off!"

Cartier rolled her eyes. Up close, she looked even more extraordinary, with her theatrically thick makeup and her outlandish outfit.

"So, my dear girl. I must say that you are the very image of your mother," said Benedict Levine.

"Thank you, Uncle Benny." Cartier smiled at him. She would be a most unusual-looking girl, even without the strange outfit. She had a wide mouth, large wide eyes, and a straight, prominent nose. Her skin was clear, and she'd removed her Egyptian headdress with the odd feathered mat on top to reveal huge quantities of dyed-blond hair.

She had a good figure that looked hard-won rather than natural. She had a short torso, long limbs, and a malleable quality that was at once interesting and, Helen thought, a little concerning. She was nearly pretty but not quite.

As Helen moved around, getting the guests their drinks and laying out the starter course, she caught bits of the conversation, which seemed to consist of Archie Hightower grumbling about the markets and the state of the world and the Levines trying to shift the conversation onto more pleasant or at least neutral topics.

"I understand your driver has just given notice," said Benedict.

"Him and the rest of Daddy's staff," said Cartier, finally looking up from the phone in her lap. "How many are left, Daddy?"

"Never mind!" said Mr. Hightower, face turning red again. "No one wants to work any more. Everyone is too damned sensitive."

"It's like Mommy said. There is actually a limit to how much abuse people will take, and Daddy's specialty is finding that limit for each and every person." Cartier laughed inanely. "Remember the pool boy? The one Mommy thought was so funny because he could hardly bend over because he was like eighty-five years old? How she said your yelling wouldn't faze him because he couldn't hear you?"

"Stop talking such foolishness," said her father.

"No. It's the greatest thing. The guy could hear just fine, but Mommy convinced him to *pretend* he couldn't hear so you wouldn't yell at him. Did you know the pool boy and Mommy used to play canasta when you weren't around? She super loved him. Danny. That was his name."

"Oh, for god's sake. Imagine socializing with the help," said Archie Hightower.

"We consider our employees family," said Dr. Levine.

"Well, they're not," said Hightower. "That's a damned good way to get taken advantage of."

"It's also a good way to keep valuable employees and create a wider sense of compassion," said Benedict Levine.

"We just finished a retreat led by our beloved Helen," said Bunny

Levine. "One of the best retreats we've ever attended, and it took place right here in our own home."

"Well, it wasn't *in* the house, per se," said Benedict. "We've created our own mediation space. You must come see it. It was a very deep experience, wasn't it, my darling?" He took his wife's hand in his.

The Hightowers stared wistfully at this display of affection. Helen wondered where Mrs. Hightower was.

"We sat with staff and friends, and Mrs. Shelton joined us."

"Really?" said Archie Hightower. "A Shelton is willing to pretend she's one with the common people?"

"Mrs. Shelton's grandparents started out running a small greengrocer," said Benedict. "Before they were the Real Foods empire. She has never forgotten her roots."

"A pittance compared to what that son of hers has made," said Hightower. "If I had to do it over again, *I* would have gotten into hedge funds and pharmaceuticals and defense contracting."

"You certainly have the temperament for those things. Especially defense contracting," said Benedict, evenly.

"Goddamned right I do," growled Archie Hightower. "But I ended up in shipping."

"What was your first job?" asked Bunny Levine, pouring herself a lemon water.

"Worked on the docks," said Archie Hightower. "And some people never let me forget it. And look at me now. I own the whole fleet. And a lot more besides."

Helen left the table and came back to set down the trays of vegetables for the bagna cauda. Each diner was given their own dipping pot with a small candle underneath to keep the sauce warm.

"What is this?" asked Archie Hightower.

"Bagna cauda," said Bunny Levine, in a voice that had commanded hundreds of nurses and other hospital staff to follow her directions.

"Fine," said Archie. He frowned at the sauce and pushed it aside. Then he shoved a carrot into his mouth and crunched it with grim displeasure.

Cartier began to heedlessly plunge her vegetables into the sauce. "It's so good. I love it!" she said on one of the rare occasions she looked up from the phone in her lap. "Could I have more bread?"

"Of course, dearest," said Bunny Levine.

Cartier cocked her head to the side. "Oh, no. Actually, I better not. Ugh. You know?" She patted her stomach, then looked at Dr. Levine. "Or maybe you don't know."

"You look gorgeous," said Benedict. "Doesn't she, darling?"

"That dress is too tight," said Cartier's father. "It's barely decent."

Cartier stared down at herself as though surprised to find that she had a body.

"It's a beautiful colour on you," said Dr. Levine. "And you look magnificently zaftig."

"That's it exactly," said Mr. Levine to his wife. "You always have the right words."

"Um, does *zaftig* mean fat?" asked Cartier.

"How do you not know this?" said her father. "Too much time on the internet. Not enough time reading books."

"Like you read books, Daddy."

Helen could sense her employers' equilibriums slipping. She found herself wanting to get the lunch over so she could re-establish the protection of silence and calm around them.

Dr. and Mr. Levine continued to try to steer the conversation away from vexing topics. They exclaimed over the bagna cauda and enjoyed the small slices of focaccia with the perfectly toothy, salty crusts.

"Helen, you must tell Chef he's a genius," said Mr. Levine.

"Truly," added Dr. Levine, before exchanging a look of mutual adoration with her husband. They were so in love it sometimes took people by surprise, and Helen had heard more than a few guests comment bitterly at their bond when they thought no one could hear. Helen understood that for some who did not have such a strong and intimate romantic connection with a partner, watching Dr. and Mr. Levine was probably like being a starving person peering through a window at a magnificent feast.

Helen found the couple not just admirable, but heartwarming, and she wished, with her usual generosity, that everyone who so desired could have such good karma.

It was clear that Archie Hightower did not share her feelings. He seemed almost repelled by his hosts' small displays of affection. Indeed, affectionate gestures seemed well outside his interactive repertoire.

The Levines' new housekeeper, Mariska, a diffident young woman Helen was training, set down the heavy white plates containing slices of Spanish tortilla pie in front of each diner, while Helen placed the dead-of-natural-causes roast chicken, already sliced, in front of Mr. Levine to serve.

Archie Hightower stared at the pie, and once again his high colour returned. He had a concerning yellowish-grey cast to his skin when he wasn't red with rage.

"Girl!" he said to Mariska, who had arrived from Ukraine only six months before.

Mariska's large blue eyes grew huge as the angry little man beckoned her with his finger, which was as rigid with outrage as the rest of him.

"Is there dairy in here?" he asked.

Mariska was too afraid to answer, so Helen took over.

"Yes, sir," she said, coming to stand beside the young woman and gradually and imperceptibly moving her out of the way of the storm she could sense was coming.

"What is it about 'allergic to dairy' that you don't understand," he said. "Huh? If I eat this, I'll be shitting all night. How hard is it to get basic directions right?"

Helen had not been informed that Hightower had a dairy allergy. She'd called his house, and the person who answered had assured her that he had no dietary restrictions whatsoever and that he was particularly fond of dairy. Dr. Levine had told her that Hightower preferred simple food. To Helen, it didn't get much more simple than Spanish pie.

"I'm sorry, sir," said Helen. She picked up his plate.

"Are you people deaf or just stupid?" he persisted. "How hard is it to get directions right?"

This was too much for Bunny Levine. "Archie, you may not speak to any member of our staff in that manner."

"Yes, exactly," said Mr. Levine. "Let's try not to be such a towering asshole for the remainder of the lunch."

And something about the straightforward clarity of their words took the steam out of Archibald Hightower.

"Sorry," he grumbled.

The interaction had even captured Cartier's gnat-like attention, and she giggled. "Oh, Daddy! You get called an asshole at every single event you go to!"

Sometimes twice, thought Helen.

Archie Hightower looked straight ahead like a bullfrog who had missed every fly so far that day.

"Helen? You and Mariska can take a break, please," said Dr. Levine. "Benny and I will finish up." She smiled at Archie Hightower as though daring him to yell at her.

"May we collect the dishes when you're done?" asked Helen.

"No, thank you," said Dr. Levine. "We've got it. Please just tell Chef that we need a dairy-free alternative to the Spanish pie. Perhaps a nice omelette?"

"And toast," said Archibald.

"We appreciate you, Helen," said Bunny, and Benedict nodded.

Helen went back to the kitchen. She was glad for her employer's words, but she felt a deep discomfort about leaving them to serve and clean up after their guests.

As a butler, she had a near compulsion to take care of any matters, large or small, that her employers might need even before they were aware of that need. But she'd worked for the Levines long enough to know that they always meant what they said and enjoyed "slumming it," as Benedict Levine called taking care of themselves, even though they had a full complement of household staff. Helen had the impression that the couple treasured their time alone in the house and they liked doing for themselves now and then.

Helen kept her earpiece on, in case she was summoned, and she assured Mariska that she'd done nothing wrong.

"Will many people talk to me like this?" asked the girl, who still seemed shaken by her interaction with Archie Hightower.

"Some will," said Helen. "If you have genuinely made a mistake, all you can do is apologize, make it right, and then move on. If you have not made a mistake, most people just want to feel heard."

"Do NOT let these client peoples bully you," said Chef. "There are some real sadies out there. Don't ever let those peoples know they got your goats." Chef was from Greece and, Helen could tell, would last about ten minutes doing table service before he stabbed someone in the neck.

"Sadies?" asked Mariska. "Who is this?"

"You tell her, Helens," said Chef. "They are like the Putin Russians. Mean. Unreasonable."

"The word is *sadist*," said Helen. "It means people who get pleasure from hurting others."

At this, Mariska nodded her head. "I know about this kind," she said. "Very common where I come from."

Helen knew that this kind existed everywhere.

Chef whipped together a perfect herbed omelette without cheese or butter and Helen brought it to the table. When she tried to offer fresh coffee, she was waved away by the Levines. She noticed that Cartier wasn't even trying to hide her phone use anymore.

A few minutes after Helen had returned to the kitchen, Dr. and Mr. Levine entered the enormous space together with the air of sixth-graders escaping an extended and unwelcome session of dodge ball.

"We're here to 'get the desserts,'" said Benedict Levine, widening his eyes and putting air quotes around his words. "Right, darling?"

"Oh yes," said Dr. Levine. "It's unfortunate that they are not quite ready, and we'll be forced to hang out here with you all while Chef finishes."

At this, Chef's head reared up in alarm.

"Is not true, Dr. Levines! The desserts are here! Including a no-dairies version!" He pointed at three slices of white cake with dark icing and a magnificent pavlova topped with coconut cream and berries.

"What sort of cake is that, Visilis?" asked Dr. Levine.

"The cake is a tres leches! Made specials for today."

"As in three-milk cake?" asked Dr. Levine, who was clearly struggling to keep a straight face.

"As in the most dairy-filled thing imaginable other than a cheese platter and a side of whipped cream," said her husband. "It all looks fantastic."

"Yes, and since news just now comes to me of this allergen to good dairy, I bring out a pavlova I made last night."

"I see. And there's no dairy in the whipped topping?" asked Dr. Levine. "Amusing as it is that we nearly served him a dairy-filled dessert, I think the poor man really is allergic."

"Coconut cream. Light as starving cloud," said Visilis, which made everyone stare at him. "And the pavlovas have only eggs whites. No cows, eggs!"

"Okay, well, it all looks superb," said Dr. Levine. "But I think we'll hang out here for a few minutes. If you don't mind."

Visilis was unsettled by their presence. "What can I feed you during your visit to my kitchen that you have hired me to run like well-oiled gear shift?" he said, throwing out his arms grandly to encompass the huge kitchen.

"Oh dear, Visilis. You are too kind, but we are very full and happy already," said Dr. Levine.

"And may I say, your food during the retreat was ambrosial," added Benedict Levine.

The two of them seemed inclined to stay awhile. They looked like satisfied cats as they perched on two of the tall stools arrayed behind the huge island with the eight burners and two sinks.

"I should really learn to cook, shouldn't I?" mused Dr. Levine.

"No one makes an apple sprinkled with granola like you, my beloved," murmured her husband.

"The secret to making an apple is to use either Envy or Pink Lady apples," said Dr. Levine.

"Shall I check on the guests?" asked Helen.

"If we all stay away from dear Archibald, we are far less likely to have issues. It's when one goes near him that the trouble starts," said Dr. Levine.

"I have to say, I think he's mellowed since he lost Bonnie," said Benedict. "He was truly unbearable when she was alive. To everyone but her, that is. She was the only person to whom he was not a complete bastard."

"He dotes on Cartier, too. It's just hard to tell because his emotional range is so . . . limited," said Bunny.

Helen felt something close to a compulsion to check on the Hightowers. It wasn't just her butler training. Some instinct was pushing her to go to the dining room.

"Visilis, darling? Any chance of an orange juice and soda, with just a teensy bit of pomegranate juice?" asked Bunny. She was slowly swivelling her chair and showed zero sign of urgency to rejoin their guests.

"Mrs. Doctors. Of course!" said Visilis, and like magic, there was a small juicer, sparkling water dispenser, three perfect oranges, a knob of ginger, and a tiny carafe of fresh pomegranate juice on the acre of countertop.

"Please excuse me," said Helen.

The Levines smiled at her like a single happy being. "Of course, Helen. We know our benign neglect of guests is very hard on you. We promise to be along in a minute. We're just enjoying being away from them right now," said Dr. Levine.

"And we're enjoying not hearing anyone being abused by the thundering arsehole that is Archie Hightower," said Mr. Levine. "I apologize, Helen. That's not right speech, is it?"

Helen smiled.

"It's a damned good thing he has control of a significant part of the global shipping sector, because he's not winning any awards for . . ."

"Human resource management?" supplied Dr. Levine.

"Human interaction," said Mr. Levine. "And I say that as a hardened businessman who has been known to stake out a firm position."

"Oh, my love. You are about as hard as a blancmange."

"And twice as delicious?" said Mr. Levine, making all the staff look quickly away in quiet horror.

Helen took that as her cue to go back to the dining room, where she found Archie Hightower sitting alone at the pink and white table, looking like the saddest man alive.

"Sir?" said Helen. "Dr. and Mr. Levine will be back shortly with the desserts. I hope you and Ms. Hightower will enjoy what Chef has prepared."

Archie Hightower, whose body in repose radiated a sort of knotty tension, looked at her without quite as much ill will as he had earlier. "My daughter will not," he said.

"Oh?"

"She has buggered off. She got some sort of news. Had to go."

"Archie?" said Benedict, who'd entered the room holding two prettily plated desserts. "Where's Cartier?"

"Gone," he said shortly and stared at his plate.

"Is she okay?" asked Bunny.

"Apparently her friends have a shoot planned. She is in a panic that she'll be left out and so she took off."

"That's too bad," said Bunny, and her husband nodded.

"Cartier is genuinely terrified that she'll be left out of any of their boneheaded, pointless activities." Archie Hightower stared down at his dairy-free dessert wearing an expression of mute, furious misery. In spite of everything, Helen felt deep compassion for this man and his giggling, uncertain daughter. "She told me to say goodbye to you both."

The Levines didn't respond but just looked at their remaining guest with concern in their eyes.

"She's got these new friends. Complete morons," said Archibald Hightower. "Shallow as plates of water. Film themselves constantly. One of them just died doing something stupid. I have no idea how to make her find new friends. How to convince her not to be a nitwit. How to force her get some sort of a life for herself."

He sighed and the Levines laid hands on his shoulders, like they were giving succour to a dying man. Which, it turns out, they were.

CHAPTER 3

An hour after Archibald Hightower headed back to his home in West Vancouver, Helen was summoned to the study.

There she found Mr. Levine standing with his hands behind his back, staring at an enormous painting of his father, Lewis T. Levine, who had been president of the Bank of the Founders, one of the most prestigious banks in the world. Benedict himself was renowned as an innovator in the world of finance and as one of the finest minds in economic theory.

Dr. Levine, who had changed into cream cashmere lounge pants and a silk top, lay on a divan in the corner. She absently fingered an antique, hand-carved mala.

Bunny Levine had ineffable grace, a generous heart, and a slightly hedonistic quality kept in check by her rigorous training as a surgeon and her devotion to the easier parts of Buddhism. Mr. Levine, a secular Jewish man, had retired early to devote himself to philanthropy, relaxing pursuits, and his wife. They were in their late sixties and were as well matched a couple as Helen had ever met. They seemed to be coming from a place of almost limitless good karma and made everyone and everything around them feel good. They were also madly in love in a way that could feel a bit uncomfortable for those in their vicinity, including their grown children and staff.

During the retreat, Helen had several times mentioned the precept against engaging in sexual activity, but thought it was fifty-fifty that the two of them had failed to remain chaste in their individual khutis.

Now that their vexatious guests were gone, they were back to being languorous and beatific.

"Helen," said Benedict.

"Yes, sir?"

"You know how much we appreciate you," he said.

"Yes, sir."

"We feel so, so fortunate that you have come to be in our employ," said Bunny. "After so many years of flawless service from Fred, we could never have imagined finding someone so perfectly suited to the position as you."

Same, thought Helen, with absolute sincerity. She took in the large, elegant room with the floor-to-ceiling windows that looked out over a large pool and carefully designed grounds planted with drought-tolerant native plants. Paddock House, as it was known, was a multi-level masterpiece with tiered landscaping. Besides the new retreat facilities, there was stabling and pastureland for the Levines' small, well-cared-for herd of off-the-track racehorses. They also cared for a large pack of retired greyhounds, including six Galgos, the badly mistreated hunting greyhounds from Spain. Two of the lean grey and white beasts lounged at Dr. Levine's feet, and a third lay half across her lap on the divan while she stroked its narrow head as it slept.

Metta, the feeling of loving-kindness, and mudita, the feeling of empathetic joy, washed over Helen as she was once again filled with a sense of her extreme good fortune. She was indeed blessed by life and by her employment.

"We want to do something nice for Archibald," said Mr. Levine.

"Yes, sir," said Helen.

"He is *such* a difficult man," said Dr. Levine.

"An extremely rich person," said Benedict. "But a truly challenging personality. He needs help. I worry about his health. Spiritual and physical."

"Benny and I were reflecting on the powerful teachings we received on generosity during our retreat," said Bunny. "We feel moved to share our blessings." She bowed her head slightly and clasped her hands together again. The dog that lay beside her released a long, whistling snore of perfect contentment.

Helen awaited her instructions. She would arrange for a large donation to a worthy charity perhaps? Maybe they would send Archibald Hightower a book that might help improve his temperament? Recommend a top therapist for him?

Earth to Helen, she gently reminded herself.

"Cartier really hasn't recovered from the loss of her mother," said Mr. Levine, his kind face suffused with compassion.

"We're very worried about her," said Bunny, "and these new companions of hers."

"So we have decided to give you to her," concluded Mr. Levine.

"I'm sorry," said Helen, thinking she'd misheard. "Pardon me?"

The Levines nodded peacefully.

"Cartier needs guidance," said Dr. Levine. "A steadying hand."

"She could do with an infusion of wisdom," agreed Mr. Levine, levelling an adoring look at his wife.

A fire burned in the fireplace and made the room feel cozy on the unusually cool June afternoon. Or was the room a hair too hot?

"Wisdom, grounding, and help with her . . ." He looked to his wife for guidance.

"Taste," said Dr. Levine. "She needs some taste. And some judgment."

"Boundaries," said Mr. Levine.

"She's a very wealthy young woman already, and when her father dies, she's going to inherit a substantial fortune."

"Archibald is not well," said Dr. Levine. "There is no time to wait."

Benedict Levine shook his head sadly.

It had never occurred to Helen that she could be given away. That eventuality had not been covered in the North American Butler Academy guidebook.

Seeing the dismay that must have crept onto Helen's face, Bunny Levine broke into a rich, throaty laugh.

"Oh, Helen, dearest one! Not forever! Consider it a secondment. Benedict and I loved the retreat so much that we've decided to go to Nepal for a month. We would like to start a children's school. Perhaps more than one. We would also like to help in the ongoing efforts at earthquake relief. We're going to need you to find us a suitable architect and an educational consultant who is accustomed to working in the region. Both of them need to be able to travel with us. And please contact the consulate and let them know we're coming. The President will likely want to be in touch. It's been ages since we've seen him and his lovely wife."

"If we're working on earthquake recovery, we must also look at how we can help in Syria," said Benedict.

"And Haiti."

"You are absolutely right. We can always do more."

The two of them clasped hands and looked into each other's eyes.

Helen produced her notebook from her pocket and took notes.

"But while we're away, we will loan you to dear Cartier. As a favour to Archie and to Cartier. It is the greatest gift we can think of for such a one as him. But only if you're willing, of course."

Helen, whose equilibrium had briefly abandoned her at the thought of leaving the Levines, quickly regained a sense of balance as she made plans for her employers' trip and tried not to dwell on her new, temporary assignment.

Pain is inevitable. Suffering is optional. Resisting this new duty would only cause suffering.

CHAPTER 4

A day later Helen sat in Archibald Hightower's kitchen, where she had been invited to wait for the man himself to see her. She had been there for an hour and a half. The housekeeper, a stocky white woman in her early sixties, wore a starchy black dress and white apron, and the chef, neatly turned-out in traditional whites, spoke freely in front of her.

"What's causing him agita this morning?" asked the chef, a Black man who was probably in his late fifties.

The housekeeper, who'd introduced herself as Lou Ellen, shrugged and took another sip of her coffee, a pour-over the chef had handed her without a word when she'd walked into the cavernous kitchen.

Lou Ellen leaned heavily on the marble-topped island. "Who cares. I've got two more days and then I'm going to work at Waffle World. Better clientele." She scratched the back of her neck. "This uniform must be made of sawdust. I told them I was a size twelve and they gave me this thing. It's an eight."

Helen remembered the much-too-small uniform the chauffeur had stripped off when he quit in such spectacular fashion. Perhaps Archie Hightower made everyone wear the same size uniform, no matter what their proportions.

"It's from the girl who was here two housekeepers ago," said the chef, sighing deeply. "Is Waffle World taking resumés?"

"Damn right they are," said Lou Ellen. "You should get out before you forget what it's like to be spoken to like an animate object."

"It's just waffles at Waffle House?"

"Yeah, pretty much. They have like twenty toppings. So that part is going to be a hassle."

Lou Ellen, who had blond hair streaked with grey, got gingerly to her feet and began idly tidying up outside the chef's range. Her movements were efficient and practised. Everything in the kitchen gleamed. Everything in the servants' entrance had been spotless. The parts of the enormous house Helen had glimpsed had been absolutely pristine. And, other than the chef and some contract gardeners working outside, this woman was the only employee Helen had seen. Helen wondered if she was the one who'd told Helen that Mr. Hightower was a fan of dairy. Somehow she thought not. Lou Ellen seemed resentful, but completely professional.

"Have *you* looked into Waffle World?" the housekeeper turned and asked Helen, abruptly. "They just unionized. Decent wages. Good hours. And waffles are—" She shrugged. "Waffles."

Helen smiled at her. "I will only be on staff here temporarily. I have a regular position elsewhere."

"You think that now," said the chef. "This was *supposed* to be a part-time job for me. A way to ease into retirement. There is nothing easy about this place. Nothing easy about the boss. And now I'm stuck here. Full time."

The housekeeper nodded. "Seriously. Nothing easy."

Helen didn't respond. To do so would be improper. But she sympathized with them.

"I'll be working for Ms. Hightower," said Helen.

The housekeeper and the chef exchanged a look.

"Oh," they said, in unison.

"Hope your insurance is up to date," muttered the chef.

"Shush, you," said the housekeeper. "All he means is that . . ."

"She has a high-risk lifestyle."

"She has a not-smart lifestyle. But on the upside, she's not as rude and igno—" The housekeeper stopped herself. "She's less . . . difficult than her father."

"That's a singularly underwhelming achievement," said the chef. Then he turned back to the housekeeper. "I trained at the CIA. Not the spy CIA. The culinary school. I've worked in Michelin-starred restaurants. And I'll tell you now, I have been a chef for my whole career. But after this gig, I do not care about food anymore. I might *inject* all my food from now on. IV-style. That man ruined *food* for me."

"Oh, honey. He can't kill your joy forever. You come with me to Waffle World and we'll fix you up. You'll learn to love again. Waffles, at least. Don't you worry."

"Waffles are simple food. Honest food," said the chef.

"Frozen food," added the housekeeper, finishing her coffee and putting the cup in the dishwasher.

"I'll eat 'em with lots and lots of dairy."

The two of them laughed.

A text buzzed and the housekeeper looked down.

"He wants to see you now," she said. "Gird your loins, girl."

"Man the battlements," said the chef. "You got this."

Helen got to her feet and readied herself to meet with Mr. Hightower again.

〜〜〜

Even before Helen and Lou Ellen reached Archibald's office, it was clear that he was having a bad day. The sound of yelling could be heard well down the hallway.

"Come in!" he bellowed at the housekeeper's soft knock.

"Mr. Hightower. This is Helen Thorpe," said Lou Ellen. Helen admired the way the woman stood her ground in the centre of the plush wall-to-wall carpet in the impersonal but lavish office, despite Archibald Hightower's rage-filled face.

"Who?" he barked.

"Helen Thorpe," said Lou Ellen.

"Why?" he said.

Lou Ellen looked to Helen for an explanation.

"The Levines sent me," Helen reminded him.

"Oh right," said Archie Hightower. "You're the big-deal butler." He got to his feet and came around his desk.

This earned Helen an impressed glance from Lou Ellen.

Helen didn't respond to his words. Instead, she focused on his body, which still looked like a series of knots tied into a single big knot. His face was red, his shoulders hunched. He leaned slightly to the side, like he was nursing a sore back. He was favouring one leg. Bad knees, perhaps. Tight hamstrings. He was, overall, the very picture of unease. Perhaps even dis-ease. Helen understood why the Levines were concerned about his health. He appeared primed to have a massive stroke, followed by a heart attack and a grand mal seizure, as well as multiple catastrophic organ failures at any moment.

Helen steadied her breath and invited a sense of broad, emotional equilibrium into her perception. As she did so, Archie Hightower was transformed into a smallish man in a large room in an oversized house on a massive property. He was no more than one collection of agitated particles in an infinite sea of particles. The ability to bring a sense of equilibrium to almost any situation was one of Helen's gifts and part of why she was so well-suited to working with rich people, who had often lost all perspective and had, as a result, contracted themselves around their wants and perceived needs.

Something in Archie Hightower responded to Helen's calm demeanour. He seemed to relax, almost imperceptibly, and some of the rancour was gone from his voice when he next spoke.

"Bunny and Benny really like you," he said, as though the entire concept of really liking someone was foreign to him. "I, uh, appreciate you coming."

Lou Ellen was looking between her soon-to-be-former employer and Helen with amazement.

"I hope to be of use," said Helen. It was true, of course. Helen's primary directive was always to be of use.

"You can go, Linda Lou," said Hightower. "But you need to tell *them*"—he jerked a stubby thumb outside his window, where one of the gardeners was trimming a shrub with hedge trimmers—"to shut the fuck up already. We just lost another tanker and I need to think."

"Yes, sir," said Lou Ellen. She was still staring at Helen like she'd seen her perform a miracle along the lines of turning water into wine.

"Now," said Archie Hightower, but there was no force in the command.

Once Lou Ellen had stepped out and closed the door behind her, Hightower stomped over and retook his seat behind a massive, dark desk. There was nothing on it except two computer screens and a keyboard.

Helen stayed where she was. It was a Sunday, so Hightower was not at his offices downtown. But he was clearly working.

He stared at the screens and then seemed to remember that Helen was there.

"I don't know what to do for her," he said, finally.

Helen waited.

"My daughter. That's who you're here for. She's . . . she's . . . a disaster. You wouldn't believe the people she hangs around with. And she's tacky as all hell. I'm sorry. I've got all the taste of a whorehouse medicine cabinet and even I can see that Cartier is . . ." Words failed him, and he sighed. "I mean, she's seriously bad."

He seemed to realize that Helen was still standing, processing his charming description of his only child.

"You want to sit down or something?"

She took a seat in the chair directly in front of his desk.

"Not there, for Christ's sake," he said. "Drives me crazy when people stare at me."

Helen got up and took a seat off to the side of the desk in a plain office chair.

Hightower seemed to relax. She wondered what, exactly, his psychiatric diagnosis was. She was sure he had one. The Buddhist diagnosis of his personality was aversive type. That much she could determine.

"My wife, god rest her soul, died three years ago. We weren't, uh, ready. I guess no one is. Cartier took it especially hard. The two of them were close."

Helen listened for what he said and for what he didn't say.

His chest heaved and his facial muscles contorted. It seemed that Archie Hightower had taken his wife's death just as hard as his daughter and was working to keep his feelings under control.

"I'm an asshole," he added. "Benedict and Bunny might have mentioned it?"

Helen made no response.

"But my wife, Bonnie? She made up for it. For me." He nodded vigorously and Helen could see that he was trying not to cry. "She was a good person. Genuinely nice. God, that woman made me laugh sometimes."

He brushed a tear away with a knuckle, and his tense, fleshy face softened into that of a man deep in grief. He stared at the knuckle and moisture on it. "What the Jesus fuck is wrong with me?" he said, clearly baffled at the release of honest emotion.

Archie Hightower turned his wet gaze to Helen. "Are you doing this? Is this why Bunny and Benedict think you're the second coming of . . . who's that guy? The Dalai Lama?" He pronounced *Dalai* so it rhymed with *rally*.

"I'm sorry for your loss," she said simply. Compassion, real compassion, not pity, flowed from her in response to his obvious pain.

"Yeah," he said, and more tears leaked from his eyes.

They sat in silence for a time while Archie Hightower cried, softly and reluctantly, and then more freely. When he was done, he collected himself. From outside came the sound of muffled voices, and then the automatic hedge clippers fell silent.

Hightower took a shaky breath.

"I don't know how I feel about this," he said. "Am I going to cry every time you're around? Because I would rather someone shoot me in the face, to be honest."

Helen smiled. It was such a genuine thing to say. And somehow, just like that, she'd found something to like in the angry, sad man in front of her, just as there was something to like and appreciate in almost everyone.

"Your daughter," she prompted. "You feel she could use some help?"

Archibald Hightower breathed out a sigh. He looked less contracted. Calmer.

"Bunny and Benedict told me what you did on that island. At the retreat centre. How you gave all those bloodsucking leeches a test to find out their character and figured out who murdered the owner? That's a helluva thing."

He was referring to Helen's last visit to the Yatra Institute, just off the coast of Vancouver Island. She'd been a manager and meditation teacher at the Institute before she went to butler school. When the owner, Edna Todd, had died suddenly and confusingly, her will had asked Helen to come back to the Institute to determine which of Edna's relatives should take over the lodge. Helen had given the participants, who at first were almost as unpleasant as Archie Hightower, tests to determine their values. In the process, she'd uncovered a murderer. She'd hoped the entire matter would stay private, but word had spread around the butlering community and apparently beyond.

"I don't want you to give Cartier any tests. She'd fail everything except maybe Going to the Hairdresser and Advanced Internet Shopping. Her self-esteem is already garbage because she's so utterly useless."

Helen blinked at his brutal assessment of his only child.

"She really is," he said, catching her expression. "Her and all those so-called friends of hers. Influencers, my ass. They say they're a content collective, whatever the hell that is. The only thing they're collecting is likes from people who have nothing better to do. They have some ridiculous name. The DipSticks? Something idiotic like that."

"I see," said Helen.

"I would never speak ill of my late wife, god rest her soul, but she turned Cartier into her best friend. Bonnie never fit in with the swells.

That's what she called the people we met. Swells. We both came from working-class families. She had trouble connecting with other women in our social scene. When the money really started to roll in, she got more and more isolated. And Cartier couldn't seem to make friends with the West Van kids at school. Bonnie kept pulling her out. The two of them did everything together." He stared at Helen through swollen eyes. "I think my daughter might be *socially delayed*." He whispered the last words as though sharing a terrible secret.

Helen nodded.

"She's been lost since her mother died. And when she gets lonely, she gets . . . down. It scares me. When she's like that, she won't get out of bed. Won't talk, not even to the doctors I bring in." He sighed. "Then she met those little bastards. Now they're all that matters to her. Them and their idiotic internet stunts."

Archibald Hightower stared at his stubby hands as though to curse them for their helplessness.

"How would you like me to help?" she asked, feeling already the impossibility of the task. Right now, Mr. Hightower needed to talk and to be listened to. It was what she could do in this moment.

"I think what I want is for her to learn a few things about being a proper . . . uh, rich lady. Or even just a proper person with some self-respect. I don't expect a personality transplant or anything. I just want someone to help her . . ." He squinted as he tried to figure out what he wanted. "Grow up. That's what Bunny suggested. She said you were just the person to whip her into shape. Give her some depth."

Helen felt her sense of dismay grow, but her expression didn't change.

"Her friends are stupid as snails and they've started getting killed taking pictures of themselves in places they shouldn't be. And they shop. Sweet mother of Christ on the cross, do they shop. I guess one of them has some store or something, and they act like his spokespeople? How's that for a made-up job. I told Cartier that taking pictures of herself doing dangerous things is about the dumbest way to die I can think of. Why don't they just drop in some backgrounds! Hire a goddamned computer nerd to make it look cool. But oh no. She doesn't want that. Told me they had to 'keep it real for Insta.' Can you believe that? What the fuck is real about Instagram?" He sighed heavily and rubbed his face again. "She's got this idea they are all going to get famous and she's going to make so much money she won't need mine. Fat chance. She'd last about three minutes without my money. Now they have this agent representing them, and so of course she thinks she's on the verge of . . . something."

He let out a huge sigh.

"Anyway, I need to get her away from that world before she gets hurt or, god forbid, decides to marry one of them." He crossed himself at the thought.

Something on one of the computer screens drew his attention. "Oh, for f—" He glanced at Helen, and something made him not complete the word. "Tsunami hit one of our ships in the South China Sea. For Christ's sake. That's four thousand luxury automobiles for the fish to drive."

He didn't mention the fate of the crew.

"This will be the third ship we've lost since Thursday. The one before broke up off the coast of Nigeria."

He hit a button on his phone and began yelling at whomever was on the other end.

"You can tell them that we are not at fault! ACT OF GOD! ACT OF GOD!"

He hung up on the person he'd been yelling at and then looked at her. "So yeah. I want you to get her out of that influencer group, teach her some manners, and help her not to be so . . . how she is. Her allowance right now is two hundred thousand dollars a month. I know it's not that much, but she squanders it as fast as she gets it. When I die and she inherits the company, she'll have billions. She needs to be ready. And she's not."

Helen took a breath and centred herself. Something about what he'd just said had caught her attention. "Do you anticipate dying soon?"

He glared at her and then winced. "As it happens, I have just been diagnosed with a bit of cancer. Maybe it's going to take me out. Maybe it's not. Whatever happens, it's going to be unpleasant as hell. But yes, there is now some urgency." As he spoke, his face was working with emotion, though it was hard to tell what emotion it was, exactly.

Helen did not ask more questions. It was not her place unless he reached out for support. Instead, she switched back to the task at hand.

"Mr. Hightower, I must tell you that I can't do much if Cartier doesn't want my help. And there is a strong chance she won't."

"If she doesn't accept your offer, her allowance is going to go down to two thousand a month. That won't even cover her hair. You need to get her out of there. Out of whatever scene she thinks she's in. Get her away from those friends. And straightened out. Drugs are involved. I'm sure of it. If you look at the garbage she posts online, there's basically no other explanation that makes sense. There's money in it. For you."

Helen thought of telling him that payment wasn't necessary. She had a very generous salary from the Levines. And her former employer, Edna Todd, had left Helen a great deal of money in her will. Helen hadn't touched it. She was waiting for inspiration. Wise deployment of money was another thing she admired about her employers. They put their generosity to excellent use. They spent freely and with joy and discernment. And they did a lot of good.

"My daughter," said Archibald Hightower, "is interested in followers and likes. And handbags that cost twenty thousand bucks. She also wants a butt implant, but I told her I'd disown her if she did it."

"Does she have any other interests?" asked Helen, who'd never even heard of such a procedure.

"Butt implants," repeated Archibald, in his scalding voice. "My own kid. People die from getting those. And no, she doesn't care about anything else. Right now, being internet famous is what she wants most. Since her mother died, she has taken courses in perfumery, fashion design, and dog training. She has also gone to school to become a makeup artist and to study cooking. She has lasted no more than two weeks at any of it. My daughter is a deleteist."

Helen thought he probably meant *dilettante* but didn't correct him.

"The perfume school in Paris cost thirty grand for the term. She left after one week because she didn't like the teacher. I greased a few palms to get her in there, but apparently that didn't do her any good. Everyone else was already highly trained and she is just someone who spends entire afternoons fucking around at the perfume counters in Holt Renfrew. Like I said, a lot of this is my fault. Mine and Bonnie's. May she rest in peace."

Helen heard the voices of the landscapers outside. One laughed. A lovely sound. A songbird trilled. She made a note of listening. Mindfulness was about coming back, over and over, to experience what was actually happening.

"Does your daughter know what my role will be?" asked Helen. "Is she expecting me?"

"She hasn't returned any of my texts, and no, I haven't gone into detail about why I want her to come home. If I did, she might head for Europe or something. I thought it would be best if she came home and I explained the situation to her. I'll make it clear that having you around is not a negotiable thing."

This was perhaps the least promising position Helen had ever been put in. She wasn't an interventionist, a psychiatrist, a life coach, or a sober coach. She was a butler with a background in meditation. She didn't believe coercion was an effective method to create change. But something about Mr. Hightower and his lost daughter made her want to help, at least in some small way.

"Cartier is supposed to be home tonight. If she's not, get Lorna May to put you in the staff quarters."

Helen was stumped for a moment. "Do you mean Lou Ellen?"

Archie Hightower had reached the end of his ability to communicate pleasantly. He fixed her with small, red eyes, daring her to correct him again. "Lana Jane," he said.

Helen got to her feet. He returned to glaring at his screens and picked up his phone, presumably to scream at someone else about the ship and all the cars lost at sea. She quietly let herself out of the large office that, in the brief time she'd been inside it, had come to feel like a handsomely appointed prison cell where Archibald spent his days indulging his greed, hatred, and aversion, as well as his bone-deep set of regrets and sense of helplessness.

Unpleasant, thought Helen, noting her feelings, or vedenā, in that moment. The practice of paying attention to feelings of pleasant, unpleasant, or neutral in response to experience was one of the four foundations of mindfulness in which she'd been trained as a monastic. She also found it useful to keep her present in her life as a butler. Noticing feeling tone, as it was sometimes called, helped people avoid getting lost in mental stories about what was going on. Noting *unpleasant* allowed one to avoid sliding down the steep and slippery slope to disliking, aversion, and even hatred. She had the suspicion that anyone who spent considerable time around Archibald Hightower would get plenty of exposure to unpleasant.

CHAPTER 5

Cartier didn't return home that night, and Helen settled into the servant's quarters with Lou Ellen and Wallace, the chef, to wait. She learned about the house, which was mostly unused, and about the care and feeding of Archibald Hightower.

"He doesn't entertain," said Wallace, the next morning in the kitchen. "And he eats like . . ." Instead of finishing the thought, he rolled his eyes heavenward.

"He eats like a working-class guy who grew up on the docks," said Lou Ellen. "I'd never hold that against anyone. But him, well . . ." Lou Ellen had her feet up on a stool as she drank her coffee.

"Helen, have you checked out Cartier's social media, by any chance?" she asked.

Helen had not. She'd always had others handle the social media at the lodge where she'd been manager. There was something about online life that she didn't trust, even though she appreciated the opportunities to connect that it had provided during lockdown. She'd gotten quite good at handling her employers' Zoom requirements and joining her own meditation teachers' Zoom sangha on Sundays.

"We think you should look at it," said Wallace.

"Get some idea of what you're in for. If she ever comes back," said Lou Ellen, taking another sip of the coffee Wallace had made for her.

"I don't know," said Helen. "I think it might be best just to meet her as she is. In person."

45

"You don't want a bunch of preconceived notions," said Wallace. "That's very fair."

"You should see what she and her friends get up to," said Lou Ellen. "At minimum, you should know what happened to her PA."

"Her PA?" said Helen. "Ms. Hightower already has an assistant?"

"Had," said Lou Ellen. She put her phone in front of Helen, and Wallace put his elbows on the counter to watch.

Somewhat reluctantly, Helen looked at the video playing on the screen. Music floated out of the tiny speaker and Helen saw glamourous young people on a low-slung and sleek white boat. They waved from their deck chairs. They held up festive-looking drinks from a hot tub under a spotless white canopy. They danced. They dove gracefully into electric-blue seawater.

Then there was footage of large, brightly coloured C-shaped kites scudding through ultramarine skies, towing people who sped along on boards. The camera moved back to the boat, where one of the men, a handsome, athletic man of Asian descent, posed with a wide harness belted around his middle. It was attached to a line and a bar, with more lines that connected to a large kite that was inflated around the edges.

"That's them. They were learning to kitesurf. Or kiteboard. Same thing, far as I can tell," Lou Ellen said.

The women on the boat wore brightly coloured bikinis, and the two men had on trunks. They all looked fit and very lean, like models, except for one of the women, who wore a yellow bikini. She had a rather stockier, muscular build. She beamed into the camera, which moved in close to her. She was darkly tanned and rather plain of face, but there was a healthy, vital glow about her. She spoke directly into the camera. The wind made it hard to hear her voice. "I'm going to teach the Deep State to go so high and so fast they will see god." Then she made some sort of surfer-looking hand gesture at the camera. The video cut to the members of the party trying and mostly failing to get up on their boards attached to their feet as the kite was launched by a Jet Ski helper at the end of the lines. None of them had much luck. The kites would go up, and the person lying or sitting at the edge of the boat would try to stand up on their boards and almost immediately plunge into the water. The wind seemed fierce and gusty. Cut to the next person. Fall. Cut. Finally, the video showed the stocky tan girl. She didn't need the help of the Jet Ski. She tossed her kite, which was the same yellow as her bikini, into the water at the back of the boat and it drifted away. When the lines went tight, she gave it practised yank, twisted the bar, and the kite lifted into the air as she rose smoothly on her board. In seconds she was slicing confidently through the water. She wove easily among the other kitesurfers. Then she did something with the bar that controlled her kite, and she and the board seemed to take flight out of the water. She twirled around and then landed smoothly on the surface.

Helen was mesmerized. Only a serious athlete could get good at a sport that put one at the mercy of the wind and the waves. It was quite beautiful, at least until something went terribly wrong. The girl twisted in the air again; this time her body was nearly parallel to the water. Before she could get right side up again, she was yanked sideways. The kite itself began to plunge up and down, clearly out of control. The girl seemed to be straining at the bar in an effort to stop or slow the kite, but it didn't work, and she remained tethered to it. The camera began to move from side to side as though whomever was filming was trying to keep the girl in view.

The kite looped up and down and plunged in and out of the water, dragging the girl with it. She seemed to be pulling frantically on the harness around her middle, but nothing happened. Every time the kite went down, she hit the water, and she was pulled out again when the kite rose with the wind. Her kite hit another kite and the other rider fell.

Then the girl's yellow kite lurched out of the water, rose sharply, and then headed toward another catamaran, still pulling the struggling girl.

Helen put her hand to her mouth as the kite shot over the boat, dragging the girl along with it. She hit the side of the hull and was dragged up and over the hard top. As the kite yanked like a bolting horse at the lines that bound her, she was slammed headfirst into the mast. The yellow kite billowed out to the side, its rampaging progress finally stopped by the girl's body, which was stuck in the rigging. Her head hung at a terrible angle.

There was a scream from whomever held the video camera, then the video ended.

"Oh no," Helen whispered. She had never seen someone die in an accident before, though she had been present for many deaths. There was a terrible difference.

She closed her eyes for a moment and then looked down. She noticed that the video had been viewed over four and a half million times.

"*That* was Cartier's PA," said Lou Ellen.

"Did she survive?" asked Helen.

"Died instantly," said Wallace. "Broken neck. Poor kid."

"Completely horrendous. Cartier was a big old mess after that happened," added Lou Ellen. "People blamed her for livestreaming it. Said she shouldn't have kept filming. But I think she just made a mistake. She wasn't thinking. Not to be mean, but thinking isn't really her forte. Also, these people, Cartier and her friends, they film everything they do."

"They tried to take it down, but the video was already everywhere," said Wallace.

"I wasn't sure Cartier was going to recover. She took it really hard. And when she finally got out of bed and rejoined her internet group, she got in trouble because people thought she didn't mourn long enough," said Lou Ellen. "Her own audience seems to enjoy picking on her."

She scrolled down, showing Helen photos of Cartier and her friends at restaurants, at swim-up bars, in fancy costumes at parties, in dance videos. "This was all posted a few weeks after her PA died. The replies are brutal. At least, the replies that tag her," said Lou Ellen.

There she was in the odd ancient Egyptian outfit she'd worn to the Levines.

"The girl is in an abusive relationship with the entire internet," said Lou Ellen. "And she's got a few seriously hostile people who are always posting terrible stuff about her. They get taken down, but people just keep posting new stuff under different names. Poor kid."

Wallace nodded.

"I see," said Helen. But she didn't see, at least not clearly. Her mind was still with the girl whose life had just unceremoniously ended in front of her eyes. She wondered how Cartier, who'd suffered with the loss of her mother, was coping with the death of her assistant.

"What we're trying to say is good luck," said Wallace. "She's not a bad kid. But she is"—he widened his eyes—"a lot."

Helen wished she hadn't watched the video or seen the rest of the images documenting Cartier's life in the aftermath or heard about the people who tormented her online. But she had. And now she would have to be mindful about treating the girl as she was, not as she appeared in her social media feed.

CHAPTER 6

By nine o'clock the next evening, Helen was beginning to doubt that Cartier was coming back. Maybe the whole plan would fall apart and she would be able to return to the Levines having done her best. Maybe she could go to New York to inspect the renovation. See whether the furniture had arrived. She was looking forward to planning the first dinner party there. She'd already researched exactly which florist they would use. The invitations would be on robin's-egg-blue parchment with silver embossing. The guest list a mix of A-listers, interesting thinkers, and wonderful conversationalists, as well as people of profound spiritual accomplishment. In some cases, a single guest was all of those things. No one would turn down an invitation from the Levines, who were renowned for their entertaining.

Be here now, she reminded herself. That sixties-era saying, attributed to Ram Dass, was extremely handy for anyone trying to live mindfully. Especially an underutilized butler who liked to stay useful and busy.

She looked at Lou Ellen and Wallace. They were in the staff quarters, which were pleasant and roomy, with space for six live-in employees. There was a large shared living room and kitchen, and they had access to a small employees-only swimming pool and exercise room, which Helen felt was a generous touch. As unpleasant as Archie Hightower was, he went above and beyond certain workplace standards. His employees worked reasonable hours and got their required time off, as well as full benefits. If he hadn't done that at least, no one would have lasted a day under his withering abuse.

In spite of this largesse, Wallace and Lou Ellen were his last two employees, and they were as bored as Helen. As she'd suspected, they were also consummate professionals.

There was no way Lou Ellen was actually going to work at Waffle World. She'd been housekeeping manager at some of the finest hotels in America and had worked for one of the wealthiest actors in the world at his private island.

Lou Ellen, like Wallace, had come to work for the Hightowers when Mrs. Hightower was still alive and, in spite of her boss's difficult personality, she was still there. But not for long.

"It's not just him. The job is pointless. He doesn't need us," said Lou Ellen. "There is nothing happening here. He doesn't use ninety-nine percent of this house."

Wallace nodded his agreement. "He could hire a fry cook from A&W to cook for him and be just as happy. I could move to New Orleans and listen to jazz until I die. Just like I planned."

The three of them were playing gin rummy. Helen was winning. She was a fine card player because she had good luck and a balanced approach. No one ever minded losing to Helen.

"This is the most soulless house I've ever been in," said Wallace. "And I worked for Alvin Rooney."

"Who?" asked Lou Ellen.

"The guy who invented those weaponized vehicles? Now he was a piece of work," said Wallace. "Everything was white. I was the only colour in that house. It was unnerving."

Helen made gin and laid down ten cards.

"Hmmm," Wallace noted. "That was another one with no real friends. Never entertained. Just played on his computer when he was at home. He was basically a fourteen-year-old in a forty-five-year-old's pasty body."

The more Helen learned about the places Lou Ellen and Wallace had worked and the people they had worked for, the more she appreciated the Levines.

Helen didn't think she could stay for long in a house like this one. It felt and looked like a chain hotel in the off season. It had no character. Helen asked Lou Ellen about the decor.

"Mrs. Hightower had her own style, but it embarrassed Mr. H. He got someone in to 'fix' the house after she died. But he left her private rooms alone. You want to see?"

Helen did want to see.

Helen and Lou Ellen ventured to the end of the house farthest from Mr. Hightower's office. Lou Ellen opened a door, and suddenly they were in a whole different world.

"Imagine being a high school kid from Northern Ontario. You come from a working-class family, then you find yourself with unlimited cash. You can visit Vegas and buy anything you see. You love a good comic-con and all craft fairs. That was Mrs. Hightower," said Lou Ellen.

Helen could see those interests, that history, all around. The late Mrs. Hightower's personal rooms consisted of a bedroom, a dressing room, a living room, and, for some reason, an actual hair salon, complete with two hairdressing stations. The walls were covered in red and pink and green striped velvety wallpaper that clashed mightily with the gingham accents on the many homemade stuffed dolls and cushions that she must have picked up at her craft fairs.

Then there were the statues. Extremely bad ones of bodacious alien women and over-muscled creatures with extra limbs, as well as various spaceships.

"Look at this," said Lou Ellen, indicating a large model spacecraft in the middle of the room. The massive silver disc held up by a tall pedestal took up nearly half the open space. There was barely room to squeeze by it to get to the sofa. Lou Ellen hit a button and light poured from the spaceship's many windows, sending rays kaleidoscoping around the room. It also emitted a strange humming noise.

"The USS *Enterprise*. From *Star Trek 6*," said Lou Ellen. "And she's got the *Millennium Falcon* over there." That model ship was suspended from the ceiling.

It was all quite remarkable, if not remotely tasteful.

There was a lot of art featuring animals wearing Renaissance clothing, and extremely realistic wildlife paintings in heavy frames that went with absolutely nothing else in the room, except the craft fair gingham.

The furniture leaned toward velvets and black leather and glass. The countless pillows were covered in a wild mix of animal prints as well as the country-style patterns. There was a lot of long satin fringe on items that would have been better off without satin fringe.

"Wow," said Helen.

"Right?" said Lou Ellen. "I can't say I understand Mrs. Hightower's style, exactly. But at least she had some."

Helen looked around at the hodgepodge of clashing items and felt somehow cheered by it all. "Are there any photos of her?" she asked.

"Right here," said Lou Ellen. She walked over to an electric keyboard, because of course there was an electric keyboard. No grand piano for Bonnie Hightower.

Behind the instrument was a large framed photo of a woman who rode the fine line between beautiful and funny-looking. She was staring straight ahead, her large mouth fixed in a lopsided smile and a lot of luxurious hair nearly hiding her eyes. The other half of the image showed a younger Mr. Hightower in profile. He stared at his wife with something like wonder on his face.

For some reason, Helen found the photo moving.

"The woman was a bombshell," said Lou Ellen. "And a truly original person. I'm sorry you didn't get to meet her. She's the only reason I'm still here. She asked me to look out for Cartier, so I stuck around. But there's no point anymore. Cartier doesn't really know me and hardly ever comes home. And when she does, I don't know what to do for her or say to her. She hasn't been the same since her mother died. They were extremely close."

Helen reflected that Mrs. Hightower must have been very isolated if she had to ask a housekeeper to watch over her daughter after her death.

Lou Ellen's walkie-talkie sounded, breaking the spell.

"She's here," said Wallace, his voice clearly audible to Helen. "You better get her before her father sees her."

CHAPTER 7

Cartier Hightower was sprawled on her back in the echoing black and white foyer. She was surrounded by luxury-brand shopping bags and oddly shaped black equipment cases. She was struggling to get up, like an overturned turtle, and having about as much success.

She made no sound as she tried and failed to right herself.

"Oh, Ms. Hightower," whispered Lou Ellen. "Let me help."

"He can help," said Cartier, blearily trying to focus on Wallace, who sidestepped her gaze.

"I am not here," said Wallace. "In fact, I was never here." Then he disappeared.

Cartier rolled over and sat up among the bags like a limp marionette. In place of the peculiar headdress she'd worn to the luncheon, she wore oversized headphones, knocked off-kilter in her struggles, and incandescent orange lipstick, also off-kilter. In fact, off-kilter seemed to be her calling card. Huge sunglasses were pushed up onto her forehead.

She wore a purple one-piece velour shorts ensemble that showed the straps of a bathing suit underneath and pink-and-white-striped leggings that did nothing to steady her legs.

"Ms. Cartier," said Lou Ellen. "Can we help you to your room?"

Cartier mumbled some unintelligible things, followed by: "She's dead." Then she stared to sob.

"Yes," said Lou Ellen. "I'm sorry about what happened to your friend. That was a terrible thing."

Cartier's head hung down, like a rag doll's.

"You couldn't have known that the accident would be so serious," said Lou Ellen, crouching beside the seated girl. "Don't you worry about what people on the internet say."

"Not Trudee," slurred Cartier. "It's Blossom. She died. This morning. She tried to flex on us and"—Cartier twinkled her fingers as though to indicate rain—"she fell."

Helen and Lou Ellen exchanged a look.

"One of her friends," mouthed Lou Ellen in answer to Helen's unasked question.

"We weren't friends, but I didn't want her to die," said Cartier, sounding surprisingly clear.

Then she slumped to the floor, out cold.

Helen slid Cartier's arm around her and Lou Ellen took the other side, and they got her to her feet.

"Lead the way," said Helen.

They walk-dragged the nearly unconscious girl to the east wing of the house, which she had entirely to herself. Her bedroom was immaculate and impersonal.

"She mostly stays downtown," said Lou Ellen. "Her father had her room redecorated when she moved out."

They gently put the girl, who looked very young in her clownish costume, on the bed.

"Should we undress her?" asked Lou Ellen. "It's not really my place. I'm the housekeeper. Not a nurse."

"We can set out pyjamas for her for when she wakes up," said Helen. She was trying to stay present in the moment and not be distracted by what Cartier had just told them. Another of Cartier's friends had died? How? It seemed like too much misfortune for one group of people.

Lou Ellen walked into a side room and soft recessed lights turned on, illuminating an enormous dressing room and a walk-in closet. She came out with a two-piece pyjama set with the word *Gucci* stamped all over it.

Lou Ellen gave the girl a final pitying look and left Helen with her new client.

Soon Helen had Cartier tucked in under the white hotel-style duvet wrapped in fresh white sheets. She wouldn't leave her alone lest she choked on her own vomit or overdosed. Helen radioed Lou Ellen and asked her to bring Helen's first aid kit. She didn't mention that she was after the naloxone.

"Everything okay?" asked Lou Ellen.

"Just a precaution," said Helen.

Soon Wallace appeared, carrying the red canvas medical bag. Lou Ellen was behind him, pushing a luggage cart piled high with Cartier's things. As soon as they left again, Helen settled herself into a chair and waited. If the girl had OD'd, she was ready to step in. From the smell of things, she was mostly drunk, but who knew what else she'd ingested. Perhaps Cartier and her friends did the sorts of drugs that were killing so many people right now.

Cartier's breathing remained slow but steady. After a couple of hours, Helen determined that whatever she'd taken wasn't going to take her life.

Helen placed a baby monitor, which she'd been taught to keep in her butler's tool kit, next to Cartier's head. She could hear the girl's breath whistling steadily in and out. Then she made her way back to the staff quarters to get her quilt and pillow.

Wallace and Lou Ellen sat in the living room. Lou Ellen had a cup of tea and Wallace one of the sugar-free sodas he drank constantly.

"She okay?" he asked.

"I think so," said Helen. "She's sleeping."

"If her father finds out about this . . ." said Lou Ellen, who had taken off her scratchy uniform and exchanged it for track pants and a T-shirt. Her feet rested on the coffee table. "Or that another one of them has been killed, he's going to lose it."

"Does she come home in this state often?" asked Helen.

Lou Ellen shrugged. "No. She usually just comes by to see her father for a few minutes and then she's gone again. Wait! What about her car?

Did she drive here? Since all the security guards and the driver quit, there's no one on the gates."

Wallace closed his eyes. He had to be in the kitchen at 4:00 a.m. to start making the fresh bread that Mr. Hightower liked. It was nearly midnight.

"I'll check," said Helen.

"I can't go outside dressed like this," said Lou Ellen. "But let us know if you need help."

Helen left via the servants' entrance and walked around to the front of the house, where a huge driveway of paving stones culminated in a massive roundabout with an ostentatious illuminated fountain in the middle. A chewing-gum-pink Mercedes convertible roadster was parked across the paving stones directly in front of the grand entrance to the house. Both car doors were open, revealing a white-leather and wood-panelled interior. As Helen got closer, she realized the car's engine was still running.

She closed the passenger door and then got in the driver's seat and drove the car around to the side of the house and up to the six-car garage. Wallace stood in the harsh light of an open bay door and waved her in.

Helen felt a flutter of appreciation. The man had the instincts of a good butler.

The garage was full of luxury vehicles. There was the white Bentley, a black Range Rover, the Mercedes, a red Audi sports car, and a yellow Jeep. She'd just turned off the pink convertible and Wallace had hit the button to bring down the garage door when the voice sounded on the baby monitor. It was Cartier and at first her words were indistinguishable. She seemed to be protesting something. Then, clear as a radio announcement, she said: "I'm not that sorry she's dead. I don't care what . . . are you okay? Maybe I don't want to be here any . . ." Cartier's voice trailed off as she apparently went back to sleep.

Helen stared at the baby monitor.

Wallace, who'd come over to stand by the car, grimaced. "That doesn't sound good," he said.

No. No, it was barely intelligible, but it definitely didn't sound good.

CHAPTER 8

After spending most of the night with Cartier, Helen went to her own room and slept for a few hours. At five o'clock she got up, washed her face, brushed her teeth, and meditated on the floor of her room for an hour.

Helen was in the kitchen pouring herself some tea when Wallace came back to staff quarters while he waited for his dough to rise.

"What's the plan?" he asked, pouring himself a coffee. "You going to do an intervention on our girl?"

Helen didn't know what she was going to do, especially now that Cartier was dealing with another death in her friend group.

"I read about it online," said Lou Ellen, coming into the room in her scratchy uniform. "According to the news reports, a woman drowned on the Bartleby River yesterday. That's on Vancouver Island, near Courtenay. A dog walker found a camera on a tripod set up to video a waterfall behind a fenced-off part of the river. No one around. Then a hiker spotted her body downstream in a log jam. Search and Rescue got her out early yesterday afternoon. They think she was posing in or near the waterfall and fell into the chute below. Apparently, that stretch of the river goes from slow and meandering to a raging torrent in a matter of feet. Incredibly treacherous."

"Oh man," said Wallace. "Poor kid."

"They aren't releasing her name, but there are tributes to Blossom all over social media," said Lou Ellen. "She's one of Cartier's people. She was also in the Deep State."

Normally, Helen wouldn't listen to gossip about a client or anyone else. But she felt grateful for more information in this situation.

"I see," said Helen. "I'm sorry to hear this."

"People have a lot to say about it. How Blossom died, I mean. She had to climb over a safety fence to get to the waterfall. Her specialty was, and I quote, 'dramatic and unexpected swimsuit looks' and she was making a name for herself with POV videos. Whatever that is. It says here that she was known for rock climbing in a swimsuit, driving a race car in a swimsuit, riding horses in a swimsuit. In other words, she wore swimsuits where most people wore . . . not swimsuits."

"Pretty normal to wear a bathing suit in a waterfall," said Wallace.

"Not if there's a deadly chute right underneath that waterfall. One of the comments said that a source reported that she probably broke every bone in her body before she drowned."

Helen closed her eyes briefly, wincing at the words. She felt compassion for the lost girl and her friends and family. Then she remembered Cartier's drunken words from the night before. Someone had tried to "flex on us and she fell." What did it mean to flex on someone?

She fervently hoped Cartier had been nowhere near the accident and had nothing to do with it. Helen also wondered what this latest development would mean for her ability to help Cartier, particularly in the way Mr. Hightower wanted. She didn't know, but for the moment, she would try to respond in a useful way to whatever happened. It was an approach that had never failed her yet.

With that in mind, she tidied up the staff kitchen and presented Wallace with the breakfast she'd seen him eat the previous morning: two boiled eggs and a grapefruit. She passed Lou Ellen a bowl of homemade granola sprinkled with dried raspberries.

"Oh girl!" said Wallace. "You are precious to me."

"And to me. There's something about being around you. Even with all this sad news. I feel calmer. And I think it's you," said Lou Ellen.

"That's a kind thing to say."

"What goes on inside your head?" asked Lou Ellen, after she poured some fresh cream onto her cereal. "It's really nice in there, isn't it?"

Helen laughed. "I try not to take what happens in my head too seriously."

Wallace made a gesture like his own head was blowing up. "Who says stuff like that? It's like hanging with a philosopher. Also, thank you for knowing how to cut a grapefruit properly." He made a humming noise as he spooned a neatly separated section into his mouth.

"I'm going to miss you when you go off to tame Cartier and I start my career at Waffle World," said Lou Ellen.

"Have you given your notice?" asked Wallace.

"Going to do it today. Even though I sort of want to stay as long as Helen is here."

Wallace nodded. "Me too."

"We have decided that we really like you, Helen," said Lou Ellen.

Wallace and Lou Ellen beamed at Helen, basking in her presence. She beamed back at them. *Metta, metta, metta,* she thought, leaning into the moment.

The feeling lasted for about twelve seconds, until Lou Ellen's radio crackled to life.

"NOW!" yelled Archie Hightower.

The golden feeling vaporized, and Lou Ellen got to her feet. "On second thought," she said, "right now seems like a good time to quit."

~~~~

When they entered his office, Archie Hightower was glaring at one of his computer screens. He angled it around to face them. It showed the bubble gum–coloured Mercedes veering into the circular driveway and screeching to a halt.

He turned the screen back. Watched some more.

"Well," he said, as though waiting for them to explain.

Neither of them spoke.

That flummoxed him for only a moment.

"Your work with my daughter begins now!" he yelled at Helen, who was unused to being yelled at. She did not appreciate it. She was not, for once, leaning into the moment.

"And you!" he screamed at Lou Ellen. "Why wasn't I notified?"

Lou Ellen's professional demeanour finally cracked.

"You didn't *ask* me to notify you," she said, leaving off the "sir" for the first time since Helen had arrived at the house.

"It's basic common sense. Any fool could—"

That, finally, was too much for Lou Ellen.

"Thank you, that will be all," she said.

"What?" Again, the raging man was befuddled.

"Please accept my notice," said Lou Ellen. "Effective immediately." She placed a white envelope containing her resignation on his acre of shining desk.

"You can't just quit! I haven't replaced the other housekeeping staff or the driver. Or the security team."

Lou Ellen, her eyes burning with fury, held back what Helen imagined was a barrage of swear words. "Yes, I can."

"If you think I'm going to give you a reference after this, you can forget it," snarled Archie Hightower. "You can go clear rooms at a Super 8 motel out by the airport. No staff quarters. No staff pool. No benefits. Nothing but hard labour." He bit off each word like a dog trying to snatch someone scrambling over a fence.

"I'm sixty-two years old. I have saved more than enough money to retire comfortably. There is nothing you can do to me. Life is too short to work for assholes. Sir."

At that, Lou Ellen turned and left the room, and all the bombast went out of Archie Hightower. Sitting in his high-tech chair, slumped in front of his oversized computer screens in the vast, personality-free office, he cut a sad figure. Not the captain of industry but an aging toddler who needed a nap.

Helen waited. It was not her job to make him feel better. Her goal was to be of use, but she also had a healthy sense of what she would put up with. While she wouldn't have done things the same way Lou Ellen or the chauffeur had, she approved of the boundary both of them had set.

"If I had anyone on staff to do it, I'd have that woman escorted out," said Hightower, almost to himself. Then he sighed. "I guess I didn't handle that right. I just, Cartier. She . . ." He gave up. He was upset and had tried to take it out on someone, and it had backfired. He'd probably been doing that for most of his life. It must be, she reflected, a singularly miserable and isolating habit. And even though she loved the Levines and had already developed a feeling of responsibility for Cartier Hightower, she would not allow this man to abuse her.

He seemed to sense that. And he had just enough self-control not to want to lose one of the few people left in his employ, even if she was just on loan.

"Can you ask Cartier to come see me when she gets up?"

Helen nodded.

"Actually, would you be willing to handle some hiring for me? I need new security staff, like I said. And I guess I need a household manager, cleaners, a driver. Someone to look after the pools. And I have a feeling that the chef is going to quit too. So I'll need a personal chef. The employment service I was using has . . . well, they are not taking my calls."

Helen shook her head. "No, sir."

"No?" he said, startled.

"I'm afraid not."

There was zero chance Helen was going to hire more people to come to this house to be berated by Mr. Archie Hightower.

He huffed out a breath. "You're *just* here for Cartier?"

"That's right."

Something on the screen caught his eye. He waved a hand at her. "Dismissed," he said. And then added, "And, uh, thank you."

CHAPTER 9

Helen went back to the employee quarters and said goodbye to Lou Ellen, who was already finished packing and had changed into orange capris and a top with a fruit motif featuring slices of oranges, bananas, limes, and pineapples. She looked like someone about to set off on a cruise to the Bahamas.

"Retirement clothes," she said. She already looked about ten years younger. "God, I feel good. Maybe I'll move to Florida. It's just too bad that Florida is in Florida."

"Amen, amen," said Wallace. "Try Georgia. All the weather, only some of the Florida." He put a stamp on a white envelope. "Notice of my retirement. Effective tomorrow morning. I'm going to mail it because I can't deal with himself."

Helen felt a pang of compassion for Archibald Hightower, but departing this house was the healthy move. She looked forward to doing it herself.

After a round of hugs and promises to keep in touch and to not take part in any of what Lou Ellen termed Cartier's more "hair-brained" photoshoots, Helen went to sit outside the girl's room. She'd turned off the baby monitor and was simply being present. Hearing, hearing. Seeing, seeing. Thinking. She was always happy for a chance to practise Vipassana in her everyday life.

She'd just noted a flutter of cold and pressure in her foot when the door to Cartier's room creaked open. A head poked out, messy platinum hair partly obscuring the large, widely spaced eyes that were also red and swollen. Upon spotting Helen, still as the furniture on which she sat, the head stopped moving.

"Hi?" came a hoarse voice.

"Good morning," said Helen. She got to her feet but didn't approach. She was surprised the girl was awake before nine.

Cartier thrust the baby monitor in Helen's direction. "What the hell is *this*?"

"A monitor," said Helen.

"Great," said the girl. "I guess Trudee was right that we should all be scared of the surveillance state. Or whatever that is when you get spied on all the time because of the internet? I thought she just needed to change her algorithm. Getting a little . . ." The girl circled a finger around her own temple, her eyes still hidden by the masses of white-blond hair. She looked like a well-tanned Muppet.

"I was concerned for you. I apologize for invading your privacy."

Cartier sniffed loudly. "It has been an extremely crappy couple of days," she said. "My friend—I mean, my colleague. Well, whatever. This girl in my group? She died yesterday."

"I'm sorry," said Helen.

"It was like a terrible shock. And I may have"—she cleared her throat—"not handled it that great."

The look Helen gave her seemed to break down Cartier's defences even further.

Cartier took in a ragged breath. "The police interviewed all of us. Dixon had to go and identify her body. At least there's no video posted online. Of Blossom's fall, I mean. She was recording but not livestreaming, thank god. We have enough accidents on the internet. I can't believe she's gone."

"That must have been very hard," said Helen. "For all of you."

"Don't you work for Bunny and Benedict? You're like a butler? What are you doing here?"

"I am," said Helen. "I'm here to help." She waited for that to sink in. "Your father wants to see you."

65

Cartier immediately stopped crying. "Can you tell him I'm busy?"

"I don't think he'll accept that."

"Maybe I could just talk to him through the baby monitor?" said Cartier, and she gave one of her nervous laughs.

"I think he wants to see you in person," said Helen.

"I don't feel up to it," said Cartier. Helen believed her.

"I have a little something for you," said Helen. She offered Cartier a tray with two small glasses on it and a selection of pills. "In case you're not feeling your best this morning."

Cartier reached out to take it. Her nails were long and pointed, painted with black and white zebra stripes.

"This is a glass of my special morning tonic and a cup of green tea. Zinc and vitamin D and a probiotic. If you'd like dry toast, I can bring you some."

"Wow," said Cartier. "That's so nice. I'll take all this in my room and be out in a few minutes." She retreated inside and closed the door. Two seconds later she opened it again. "Shouldn't be more than five minutes, max. No toast for me. I'm already puffy."

The door closed and opened again five seconds later. "Does my dad know about Blossom?"

"I don't think so," said Helen.

"Good. Don't tell him or he'll have a total shit," said Cartier. Then she disappeared again and didn't come out for another hour and fifteen minutes.

When Cartier emerged, Helen found herself enveloped in a cloud of floral perfume that would have been quite pretty if less liberally applied. Cartier wore a shamrock-green track suit and fluorescent-yellow trainers. Full makeup. Hair in a purposely messy bun, massive sunglasses perched on her head.

"That stuff you gave me was like a miracle," said Cartier. "I think it even helped with my grief."

"That's good," said Helen.

"What was in your special mix, again?"

"Watermelon and coconut water, with a dash of pickle juice."

Cartier nodded, as though she was committing the ingredients to memory. "Okay. Well, we should talk about starting a business so we can sell it. But first, I guess I'll go talk to my dad." She headed down the wide, cold hallway, going faster than most people probably did when on their way to meet Archie Hightower. Helen followed, wondering whether the girl had taken more than just the hangover remedies she'd provided.

Cartier stopped suddenly just outside her father's office, squared her shoulders, and blew a strand of hair out of her eyes.

Then she put her sunglasses on, flung open the door without knocking, and walked in. Helen went after her.

It was like a bird of paradise had been blown off course by a tropical hurricane and landed in the middle of a generic rich-guy home office.

"Daddy," said Cartier.

Archie Hightower waved a hand at her, indicating that he was busy on the phone.

"You wanted to talk to me?"

"Jesus Christ, Lockhart. Let me call you back," said Hightower. He clicked off his headset and glared from Helen to his daughter.

Helen realized she wasn't breathing and reminded herself to start.

The silence was heavy with electricity.

Archie Hightower broke first. "What was that last night?" he demanded.

"You told me to come home. I came home."

"NOT LIKE THAT!" yelled Hightower. "I DIDN'T TELL YOU TO HAVE YOUR WASTE OF SPACE FRIENDS DUMP YOU OFF IN THE DRIVEWAY LIKE A BAG OF RECYCLING."

Friends? thought Helen.

"I've told you and told you that things have to change. And now, they're going to," he said, sounding self-satisfied.

"Uh, okay?" said Cartier, before letting out a fatuous little giggle.

"You think I'm not serious, but I am! You are going to work with Helen here and get yourself straightened out and put your life in some sort of order. *You are going to do what Helen says.*"

Cartier whipped around, slack-jawed, to gawp at Helen.

"That's right. Helen is going to teach you to be a useful member of society."

Helen thought of the protocol lessons she had originally imagined giving the girl. She'd envisioned giving her books about architecture and interior design. Providing information on taking care of body, mind, and soul as well as running philanthropic enterprises and large personal estates. None of that would make Cartier Hightower useful, exactly. Helen wasn't going to teach her to administer medical care in a refugee settlement or to design innovative measures to combat climate change, but she would at least be better able to operate successfully in her own social sphere.

"I *am* useful," said Cartier. "I do things."

"You do pointless things," said her father. "Since you dropped out of school, you are of no help to anyone who is not selling overpriced clothing or scrolling around on the internet looking for pictures of people doing things no sane person would do."

Cartier's mouth still hung open in protest. "I don't want to learn things," she said, with a fierce and rather touching determination.

"I know. That's exactly why Bunny and Benny are loaning you their prize butler for a month. When *she*"—here, he jabbed a finger at Helen—"is finished with you, I want to see real change. Or you are cut off. You can try to make a living off . . . whatever idiotic internet thing you're into at the moment."

"I'm learning to DJ," said Cartier. "And I'm basically a full member of the Deep State now. I'm on Instagram. TikTok. I'm a popular creator and I have quite a few followers, Daddy. Or some, anyway. I'm building my brand."

"I don't care," said Archie Hightower.

"Look, Daddy, I'm also like *in mourning*. We *all* are. You could be a little more understanding of our *grief*?"

Hightower stared at his computer monitors and seemed to ignore her last words. "You have one month. You and Helen can work here or somewhere else. I don't care. But if I don't see real change in you, Cartier, that's it. I've been disabling you."

"What?" Cartier's head tilted and Helen found hers following suit.

"I've been doing that thing where you give someone money and allow them to be a freeloader. It ends now."

"*Enabling*, Daddy. And there's nothing wrong with it. All my friends get enabled. It's totally normal."

"Goodbye," he said. Then to Helen, he added, "I look forward to weekly reports on her progress," fixing her with a glare before picking up his phone.

The conversation was over.

"Oh my god," huffed Cartier. She turned and flounced out of the office. Cartier rushed into her bedroom and slammed the door in Helen's face.

Oh my god is right, thought Helen. She took a seat in the hallway and readied herself for another long wait.

Five minutes later, Helen was halfway through composing a message in her head for the Levines about how her services had not been accepted by the Hightowers and she would be waiting for them at home when they returned from doing good works in Nepal when the door was flung open again.

"Come on," said Cartier. "We're *outta* here." She clutched an oversized yellow purse that looked like an enormous banana.

Helen got up, but not quickly enough for Cartier.

"Can't you like *hurry*? I don't want to see my dad again."

Helen had never been one to rush, and reflected that she found it unpleasant.

Cartier practically ran through the house and out the front door. She looked around and saw that her vehicle was not in the driveway.

"Where is my car?"

"In the garage," said Helen.

The sky was a flat white and the day was warm. The massive, architecturally undistinguished house loomed over them. Cartier peered at Helen through her mirrored glasses.

"That one," said Helen, pointing at the middle bay.

Cartier nibbled a knuckle absently while the other hand fished around in the large purse. She must have found an opener, because the door to the correct bay rose, revealing the bright-pink car. Cartier flounced over to it. "Come on!" she said. "Let's blow this dumpsicle."

Helen hesitated, then got into the passenger seat. She'd had the forethought to keep her small suitcase with her as she waited for Cartier this morning, and she had it now, but there was no place to put it in the tiny car other than on her lap. She had barely closed her door when Cartier threw the car into reverse and accelerated out of the garage, nearly taking off one of her chrome-plated mirrors as she went.

"Bye-bye, Shitville!" yelled Cartier as she hit the brakes, then stomped on the gas, making the tires squeal.

CHAPTER 10

Helen kept her eyes squeezed shut as they raced down the long drive-way and through the unmanned security gates, taking the corner leading out of the estate at an unsafe speed. As Cartier wove in and out of traffic, Helen finally got her seatbelt fastened, after which she alternated between clutching the dashboard and her small suitcase. She let out a long breath. Her first order of business, if they survived this trip, would be to take over the driving or hire someone.

The wisdom of her vow was confirmed when she looked over to see Cartier swallow several pills that she'd apparently fished from the depths of her banana purse.

"Vitamins," Cartier said, unconvincingly, when she noticed Helen watching.

When traffic finally forced the car to slow down, Helen turned to her new client.

"Are you okay to drive?" she asked. Obviously, the answer was no. Cartier Hightower was not okay to drive.

"What?" asked Cartier, checking her rear-view mirror for the first time since they'd set off.

"Are you safe to drive?" repeated Helen, enunciating each word.

"Do you mean am I loaded? Because the answer is none of your bees-wax, Hannah," said Cartier, who clearly shared her father's predilection for calling people by the wrong name.

Her driving seemed to improve as whatever it was she'd taken kicked in. There was nowhere to pull over, so Helen's life was in the hands of fate for the moment.

"Where are we going?"

"To my place," said Cartier. "It's downtown. It's, like, so dope. You're going to love it. Way cooler than my paterfamilias's pad." She pronounced it "potter-families," so, at first, Helen had no idea what she'd said.

They'd taken Marine Drive out of West Vancouver and were now making their way across the soaring expanse of the Lions Gate Bridge. The grey water below was punctuated with rust-coloured freighters. Float planes buzzed overhead like robotic insects. At the far end of the bridge rose the dense green tangle of Stanley Park.

"You live in Vancouver?" Helen asked.

Cartier ignored the question. She was staring at her phone screen, which made Helen's heart race. Cartier began to compose a text while the little car moved drunkenly from side to side, and Helen found her voice. "There's a police car two down from us," she said.

Cartier tossed her phone into her lap. "Crap." She looked into her mirrors. "I don't see it."

"Undercover vehicle. I saw the officer when we were merging," lied Helen. Cartier Hightower would probably not respond well to being told not to text while driving. But she probably wanted a sobriety test from a police officer even less. Work *with* the client, not against them.

Cartier began fidgeting with the stereo screen and Helen had to stop herself from reaching out a hand to take the steering wheel, which was encased in soft white leather.

"Anything I can help you find?" she asked. In the wind of the convertible, her hair was coming loose from its ponytail. Helen didn't care for the sensation of being messy.

"I want to play you a new track. I am going to say it's in Blossom's honour, even though she was still alive when I made it. It's like the thought that counts, though, right? You can tell me what parts you like the best," said Cartier, now leaning forward to stare nearsightedly at the screen in the dashboard. Helen looked up and gasped. They were inches from the car in front of them. Cartier slammed on the brakes and Helen's head whiplashed back into the seat.

"Allow me," Helen said, when they started moving again.

She clicked on the song Cartier pointed to, and soon the car was broadcasting a techno beat that sounded, to Helen's untrained ear, like every other techno beat she'd ever heard. It sped up in some places. Slowed in others. New sounds came and went, presumably in the spots where people were supposed to wave their arms or flick on their lighters. Raise their glow sticks? Something along those lines.

Then came the chorus, which had been altered so the voice sounded robotic.

"Uh-huh. We miss you so. Oh yeah. Uh-huh. Oh yeah. That's right. We miss you so." Over and over.

"That's me on vocals," said Cartier. "Smith produced. He's worked with some big people." She reached over and turned up the volume. "It's whack how perfect it is for a memorial song." Cartier shook her head in wonder at the synchronicity.

Helen nodded as though she, too, had deep appreciation for the sounds coming out of the speakers. The screen showed that the song was almost twenty minutes long and was called "Cloven Grooves in Sad Times." It would have to be renamed, obviously. The drivers who passed them in the next lane gave them looks, presumably for the wanton noise pollution they were emitting.

They had to stop due to traffic volume on the Stanley Park Causeway that led into the downtown core. The looks they got from people in other vehicles grew nastier. Several people rolled their eyes as they made a big show of putting up their windows. Cartier bobbed her head, oblivious.

After several minutes, she turned down the volume after perhaps the twenty-fifth repetition of "Uh-huh. We miss you so. Oh yeah. Uh-huh. Oh yeah. That's right. We miss you so."

"I wear a costume," she said, out of nowhere. "When I perform."

"You do?" said Helen, feeling dazed.

"A deer's head. That's my DJ name. Deer Head."

Helen found herself giving Cartier the same look the other drivers had given her. "Really?"

"Yeah. I like the way it sounds. Also, the band Deer Tick is super dope, even if they aren't EDM. Do you know them?"

Helen did not. She was happy to admit it and have a long discussion about ungulates if it meant that the volume on Cartier's song was turned down.

"They're like pretty old and alternative and stuff. But I like them. Or maybe it's just one guy? The producers said I have electric tastes and that's helpful. For a DJ?"

Helen did not correct her. She had a whole month to teach Cartier the difference between *electric* and *eclectic*. A month was a long, long time.

"That's good," said Helen. She decided to press her luck. "I'm sorry about your friend. Music must be a comfort to you."

Cartier went still for a moment, then she turned her mirrored gaze back to Helen.

"Yes," she said. "That's it exactly. If I get lost in the moment, then I can forget what happened to Trudee and to Blossom. Plus, I really love dance music?"

Helen had questions but wasn't sure this was the right time.

"I was already having trouble with how Trudee died. It was such a nightmare. People have watched that video of her hitting the boat millions of times. Literally. Every time it's taken down, it gets put right back up. So gross and, like, disrespectful. And now Blossom. I'm so glad that video isn't public."

Around them the traffic began to edge forward again. Dark steel and gleaming copper buildings towered ahead of them on Georgia Street.

"It's all so messed up," said Cartier. "Trudee was my PA. She was *so* sweet. She got me started on all of this. Introduced me to everyone. What happened to her was horrible."

"It sounds it," said Helen, gently.

"Yeah. We all went kitesurfing. I mean, she tried to teach us how, but we sucked at it? And then she did it herself, and even though she was really good, she . . . well, she sort of hit a boat? She got tangled up and one of her lines broke. After, investigators said that her harness release didn't work because it wasn't maintained properly. They also said a lot of small things went wrong. An error chain? Maybe that's what they called it? She went into a death loop. It was awful."

Sort of hit a boat. Death loop.

"People said I shouldn't have kept filming, but I didn't do it *on purpose*." Cartier's voice rose and she sounded like an outraged teen. "Trudee wasn't just my PA. She was my *friend*. I was just so shocked, you know? That's why I kept filming. I never thought she was going to get seriously hurt. She was a really good kitesurfer."

Cartier blinked back tears. "She was probably my best friend. I mean, even though she worked for me. I'm sorry if that sounds pathetic. But she was really *there* for me. Even when I was having a hard time."

"Blossom was another of your friends?" asked Helen in a soft voice.

"Not like Trudee. We worked together, but we weren't friends, exactly. It's still terrible that she died."

"I'm sorry," Helen said, curious about Cartier's refusal to call Blossom a friend.

Cartier didn't seem to register Helen's words. "Blossom was actually sneaking around on us. We were all supposed to shoot a video in the potholes later that afternoon. But Blossom went out by herself super early, before the rest of us were even up. She climbed the fence to get into that waterfall. It wasn't cool. I mean, we already had a shoot planned for the day. In a way, she was sort of stealing our thunder. Or would have been, if . . . well, she hadn't fallen."

Helen didn't understand why Blossom's waterfall video would take away from the planned pothole video, but she decided she would not ask for an explanation.

Cartier sighed and her head swivelled around to take in the cars and buildings around them. She got into the left-turn lane and veered off Georgia, heading back toward the water.

"Like I said, Blossom and I weren't very close. I'm new in the group and I don't think she liked me very much. But I'm still sorry about what happened to her."

Before Helen could ask any questions about Cartier's relationship with Blossom, Cartier wheeled the car into a hotel entryway, which was crowded with gleaming luxury vehicles under a soaring steel and glass overhang. "Here we are!" said Cartier. "Hotel sweet home."

A doorman wearing a dark vest, trousers, and a fedora with a feather in the brim rushed over to meet them and open Cartier's door.

"Ms. Hightower!" he said. "So good to see you."

"Thanks, Joseph." Cartier handed him a twenty-dollar bill along with her keys.

A second valet opened Helen's door and took her small suitcase.

Around them other guests and drivers craned their heads to get a look at the wild-haired girl with the electric-green track suit and banana purse as she made her way through automatic doors. Inside, uniformed staff were using iPads to check people in. Other guests were lined up at a front desk lit like a movie theatre. On the other side of the foyer was a long, narrow restaurant flooded with light from the two-storey windows that showed the street outside. The reception area was separated from the restaurant by a waist-high hedge of fake foliage. An enormous pair of pop art statues rotated twenty feet off the ground over the restaurant's bar.

"Ms. Cartier," said a desk clerk as Cartier swept past, with Helen following in her wake. They passed large glass cases containing glittering formal ballgowns. Wide stairs led up to what looked like a bookstore and an atrium with more carefully lit artwork on the second floor. Cartier paused at the stairs as though expecting to see someone.

"Do we recognize her?" a sixtyish tourist with dyed black hair whispered to her husband, who toted several shopping bags.

"How the hell would I know?" he said. "I'm half dead from going to so many stores."

"I'm sure she's someone," said his wife, unconcerned with her husband's half-dead status.

The lobby of the hotel smelled overpoweringly of clashing perfumes and colognes. The well-fed and highly polished guests who moved through it were all ages, but there seemed to be a preponderance of thirty- and forty-somethings in tight, self-consciously fashionable clothing. Many had dark tans and spoke languages other than English. Even the older people were dressed in bold colours and patterns. There were young women in leather pants and white bustiers accompanying tall men who had the supersized look of professional athletes, as well as gaggles of young women with long, dark hair. The remnants of a wedding party hung around the carefully lit white bar. Two men in unbuttoned suit jackets and yarmulkes told jokes to the appreciative audience of a woman in a tight red dress.

The hotel lobby was, in a word, a scene, and Cartier moved through it like a famous director. She led Helen to the bank of elevators. Inside, she swiped her key card and pressed a button for the eighteenth floor.

"I heard that some famous people have died here," Cartier said, apropos of nothing, before checking her makeup in the floor-to-ceiling mirror and striding off when the elevator opened again.

Cartier led Helen down the silent hallway and into a dark corner alcove. She tapped her electronic key and opened the door to reveal a huge, carefully lit suite with Scandinavian wood accents and modern furnishings in light colours. It was a handsome space and somehow not what Helen had expected.

"How long have you been staying here?" asked Helen.

"I don't know. Nearly a year? Come in. I'm sorry it doesn't have a butler's pantry," said Cartier apologetically. "Only the Chairman's Suite and the Prime Minister's Suite have those. And those rooms are pretty unaffordable. Fifteen thousand dollars a night? This is only fifteen hundred. I could buy one of the condos upstairs, but I'm not really feeling that kind of commitment right now?"

Helen found herself blinking. In spite of her job, she sometimes forgot just how much money wealthy people spent. During the height of the Covid-19 pandemic, she'd mostly stayed home with the Levines. The public-facing aspect of their lives had been set aside as they hunkered down and followed health protocols, content as two highly pampered clams. Also, Dr. Levine did not like hotels. When they travelled, she preferred to go to places where they already owned property. "It's a comfort thing," she'd explained to Helen.

Perhaps Dr. Levine had the right idea, thought Helen, watching her young client, who stood in the middle of the beautifully appointed room, suddenly looking lost and somewhat deflated.

"Is everything all right?" asked Helen.

Cartier made a face and Helen saw that her long eyelash extensions were wet. "Yes. Sure. Of course," she said and gave one of her little giggles. "It's all just hitting me. I guess I'm not used to being here without my friends."

"Ah," said Helen.

"The Deep State, I mean. Me and Amina and Dixon and Keithen. And Blossom." Her voice wavered dangerously. "Blossom had this bathing suit she showed us the night before she died. Said she was going to wear it to the pothole shoot. The fabric had this sunrise on it. Maybe that's why she went into that waterfall in the morning. Morning suit in the morning." Cartier wiped her eyes with the underside of her wrist. "I'm ruining my makeup."

"It's okay," said Helen. The girl had lost so much in the midst of such plenty.

"Check out the view," said Cartier, changing the subject abruptly.

Helen removed her shoes and went farther into the suite. The windows along one side of the corner suite gave a view of the hotel pool deck. The other wall looked out at the grass-covered roof of the float plane terminal, the ocean, and the North Shore mountains.

"Dope, right?" said Cartier.

"Yes. It's a fabulous view," said Helen. All at once she could feel the girl beside her shrinking, even though she hadn't moved. "Can I get you something to eat?"

"Huh? No. I'm not hungry. Actually, I think I'm going to take a nap."

"Of course. Can I unpack for you?"

"That's okay. I'm just going to lie down real quick."

Helen nodded.

"Oh yeah, and can you arrange to get your own room? Just tell them to put it on my bill. Try to get one close."

Helen nodded.

"I'll text if I need anything? Is that okay? You're welcome to hang out here until your own room is ready. Get a suite if you want. I don't care." This girl seemed nothing like the one who'd strode through the lobby. Every part of Cartier seemed diminished. Her energy seemed to have retracted. What was left was a track suit and a hairdo. It was uncanny. Helen already missed the girl's irritating laugh.

"Shall I get some groceries in case you'd like a snack later?"

Cartier shook her head. "No, that's okay. I really just want to go to bed." And with that, she walked into the bedroom and closed the door.

CHAPTER 11

If you want success, you have to understand what people want. Of course, people *say* they want world peace and spiritual tranquility and optimal health, but obviously they don't or the world would be a lot more peaceful, tranquil, and healthy. What they really want is sex, money, power, and fame. Those are the basics.

They also want exciting stories that trigger their emotions, good and bad. The ratio there is about 20:80. If anyone doubts that, just look at the internet. It's twenty percent cat videos, wholesome memes, impressive dance moves, and inspirational animal rescue stories, and the rest is filth. Anger. Hatred. Fear.

The internet is a reflection of the human mind. It's a story machine and an emotion generator. It puts everyone's base instincts on display. Unfortunately for Cartier Hightower, one of people's oldest and deepest instincts is to go after the weak and drive them out of the group.

All you have to do is spend five minutes on any social media platform with loose moderation standards and you can see it in action. Or you can spend ten minutes with a group of eighth grade girls and watch them sniff out and begin to torment the one who doesn't fit in. Human cruelty is a fact of life, but Cartier Hightower didn't seem to understand what was happening to her or why.

She was unpopular with the fans. She wasn't just ignored but actively disliked. One major issue was that she wasn't particularly good in front of a camera. Her need to be liked was painful to watch. It only got worse after Trudee died. Cartier recorded her own tribute video and it went over about as well as a diaper floating in a public pool. She was genuinely upset, but according to the fans, she "made it all about herself." She made excuses for continuing to film when she should have stopped. She pointed out that at least four other video cameras had been going that day and had filmed the accident and posted videos. But the internet still blamed Cartier. After that, Cartier went to pieces. Wouldn't get out of bed. Stopped posting. But the fans didn't believe that she was genuinely upset. When she was back on her feet, they said she hadn't mourned for long enough.

In other words, the internet was the biggest, meanest group of eighth grade girls on the planet, and it was an easy thing to stoke and shape that hostility.

Sometimes a great story takes shape and the creator has only to watch and guide. It was like that with Cartier. Taking a girl who seemed to have everything and showing that she really had nothing made for a fascinating story. After all, what's not to hate about a girl who is richer than god and desperate for love?

The key was to let the story develop naturally. Make sure Cartier was under chronic stress. That everything she touched turned to shit. Have her do something really bad and worthy of scorn. Any sensible person would get off the internet before things got any worse, but Cartier Hightower was not and never would be a sensible girl. But she *was* going to be the biggest villain on the internet if everything went as planned, and that made her a very valuable commodity for the person who knew how to monetize the attention economy.

CHAPTER 12

Helen went to the front desk to arrange her own room. She explained to the clerk who she was, and the clerk called up to get Cartier's permission to add Helen to Cartier's account. While she was waiting, a lean man wearing a well-cut black suit and a neat black turban approached her.

"Hello, Ms. Thorpe? I'm Gurdeep Bal, the manager here." He didn't extend a hand for her to shake, a pre-pandemic norm that not everyone had returned to, but he managed to make her feel as though she'd been warmly greeted.

"I'm so pleased to meet you," he continued. "I understand you are staying with Ms. Hightower?"

How had he gotten that information so quickly? She hadn't seen the clerk call anyone. At butler school they'd been told that fine hotels know everything that happens on their premises, at least until guests go inside their rooms. The best hotels research each guest before they arrive. Was something like that going on here?

"In a professional capacity. I'm Ms. Hightower's butler."

Bal's finely shaped eyebrows went up.

"I see," he said. "It's good to hear that Ms. Hightower will have some, uh, help. Yvette will be happy to finish booking your room. In the meantime, would you mind joining me in my office for a moment?"

Somewhat nonplussed, Helen followed Mr. Bal down a plain hallway, through an unmarked door, and into a frills-free office.

82

"Let me begin by saying how much we enjoy having Ms. Hightower as a guest," he said after they'd both taken a seat. "She and her friends are very . . . lively. And generous about tagging us in their social media."

Helen nodded, waiting for the other highly polished loafer to drop.

"In the months that she has been with us, I have expressed a few concerns to Ms. Hightower. But I feel that she may not have *heard* me."

A framed photo of the manager with his family—a wife and two giggling children—was the only decoration in the plain office.

"We would like to avoid deliveries from . . . certain parties."

Helen waited.

"Specifically, Mike on a Bike."

"Mike on a Bike?" said Helen.

"Yes. It gives the wrong impression, particularly for our older guests and some of our international guests. Especially when he parks his heavily branded marijuana trailer right outside the front doors. It stands out."

"Ah," said Helen, feeling embarrassed in a way that was not very spiritual. What was it the people who tried not to be codependent said? Not my circus, not my monkeys? At this moment, Cartier Hightower unfortunately was Helen's circus as well as her monkey.

"I understand," said Helen.

"And we have also asked Ms. Hightower to confine her DJing efforts to dedicated spaces. Off-site spaces. Our suites are soundproofed, but they can't keep electric dance music out. And not everyone on the pool deck wants to listen to someone working out a beat. We have our own stereo system and playlists."

Helen nodded.

"The same principle applies to the more elaborate photo and video shoots in public spaces. Of course we want people to share images of our hotel. We're proud of it and glad guests find it photogenic. But it's not . . ."

". . . a film set or a photo studio?" Helen said.

"Exactly. When there are large lights and makeup people and photographers milling about in small spaces, such as elevators, it becomes . . ."

"Disruptive."

He looked relieved. "I'm so glad you understand."

"I will do everything I can," said Helen.

"Wonderful," he said. "We hope that Ms. Hightower will continue to be a valued guest. For as long as the relationship works."

Implicit in his careful words was the clear message that Cartier Hightower was on thin ice at the hotel.

"And finally," he said, "are you ready for Clarice and Miggs and Jack now?"

Helen leaned forward, more concerned by this than anything else she had heard so far this baffling morning.

Before she could ask whom he was talking about, there was a knock on the door, and a somewhat wild-eyed young woman in a rumpled suit came in, accompanied by what looked like three wigs on the ends of leashes, each of which seemed to be twisted around her legs. "Mr. Bal. I'm so sorry. Miggs just pooped."

"He did what?" asked Gurdeep Bal, allowing his own stress to show for the first time. "Inside?"

"Yes! I took them for their walk and he seemed fine. But as soon as we got inside, he just started going! I tried to, you know, make him stop, but he got out of his collar and started running around in front of the check-in desk. And pooping! Right there, with all the guests! We had to evacuate everyone while housekeeping came and cleaned up. It was so disgusting. I took him outside again, but I guess he was done."

Helen was grateful she'd missed the performance.

Gurdeep Bal looked at the dogs as though they were unexploded ordnance. "Which one is Miggs?" he asked.

The young woman pointed to one of the dogs. To Helen's untrained eye, it looked the exact same as the others. "This one."

"Is he *ill*?"

"I don't know," said the young woman, sounding on the verge of tears. "I'm sorry, Mr. Bal. Our dog at home doesn't do that."

"It's not your fault, Ms. Coniber."

He fixed the Pekingese responsible for the incident with a stern look.

The little dog was lying down, panting happily as though having successfully completed an important day's work. He appeared unrepentant about the recent episode of incontinence.

Bal turned to Helen.

"I'm afraid we will not be able to provide dog-sitting at late notice for Ms. Cartier any longer. In fact, we will not be able to provide dog-sitting under any circumstances. We are also going to have to give some serious thought to limiting how many dogs can stay in a suite. Unless it's the Chairman's Suite, of course. Or the Prime Minister's."

Ms. Coniber handed Helen three leashes studded with rhinestones. Helen looked down at her new charges.

"Oh," she said. Three interested little black faces pointed up at her.

The hotel clerk, looking immensely relieved to be free of the dogs, gave Gurdeep Bal several brochures, which he handed to Helen.

"Nearby pet care services. And the name of a veterinarian in case there are any further . . . incidents. Thank you so much for coming in. I hope your time with Ms. Hightower is . . ." Words failed him, and he didn't complete the sentence.

Helen nodded. And with something less than her usual discretion, she struggled to retrieve tip money for the clerk who had been looking after the dogs and dealing with their digestive crises.

Gurdeep Bal held out a hand. "Not necessary, but thank you. We have added a thirty percent gratuity to the fee. Which is considerable."

One of the Pekingese had gotten to its feet and was attempting to lick its own behind, but it was too short and too fluffy, and it ended up keeling over, whereupon the other two jumped on it. Soon there was a sweetly snarling, yapping knot of hairy dogs at Helen's feet. She stared.

"Treats," said Ms. Coniber, sounding surer of herself now that she was free of the clutch of dogs. She gave Helen a handful of soft pellets that smelled overpoweringly of fake bacon. "Just sprinkle them around," she said. "Like so." The girl dropped a small handful of treats on the ground as though she was feeding goldfish. The dogs stopped play-wrestling and began snuffling for the small bits of food.

Helen pulled a fifty-dollar bill from her dedicated gratuities wallet and handed it over.

"Here you go," she said. "I believe you've more than earned this."

As she led the dogs down the hallway, she reflected that both Mr. Hightower and his daughter had neglected to mention that the job came with three dogs. She would need help with them, and she knew just who to ask.

CHAPTER 13
NIGEL

When the call came from Helen, it was like deep fate and karma. Or were those the same thing? Nigel wasn't sure. In any case, it felt meant to be and also like a major shock. Nigel considered himself essential personnel at the Yatra Institute, where he had worked since Helen had hired him on a temporary basis to help out not long after the owner of the lodge had died under mysterious circumstances. Helen and two friends she'd met at butler school had solved the case. It was a crazy story and one Nigel loved to tell, even though he knew he should be more discreet, especially now that he planned to attend the same butler academy Helen had gone to.

Everyone seemed to think that he needed more high-end experience, probably due to his underprivileged background. Nigel had grown up in Port Alberni and his parents didn't exactly write etiquette manuals in their spare time. They *had* written quite a few angry letters to the local newspaper about tax increases, noise pollution, and the weather.

When Helen called and said she needed some help with a short-term client, Nigel asked Murray and Gavin, Helen's butler friends who had stayed on at the Yatra Institute after Helen left, for advice, and they had enthusiastically said he should go. A bit too enthusiastically, now that Nigel thought about it.

Nigel had researched the client and learned that she was an ultra-well-off influencer who was mostly good at influencing the angry blob that was the internet to despise her. But she belonged to a group of creators who were huge on YouTube and Instagram and everywhere else. He'd been shocked to find out that Helen was working for someone who would do anything for attention. Nigel would have bet that Helen didn't even know what Instagram was. He was also floored to learn that her main employers had loaned her out to the influencer. Loaned her out! It was enough to make him reconsider wanting to become a butler. What if his employers lent him to a criminal kingpin or someone who had a lot of screaming fits and threw things at staff?

Nigel wondered whether he was equipped to assist Helen in looking after an influencer. After all, he'd spent over two years living at the Yatra Institute, which was a very spiritual place with slow internet. Sure, he went on Reddit a few times a day and checked Twitter when he wanted to lose all hope for humanity. He also looked at Facemeta, or whatever it was called now, about twice a year, when he wanted to see old people yell at each other. But he was not in the same league as the new client, who was several ticks beyond highly online.

It also seemed relevant that two members of the client's content group, the Deep State, had died recently. One had had a horrific accident while kitesurfing. The other one was RIP after falling off a ledge in a waterfall and into a raging river. Nigel didn't want to be insensitive, but that kind of body count suggested that the new client and her friends were not "safety first" people.

Even before the accidents, the stupidly named Deep State was famous in the way that didn't totally make sense, which was a very internet way to be famous. Each of them made a different kind of content and didn't seem to have much in common, other than being in their twenties.

There was Amina Njie, who specialized in makeup, street fashion, and being ridiculously good-looking. Dixon Cho was the owner of a unisex athleisure company called, unsurprisingly, Dixon Cho. He was, if anything, better-looking than Amina, which was lucky because his clothes were some of the ugliest Nigel had ever seen, and Nigel was an aficionado of ugly fashion. Dixon Cho's clothes cost more than any normal person could ever pay. Then there was Keithen McNair, a major star thanks to his talent for "shaming people who needed it," according to his bio. If anyone got caught on video acting like a racist a-hole at a fast-food restaurant, it took about three minutes for people to start tagging Keithen, asking him to find the culprit's name, employer, and in the worst cases, their address. Keithen, with his square jaw, long red hair worn in a ponytail, tattoos, and ever-present backwards baseball cap, looked like a guy who worked in the Alberta oil patch, which is exactly what he'd been before devoting himself full time to shaming people. Part of his appeal was that he was surprisingly, if inconsistently, liberal, which people seemed to love.

There was Blossom, an amateur swimsuit model who differentiated herself from all the other amateur swimsuit models by wearing bathing suits in unusual circumstances. She wore tiny bikinis to a go-cart track, while riding a mechanical bull, and on a unicycle, as well as the usual activities involving water. In recent months she'd been taking part in some popular video trends, and Nigel had liked that material more than her swimsuit content because she came across as smart, funny, and self-aware, if a little mean.

Cartier, Helen's new client, was the newest member and, according to fans of the Deep State, a poor choice for the group. She hadn't brought a large base of followers with her and she was, as the Deepstatestans put it, "coasting on their content." The audience seemed to veer between thinking Cartier was merely boring to actively hating her for a variety of alleged offences. Nigel couldn't figure out why she participated with the group at all. She didn't need the money, but she did seem desperate for approval and attention.

As a content collective, the Deep State had a number of specialties. They recorded a series called the Deep State Reacts, where they listened to music or watched films that the audience had suggested and they all reacted. Another series was called the Deep State Tries, where they all tried some new, preferably difficult or unusual activity, like heli-skiing, driving a Zamboni, ice fishing, searching for snakes in the Florida Everglades, or kitesurfing. The last one was the activity that had gotten Cartier's personal assistant killed several weekss before. They also did stunt philanthropy, where they gave away money in ways that were designed to bring maximum attention to them and their largesse. There were also Deep State Re-enacts, which involved them acting out famous scenes from films and TV shows.

Nigel found them and their endless output fascinating, entertaining, and a little tiring, and he couldn't believe he was going to work for one of them, or at least assist Helen as she worked for one of them.

〜〜

The cab stopped in front of the fanciest hotel he'd ever seen, and he felt totally overwhelmed until he saw Helen waiting for him in the lobby. She gave him a kiss on each cheek and then held him at arms' length to get a good look at him. He did what he always did in her presence. He melted a little. Swooned a little. Not in a romantic way, but in the way you do when you've been in the cold and dark for a long time and you step into the warm sunlight. That's what Helen was. Warm sunlight. When Helen looked at you, you felt seen.

"You look good," she said.

Nigel expanded like a flower under her attention. A somewhat portly flower, but a flower nonetheless.

Helen also looked well. She had some mysterious quality about her that allowed her to look at home in most environments. Nigel thought it had something to do with clean living and meditation. She was always poised, always attentive. Never a hot mess, the way he often was.

"I'm at your service!" he said. "Gavin and Murray and Rayvn and everyone at Yatra send their love."

Helen nodded and reached for his bag, which he would not allow her to take. "Nope! Nope! I'm the bag-carrying guy around here. The valet tried to get it too and I told him, 'No, sir! I'm a helper too. Like you!'"

Helen gave him a quizzical look and he realized he was babbling incoherently, the way he always did around her. Helen made him want to share.

"Anyway, I'm ready for action," he finished, feebly.

Helen smiled at various people on staff at the hotel and many of them greeted her by name as she went. In fact, they also seemed to light up in her presence. Good old Helen still had it.

"I am not sure exactly how this is going to work, but I'm glad for another pair of hands," she said.

Nigel held out his hands. "These are soft, and they can't build anything, but they're right here on the ends of my arms. Two of them."

"That's good," said Helen, laughing softly.

"I'm excited to meet your . . . boss," said Nigel.

At that, Helen stopped laughing. "Ah. That might not happen right away," she said.

By this time, they'd taken the elevator up and it had opened silently onto a softly lit, thickly carpeted floor.

She slid a hotel keycard over a pad, and it turned green. She ushered him into a spotless room that looked out over the float plane terminal. "You'll be staying in here," she said. "I'm right next door. And Cartier, our client, is in the suite next to us. In the corner suite."

"Whoa!" said Nigel, in the entry-level luxury of his room. "This is incredible."

"I'm glad you like it."

Helen took his suitcase from him and set it on the built-in wooden shelf near the door.

"There is someone I'd like you to meet. Well, *someones*, really."

He turned. "I thought you said we couldn't meet the client yet."

Helen was already on her way out of the room. She walked into an alcove in the hallway and swiped open the door.

"This is Ms. Hightower's suite. She's not feeling well at the moment. But—"

She moved over behind one of the white couches in the large room, bent over, and began doing something that he couldn't see.

There followed a pandemonium of ankle-height dogs with flowing red hair. They panted happily and jumped up on his pant legs, on Helen's pant legs, and on each other's pant legs, if they'd had pants.

"These are Jack, Miggs, and Clarice," said Helen. "Ms. Hightower's dogs."

One of them lifted a leg and was about to begin peeing on a cream-coloured ottoman.

"Uh-uh-uh, Miggs!" admonished Helen as she scooped him up. "Wait, please." She pointed at a row of leashes folded neatly over a coat rack hook. "Help me get them outside."

"Where is Hannibal?" asked Nigel.

"Pardon me?" said Helen, as she hooked up the little dogs.

"They're named after *Silence of the Lambs*. The collection isn't complete without Hannibal."

"Ah," said Helen. "I wondered why Ms. Hightower referred to them as the lambs. They look more like . . ."

"Wigs?" said Nigel.

Helen laughed softly. "Yes. Also, they are not particularly silent."

The phone in the room began to ring and the dogs began to bark, as though to illustrate how much noise they could make.

"Should I get that?" Nigel asked.

Helen hesitated. "No. That's fine, thank you, Nigel. We'll take the dogs out to do their business and then we'll have a chat about what we're doing here."

He carried one dog and she carried the other two into the elevator, through the lobby, and out the front door. Staff waved fondly at Helen, but a darkly tanned guest dressed in golf clothes said, "Isn't that one of the dogs that shat all over this place when we were checking in?"

"Oh, god yes, it is. Filthy little thing," said his companion, a leathery woman likewise dressed for golf.

Nigel glanced at Helen, who shrugged her shoulders and made an *oops* face. It was as close a gesture to sheepish as he'd ever seen her make.

They'd nearly made it to a dog-friendly-looking section of grass in a small plaza between two massive buildings when two tall, thin people, both wearing large sunglasses, approached. They were, for lack of a better word, hot. Maybe even smoking hot, if Nigel was not mistaken. The man wore his thick, perfectly cut black hair in a super-tight fade that went well with his chiselled bone structure and outstanding teeth. His good looks were barely marred by the hideousness of his barf-coloured velour track suit. The woman's hair had been dyed a shade of fairy silver that it wouldn't turn naturally for another forty years. It matched perfectly her clinging, silvery-grey jumpsuit that would look good on point-one percent of the world's population.

"Excuse me," said the woman. "Helen, right?"

"That's right," said Helen.

"Hello, Helen. Why aren't you letting us see Cart?"

"I'd say it's a fair question," said the man, as though Helen had suggested it wasn't. He had an indeterminate accent of the kind that came from either acting school or an expensive boarding school. He slid his sunglasses up his face to reveal accusing eyes framed with long eyelashes. Was he wearing lash extensions? If so, they were really working for him.

"We would very much like to see her," said the man.

"We're almost family to her," said the woman.

"As well as business associates," said the man.

Nigel was speechless. Two of the most internet-famous people were standing right in front of them. And Helen seemed to have no idea who they were! This was going to be good.

CHAPTER 14

Of course, all three of the dogs chose that exact moment to relieve themselves, which Helen, emotionally stable though she was, felt undercut her natural dignity. She handed the leashes to Nigel.

"Ms. Hightower isn't feeling well," said Helen. "She asked that she not be disturbed."

"She's depressed again," said the woman. "It's only natural. We're all depressed after what just happened to Blossom."

"And Trudee," said the man.

"But the show must go on," said the woman.

The man nodded and the thick swoop of hair on the top of his head stayed in place. "That's right. We've got to support each other through this."

Nigel was staring, open-mouthed, at the newcomers. It was as though he'd never seen a certain kind of stylish, well-groomed, international Vancouverite before. He'd get used to it, Helen thought. The hotel was full of them.

"We've called her cellphone but it just goes through to voice mail. We've called up to her room but no answer. Same thing when Keithen tried. Even Bryan hasn't been able to get through. And you see, the thing is, her absence is having an effect on all of us," said the man. "I'm Dixon, by the way. Dixon Cho. This is Amina." He held out a hand for Helen to shake. Even his hand seemed fit and stylish. Helen shook it and noted that his watch was a Patek Philippe Nautilus. It probably cost as much as Cartier's pink car. A stunning piece of watchmaking.

"I'm Helen Thorpe. This is my colleague, Nigel."

"It's so nice to meet you," said Amina. She sounded sincere. Her makeup had a metallic sheen. She'd painted shiny peacock hues around her large eyes. Even without that, she would be a head-snappingly beautiful young woman. "We aren't trying to be confrontational. It's just that we're worried."

"That's right," said Dixon. "We know Cartier gets in the dumps and isolates. We don't want her to feel alone."

Helen remembered how Cartier had been dropped off at her father's house like a load of laundry, presumably by these people. Then she reminded herself that she didn't have all the facts. She should not make assumptions.

"We understand that her father hired you?" said Dixon. "For security purposes?"

One of the hotel staff must have talked to them about Cartier's new staff member. That showed a distinct lack of discretion and loyalty to their guest.

"I've been hired to assist Cartier," said Helen.

"So you're her new security person?" pressed Dixon. "Or a new PA?"

"I'm helping her in a personal capacity," said Helen.

"Well, we're glad she has some help. She seemed more—" Amina looked to Dixon for assistance.

"Balanced," he said.

"Yes. That's the word. She seemed more *balanced* when she had Trudee. Can you please just tell her that we're here for her. All of us."

"She doesn't need to go through this alone," added Dixon.

Helen looked from one to the other. They both had a way of looking at her that felt both too intense and oddly unfocused. She could hear their phones buzzing with notifications as they tried to maintain eye contact.

"Some of your videos are legendary," said Nigel, surprising everyone.

That caught the pair's full attention.

"Any one in particular?" asked Dixon.

"A lot of them. That time you handed out hundred-dollar bills to the seniors who were getting back on the bus after being at the casino all night? That was amazing," said Nigel.

"Especially when most of them turned around and went right back to the slots," said Dixon, making a wry face.

Obviously Nigel had been researching Cartier's group. Why hadn't he told her that? Probably because he worried that she wouldn't approve.

"Oooooh, thank you, babes!" Amina cooed. "Always good to meet a fan of the Deep State."

Dixon nodded. "You know, Cartier really helped with that one, even though she was just coming off another . . . bout."

Helen wondered how Cartier had helped. Had the hundred-dollar bills they'd handed out been hers?

"Poor Cartier. People have been really hard on her. What happened to Trudee was no one's fault. We don't take unnecessary chances. I mean, obviously we didn't know much about kitesurfing, other than what Trudee taught us. It was our first time. What happened to her was just a terrible accident," said Amina. She sounded as sincere as she could while sneaking frequent glances at the phone she clutched.

"We will give you our numbers and please let us know when Cart is ready to see us. I really think she'll feel better if she comes back to work," said Dixon. His gaze had also begun to slide down to his phone. "We have a number of important commitments coming up. *Contracted* commitments."

"Certainly," said Helen. She hadn't intentionally kept Cartier's friends away. She'd simply respected her client's wish to be left alone. Was it a sign of friendship that these two people had gone to so much effort to get in touch with Cartier? Or were they just protecting their contracted commitments?

Either way, Helen gave them her own cell number, which they punched into their phones. While they were doing that, four teenage girls approached. "Oh my god. It's the Deep State, bitches!" said one girl. Her bobbed hair was dyed silver, or she might have been wearing a silver wig. She had on a bright-green track suit and red sneakers. She also carried a bag shaped like an apple. Now that Helen thought of it, Amina carried a purse shaped like a . . . was that a watermelon? Was this an Instagram thing? To carry purses shaped like fruit?

"Deep State, bitches!" called another one and threw up a hand sign that Dixon and Amina returned. It was the same gesture, a hang ten followed by a talk to the hand, that Helen had seen Cartier and her friends make in their videos.

"Can we get a picture with you?" asked a girl dressed like a frumpy preppy at gym class, circa 1985.

"Or do a TikTok?" asked the girl with the apple bag.

"Can you do the dance? The one you made about tea? With that cool guy who makes the tea and smokes weed?"

Amina nodded her head sagely. "Minty Bongwater. He's such a beautiful spirit, isn't he?"

The girls nodded vigorously. "His grillz are amazing. I didn't even know you could get turquoise."

"Why did Cartier keep filming?" asked one of them, abruptly changing the subject. "Was it because she didn't care what happened to her assistant? I heard she just wanted the views."

"She's not even actual Deep State. She's only with you guys because of her—" The rest of the sentence was drowned out when more passersby, mostly teenagers, joined the original girls and started calling out questions and comments to Amina and Dixon. For all the attention Amina and Dixon got, most of the questions pertained to Cartier and her shortcomings.

"Is it true that Cartier did something to Blossom?"

"Is Cartier jealous of the rest of you?"

"Are you worried about your own safety around her? Because it seems like she's kind of, like, bad luck?"

The young people in the crowd seemed to relish disliking Cartier as much as or more than they enjoyed liking Amina and Dixon.

Helen watched as Amina and Dixon gave autographs and posed for photos and videos with their fans, and tried to deflect the anti-Cartier commentary. Cries of "It's the Deep State, bitches," rang out.

Eventually, Helen gestured to Nigel that it was time to get back to the hotel. Dixon noticed and mouthed "Call me" and held his hand to his ear.

"It was so crazy to meet them in person," said Nigel when they were a half a block away.

Helen untangled two of the dogs, who'd gotten themselves wrapped around a pole. "Who are they?"

"They're the rest of the Deep State. Well, two of them, anyway."

"I gathered that," said Helen, who would not have recognized them from the photos and videos she'd seen. People looked so different in person. Larger, for one thing. More vital and complicated, for another.

"They're really famous on the internet."

"I also gathered that," said Helen. "Maybe you should tell me more about what you know about them."

So he did.

CHAPTER 15

After apologizing for being "snoopy" about the client, Nigel recounted essentially the same story Lou Ellen had given her, but with more detail. About six months before, Cartier had joined the group known as the Deep State, and they were sort of like the internet version of a musical supergroup. Only they were like a supergroup in which one person played classical music, another jazz, a third death metal, and the fourth pan flute solos.

"They don't really fit together, but basically, they show people what's cool," said Nigel, when he and Helen stopped at a food truck. "People copy them. Try to be like them. Their audience loves them. A lot."

"Not all of them," said Helen.

"No. They resent Cartier. They have a lot of conspiracy theories about her. At minimum, they think she's not legit." He pulled two napkins from a dispenser as they waited for their food.

"It doesn't sound like any of it's legit," said Helen.

"Maybe that's not the best word. Everyone is really into authenticity now. You have to be cool and creative and funny and not boring *and* real. Like super raw and honest. But not needy. Everyone thinks Cartier is needy. But they are definitely fascinated by her."

"That's a lot," said Helen. "To ask people to be all of those things."

"Yeah," said Nigel. "Popular creators make a lot of money but they work for it. And when things go bad for them, they often go *really* bad.

You know, if they make a mistake or do something the fans don't like. Their careers can go up in flames in an hour. It's incredible."

They stood at the side of the truck to wait for their orders.

"Does the Deep State tell people they should carry bags that look like fruit?" asked Helen.

"Kind of," said Nigel. "It's more like if they carry a type of bag and just happen to drop the name of the bag company in the comments, they get paid for that. But they have their own line of fruit bags that they sell. The creator economy is super complicated. I read a couple of articles about it and I still don't understand how it all works."

He took the wraps from the outstretched hands of the food truck employee and handed one to Helen.

"So that young woman who just approached them, was she carrying one of their bags?"

"Naw," said Nigel, his mouth full of bahn mi. He finished his bite. "Dixon has a line of boutique fruit purses he sells in his store. Deep State Fruit. Those bags cost like two grand each. That girl we just saw, the one with the apple? Who knows where she got that, but it's not real. It's just *inspired* by the real Deep State Fruit."

"Aren't they upset that someone is copying their idea?" asked Helen. They moved to sit on a bench in the plaza near the hotel. She fed a tiny bit of the soft, chewy wrap to each of the attentive Pekingese. Not too much, because she didn't want a repeat of the incident in the lobby.

"Nah. Most of their fans, especially their younger fans, can't afford their merch. The most important thing is followers. Eyeballs. Attention," said Nigel. "You know, attention economics. Everyone online wants your attention."

Attention economics was something Helen could instantly understand. Though the idea of monetizing attention felt deeply distasteful to her.

"Probably after they sign all those autographs, they'll film themselves giving a Deep State Fruit bag to one of those kids in the crowd. Free advertising for themselves, and the kids will post about it everywhere. You know how it is."

Helen didn't know how it was.

"Everyone wants to be rich, famous, and beautiful. They want to influence people with their taste, I guess."

"Do you?" she asked him.

Nigel, who was one of the speediest eaters Helen had ever seen, crumpled up the foil from his sandwich. "Influence people? No. Rich would be okay. And I don't care about famous. I'm already beautiful." He laughed and she joined him, delighted in his delight in himself.

"What do people get from it? Watching the Deep State, I mean," Helen said. She felt—what was the word people used to use? Square. That was it. She felt square and she sounded square. The sensation was new. She'd sometimes thought she was too quiet and maybe a little too earnest. But she wasn't used to feeling dull. It was an unpleasant sensation.

"I like seeing what they do. It's always sort of extreme. Not like real life. Sometimes I just watch to see how terrible my life is compared to theirs."

"Do you really think that?" said Helen, appalled.

"Only when I go on my socials for too long," he said, philosophically. "Also known as the place where people feel less lonely and also more lonely, all at the same time."

Helen regarded him. "I really appreciate you," she said.

He blushed. "Then there are the hate follows." He hastened to clarify. "Not me. *I* don't hate anyone. But sometimes people follow people they dislike because it . . ." He shrugged. "I don't know why. It kind of makes you feel superior, I guess."

Helen sighed. This was the world in which Cartier lived. A world of unreality. Of unmet desires and ceaseless demands for attention. A world of hate follows.

"Let's go see if she's up," she said, finally, getting to her feet.

"Boss?" said Nigel.

She looked at him. He was so strange and insightful and so perfectly precious in his oddness. He and the three smiling Pekingese at his feet made her heart happy.

"Yes?"

"What are we supposed to do for this girl?"

"Her father has asked me to try to help her."

"Right. With butlering stuff?"

"With life stuff," said Helen.

"Maybe you should invite her to the Yatra Institute? It's going to be hard to do anything for her here." He waved around them at the clamorous downtown street and the rows of high-rises.

"I don't think she'd agree to go to the Institute. And it's busy with programs right now."

But she'd lost his attention.

"Clarice! Don't eat cigarette butts," said Nigel. He bent down to take the crumpled filter from the dog's mouth. "Gross." He flicked it into a garbage can and Helen was proud to see him reach into his man bag and take out a small package of wet wipes to clean his hands. A man bag and wipes! How far he'd come. She noticed her own attachment to Nigel's development as a domestic professional. Was her ambition for him to become an accomplished domestic professional really any different from the ambition of influencers who wanted people to follow their example? Perhaps not.

"I'm not exaggerating when I say that Deep State fans don't like Cartier very much. You heard those kids. They were mild compared to what people say online. When they're not accusing her of having something to do with the accidents, they're saying that she's using Trudee's and Blossom's deaths to get attention for herself. Which is bizarre. They also think she's only part of the group because of her paper."

"Paper?" said Helen.

"Money."

"Ah," said Helen.

"If people don't like you on the internet and you're like, an internet person, you need majorly thick skin. Does she have that?"

Helen thought of the soft, awkward young woman currently being crushed by her own dark feelings. No. Cartier Hightower did not have thick skin. She sometimes seemed barely to have any skin at all. With luck, the so-called Deep State would move on without Cartier, and Helen would get a chance to help her. But Helen was starting to think that Cartier Hightower was not a lucky girl.

CHAPTER 16

When they got back to the suite, Helen knocked softly on Cartier's bedroom door. There was no answer, so she sent her a text letting her know that Amina and Dixon had reached out and were asking whether she needed anything. Helen also invited her to come out and meet Nigel and said the two of them would be in the living room of the suite for the next thirty minutes, just in case.

Helen was explaining invitation and seating protocols for state dinners to Nigel when the door to the bedroom swung open and Cartier emerged, looking both puffy and half-starved.

Nigel and Helen got to their feet.

"Ms. Hightower," said Helen. "This is my colleague, Nigel. He has come to help out."

Cartier yawned massively, barely bothering to cover her mouth with her fist. "Oh, hey." She looked around. "It's just you guys here?"

Helen nodded.

"You said Amina and Dixon came by?"

"They did. We met with them earlier. Outside."

Cartier had on fuzzy sweatpants, bagged at the knees, and an oversized pale-peach sweatshirt decorated with a number of stains.

"I don't want to see anyone right now. I'm just too . . . tired."

"Of course," said Helen.

"I'm not looking my best. Plus, I'm kind of hiding. From my emotions? My mom did the same thing. She called it 'going full fort.' As in blanket fort." Cartier gave a half-hearted laugh. "We used to make these epic blanket forts when I was a kid. She'd get the help involved, like the gardeners and the housekeepers and whoever else was around. We made whole blanket rooms and hid out in there. Reading books or watching our phones or just sleeping. My mom could stay in a blanket fort for a really long time. Days, even. Especially after she got sick."

Helen felt deep compassion for the girl, thinking about her with her ill mother, who was also her best and only friend. She wondered if she should offer to make a blanket fort for her client, but thought perhaps their relationship wasn't at that stage yet.

"You know what would be cool?" said Cartier, after another enormous yawn. "Doing blanket fort TikToks. Take it to the next level with fairy lights and wine and music. I don't think this place is big enough. We might need to rent a house." Then the girl's glassy eyes landed on Nigel. "Has he signed an NDA?"

"He has not," said Helen.

"Have you?"

"No. But we are both happy to do so."

"Can you ask Daddy to have his lawyers draft something? It's not that I don't trust you. I just . . . you know, it's what everyone does now. With staff."

Cartier shuffled over to look out the window. She gazed down at the pool deck, with its rows of lounge chairs and potted palm trees. People in bathing suits and robes were lined up at a small drinks station. Some floated on their backs in the pool. Others lay on their loungers under striped umbrellas, speaking or staring into their phones.

"Ugh," said Cartier. "I hate the sun. And bathing suits."

It was an odd thing to say, given her decision to live in a suite overlooking a pool, and the very recent death of her swimsuit modelling colleague.

She plopped down on one of the pale leather couches. "What's new with you guys?" she asked. Then she looked at Nigel, surprised by his presence all over again. "Who are you again?"

"I'm Nigel. I'll be helping Helen with the dogs and anything else that's needed. I'm an extra pair of hands."

Helen was proud of how clearly and simply he'd spoken. He'd made no strange confessions about his checkered work history and wasn't wearing half a gallon of horrific cologne, as he had been when she first interviewed him for a job. Gavin and Murray were doing a fine job of preparing him to go to butler school in the fall.

"The dogs!" said Cartier. "Oh my god, where are my babies?"

"Shall we get them for you?" said Helen. She and Nigel had left them in Nigel's room after their walk so they wouldn't disturb Cartier.

"Uh, yes. Of course!" Then she gazed into the middle distance for a long, searching moment. "Actually, before you do that, can you do something else for me?"

"Of course," said Helen.

"There's this guy called Mike on a Bike? He has a courier business. I'd like to, uh, purchase a few things. Maybe you could get him to come by?"

Helen was glad that the hotel manager, her training at the North American Butler Academy, and her own internal ethos had prepared her to handle this sort of scenario. Yes, cannabis was legal in BC, but no, she was not going down this road for any client and especially not one she was trying to prepare for a life in which funds would be unlimited and boundaries scarce, one whose father was worried that his only child was on drugs. If Helen started ordering Mike on a Bike for Cartier, she'd be tracking down MDMA dealers and who knows what else for her new client in no time. Best to nip this in the bud. So to speak.

"I'm afraid the terms of my contract prevent me from ordering drugs for clients."

"Um, pot is legal now, Hel. You would probably get me *booze*, right?" said Cartier.

"I've been hired by your father, and he was very clear about substances."

"Are you like a sober-coach butler?" asked Cartier, her long eyes narrowing. "Planning to narc me out to my dad?"

"Not unless there is a serious health concern," said Helen.

Cartier puffed out an annoyed sigh. "Fine. Whatever. I thought you were cool. Not some babysitter my dad hired."

Helen could feel Nigel's eyes darting between her and the client. "You are welcome to make your own arrangements with, uh, Michael," said Helen.

"The hotel said Mike and his bike can't come on the property anymore," groused Cartier. "Even though his trailer is super tasteful. It's so dumb. They wouldn't know if a coke dealer came by. Half the people in this city look like coke dealers."

Helen nodded. That was true enough.

The phone in the room rang.

"Shall I get that?" asked Helen.

"I guess. Whatever." Cartier slumped back in her seat and pulled up her legs.

"Who is it?" asked Cartier.

"The front desk," said Helen. "A Mr. Bryan Ulrich and Keithen McNair are here to see you."

"Oh. My. God!" stage-whispered Cartier. "Bryan? He's here?"

"It seems so," said Helen.

"Fuuuck." Cartier drew her long black-and-white nails through her nest of platinum hair. "I look like such trash."

"Shall I ask them to wait for fifteen minutes so you can get ready?"

"What? *No!* I can't ask Bryan to wait. He's Bryan Ulrich, for god's sake." Cartier spoke as though his was a household name.

Helen sighed internally. First she'd never heard of the supposedly famous Deep State, at least not the content-creating version. She *had* heard of the conspiracy theory version. And now she'd never heard of Bryan Ulrich.

"I would be happy to get them settled while you freshen up in your room."

"Oh god," sighed Cartier. "Okay. Okay. Tell them to come up. And then be nice to them for a little while so I can get my face together. Fuck. Fuck."

And with that, she got to her feet and rushed messily into her room.

Helen looked at Nigel, who was typing furiously on his phone.

"Bryan Ulrich is an agent who represents influencers and brands. He works with the Deep State." He looked up. "And Keithen is in the group. He's the vigilante one."

"The what?" asked Helen. But it was too late.

A soft knock sounded, and Helen opened the door to two white men, one in stylish and well-preserved middle age, the other in his early twenties, with long red hair, tattoos, and the confident demeanour of someone who has never had a moment's doubt in himself.

"I'm Bryan," said the older man, holding out a hand, which Helen shook.

"Keithen," said the younger.

Helen invited the men in, introduced herself and Nigel, and let them know that Cartier would be with them shortly. They sat down and Helen offered them refreshments, which Nigel prepared.

Bryan had an easygoing manner and an open face. He took the luxurious surroundings in stride, neither impressed nor unimpressed. There was a sturdy solidity to his physical presence. He met Helen's eye easily but didn't stare. When he smiled, his teeth were straight and white. All in all, he looked well cared for and easy to like. The sort of person other people would like to deal with.

Keithen was different. His tattoos extended down onto the fronts of his hands. He was tall and looked strong, like a man who made his living with those heavily-inked hands. He wore Dickies, a grey T-shirt, and green Chuck Taylors. His bright-blue eyes had an appraising quality that wasn't exactly off-putting but certainly made Helen feel as though she was being assessed. He reminded her of many of the slightly mean popular boys from her small-town high school.

"Cart's dad hired you?" asked Keithen.

She smiled. "I'm working for Ms. Hightower for a time."

"You're a genuine butler?" There was an edge to this question that Helen had heard before. The term *butler* set people off, triggering their internal prejudices about wealthy people.

"Now, Keithen. Enough interrogating," said Bryan. "We're not on TikTok. Nobody here has kicked a dog or bullied a clerk at a 7-Eleven."

Keithen made a sour face but didn't respond. He was very pale.

Bryan smiled at Helen. "Keithen is a legend in the social media world for his finely honed sense of outrage. And rightly so. He's very good at finding out everything about people who have violated his sense of right and wrong."

Keithen made a huffing noise. "I should fire you."

"But you won't," said Bryan easily. "Because you love me."

"Yeah, man. I love you. Everything's been going so great since you came along."

Bryan seemed about to respond when Cartier came out of the bathroom. She had on a clean track suit and still looked tired, but somewhat less like a girl who had spent the better part of three days in bed.

"Bryaaannn!" she said.

"Oh, Carty. Our sensitive girl," said Bryan, and he got up and gave her a gentle hug. "How are you holding up?"

"She's clearly barely coping up in here," said Keithen. "Scraping along, grinding it out. What is this place? Two grand a night?"

"You're an asshole," said Cartier, as they exchanged insincere cheek kisses.

The three of them took seats on the pale leather furniture, and Nigel got Cartier a cup of tea.

"You don't need to stay," Cartier told Helen.

"We're just going to have a little debrief here. Talk things through," said Bryan. "It has been a challenging time for everyone."

"Helen, I'll text you when we're done," said Cartier. "Maybe go for a walk or read or do whatever it is that you like to do?" It was obvious that Cartier couldn't quite fathom what someone like Helen might enjoy.

"Maybe you should get some food?" Bryan said to Cartier. "You look like you haven't been eating."

"She already has a butler. She doesn't need a dad, too," said Keithen.

"That's enough, okay," said Bryan, and this time he sounded like he meant it. "Save the class warrior stuff for your videos."

"Fine," muttered Keithen.

And with that, Nigel and Helen let themselves out of the suite.

They decided to take the dogs for another walk, this time along the seawall, starting at Coal Harbour. They made it out of the hotel without incident, with all the staff greeting Helen like she was the hotel GM.

"God, how do you do that?" asked Nigel. "Everyone in that place loves you so hard already."

Helen just smiled. She tried not to take other people's reactions, good or bad, personally.

"The younger guy? That was Keithen," said Nigel, unnecessarily. "He's probably got more clout and more followers than all the rest of them put together."

"Ah," said Helen, who was still processing the interaction between the three people upstairs. She understood why Cartier's father was so worried. The dynamics between them felt off. Now that she'd met all the members of the Deep State and their agent, she thought she'd seen all of the five Buddhist poisons on display: pride, greed, attachment, aversion, and jealousy. They seemed possessed of precious little of the qualities that might counterbalance the poisons, such as love or joy or compassion or equanimity.

"Keithen's whole thing is being outraged and finding out the identities of people who do bad things. He's sometimes pretty funny online. Seems like not so much in person, though."

True. Keithen had not seemed funny or entertaining in person. But his outsized confidence going up against a target would likely be compelling.

Helen bent down to feed each of the dogs a small liver-flavoured treat. None of them had experienced any digestive upset since she and Nigel had taken over their care, and Helen felt good about that, as well as relieved.

"Does Bryan go on camera too?" she asked.

Nigel shook his head. "No. I've never seen him. I think he just . . . I don't know. Advises them? Gets them business deals. Ad campaigns.

Endorsements. Stuff like that. Word is that the Deep State is on the verge of making bank, thanks to him. He's a big deal, I think."

Helen looked at him. "Making bank?" she said.

"That means making a lot of money. Keithen, for instance. He's nowhere near the level of a PewDiePie or one of the Paul brothers or the Kardashians. He's not even Liver King level. But he already probably makes at least a few hundred grand a year. Maybe more. If they get to the next tier, they could make millions."

Helen found that information startling. Who paid them? She still didn't understand what was in it for Cartier. She didn't need the money. Was it the attention she craved? Companionship? What made her willing to put up with being belittled by Keithen and shunned by large parts of the audience? Her so-called friends in the Deep State had dumped her off in her hour of need and hadn't even bothered to turn off her car. The relationship did not appear to be one based on mutual care. "Is Cartier famous?" Helen asked.

"She's more infamous," said Nigel.

Helen's phone buzzed with a text from Cartier.

Can U Come bck in? And bring t Lams

Helen and Nigel had only been out for about twenty minutes, but they turned back right away.

CHAPTER 17
NIGEL

When they got back to the suite, it was filled with the remaining members of the Deep State. Keithen, Dixon, Amina, and Cartier lounged in various positions around the suite and stared at their phones. Bryan sat off to the side, like a popular, easygoing teacher taking a middle school class on a field trip.

It was after one o'clock and they appeared to have settled in for a good scroll session. For once, Helen seemed unsure what to do. The group's silent focus on their devices was probably unsettling for her. Nigel thought everything about the situation was unsettling for his boss. After all, Helen was the anti-internet. She was calm focus and gentle attention. She was the praying hands emoji in human form. She definitely deserved better than these people.

Helen, who was obviously baffled by the Deep State, didn't seem to realize that they found her, with her plain navy outfits and quiet, grown-up manner, a joke. And Nigel hated that for her.

He was used to people thinking he was goofy. That was fine, since he *was* goofy, at least most of the time. But Helen was a serious individual. A good person. And this whole influencer scene was the opposite of that. He felt overwhelmingly protective of his earnest and gentle mentor. She was like a fourth Pekingese in a room full of pit vipers. No. That wasn't quite right. She was more like a sloth in a room full of hyenas. Nope. That wasn't it either. Helen defied comparisons.

"Hey, Hells," said Cartier, taking what Nigel considered to be outrageous liberties. "We were wondering if you could order us some smoothies? I think we're going to go out in a bit and we need some fuel." The Deep State looked up from their devices, except for Bryan, who kept texting away. Was Dixon *filming* Helen?

"Of course," said Helen.

Cartier immediately reeled off the most detailed smoothie order Nigel had ever heard. Halfway through, between the ground white chia and the matcha powder, Helen took out her notebook and began writing it down. Not even her excellent memory could handle a fifteen-item ingredients list.

The others gave their own, slightly less complicated orders, except Bryan, who was fully engaged with whatever was happening on his phone.

"Very good," Helen said, after reading back the smoothie requests. "Is the hotel kitchen familiar with this order?"

"Uh, no. You'll have to get them from Juiced. It's a couple of blocks away."

"Hey," said Amina. "Could you call Mike on a Bike for us?"

"I could go for some flower. I'll take El Chapo Popcorn," said Keithen. "Just seven grams."

"Edibles for me, please. Watermelon," said Dixon.

"Not going to happen," said Cartier. "I already tried. Hells won't order us weed."

"Why not?" asked Amina, as though any answer would be highly offensive.

"I don't know," said Cartier. "Something to do with my dad."

"I'll call him," said Dixon. "Mike," he clarified, seeing Cartier's horrified expression. "Not your dad. Jesus."

The others nodded.

"No one is *ever* calling your dad, Hightower," agreed Keithen.

"For any reason," agreed Amina.

"You dad could have a million dollars to give me, and I still wouldn't call him," said Keithen.

"Oh, be quiet, you guys," said Cartier. "He's just . . . you know." She shrugged.

"Yell-y?" said Amina.

"My grandma would have said he was mean as six cats in a one-cat carrier," said Keithen. "My gram saw everything through the lens of cats."

"Okay, that's enough," said Bryan, finally tuning in. "Let's get the smoothies happening so we can start knocking items off the agenda. There are commitments to be kept." He looked down at his phone. "There's Stephanie. I better take it."

He got up and waved as he let himself out.

"He really signed Stephanie Murphy?" said Keithen, after the door closed behind Bryan.

"Apparently," said Dixon. "And he's working with the Kanuckle twins. You know, those identical twins who do the toy and game reviews? And they dance and make slime and whatever? They've already been signed by Nickelodeon and I think Bryan is working on a major deal with TotalToys for them. They have nearly eight million followers, if you can believe that."

"Ugh," said Amina. "That whole kidfluencer thing icks me out."

"God, we better up our game or he's going to drop us." Cartier grinned weakly.

Nigel caught the look Amina levelled at Cartier. The look said that the only person who needed to do better was Cartier.

"High-profile clients just mean he has that much more power to help us," said Keithen. "He's already got us more and better contracts than we ever had before on our own."

"He's awesome at image management," said Amina. "Super useful."

"Cartier's right," said Dixon. "Hard to manage our image if we're . . . well, if we—"

"If we keep dying," said Keithen. "And botching everything we touch. No brand wants to be associated with scandals. Even your basic misfortunes bum people out."

"Yes and no," said Amina. "Everyone loves drama."

"But they don't want their Mercedes advertisement anywhere near some misery train."

Nigel followed the back and forth with more interest than was strictly appropriate. An old rule of domestic service is that one should hear but not listen, but he loved to listen.

"He told me in confidence that we're being considered for a major new campaign. But he wouldn't give me any details," said Dixon.

"If he's signing people like Stephanie Murphy, we should start aiming higher. Commercials. Acting gigs," said Amina.

The others nodded.

"In the meantime, let's just get through the day," said Keithen. "We've got some catching up to do."

With that, Cartier and her friends went back to their phones and Helen ordered the smoothies, which between them had a total of sixty-three ingredients. Only Keithen had kept things simple by ordering a coffee and an orange juice.

While all of this was happening, Cartier and her friends kept taking photos of Helen when she wasn't looking. Nigel wanted to say something, but he didn't want to undercut his boss's authority. The situation made him feel itchy and stressed out. He hadn't felt this tense since he and Helen were nearly murdered at the Yatra Institute back on Sutil Island. These people gave him the creeps and not just because, except for Cartier, they seemed totally unaffected by the fact that people in their group kept dying.

CHAPTER 18

Helen waited patiently for something to happen. She had caught each of the members of the Deep State staring speculatively at her several times before looking away. They kept filming her when they thought she wasn't looking, and she wondered why but decided not to ask. Just as disconcertingly, every so often one of them would ask her a question and then appear to lose interest halfway through her answer.

"So, Helen, what's it like being a butler?"

"What's the hardest part of butlering?"

"Do you sometimes wear a uniform? Like a tuxedo or anything?"

"Have you worked with a lot of royalty or famous people?"

"Have you ever considered a different"—hand wave—"skin care regimen?"

She answered each query politely. Helen was a former monastic. She was trained to be still and to avoid resorting to distractions. She wasn't bothered by being treated like a not-very-popular attraction at a zoo, but the dynamic was clearly upsetting for Nigel, who seemed to be struggling not to say something. As usual, his feelings showed clearly on his face.

"Do you even *have* a phone, Helen?" asked Dixon, even though he knew she did. "Why don't you use it? Is digital self-denial some butler rule?"

Mostly what happened was that Cartier and her friends drank smoothies, ate cannabis edibles, which Amina had gone outside to collect, and monitored their phones like NASA scientists watching the launch of a space shuttle. Their fingers moved constantly against their screens as they scrolled, flipped from account to account, refreshing, refreshing, refreshing.

Sometimes they spoke about what they were seeing, but mostly they stared. Their expressions had a contracted quality and the sort of intense focus that crowded out the rest of the world.

Helen watched. And waited.

After about an hour of intense scrolling, they all looked up at the same time. It was 3:30 in the afternoon.

"Okay," said Amina. "Let's move."

They got up and organized themselves while Cartier disappeared into her bedroom.

After five minutes, Amina started to lose patience. "Could someone please tell Cartier to hurry up? We're going to miss our appointments. Tandy only got us in as a huge favour to me."

"The video for Blossom's memorial," said Keithen. "We have got to get that shit done."

Helen was about to offer to knock on the door when Cartier emerged in full makeup and wearing a soft-pinkish track suit.

"Oooh, you're wearing our Mountbatten pink. Looks good on you," said Dixon.

Cartier looked pleased and blew him a kiss.

The entourage began to move like a single organism. Helen followed them and waved at Nigel, who was staying behind with the dogs.

They filled the hallway outside the elevators with the scent of perfume and the soft rustle of expensive athleisure wear. Every eye in the lobby tracked them on their way out the front doors, where Joseph and another valet waited to open the doors of an enormous Range Rover painted matte black. It looked like the sort of thing a private military contractor might drive on their way to do war crimes.

"Thanks, Joseph," said Cartier, giving him an air kiss.

On her way into the vehicle, Helen handed Joseph a ten-dollar bill. After a moment's thought, she added another ten.

Dixon got in the driver's seat and Cartier climbed up into the passenger seat, presumably because it was her vehicle, not because she was the most valued member of the group. Helen, Amina, and Keithen climbed into the back seat, where they fit with room to spare. Moments later, the tank-like vehicle turned out into the flat white light of the Vancouver afternoon.

"So are we going to Blossom's service? Or just sending flowers? Can we please just make a decision?" asked Dixon. He spoke as though picking up a conversation that had been going on for some time.

"I can't face it," said Amina. "Too emotional. It triggers my PTSD."

"You only have that on Instagram," said Keithen.

"She also has it on her TikTok," said Dixon.

"Shut up, you guys," said Amina, apparently unperturbed. "Overwhelming emotion is bad for me."

"Some genuine emotion might actually do you good," said Keithen. "A little time on the struggle bus would help you relate to the common people."

"Oh, shut up, Fucker Carlson," said Amina.

"Harsh burn," said Keithen. Their bickering had a rote quality and wasn't particularly charged with animosity.

"Is anyone going to answer my question?" asked Dixon, stopping in the middle of the Robson Street intersection. Horns sounded and other drivers swerved around them. None of the others seemed to notice, or care.

"I've forgotten what the question is," said Cartier.

"Are we going to Blossom's service?"

"We didn't go to Trudee's," said Amina.

"Yeah, but she wasn't exactly one of us. She was an assistant. Your assistant," said Dixon to Cartier. "It was a mistake for you to miss that."

"Stop blaming her. Trudee's folks lived somewhere super random," said Amina. "Like Williams Lake or David Lake or Gerald Lake. One of those lakes up north with a white settler man's name on it."

"You mean 100 Mile House?" said Keithen. "Jesus. You really didn't know her at all, did you? We all should have gone. People noticed that we didn't. And we should go to Blossom's."

The way these people interacted with each other was exhausting. Realizing that was somehow a relief to Helen. For the millionth time, she recited the refrain that she'd been taught to bring herself back to the present: *Never again this moment.* Each moment with the Deep State was one she would not have to repeat. Or would she? There was a strange, stuck quality to the group. It was in the entrenched, backwards-looking way they spoke to one another and in how they stared fixedly at their phones any time they weren't reaching for something else to change the way they felt.

"Okay, we're here," said Dixon. This time he braked in the middle of a narrow laneway. "Let's go, bitches, it's hair time."

And with that, Cartier, Keithen, and Amina piled out. There was more honking, and Dixon turned around and threw the keys into the back seat for Helen.

"We'll be in the salon," he said. "Cartier wants you in there after you park." The honking grew louder. More insistent.

Helen took a deep breath and got out of the back and into the driver's seat.

CHAPTER 19

It took Helen fifteen minutes to find parking and then walk back to Blow It Out Your Salon.

The assault of blow-dryers, gossip, pop music, and chemically scented beauty products was immediate. The decor was entirely white and pink.

Helen went to the counter, where a young woman with long pink and black hair and debilitatingly long eyelash extensions waited.

"Can I help you?" asked the girl. At least, that's what Helen thought she said. She couldn't hear what she actually said over the music.

"HELLO. CAN YOU TELL ME HOW LONG CARTIER HIGHTOWER WILL BE?" Helen yelled.

"I'm so sorry. We're fully booked," said the receptionist. She seemed to be staring at Helen's hair, and her expression said she found it concerning.

"WHEN WILL SHE BE DONE?"

"Aw," said the receptionist. "Thank you."

"I'll wait outside," said Helen, giving up.

The door closed and she felt instantly better away from the noise and the scents. The afternoon had suddenly turned lovely. The white cloud cover was gone, revealing a soft-blue sky. The people on the streets of Yaletown seemed happy and prosperous in a way Helen associated with wealthy areas in California. Every second or third person had a small dog or two at the end of a fancy lead.

She was about to embark on a short stroll when her phone buzzed. It was Cartier.

Can U cum here Now

In spite of her best efforts to remain neutral, Helen winced. Then she texted back.

If you're ready I will get the vehicle and pick you up.

No car Just U

I will be there shortly.

Helen sighed and walked the few steps back into the deafening salon, where she was greeted by a staff member in a black apron. The young woman had a black bob interspersed with white chunks, reminiscent of piano keys.

"Helen?" the piano key–haired girl yelled over the din.

"That's right. I'm here for Cartier Hightower."

"Come with me," said the girl.

Reluctantly, Helen followed the girl deeper into the salon, where Cartier and Amina sat side by side in white leather chairs. Amina's stylist was putting her hair into an elaborate updo, accented with several braided attachments that wound around a topknot. In one of the rows of chairs behind them, Dixon appeared to be receiving an elaborate head massage. Two chairs over, Keithen was being shaved. The place was packed and much bigger on the inside than it appeared from outside.

Amina waved languorously at Helen and went back to her conversation with her stylist.

When Cartier noticed Helen, she leapt out of her chair, startling the girl behind her, who'd been about to do something with a hot iron.

"Helen!" Cartier cried. "You came." She spoke as though Helen had a choice.

"Are you ready for me to bring the car?" Helen asked.

She noticed the people in Dixon's row of chairs had their feet soaking in small sinks of bubbling water. Everyone in that row who was not a worker was sipping at tea and staring at their phones while black-clad technicians dried and painted their nails or massaged their heads or hands.

"I had the greatest idea!" said Cartier. Half of her long white-blond hair had been curled into ringlets that wound their way down her back. The other half was twisted into clips.

Helen's own favourite hairdo had been the shaved head she wore after she became a monastic. When she left the order, she'd grown her hair back to shoulder length. These days her hair care routine involved washing, brushing, and putting her thick dark hair in a simple ponytail. She thought that the part of Cartier's hair that had been blown out made it look like she was wearing a wig, but it seemed to have done wonders for her confidence. Or perhaps Cartier had taken another pill. Either way, the girl seemed positively giddy.

"You are seriously not going to believe this idea I had," said Cartier.

Helen noticed that the other members of the Deep State were watching them carefully while pretending not to.

In fact, the attention of everyone in the salon seemed to have sharpened when Helen arrived. Even the volume on the music had dropped.

Cartier beamed at Helen. "We're going to get you a blowout!"

Helen, caught entirely by surprise, didn't know how to respond. This, once again, was not something that had been covered in butler school.

She briefly closed her eyes and focused on her breath. Deep breath in, soft breath out. Repeat. Receiving a blowout would fall under the category of gifts. Butlers did not take gifts. Nor did they want to be the centre of attention. Helen was even less keen on being the centre of attention than most. She had never, ever wanted that. *Aversion*, she noted. Powerful aversion.

"Thank you so much," she said. "That is very kind, but not necessary." Helen looked at the group of blowout artists standing behind their clients. Everyone was staring at her.

"Um, hello, Helen. I don't want to pull rank or whatever, but I'm basically your boss," said Cartier in a voice that was both bullying and cajoling. "And I insist that you do this. For me. After all, we're"—she waved a hand around as though speaking for everyone at Blow It Out Your Salon, as well as everyone in Yaletown and in the greater Vancouver area—"in the public eye. Which means that *you* are in the public eye. We *all* need to put our best hair forward. For the team."

Helen felt the current of resistance coursing through her strengthen. She really, *really* did not want anyone messing with her hair. Or any other part of her. Not in this sort of place, which was very much not her style.

Resistance, she reminded herself automatically, is the source of most suffering. It wouldn't hurt her to sit in the chair and allow someone to interfere with her hair. She could use the experience as an opportunity to understand her young client better.

Helen nodded and the stylist with piano-key hair asked her to sit in one of the white leather chairs. *Stay interested*, Helen told herself. How bad could it be? She tried not to look at herself in the mirror, and instead focused on the new stylist. Helen smiled at her, and the stylist smiled back.

"Do you know what you'd like to do with your hair?" asked the stylist. "I'm Tandy, by the way."

"I'm . . . I think my hair is fine," said Helen.

"Oh no," said Tandy, slowly shaking her head. "It's not." She smiled sweetly. "Don't worry. Cartier has given me some great ideas."

"Thank you, Tandy," said Helen. Then she closed her eyes. She kept them squeezed shut while Tandy put a cape around her neck and only opened them again to get to one of the wash stations.

"Put your head back, please," said Tandy, after Helen had taken a seat. "There. Is that comfortable?"

No, thought Helen. It most certainly is not comfortable. But she didn't say anything. If Helen hadn't felt so rattled and off-kilter from spending time with Cartier and her internet-addicted friends, she surely would have found a way to get out of this situation gracefully. *Regret*, she noted. *Unpleasant.*

Tandy washed her hair and put many products in it, only to rinse them right out again, and then she gave Helen an elaborate head massage, which was quite pleasant. Then Tandy wrapped Helen's head in a towel and brought her back to her station.

Cartier and Amina had disappeared. That made Helen uncomfortable. She was meant to be on duty, helping her client. And instead here she was, getting her own hair done! It was preposterous. Unprofessional! If her fellow butler graduates could see her now.

Tandy removed the towel and Helen's wet hair fell to her shoulders.

"Virgin?" said Tandy.

"I beg your pardon?" said Helen, who was finding out that she did still have the capacity to be shocked.

"Your hair looks virgin. You've never dyed it?"

"No," said Helen. Nor had she ever curled it or put hairspray in it or given it more than a fleeting thought. Every so often she would drop into an inexpensive no-appointment-necessary salon and get it cut. She always turned down the wash and blow-dry.

"Do you mind if I put product in it?"

"I suppose not," said Helen, who couldn't imagine what more potions could be added that hadn't already been applied in the washing sink.

Around them the salon had refilled with a new batch of people getting their hair washed and styled. Perfectly decent people indulging their natural vanity. It was all okay. Perfectly normal. So why did she feel like running, screaming out of the salon, chased by her own dislike of her present circumstances?

"Can you make it like it was?" asked Helen, meaning straight and pulled back into a simple low ponytail.

Tandy, who was perhaps nineteen, made a face. "To be totally honest, Cartier and Amina already sort of told me how it should look," she said.

"So you were just asking me to be polite?" said Helen.

"Yeah, basically," said Tandy.

"Well, go ahead, then," said Helen. "I'm sure whatever you do will be very nice." And with that, she closed her eyes and dropped into a concentrated state, which was a blessed relief.

"Done!" said Tandy about twenty minutes later.

Helen gaped at the sight in the mirror. Her entire head was covered in tight corkscrew curls. She looked like Shirley Temple, only much older and with a face that really, really didn't suit little-girl curls. Tandy was biting her lip. Helen didn't want to hurt the girl's feelings, no matter how appalling she found the hairdo.

"I hope you like it," said Tandy.

"Are *you* happy with it?" Helen asked.

"Yes?" said Tandy, whose face said otherwise.

"Well, good, then," said Helen. "Thank you. It looks very interesting."

"I need to add some more spray," said Tandy. "Cartier said she wants the curls to last."

Helen wondered briefly what was happening that evening that would require her to look like a Portuguese Water Dog. She found she really didn't want to know.

"I think there is enough hairspray in it already," said Helen firmly. There were limits.

"Don't worry. The curls will relax on their own. Eventually."

Before Helen could say that sooner rather than later would be better for her, in terms of curl relaxation, there was a honk from the street and the receptionist ran over. "It's Cartier," she said breathlessly. "She says you have to go."

"Payment?" asked Helen, who was already up and out of the chair.

"Cartier took care of it."

"Tip?"

"She left a huge one."

"Thank you again," said Helen, rushing out and toward the street, sausage-y ringlets bouncing as she went, rows of heads turning to follow her. As she exited the salon, she thought she heard peels of laughter behind her. *Unpleasant. Unpleasant.*

CHAPTER 20
NIGEL

What they had done to Helen was a crime. There was no one Nigel respected more than Helen and even *he* had a hard time taking her seriously with that hairdo. He didn't know which diabolical clout chaser among them had decided to fuck up Helen's hair, but the Deep State Instagram account started posting about it as soon as they hit the salon.

The first photo showed shots of Helen looking like her normal, gentle, hyper-organized and strangely calm self. Something about the light or the angle or maybe just the platform itself made it clear that she was not a heavy makeup user and that she didn't give a single shit about her hair. But not in a bad way. More like in a regular, professional, older-fashioned gal kind of way.

The next shot was Helen with *the hair*. She was caught in mid-stride, and she must have been moving pretty fast, because the lumps on her head were all in flight. It looked like someone with a good arm had thrown an entire tray of cocktail sausages. And her amazingly kind Helen face was all concerned about being late or whatever.

The photo was captioned: *Daddy got me a butler.*

Fuck these people, thought Nigel.

The Deep State's audience ate it up like Gruyère in the fondue pot. A few of their followers, the ones who had an iota of decorum about the fact that one of the Deep State had just died, tried to put a lid on the bitchy festivities.

Maybe show some respect for Blossom. She just died, in case you forgot. #RIPBlossom

And:

Sorry, Blossom. Seems like your so-called friends don't care. #RIPBlossom #RIPMourningProperly #dobetter

But the rest of the internet was like: Naw, let's make fun of the butler and her sad hair.

One account, RUOkay2212, tagged Cartier's personal account and wrote:

Everything Cartier touches dies. Just look at that poor b&%^'s hair. #countdowntodead

The comment was removed, but minutes later, there was a comment from someone called RUOKAY4Real1z.

Cartier Hightower has to pay people to hang out with her #thentheydie

It was preteen-level bullying, but it was relentless and personal and aimed directly at Cartier. What, Nigel wondered, would it be like to have that kind of stuff directed at you all day, every day. He would have given up after an hour of it. No more internet influencing for him.

Nigel wanted to text Helen but couldn't figure out what to say or how to warn her. He finally settled on:

Hey. How's it going? Everything okay?

All is well. Thank you. Please have housekeeping change the linens in Ms. Hightower's bedroom and order flowers for the suite.

Then she sent him a list of the flowers she wanted.

That was totally Helen. Busting her balls for a girl who was making fun of her. Nigel decided he had to get more direct with Helen for her own good.

Sure. Right away. Also, Helen? Maybe stay out of range of their cameras?

He could see that she'd read it. But it took a couple of minutes for the reply to come through.

Thank you.

That was it.

Anyone who would target Helen was capable of anything, as far as he was concerned. Maybe what people were saying about Cartier being a psychopath was true. Nigel decided right then and there to make sure that nothing bad happened to good, gentle, kind, extremely offline Helen.

CHAPTER 21

After they left the salon, they drove to a dimly lit Gastown store crowded with denim and people wearing denim. Next, the group went to a nearly empty store selling wildly expensive, cheap-looking clothes. It was Friday and so stores were open until 9:00 p.m. A tiny sign over the door read: *Dixon Cho*. So this was Dixon's boutique.

Inside, Cartier chose a pair of zebra leggings with side openings (a cool thousand dollars) and a tank top (five hundred and twenty-five dollars), as well as a purple acid-washed jean jacket with a lot of studs and rips (twenty-five hundred dollars).

"It's perfect for tonight. Oh, and can you grab that Clot for me?"

Helen picked up the white hat with the word *Clot* emblazoned across the front.

"Dad hats are everything, aren't they?" said Amina, coming over to admire the hat.

"Hells? Can you try it on for me?" asked Cartier.

"I'm happy to take a photo of you while you try it on," said Helen.

"I need to see it on someone else to know whether I like it," said Cartier.

Helen accepted her fate and put on the hat. Cartier and Amina quickly snapped photos. Helen closed her eyes, noting her aversion. How did her negative reaction to having her hair curled and being made to wear dad hats emblazoned with unpleasant words fit into the Buddha's teachings? Did the Eight Worldly Concerns of gain and loss, praise and blame, fame and disgrace, and pleasure and pain apply? Or should she refer to the teachings on suffering? Was there something in the butler handbook about this situation if the Buddha's teachings did not apply?

Helen knew Cartier and her friends were making fun of her and trying to humiliate her. It made sense. They were surrounded by chaos. They didn't seem to like one another very much, and they couldn't pay attention to what was happening in the real word long enough to make a genuine connection with others. People around them were dying in sad and seemingly preventable ways. Her calm probably felt like an affront. So did her lack of vanity.

Should she simply quit this terrible and seemingly impossible job? She didn't think the Levines would blame her. But perhaps they would think less of her? How attached was she to their good opinion? Very.

Helen looked at the remaining members of the Deep State, shopping with a sad, frantic intensity, while Dixon did some kind of livestream, talking about his vision for his store. She realized she didn't care if they found it funny to dress her up and take her photo. She could see the humour in it, even if she didn't enjoy the experience. She would take her cues from the Dhammapada, or Treasury of Truth: "As the wind cannot stir a solid mass of rock, so too blame and praise do not affect the wise."

That was her. She was the rock. The rock with curled hair. The rock who had been taken on an unpleasant shopping trip. All would be fine. But she would have to make sure that she was not led by them into some activity that would end with her smashed to bits in a river or dashed into the side of a boat. Even rocks can be broken.

Helen, arms weighed down by Cartier's purchases, moved over to her client. "Shall I take these to the checkout? And perhaps I should call and order a floral arrangement for Blossom's memorial service, since you have decided not to attend?"

Cartier rolled a blue-beaded bracelet up and down her arm. It looked like the sort of thing seven-year-olds make for one another. The price tag revealed that it was over a thousand dollars.

"Sure."

"Do you have an address for where the flowers should be delivered?"

"Try Dixon. He's a business guy, so he's super organized."

Helen went to where Dixon was admiring himself in a white and brown velour track suit with oddly shaped appliqués on the sides of the legs and the chest. He was a good-looking man, but the track suit made him look like he was wearing a scrawny cow costume. Then again, Helen was not in a position to judge. Her curls remained high and tight and reminiscent of toilet paper rolls. The extremely on-trend sales clerks kept giving her horrified glances. Fair enough. Every time she caught sight of herself in the mirror, she recoiled in much the same way before she remembered that she was a rock.

Not me, not mine, she repeated when another wave of embarrassment washed over her. She might be a rock, but she had to admit there was a certain level of erosion happening.

"Do you have an address for where I should send the flowers?" she asked Dixon.

"Isn't this incredible?" he said, indicating his cow track suit. "This one is called Yes You Can't."

"Ah," said Helen. "I see."

He turned to look at his rear end, which was not remotely enhanced by the brown and white velour. But he seemed pleased.

"Would you mind?" he asked, handing her his camera.

Helen stared. Her arms were still loaded with potential purchases.

"Take a picture of my booty?" said Dixon.

"Of course," said Helen. She set down the pile of clothes with nary a natural fibre among them and took his camera.

"Take it head-on," he said. "So to speak."

What on earth was he talking about?

"Get low. Butt level."

At that moment, Helen decided to allow herself to stop being fully present.

She was so tuned out, she barely heard Dixon when he next spoke.

". . . I'll get that address for you. Can you make sure the card has all of our names? And hey, Helen?"

She gave herself a little shake to bring herself back to the unpleasant present.

"What are you *really* doing here?" he asked.

For once, she had Dixon's full attention. There was nothing friendly or curious in his question. It was an accusation.

It was not Helen's place to explain Mr. Hightower's reasons.

"I'm just here to help Ms. Hightower," she said.

"Are you a butler or a spy or what?"

"A butler," said Helen.

"Right. But that's not *all* you are. I can tell. There's something else going on with you." He stared at her intently. "You remind me of someone."

"Shirley Temple?" said Helen, touching her hair. She wasn't one to make a lot of jokes, but the overstimulating environment and irregular schedule were creating opportunities for her to try new ways of being.

"Naw." He smiled his million-dollar smile. "I don't think so. Like I said, there's something about you."

Helen had heard that many times before.

"If you are spying on us for Cartier's dad, you're going to be disappointed. She's the one who needs us. It's not the other way around." His friendly expression remained fixed on his face even as he issued his warning.

"Look, she's only been with us for, I don't know, six months? Eight? And we only brought her on because Trudee vouched for her. Vouched hard."

Helen listened.

"But Trudee's gone," he said. "And Cart's not really landing with the fans. Once things settle down, we need to have a talk about whether the Deep State is the right fit for her."

Helen had questions, but some instinct told her not to push. So she just nodded and collected Cartier's items off the table where she'd set them.

"I'll get you that address," he said, then added, "Good chat."

Helen felt deep compassion for her client, who was going to be removed from this group of people who didn't like her, but whom she clung to for reasons Helen didn't understand. What did Cartier like about being in the Deep State? What did she get out of being disliked by numberless faceless people on the internet?

Helen retreated with Cartier's purchases to a corner of the store. Maybe Nigel was right. Some time in a new environment would help her client to see how self-destructive the dynamic was. Or maybe not. Helen decided to contact the Levines and ask if they could suggest a place she could take Cartier for a getaway.

She was discreetly finishing up the email to her employers when she received the promised address from Dixon. The flowers were to be sent to Telkwa, a tiny community near Smithers, in the northern interior of the province. The fact that Blossom had been a small-town girl came as a surprise, but maybe it shouldn't. Maybe people from everywhere wanted the dubious benefits the internet could provide.

Helen walked over to where Cartier was vigorously debating with a clerk in a sparkling white track suit over the merits of the leather high-top sneakers that appeared to be covered with paint splatter versus a metallic leather pair with an appliqué of some sort of rodent (rat? mole? capybara?) applied to the toes.

"What kind of flowers did Blossom like?" Helen asked.

"Huh?"

Helen repeated the question.

Cartier was stumped. "I really don't think about Blossom when I think about flowers," she said, not appearing to notice the irony of her statement. "I mean, she was more into . . ." Long pause. "Purses."

"Purses?"

"Yeah. Like where other people put flowers, Blossom showed off her purses. She had some okay ones. But not exceptional. She only had one Fendi Baguette and it wasn't even one of the really good ones. A lot of Coach and . . . who was that designer who died? Blossom had a lot of her stuff."

"Kate Spade," offered Amina, who was listening in while trying on bizarre spectacles.

"That's right. Anyway, her bags are what she showed off."

"And her tatas," said Amina, dryly. "She definitely wasn't leading with her face."

The nastiness of the comment caught Helen by surprise, and it must have showed in her expression.

"What? I'm not saying she was a dog or anything. But she used a lot of filters on her face." Then Amina showed off her smile, which certainly didn't need any assistance.

Rock, Helen reminded herself.

"If you want inspiration for her flowers or whatever, just check her personal Instagram," said Dixon, who'd come over to listen. "It's still up. Like in memoriam? @BlossomSwimz4u."

Helen didn't want to look at Blossom's Instagram. Or Cartier's. She didn't want to look at anything the Deep State posted. But she knew who would. She texted Nigel and asked him to review Blossom's social media profiles to decide what sort of flowers they should send.

Back in the car, the Deep State began to bicker.

"We've got to shoot the memorial video," said Keithen. "The fans are going to notice that you guys posted about shopping instead of about Blossom."

"Oh, and you didn't post anything over the last few hours?"

"No, I didn't. I have some class. Obviously, I did post about that situation in the Nissan dealership. The girl who got dragged out by the RCMP on a livestream because she was acting the fool?"

"Ah, you doxed a mental case. Much better than doing product placement for Ramen T Ramen, like Bryan told us to," said Amina.

Helen noticed that Cartier stayed very quiet during these flare-ups.

"He said we shouldn't go silent," said Amina. "We should acknowledge our loss, then keep moving with our commitments. We have contracts to fulfill. And people want to see us. Hear from us. We'll go to RTR tomorrow. I can't eat anything else today."

"Pretend to eat, you mean," said Dixon.

"Whatever. We'll go do the video now. I won't have much time to edit, but that's fine. It'll look more authentic if we leave it looking a little raw," said Keithen. "I mean, obviously we *are* authentic." He shot a look at Helen from the passenger seat.

Something told Helen that Keithen knew just how inauthentic they were.

CHAPTER 22
NIGEL

Would he be willing to look at countless photos and videos of an attractive girl in a bathing suit? Why yes, Boss, he would. For a minute, he even thought it would be fun, until he realized that looking at pictures of Blossom looking happy and young and very much *alive* made him feel incredibly sad.

Blossom was a white girl with long brown hair. Her photos were so expertly shot and edited that it was hard to tell from them how she might have looked in real life, other than fit and pretty and fond of wearing a swimsuit in locations where other people might wear pants. He got a clearer sense of her as a real person from her POV videos.

In those, she played the roles of people in absurd situations. She made a series called Friend of a Creator, where she played the role of a person trying to do normal things with a friend who was an influencer. Blossom played both the creator, who turned every social occasion into an opportunity to make content, and the friend, who got left out in the process. In one video, the set-up was a lunch. She was the influencer, making over-the-top reaction videos about every item on her plate, and the friend, who was stuck basically eating by herself with no one to talk to. Her Friend of a Creator POVs were extremely meta, as she often spoofed things she and the rest of the Deep State had recently done on the internet. Nigel thought Blossom had a wonderfully expressive face in her videos and that she had probably been quite fun to be around. She was clearly very smart.

One of her most popular video series was titled Rich Friend, Poor

Friend. In those, she played a character who was clearly an exaggerated version of Cartier and a friend with no money. As the rich friend, she walked around with fake bills falling out of every pocket as she moved. She used money to swish away bugs. She took a match to fake hundreds as though it was an unconscious habit. The poor friend kept trying to find a way to ask to borrow money but was too embarrassed. It was scathing but also made a sharp point about how it felt to hang out with very wealthy people.

Nigel wondered how the video had gone over with the rest of the Deep State and how Cartier had felt about being lampooned by someone in her own creator group. Once in a while members of the Deep State filmed themselves reacting to Blossom's POV videos, which made the whole thing feel like a joke that everyone, except maybe Cartier, was in on.

How, Nigel wondered, did a girl who was sharp enough to come up with those videos end up climbing a fence to stand at the edge of a highly dangerous chute in a river? After her death he'd looked up a few articles about the Bartleby River and the part of it that lay directly below the waterfall. Someone had posted drone footage. The channel below the waterfall cut deep into rock, and the river went from wide and slow to narrow and boiling with water pressure. Massive logs had been hurled into the chute when the water was high, and they were lodged against the walls, presumably until another major storm tore them loose. He couldn't imagine going anywhere near it. Why had she taken the chance? She could have taken her bathing suit shots almost anywhere else on the river and it would have been safer. Had she not seen what lay just beyond the waterfall? The whole thing was a mystery.

An idea occurred to him, and on a whim, he downloaded a reverse image search app to look for any photos of her that were not affiliated with her social media feeds or the Deep State. It wasn't going to help him decide which flowers they should send to her memorial, but it would satisfy his curiosity. Who was Blossom when she wasn't making content for the public?

Most of the images that the program returned were related to her career as an influencer. Shots of her posted by friends. At industry events for influencers and swimsuit manufacturers. There were some older shots of her posted by her family to Facebook. High school pictures posted by old friends on their own social media. Her as a teenager, cradling an extremely large cat. Her prom date, an Asian guy who wore skate shoes with his black suit, had posted a picture of the two of them. In one, they were both on his board, Blossom in a short, champagne-coloured dress.

He kept scrolling. There were a lot of images of Blossom on the internet. But one caught his eye. It was a photograph of two girls holding hands and laughing at each other in a way that suggested deep delight. Nigel was startled to realize it was Blossom and Trudee, Cartier's PA. The girl who had died only weeks before Blossom.

Where had this photo come from? Were there any more? Was this just two friends telling jokes? It looked like more than that to him. But what did he know? He wasn't exactly Relationship King.

He fed photos of both of the young women into the app and waited. There were more photos of them. Trudee and Blossom lying in a rumpled bed. Nothing explicit, but they were very obviously together. Trudee helping Blossom zip up a dress. None of the photos had been taken in public. All of the photos were just the two of them. They looked happy. They looked private. He had no idea who'd taken them or where they'd originally been posted.

Had they been keeping their relationship a secret? If so, why?

He checked the memorial photo pages set up by the funeral homes for each girl. Trudee's photo gallery included some of her with members of the Deep State, but none with her and Blossom. Blossom's gallery had none of her with the other members and none of her and Trudee. It seemed that Blossom's parents didn't want to feature her career on social media.

He couldn't think of a good reason for Trudee and Blossom to hide their relationship, but then again, he didn't know much about them, or about the group as a whole, for that matter.

Which reminded him, he should check to see what they were up to. He set down his phone for a minute so he could appreciate the dogs.

Jack and Miggs were asleep beside him. Clarice lay on the other side, chewing on a small toy. Nigel had decided he was very much a Pekingese guy. The dogs, like him, were cheerful and enjoyed napping and snacks. One day when he was established, he thought he might get a Pekingese or two.

After the short respite, he picked up his phone and checked Instagram and TikTok for what felt like the fortieth time that afternoon. The Deep State account had posted yet another unflattering shot of Helen. It showed her bent over taking a close-up photograph of Dixon's rear end. Dixon's fake-shocked face was turned to the camera, mugging as though Helen was some sort of pervert.

Under the photo, Dixon had written, *Does this butler make my butt look big?*

"Asshole," muttered Nigel.

There were dozens of laugh emojis, fire emojis, and then someone had written:

Does she know you guys are posting her pics? Seems like she doesn't. Not cool. #savethebutler

That comment got forty-two likes.
There were other critical comments.

U sure don't seem to be mourning your friend. #RIPBlossom

Using Jewellery's butler as a flex. Lame.

Jewellery was what Cartier's non-fans called her. Charming.
Then there was another RU account, this one called RUnotokay34!

At least we don't have to look at old Fish Eyes @CartierHightower if we're looking at @DixonCho's fine a%$.

Man, RU was relentless in tormenting poor Cartier. It was depressing.

Nigel looked at the photo again, and something about Helen's expression, focused and earnest, told him she would be fine. The guy had obviously asked her to take the picture, and she'd done so while one of the others had surreptitiously taken her photo. It didn't matter. Helen wasn't going to be thrown off course by these people. The entire internet couldn't unbalance Helen.

Nigel sighed and considered going for a swim. Or maybe he should take the dogs out for a pee. He made a mental note to ask Helen whether she knew that Trudee and Blossom had been in a relationship and whether she had any insights into why both of them had ended up dead.

He gave a little involuntary shiver, and Miggs, the most empathetic of the Pekes, kindly licked his hand.

Nigel patted the little dog and then called Creekside Floral Collective in Telkwa, BC, and ordered the largest bouquet they made to be delivered to Blossom's family the next day.

CHAPTER 23

The plan for the night was genius, even if it was going to be complicated to execute. The Deep State was teed up to become one of the hottest stories in the world. There were already two dead girls! The audience was ready for some fresh developments. It would be ideal if they all looked responsible, at least for a while. Then, as the dust settled, the finger-pointing could get more specific.

They had borrowed the key to the black box theatre room from a bartender and planned to sneak in there and shoot while the ReVibe room next door was in full swing. If everything went as planned, they'd get caught in there, at least most of them would, and they would be blamed. Everyone expects influencers to do stupid things, and tonight they would oblige.

Of course, there was a risk that the audience would turn on the wrong person, but it wouldn't take much manipulating to make sure most of the anger landed on Cartier. As any dictator knows, it doesn't take a lot of effort to set the mob on an easy target. The main thing was to make sure that Cartier's butler (butler, for god's sake!) and the butler's strange, unsightly assistant didn't get in the way.

Those two were an unexpected and unwelcome glitch. So far, the assistant seemed to be mostly stuck at the hotel with all those awful little dogs. Unlike the butler, the assistant seemed to have half a clue about the internet. But the butler had other disturbing qualities, like noticing everything that was going on around her because she wasn't on her phone.

She was so offline she didn't even realize that she was getting famous, at least among the followers of the Deep State. Fortunately, Cartier didn't seem to listen to Helen, which meant the butler wouldn't be able to convince Cartier to do something stupid, like take a break from the Deep State or go offline before the story had played itself out and captured the attention of every person with an internet connection. Everyone had a role to play, whether they knew it or not.

CHAPTER 24

After they finished shopping, the Deep State had Helen drive them to something called Graffiti Alley, around Broadway and 7th. After she parked, they instructed her to come along.

"We're going to shoot our memorial vid," said Dixon.

"It's going to be lit," said Keithen.

They unloaded two tripods from the vehicle and, after some discussion, set them up in front of a black and white mural showing bizarre skateboarding figures with fingers coming out of their eyeholes.

Back at Dixon's store, Cartier and the others had gone into the change rooms and come out wearing black and white outfits with only small pops of colour, on their shoes or hats.

The four of them arranged themselves against the wall, grim looks on their faces. Every so often one of them would leave the wall, look into the cameras, and suggest that someone lean left, or someone else lower their chin or adjust their hat. Then the person would rejoin them.

"How does it look?" called Cartier to Helen, who stood off to the side.

"Good," she said. Did they? She wasn't sure. Also, was this how people mourned now?

She watched as they posed together in front of the mural. Leaning against each other. Standing apart. Looking solemn. Looking fierce.

Sure. Why not mourn like this? Whatever ritual helped. Watching them, Helen was reminded of the lines James Joyce had written about one of his characters. "He lived at a little distance from his body, regarding his own acts with doubtful side glances. He had an odd auto-biographical habit which led him to compose in his mind from time to time a short sentence about himself containing a subject in the third person." She'd always found that to be a profound description. These young people also seemed to live outside themselves, but they gave no doubtful side glances at their own acts. Instead, they seemed strangely oblivious to reality as it unfolded around them. They lived not just out-side themselves, but *inside* their devices. They were constantly creating their own autobiographies as they documented highly stylized versions of their own lives.

It was, thought Helen, the opposite of her training, which had involved using mindfulness to be as present in the body and as alert to the fleeting, unreliable sensory nature of life as possible.

Her teacher Sayadaw U Nandisara and her favourite teachers from Hawaii often quoted the words Buddha had spoken to Rohitassa, a deva who could not reach the end of the world no matter how hard he tried.

> *Thus have I heard: The end of the world can never*
> *Be reached by walking. However,*
> *Without having reached the world's end*
> *There is no release from suffering.*
>
> *I declare that it is in this fathom-*
> *long carcass, with its perceptions*
> *and thoughts, that there is the world, the*
> *origin of the world, the cessation of the*
> *world, and the path leading to the cessation of the world.*

How, Helen wondered, would these people, who had not put down their phones for more than a minute or two since she'd met up with them many hours before, feel about the news that their fathom-long carcasses held everything they would ever need to know?

It was a thought far too esoteric for the moment and definitely too cerebral for the crowd. She caught in her own thought a barb of the judgment that she preferred to let go. In truth, she felt somewhat checked out of her own fathom-long body as she stood watching the photoshoot that seemed so entirely inauthentic.

One by one, Cartier, Amina, Keithen, and Dixon walked up to the camera and spoke into it. Had they rehearsed their words? Their poses?

They behaved with extreme unselfconsciousness, as though being influenced by a director with an overwhelming vision.

When they were finished filming themselves, the four of them huddled around and watched the footage on small monitors they'd attached to each camera. They discussed what they saw in hushed tones, pointing out details and making further suggestions.

After a time, Amina left the huddle and came to stand beside Helen. They watched in silence for a moment. Cartier had walked away and was looking at her phone. Keithen and Dixon continued discussing the video.

"Busy day," said Amina finally.

"Very," agreed Helen.

"Sorry about your hair."

Helen glanced at her. "Thank you. It's taking me awhile to get used to it."

Amina laughed. "You're quite a good sport, aren't you?"

"I hope so," said Helen.

Then Amina's face grew serious. "The online world can be kind of awful. I hope you know we realize that."

Helen didn't respond. It was her experience that all parts of existence had their challenges.

"We're not children anymore. We know the risks. Well, some of us know the risks more than others." Here, she gave a meaningful look in Cartier's direction. "Being an influencer isn't necessarily the healthiest way to live. Emotionally, I mean. And spiritually."

"Oh?" said Helen, thinking about the day she'd just spent with Amina and the others. The members of the Deep State had bought things, they'd recorded themselves in a variety of places. They'd staged moments for their fans. But as far as Helen could tell, they hadn't had a truly present moment with themselves or anyone else. Their focus had always been pulled in multiple directions.

"No digital native is completely naive to the downsides of online life," said Amina, sounding for the first time like the daughter of an intellectual rather than someone who sprang fully formed from Instagram. "But she"—Amina pointed toward Cartier—"sometimes acts like she grew up with the Amish or something."

An Amish community was just the sort of place Helen would have liked to take Cartier, but she didn't say so.

"This is a business for us," said Amina. "Obviously, there's an art to what we do. You know, coming up with content. But we're in this to make money and because we're good at it. Why is *she* doing it?"

Helen turned to face Amina.

"Are you sure it's just about money for you?" she asked.

Amina's face seemed to freeze momentarily, and Helen saw a formless shadow cross the young woman's flawless features before she looked away. Helen had seen such expressions on the faces of retreat participants who were starting to get in touch with some aspect of their lives that was very painful to them.

Amina sighed. "I'm here for the money and the fame. And the constant reinvention."

Helen gave her a wry smile. "Reinvention seems like a powerful incentive," she said.

They both watched Cartier, who'd gone back to talk to Dixon and Keithen. For a moment, Helen considered the two young women who'd been killed. No reinvention was possible for them.

CHAPTER 25

At nine o'clock that night, Helen knocked on the door of Nigel's room and he answered wearing the fluffy white hotel bathrobe and the branded complimentary slippers.

She felt a pang at the sight of him. For the first time in her life, she longed to lounge around in a hotel in a complimentary robe while surrounded by dogs that looked like Tribbles. Something about the experience of zigzagging around the city with Cartier and the rest of the Deep State had exhausted her. Everything in Cartier's life was loud and public and hectic in a way that Helen, who was by nature quiet, centred, and calm, found disorienting. Cartier and Helen had just come back to the hotel for what Cartier had said would be a "minute" so she could change into her outfit for the evening and get her gig bag.

Helen would have given a lot to switch places with Nigel, and briefly considered asking him to finish out the evening in her stead. But she didn't. Instead, she asked him how things were going.

"Oh good. I just got out of the pool. This is a crazy nice hotel. Me and the dogs ate out on the pool deck while the sun went down."

"Right," said Helen.

"The dogs are settled in for the night. The flowers have been ordered and will be delivered tomorrow morning. I am ready to do whatever needs to be done. You know, Helen, have *you* considered going for a swim?" Nigel gave a meaningful look at Helen's still ringleted hair. "You could do some *underwater* swimming. Then have a shower. Then get into a hotel bathrobe. I can look after the client while you and your hair are . . . recovering."

"Thank you, Nigel. That sounds very nice. But I've just ordered Cartier room service and then we will be going out for the evening. Her group has an engagement of some kind."

"You *sure* you don't want me to go in your place?" he asked, intuiting her desire. "You could stay here with the dogs?" He gave another skeptical look at her curls. "You could do a little meditation or some yoga or maybe some primal screaming?"

"Ms. Hightower has asked me to accompany her this evening. But there is something you can do for me. I am going to send you a number. Dr. and Mr. Levine have suggested a place where Ms. Hightower can go to get away from all of this. It belongs to their friend Mrs. Ban. Please contact Reynolds and let him know that we will be visiting the ranch in the next day or so. I am going to invite Ms. Hightower to take a break from her current . . . uh, schedule, and regroup at the Ban estate. It's quite remote, I gather. Reynolds will make sure everything is in order for our visit."

"Are you inviting her friends, too?"

Helen had concluded that the other members of the Deep State were definitely *not* Cartier's friends, but she didn't say that. "No. It will just be Ms. Hightower, you, me, and the dogs."

"Do they have 5G up there?" asked Nigel, his hands deep in his roomy terry cloth pockets.

"I don't know what that is," said Helen. "If it's about computers, I hope not."

Nigel made a face like he'd just seen someone touch an electric fence. "Oh. Wow. Bad internet is not going to be popular with the client."

"We shall see," said Helen. "Ms. Hightower might not agree to come."

"Who is Reynolds?"

"Mrs. Ban's butler. It turns out I know him. When I was in school, he gave us a workshop on butlering in rural versus urban environments. The Bans own a number of large ranches, so he's an expert."

"Do you think the client will like being in a rural place?"

Helen didn't answer, because her phone was buzzing with a summons from Cartier.

"You are okay staying by yourself this evening? You are welcome to join us."

Nigel considered. "You know, I'll pass. Miggs needs a quiet night at home and I think Clarice is feeling tired." All three Pekingese were passed out contentedly on his king-sized bed, surrounded by small toys. They'd barely roused when Helen had come in. They were all freshly brushed, and their luxurious coats were spread around them in silken swirls. They were like advertisements for hair.

"You are doing a wonderful job with them," said Helen.

"We have an understanding," said Nigel. "Me and these dogs are deeply in sync. I think I might be a dog person now."

"Enjoy your evening and let me know if there are any issues after you speak with Reynolds. And please be ready to travel at short notice. You and the dogs."

Nigel looked past her into the hallway as her phone buzzed again. Cartier was anxious to go.

"I found something sort of interesting when I was looking at Ms. Hightower's feed today. Well, not her feed. Blossom's." Before he could say any more, Helen held up a finger to Nigel while she looked at her phone screen. "I've got to go. We can talk when I get back this evening or tomorrow morning."

With that, Helen headed back to the suite and the client.

~~~~

Helen drove the two of them through downtown Vancouver to the club. The others were going to meet them there. The night was warm, and the streets were thronged with people. Helen had little experience of going out to nightclubs, other than a few times when she'd been in butler school. She'd chosen to take the robes and join a monastery when she was just out of her teens. A late night in those days had meant attending the 9:00 p.m. sit. After she left the monastery and went to work at the retreat centre, her schedule had stayed much the same. Helen was not a night creature, but she found the city and the energy coming off her passenger exhilarating.

The feeling grew when a small valet in a satin jacket that made him look like a jockey took the Range Rover after they pulled up outside a huge, featureless building with a tiny neon sign that said *Gooey*. An enormous South Asian bouncer in a track suit stamped with the Gooey logo ushered them inside. He led them down a dark hallway, up a back stairwell, and into a dimly lit dressing room. Bass was thumping through the walls and floor. Helen could feel it in her feet. In her heart.

"You need anything?" the bouncer asked, looking between them.

Cartier ignored him, but Helen thanked him and gave him a nice tip.

"We don't get too many like you in here," he said, still staring at Helen intently.

She thought he probably meant her hair. She doubted many people went to nightclubs looking like the overfed children of successful shopkeepers circa 1892.

"You got that thing," he said. "My grandma has it too."

Helen nodded. It seemed there would be endless opportunities to feel humble during her time with Cartier. Being compared to the large man's grandmother was somewhat galling, given that he was probably nearly her age.

"I don't mean that you're old. I mean, you got that really good energy." He slid his hands out to either side of him. "Smooth. Calm. Deep. I'd be a happier man if this club had about two hundred of you coming here every night." He was nodding to himself, obviously enjoying the thought.

"Thank you," said Helen.

"Is my head here yet?" asked Cartier, who'd been staring at her reflection in the mirrors that stretched the length of the room.

"Right here, bitches!" said Amina, coming into the room. She swung a large black case onto the dressing room counter and clicked it open, revealing a giant deer head, which Cartier immediately slid on and then off her head, as though to make sure it fit.

The bouncer watched all of this with a pained expression on his face, then put his hands together, bowed at Helen, and left. She found the interaction reassuringly familiar, if unexpected. The happy feeling evaporated when the rest of the Deep State arrived. Dixon and Keithen hung up what looked like costumes, and Amina stood in front of the mirror and touched up her hair and eye makeup.

A man in an Avicii Lives T-shirt came in and held up ten fingers. "Ten minutes," he mouthed and disappeared again.

Dixon and Keithen whispered something to Amina that Helen couldn't hear and then also left.

Cartier took off the head, revealing a pale and sweaty face. She looked at her phone. "I hope he comes," she said.

"Would you like some water?" Helen asked her client.

Cartier ignored the question. "As soon as the set's over, I've got to come back here and get dressed for the video. Like, right away," she said. "So can you stay close?" Cartier frowned at her phone. "Damn. He can't make it."

When the man in the T-shirt came back and gestured that it was time, Cartier slipped on her deer head and Helen followed her out of the room.

"Marni S. is on the lights," their guide yelled as they walked down a dark, empty hallway and then veered into what turned out to be the backstage area of a performance room. "She'll do you right."

Out front, the announcer said something and the crowd cheered. Then Cartier, a.k.a. Deer Head, slipped through the curtains and took the stage.

There was a spattering of applause, and a few boos, which made Helen's heart hurt for her client.

The stagehand crooked his finger at Helen. He led her to a spot out of the way, where she could see the smallish stage and the crowd without being visible to them. Phones and glow sticks lit up the space, like firebugs who couldn't quite get liftoff.

The stage went black, and then a single laser light hit the decks onstage. More lights drilled down until they reached Cartier, who had been standing in a pool of darkness at the back of the stage.

Cartier, in her deer head, strode to the electronics, and Helen watched, fascinated, as she started playing her music. Instead of looking ridiculous, the head looked quite dramatic and even frightening. Cartier yelled something into the microphone and then started turning knobs and pumping her fist while lights exploded around her. Reds, oranges, greens, pinks, purples. The lights pulsed and strobed and shot out into the audience. On the walls, images of deer kept appearing and disappearing. Cartier looked perfectly confident and in command.

The same sort of sounds that had given Helen a slashing headache when Cartier played them in the car now felt appropriate.

Helen didn't *like* the music, exactly, but she felt gratified by Cartier's abilities as a performer. There was a fierce grace in her movements. She seemed in control of the music and the crowd, which had appeared ambivalent at first. Now they jumped up and down and punched their fists in the air and shouted when she urged them to do so.

Empathetic joy, known as mudita in the Pali language, is the feeling of happiness for the good fortune of another, and in that moment Helen felt it for her client, who was a good DJ, even if she had to dress like a ruminant to get attention.

Fifteen minutes later it was over, and Cartier was leaving the stage in her head.

"Yeeeessss. Thank you, Deer Head, for that banger to get us warmed up tonight," said the announcer.

Roar from the crowd.

"Deer Head is new and we predict great things for them."

More cries of agreement.

So Cartier *was* good at something. That was welcome news. With a lighter heart, Helen followed the stagehand and her client back to the green room.

CHAPTER 26

Cartier's face was flushed and young when she emerged out of the enormous head.

"That went good, right?" she said.

"Yes, very," said Helen. "The audience was extremely appreciative."

Cartier's smile grew. "Yes," she said, and she gave a little fist shake of triumph. "Okay. I better get changed." She grabbed some clothes from the rack and disappeared into the bathroom. Two minutes later, she was heading for the door at a speed as close to a run as her red high heels would allow. She also had on an oversized purple suit with huge shoulder pads and oddly shaped dress trousers, and she'd covered her sweaty hair with a brown, curly mid-length wig and added a swipe of glitter under her cheekbones.

"Come on," she said and made her way quickly along a dim hallway. "We're doing a recreation in a side room next to the ReVibe Room downstairs. We're going to coast off what the DJ in the next room is doing."

Helen had no idea what any of that meant. A recreation of what? And what, exactly, did it mean to "coast off" something? She found the layout of the club confusing. It was multiple levels and seemed to be full of performance rooms for different-sized crowds, backrooms, and side rooms. They made their way back down to what seemed to be the ground level of the club until Cartier stopped in front of a heavy door. Helen opened it, and the two of them entered a much larger room than the one Cartier had performed in. It was crowded with people dancing to the sped-up sounds of George Michael.

Cartier and Helen edged their way along the wall until they reached an unobtrusive door near the back. Cartier knocked twice and the door swung open.

"Welcome," said Keithen, and he ushered them inside a small, square space. It was painted black and was empty but for the rest of the Deep State and some equipment. The music from the room outside was clearly audible inside.

Black rehearsal cubes had been arranged to form a stage against the back wall. There was a catwalk, also made of painted cubes. Beside that was a small table with two chairs. Near the back of the stage was a backlit white projection screen. The scene looked vaguely familiar to Helen, but she couldn't tell from where.

Dixon was checking the cameras on tripods pointing at the stage from different angles.

"Our music will come on right after the 'Girls Just Wanna Have Fun' remix," he said over the music that reverberated through the room. "I'm going to sneak into the ReVibe Room, get some shots of the crowd, then come in here for the recreation. Ready to go?"

Cartier smoothed the front of her suit jacket.

"Positions, everyone!" said Amina as she walked behind the projection screen, her silhouette clearly visible.

Cartier rushed over, climbed onstage and behind the screen, and took the same posture, so that their silhouettes faced each other.

"Three, two, one: rolling," called Dixon. Keithen opened the door so Dixon and his video camera could slip into the larger dance room just outside as the insistent sounds of the synthesizer track from Cyndi Lauper's most iconic song were replaced with a slower beat. After twenty seconds, Dixon rushed back into the room, put down his camera, and took a seat across from Keithen at the table.

The silhouettes of Cartier and Amina began to dance.

At that moment, a girl dressed like a baby in a white diaper and

T-shirt, holding a glow strip shaped like a soother, stumbled through the door from the party room. "Oh my god! Here's the real party!" she said, staggering toward them.

"Helen! Stop her!" hissed Dixon from his little table.

The girl dressed like a baby started grooving toward the stage. She was clearly very intoxicated and so unsteady on her feet she looked like an actual toddler. Her diaper and soother and large teeth glowed in the black light, creating an unsettling effect.

Keithen and Dixon pretended not to see her and instead stared at the dancing figures behind the screen.

"Excuse me," said Helen, approaching the girl and trying to stay out of view of the cameras. Here was another situation that the North American Butler Academy had failed to prepare her for. "Can I help you find something? Perhaps you're looking for a washroom?"

The girl held out her arms like she was either going to boogie down or put Helen in a bear hug. "Dance with me!" she cried. "I'm so high. Are you so high? Don't you just love eighties music? Oh my god! Look at you! You're so old, poor thing!"

"Yes," agreed Helen, "I am quite old."

"And your hair! Look at your hair. Awww."

The DJ's turbocharged version of what Helen now recognized as "He's a Dream" continued and Helen and the drunk girl baby watched, mesmerized, as Amina and Cartier stepped out from behind the screen, made a few moves, and then ripped off their suits in not quite perfect unison, revealing red baby-doll lingerie.

"Duuude!" cried the baby girl. "It's that scene! From that movie! They're doing a recreation!"

Finally, Helen understood. They were acting out the iconic dance number from *Flashdance*. Helen hadn't seen the film since she was a teenager, and this scene was one of the only parts she remembered.

As the song built, Amina, who was a good dancer, and Cartier, who wasn't particularly, acted out the famous performance. They pounded their fists on the two chairs, then got up and sat in them. Amina slid gracefully out of her chair onto the floor and Cartier awkwardly levered herself to the ground. There was a bit of rolling around on the narrow stage in their negligees and high heels. Helen was worried one of them would fall and hurt themselves, but she was also impressed by their commitment to their parts.

In the room beyond, the DJ added in another layer of beats so that some parts of the song seemed to speed up and others were repeated for emphasis. Cartier and Amina were again flailing around on the folding chairs while Dixon and Keithen made a big show of staring at them, mouths open, imitating the men in the movie.

At a predetermined moment, Cartier and Amina pulled overhead cords rigged up on poles and, right on cue, water spilled all over them. It wasn't quite the epic wave that cascaded over the dancer in the film, but Cartier and Amina had clearly been dampened with at least a few water balloons' worth of liquid.

"Is this real?" squealed the baby. "Or am I just way too high!"

It was real, as well as a strange combination of hokey and impressive.

Amina and Cartier stomped up and down the little makeshift runway, splashing small puddles of water right and left. They windmilled their arms and bobbed their heads until the DJ shifted into "Somebody's Watching Me." This was the signal for the members of the Deep State to high-five each other. The drunk baby beside Helen held up her hand, and after a moment of confusion about what she was supposed to do, Helen gently slapped it.

Meanwhile, the door that led into the larger room, which must have been left ajar by the drunk girl, opened and people began to trickle into the small space.

Keithen and Dixon rushed to rescue their cameras and tripods, and Amina and Cartier collected their things from the stage. Helen moved forward to help, but before she could reach them, an alarm loud enough to drown out the music went off in the ReVibe Room.

Everyone looked around, alert but not quite afraid, wondering whether it was real or part of the music.

The girl dressed like a baby seemed to take the noise as a cue to begin some dance only she knew. She held up a raised fist and began stomping around in a circle.

Someone just outside the room yelled, and the cry was taken up by others.

"Fire!"

"Fire!"

"It's a fire!"

Then the pushing began.

CHAPTER 27

People began to squeeze into the tiny room, and as they did so, they turned from individuals into a crowd.

"There's a door to the outside here!" screamed someone near the stage.

In what felt like a minute, Helen was pressed so hard by the mass of bodies moving toward the back wall, where the screen had been, that she was picked up and carried.

Was there a way to get outside from this room? Where?

Helen was shoved far enough toward the makeshift stage that she could see that the cubes had been shoved out of the way and the white screen torn down. Behind it was a door and an exit sign. People tugged on the handle, but it didn't open.

Surrounded on all sides by panting, sweating, screaming people, Helen couldn't see Cartier. All she could do was try to make sure no one near her fell. If they did, they might not get up again.

Pressed in from every direction and being rammed into the immovable wall of people in front of her by the wall of people behind her, Helen told herself to remain calm. If she was about to be crushed, or worse, crushed and burned, she didn't want to meet her end feeling sick with terror. *Breathe*, she told herself. Mini breaths. In through the nose, out through the mouth. Tiny sips of air.

Do not panic.

Do not fall.

Stay on your feet.

She spotted the drunk girl, who, sure enough, seemed to be going under the concrete tide of people who were still pressing into the small room. Why were they all rushing in here? She'd seen at least two exit signs in the bigger dance room. No time to think about that. Helen reached out and, with great effort, managed to grab the girl under her bare arm.

"Stay up," she yelled, but she couldn't tell if the girl had heard her.

The crowd was a single open-mouthed, screaming, panting creature. Helen looked around to see if anyone would meet her eyes. A young woman with short blue hair and a glittering nose piercing did. "We need to keep her up!" Helen yelled. The woman, who had the sort of composure that Helen associated with first responders, nodded and grabbed the girl, who appeared to be starting to pass out, by her other arm.

Helen couldn't see the door in front of them anymore.

The press of bodies got heavier, and the crowd began to sway back and forth. What was it called when crowds began to trample people? Progressive crowd collapse. That's what this was, and this is how it happened. Was there even room in here for people to go down?

She lifted her head and tried to keep her voice calm and steady, but louder than she'd ever been in her life.

"There are multiple exits in the other room. Turn around! Turn around! Don't fall! Be careful with each other."

Something about the quality of her voice caught the attention of the people who were closest. A few shook their heads like they were coming out of a dream. Or a nightmare.

"Back!" yelled someone. "Go back!"

The cry spread, taken up by those who had breath left to scream.

And seconds later, the pressure eased incrementally as the crowd began to flow in the other direction.

The mass of people who had been pressing into the small space became lighter. A hundred people, then fifty. Thirty. Helen nodded at the girl with the nose ring, who still had a hold on the drunk girl, who went limp as soon as the crowd of people around her thinned.

Helen began to push her way toward the exit door that presumably led to the street. It was still locked.

Why on earth had the Deep State set up their stage in front of the door? Why had they locked it?

Around the small room people sat with their heads in their hands. Some were on their hands and knees, trying to catch their breath. People leaned against the wall, bent double with relief or having panic or asthma attacks. Injured people were being seen to by their friends. They were individuals again. No longer part of the instinct-driven horde.

Helen shoved the cubes completely out of the way. A young Black man wearing George Michael–style shorts and a tank top helped her.

"Who the fuck locked this door?" he asked. "We all nearly died in here."

Helen felt sick. Where was Cartier? Where were the other members of the Deep State?

She tried again to open the door, again with no success. Meanwhile, the fire alarm rang and rang and rang. Then she heard banging on the other side of the door. There was a loud crack, and a beefy white security guard in a bright-blue shirt flung the door open and the night air flooded in. He had a crowbar in his hands. His face was bright red, and he was panting as he looked around.

"How did you people get in this room?" he said. "Jesus Christ." He peered in and saw the remnants of the crowd staggering around or slumped onto the floor with people attending to them. He rushed across the small space and through the door into the larger dance hall.

"Call an ambulance," Helen said to the man in the George Michael shorts as she bent to help a girl who was gasping into her inhaler.

The alarm stopped and the space turned oddly silent but for the ringing in Helen's ears and the panting breaths and whispers of the injured.

The security guard who'd broken open the door came back, accompanied by three other security people.

"Someone messed with the exit doors in the ReVibe room," he yelled. "Glued them shut or something. Staff were trying to get them open from outside when the alarm sounded. Somebody yelled fire and directed people in here. Goddamned room is for black box theatre productions. Weird performance art and poetry readings. Stuff like that. It's always supposed to be locked when the club is open." He held his palms up to his temples. "Jesus. Thank god it was a false alarm. This is no joke. This could have been so fucking bad."

Looking around at the dozen or so people who remained in the little room, which was rapidly cooling off, Helen thought it was already plenty bad. Where were Cartier and the others?

It takes fifteen minutes for an adrenalin rush to clear the human system. Helen wondered how she and everyone else would feel after that. Not good, she suspected. While the bouncers looked people over, Helen followed a hunch and poked her head behind a half wall at the back of the room. It looked like it might be used as a place to hang coats or take tickets. She found Cartier, still in her lacy red negligee, huddled behind the wall.

"Are you okay?" she asked.

Cartier sat on the floor, her arms around her knees. Her heavy makeup was smeared over her ashen skin. She looked like a creature from a horror movie. Victim or villain. Helen felt a surge of empathy for her client, and some wonder at her life choices.

"Where are Dixon and Keithen? Where is Amina?" asked Helen.

"I don't know," said Cartier. "I saw them trying to move the black boxes and then I freaked out and hid in here."

Helen saw paramedics and uniformed police officers rushing in, accompanied by staff members from the club. The paramedics squatted and began speaking to some of the injured people while other people waved for attention. The police conferred with each other and then approached people, telling others to stay where they were.

It was time to deal with this. Helen draped a suit jacket she'd picked up off the floor over Cartier's shoulders.

Then she offered her a hand up.

"The police are doing interviews. Are you ready to speak to them about what happened?" she asked.

Cartier stared at her.

"No?" said Cartier.

Before Helen could decide what to do, a police officer with a Princess Diana haircut stuck her head behind the half wall. "Got two back here," she called, and gestured for Helen and Cartier to come out.

The black box theatre room now had a bleak bus station energy as paramedics escorted people who were holding parts of their bodies or breathing into oxygen masks outside. The lights had been turned up, exposing the dinginess common to all-black rooms. Uninjured people were gathered at one end of the space, and a couple of officers stood talking to them.

"Tell me what happened," a muscular cop said to a girl who was dressed like Elton John, complete with a checked suit jacket and huge glitter-framed sunglasses. The crowd's outfits were so outlandish it had the effect of making the cops look like they were also playing dress-up.

"You two can go wait with the rest of them," said the officer, directing Helen and Cartier to the crowd of people waiting to be interviewed.

"Was this some kind of terrorism?" someone asked.

"We don't know anything yet."

"Not terrorism. Instagram," said the muscular officer, sounding like he had been waiting his whole life to speak that line.

"That one was involved," said the girl in the diaper, who'd once again appeared, like an avenging baby. She pointed at Cartier. "There was her and another girl and two hot guys. They were doing a shower scene, you know? Then it all went—" She broke off and waggled her finger around to show something spiralling out of control. "Weeeee-ooooo. Total shitfest. Very uncool."

"Shower scene?" asked the muscled officer. He had a look on his face that made it clear he was ready to bring down maximum disapproval on whatever explanation was forthcoming.

The older officer with the Princess Di hair gave the drunk girl an exhausted look. "Weeeee-ooooo?" she said. "Can you provide more detail? What did these two do, exactly?"

The thump of music started up in the ReVibe Room and thirty seconds later stopped abruptly. The whole club had the feel of a hideout that had just had its roof ripped off.

"Noooo!" said the drunk girl. "Don't stop the music! Never stop the music." Then she made a noise that sounded like a series of burps. Quite disconcerting. The rapid sobering she'd undergone was apparently reversing itself.

"What?" said the cop, then thought better of it. "You say these two"—he gestured at Cartier and Helen—"had something to do with what happened here tonight?" He looked like a man who could easily deadlift two or three influencers.

Helen didn't care for the sensation of being helpless or being talked about as though she wasn't there, but she didn't interrupt.

"That one," said the girl, pointing at Cartier, "and her friend were dancing on the stage. The old one?" She pointed at Helen. "She tried to help me find a bathroom, but I didn't need one. At first I thought, wow. Cool, right? They were acting out the scene. But then we needed to *use* the door over there because of the fire alarm. Then it wasn't cool anymore. Everyone was pushing. I was nearly squished to literal death." The girl made an exploding noise and flapped her hands around to illustrate her point.

"Okay," said the muscled cop. "How much have you had to drink tonight?"

The drunk girl shook her head. "Nothing."

"Great," he said.

"You," said the female officer, pointing at Helen and Cartier. "Don't move. We are going to need to speak to you. Where are your friends?" she asked Cartier.

But Cartier wasn't listening. She was staring at her phone. "Noooo!" she cried, instantly securing the attention of everyone in the room. She held her phone inches from her face as though she'd suddenly gone nearsighted.

"This is NOT FAIR!"

"Miss? You're going to need to calm down," said the older officer, who was joined by a third officer with a grey flat-top. Like the other muscle-bound cop, he looked like he went for a workout to celebrate each of his workouts. The three of them glared hard at Cartier, who hadn't registered their words or even their presence.

"WHY IS EVERYONE BLAMING ME?" cried Cartier.

That's when Helen noticed multiple people around her, witnesses and staff, also on their phones. It was disorienting to realize that in spite of the recent, very real trauma lingering in the room, there was something unfolding on their phones that felt more compelling than the reality in front of them. She understood with a sick feeling that the story of what had just happened at the club was starting to spread. It was going to reach far beyond this room and these people. And it involved Cartier.

Helen gazed around. One of the nightclub security staff was filming her client. He wasn't the only one.

Helen didn't want to startle the police. She could tell that they were on edge. But she couldn't allow this to continue.

Where *were* the others? How had they escaped? And why had they left Cartier?

"Excuse me," she said in a voice that carried. "May I speak to my client?"

"Who are you again?" asked the officer with the ladylike hair.

"I take care of Ms.—" It occurred to Helen that it would not do to give Cartier's full name in front of a room full of cameras. "I take care of personal matters for her."

"Are you her attorney?"

"I liaise with her legal representatives," said Helen, which was probably true. She would need to see about getting a lawyer for Cartier as soon as possible, just in case. And she needed to get her out of here. "May I have a brief word with her?" asked Helen.

The police exchanged a glance, but something about Helen, about her presence, seemed to reassure them. The female officer nodded. "Don't go anywhere."

"Cartier," said Helen when she was close enough that only the officers could overhear. "You are being watched. Recorded."

Cartier looked at her with wide, wounded eyes. "They're saying—"

"They are wrong," said Helen. "Give me your hand." Like a child, Cartier allowed Helen to take her hand.

"Does she need to give a statement now?" Helen asked the waiting officers.

"Yes. You both do."

"Here?"

"You can come down to the station if you want."

At this, Cartier tightened her grip on Helen's hand as though it would stop her from being pulled underwater.

"Yes, please. We're ready," Helen told the police. Two officers led the way outside, away from the stares of the survivors and their cameras. The enormous bouncer who'd compared Helen to his grandmother cleared the way for the group.

"I didn't do it," said Cartier, speaking into Helen's shoulder. Helen was shielding her face from view. "I had nothing to do with setting this up."

"You're all right," the bouncer told Cartier kindly, noting her tear-stained face. "You got this lady on your team. Nothing can go wrong."

That, Helen thought, was manifestly untrue.

"Can you arrange to have our vehicle brought to us at the station?" she asked him as he walked beside them.

"As soon as you ladies are ready for your vehicle, you just text me. Me or one of the guys will be over with your car." He handed Helen a card with his number on it, and she slipped him a hundred-dollar bill and the parking slip.

"Thank you," she said.

"No. Thank *you*. You got that good energy. It comes off you. Like my grandmother," he said. "I'm Issan."

"Helen," she said.

"I bet if you weren't in that room, we'd have dead people. That's what I for sure think," he said. Issan walked beside them all, overwhelming the officers with his size and emanating a stable gentleness that was probably singularly effective in defusing any situation that might arise in the club. He waved when they reached the exit, and it felt like a benediction.

CHAPTER 28
NIGEL

He'd spent the night checking the various feeds for the Deep State. Before Cartier and the others had even arrived at the club, some of their followers had been calling them out for shopping all day and getting drinks and having their hair done so soon after their friend had died.

Ever hear of mourning, you psychos? #DeepstateDeepsuck

Decorum isn't just an eyeshadow shade, dipsticks.
#Deepstatedummies

That sort of thing. But most of the attention was on the novelty of Helen and the idea of having a butler. Then the headlines began to appear.

Social media "influencers" known as the Deep State cause panic. Multiple injuries reported.

Nigel clicked on the story and saw a photo of Cartier, Amina, Dixon, and Keithen smiling into a camera. They appeared to be in a tropical location. So this wasn't a recent photo.

He skimmed the article.

*The self-proclaimed "content collective" known as the Deep
State nearly caused a mass casualty event at Gooey nightclub in
Vancouver when they blocked the doors of the dance club in order
to film a TikTok video and a fire broke out.*

Fire? What the hell?

Nigel, heart racing, looked away from the news feed and finished his
text to Helen.

Are you okay? Has there been a fire?

No answer. It didn't appear that the message had been delivered. The
article said they "nearly" caused a mass casualty event. Did that mean
everyone was all right?

Nigel checked the #Deepstate hashtag.

A flood, a tide, a tsunami of new posts.

Posts about the events at the nightclub were coming fast and furious.
There was a video of the Deep State acting out a scene from *Flashdance*,
complete with splashing water.

Nigel paused the video. The article said Cartier and her friends had
blocked the doors. Where were those doors? Behind the screen? Why had
the club let them do something so dangerous?

The room their video was shot in appeared small. Had they been in
there alone? Why was there a small empty room in a nightclub? Then he
remembered that even modest clubs and theatres often had areas they
didn't use. But how had a riot broken out in a tiny room where they were
the only occupants?

He didn't understand what had happened.

He found a video posted to Twitter and hit play. It was dark
and full of heaving bodies and a fire alarm. "Can't get out. Doors are
blocked," panted whoever was filming. The hashtags were #GooeyFire
#GooeyStampede.

Then people started to post photos and videos to Instagram, TikTok,

Facebook, Twitter, and Reddit in the aftermath. The room was the same one the Deep State had been filming their *Flashdance* recreation in. People were huddled against the black walls. There were uniformed police and club staff in their blue polo shirts walking around. Ambulance attendants.

"Jesus," whispered Nigel again, horrified. Where was Helen? He couldn't believe she'd allowed them to block the doors. Miggs, who'd been asleep beside him, gave his hand a concerned lick. "It's okay, buddy," said Nigel. But it wasn't.

Another version of the RUOkay account posted a video to Twitter.

Moron influencer upset that people nearly dying ruined her video.

Nigel clicked on the new video.

It showed Cartier screaming into her phone. She looked totally deranged, howling at her device. Then Helen appeared, shown from behind. She put her arm around Cartier and spoke with two police officers who stood nearby. And the video cut out.

Oh man. This was all kinds of bad.

Nigel had already packed his things, as Helen had instructed, and something told him that they would need to be ready to go as soon as Cartier and Helen returned. *If* they returned. Could they be charged for an incident like this? This was the clusterfuck to end all clusterfucks. What had Cartier done? What had Helen allowed her to do?

He gave his head a little shake. No. People on the internet were making accusations. The first rule of modern life was don't trust the internet, at least not right away.

In a situation like this, where everything seemed to be going to hell, Nigel would follow Helen's example. He would wait before making judgments.

He would also put his bags near the front door and pack up everything the dogs would need.

CHAPTER 29

After Helen finished giving her statement, she was told that Cartier would be at least another hour. Helen texted Issan, the bouncer from the club, who responded right away.

> Nhung's got ur car. He's just down the street from the station. I'll tell him to meet u outside.

Helen texted her thanks.

> Everything ok?

> I think so.

Five minutes later she reached the sidewalk outside the police building. The valet pulled over in a no-stopping zone and put on the hazard lights, and a heavily tattooed young Vietnamese Canadian man got out.

"Miss Helen?" said the driver.

"Yes," she said.

"Here you go. Issan said VIP for you. All the way."

Helen slipped him a generous tip. "Half for you and the other half for Issan, please."

He looked down at the money between his fingers, eyebrows raised. "Wow!" he said. "You have a good night, miss. Probably be better after you get away from this place." He looked up at the deceptively cheerful pile of red brick and grey glass boxes.

A cop walked out and glared at the illegally parked vehicle.

"You need anything else?" asked the driver.

"No. Thank you. Can I give you a ride back to the club?" she asked.

Nhung blinked. "Wow. So nice. That's okay, miss. Got a guy coming to get me."

As if summoned by an invisible hand, a white Corvette pulled up. Nhung waved at her, ran over, and got in.

She found a place to legally park the Range Rover on the street and considered for a long moment what to do next. The city had grown cool and quiet. What was she supposed to do with her client? About this situation? It was clear that someone was targeting Cartier. Why?

Helen had a sudden overwhelming urge to speak to her teacher. It would be late morning in Thailand, where Sayadaw U Nandisara was team teaching with some renowned Vipassana teachers from Hawaii. If she tried to go through his senior monks, it might be days or even weeks before she would be allowed to speak to him. But there was a way to bypass the queue. Like her current client, Sayadaw enjoyed his cell phone, specifically WhatsApp, which he checked each morning with the excitement of a child at an elaborate Easter egg hunt held in a perfect meadow. Maybe she would get lucky and catch him with his phone nearby.

She entered his number, and after two rings his wrinkly, joyous face appeared.

"Hello?" he said.

He moved the phone around so at first she could see his chin and teeth and then the top of his head, and finally he held it so his eyes gazed directly into hers. He was the head monk at the monastery where she'd been a nun before she left, and she knew she had a special place in his heart, which was more or less an immeasurable expanse.

"Hello, Sayadaw," she said, and bowed.

When she looked back into the phone, his eyes were alight with happiness.

"It's Helen!" he said, as though the fact might come as a surprise to her. Maybe it did. She'd felt lost since she arrived in Vancouver. There was good no-self, and then there was the kind of no-self where one felt that one's component parts had accidentally been taken out with the recycling.

"I know you're teaching at the retreat," she said. "I'm sorry to bother you."

"You need help," he said, nodding. "I can see it in you."

That stopped her. "You can?"

"Oh yes. One of the Canadian monks told me this morning about your hair and that you are famous on the internet now."

Helen now felt like someone had flushed what remained of her equilibrium down the toilet. "They did? The news has already reached Thailand? That's . . . well, I'm sorry to hear that."

"We have the internet here," he said, somewhat breezily. "And there are monks who use it too much, I think. "

Helen tried to think of what to say to this man whom some called an arhat, or enlightened being, about the fact that she was now perhaps a global meme.

"That is not important, of course. The hair. But I see that you are wobbled."

Wobbled. That was the perfect word for how she felt.

She closed her eyes and sighed. It felt good to have someone pay attention to her. It was one of the great gifts that good butlers and spiritually attuned people gave others. The quality of attention in someone like Sayadaw U Nandisara was a rare and special thing. But she must not take too much of his time.

"My employers asked me to work with a young woman," she said, "to help her."

"Ah, yes. The same monk told me that you are now a butler to a new person."

The man never failed to amaze her. Just how much time did he and his monks spend on social media? Had it captured Sayadaw, too? Could the internet take away a person's enlightenment?

"It's a temporary position. Her father asked me to work with her. She's quite . . . untethered. Addicted to her phone. Experiencing some terrible things online. Bullying. Her life is very chaotic. I'm supposed to help her become more grounded. But there's the issue with the phone and her reluctance to disengage, and there is a lot of trauma surrounding her and her friends. Two of them have died."

Helen's teacher stared at her with an intensity that made her want to cry. He was listening with every fibre of his possibly enlightened being.

"I want to help her. But I don't know how. I'm her butler. There's a limit to what I can do. I work *for* her. I am not in charge."

Another long beat while Sayadaw considered the problem. "You say you are employed by her father?"

"Yes. I agreed to help her prepare for life after he is gone. He is not well. He may not have much time."

"Her father thinks she is not ready for the life she will have after he is gone?"

"He's right. She isn't."

"What do we do with the highly distracted students who come to us for the retreat?" he asked.

Helen thought. "It depends on what they need. We consider each one and consider what might help them to find peace."

"That's right. You were always good at knowing what people require, Helen."

"Thank you, Sayadaw."

"What does this girl need?"

"She needs to get away from here. She needs to get off her phone. She needs to disconnect from social media and the entire internet. She needs the brahmavihārās. Like we all do. She needs to get outside and return to her true nature. She needs to understand how other people live."

Sayadaw's eyes nearly disappeared as his face crinkled into a huge smile.

"Yes. So you will take her away. And get her off her phone. Help her to be useful. Take her for some nice walks, I think."

It would not do to argue with her beloved teacher, but he wasn't getting it.

"I don't think—"

He held up a finger in front of the screen. "She won't like it. You will have to be a bit creative!" His face grew more serious again. "Many students we see now are like this with the phones. With the online. We find a way to coax them into the here and now. Some of them, we have to get tough. Make them go cold chickens."

Ah, Sayadaw and his perfect malapropisms. How she loved him.

"You give this girl a chance to be with what is real. To do what is real. To be of service. It is the most freeing thing there is for one who does not abide in the refuges. To do this, *you* must remember what is real."

She had no idea what he meant, but she also knew exactly what he meant. Helen bowed at the phone screen.

"It is too bad your hair is not quite as fancy anymore," he said. "I would have liked to see it here on the WhatsApp."

It was true. Helen's curls had relaxed over the course of the evening thanks to the heat of the club and the terror sweats she'd experienced. She'd also run her hands through her hair at least a hundred times. But the curls had not given up entirely and a few buoyant ringlets remained.

"Thank you, sir."

He chuckled. "Now I will turn off this phone."

And then he was gone, and Helen knew what she had to do.

WEEPING CREEK RANCH

CHAPTER 30

They drove all night, Helen and Cartier in the Range Rover, Nigel following in the pink Mercedes, to reach one of the oldest and largest ranches in British Columbia. The ranch house was located about eighteen kilometres off the main highway along a dirt road. To reach it, they turned off the gravel road and onto a long driveway flanked by split-rail fencing. Shade trees planted on either side of the road blocked the view until they turned the final corner and saw a sprawling stone and wood house nestled below gently rolling hills covered in lush green grass. The sky was the signature blue of a Tiffany box, and fluffy clouds hung high overhead, as though placed there by a designer of sentimental postcards.

Cartier had barely looked up from her phone for the entire six-hour drive. When they had lost service at different points in the drive, the girl had kept the phone in her hand and stared at it as though willing the connection to vibrate back into life. Helen found the girl's fixation with her phone almost as disturbing as what Nigel had told her was happening online.

Maybe the constant monitoring of the phone made sense given the level of abuse Cartier was receiving. It is a terrible thing to be run over and perhaps even worse when you can't see what's coming next.

All Helen could do was be a stabilizing presence. She'd ignored the barrage of messages from Cartier's father that had started coming in at five thirty that morning. She would deal with him later.

179

"We're here," said Helen, when she stopped the Range Rover in front of the house.

Cartier didn't respond.

"I'll bring your bags inside. There should be someone waiting for us. Would you like to wait out here?"

Nothing.

Helen sighed. *Compassion*, she reminded herself. *Compassion*. Then she got out of the vehicle and watched as Nigel pulled up behind them in Cartier's pink Mercedes. He had put on a rather dashing driving scarf and goggles. His ability to rise to any occasion and then wildly overshoot the mark, at least in fashion terms, was one of his finest qualities.

She walked over to the car, and he looked up at her. "Too Isadora Duncan?" he said.

"Not if you made it here alive."

"Touché!" he said. Then he looked toward the Range Rover. "How is she?"

"Quiet," said Helen. "Let's go in."

Together they carried some of the bags up the flagstone stairs to the oversized wooden front door.

A young woman dressed in jeans and a T-shirt let them in before they could knock. "You're here with Ms. Hightower," she said. "I'm Mabel. Reynolds told me you'd be along."

"I'm Helen Thorpe. This is Nigel, my assistant. We're very grateful for the use of the premises."

"Of course. Reynolds said to pass along Mrs. Ban's regards. She is very fond of the Levines."

Mrs. Ban, the owner of Weeping Creek Ranch, was a billionaire from Singapore who was a close friend of the Levines. They'd been on many a charitable board together. Mrs. Ban owned ranches in Canada, Australia, Brazil, and the U.S. Her life involved going from one ranch to the next, accompanied by her adult sons, both of whom loved everything about cowboy culture and were famous for insisting that all the staff on their ranches take part in cowboy poetry slams and singalongs.

After Helen had emailed the Levines asking if they had a recommendation for where to take Cartier, they'd suggested Weeping Creek Ranch, which was a long but manageable drive from Vancouver. Helen had met Mrs. Ban twice before. She was a pretty woman in her late sixties who lost no opportunity to bemoan the life choices of her children.

Helen remembered the last time the Levines had entertained Mrs. Ban in the garden at their home in the south of France. Mrs. Ban had gone into full lament mode about her daughter, who was trying to become a plus-size catalogue model in New York. This goal baffled Mrs. Ban, who was committed to being undersized and found catalogues in general to be distasteful.

"We have the ranches," Mrs. Ban had said from under her gargantuan hat and sunglasses. "Mining interests around the world. Liquid natural gas. And she is going around, hat in hand, to be photographed in bad clothing for big, tall girls! But she is not tall! Barely five feet. We could buy all the clothing companies ten times. But she won't hear of it. Why not be a kindergarten teacher if she wants to make no money? Why not be an opera singer if she likes to fail and be rejected! Ah."

Under the shade of a magnificent old hornbeam tree, she'd gone on to tell the sympathetic Levines that her sons showed little interest in business other than the publishing company they'd started that was devoted to preserving Western poetry and songs.

The Levines, whose children weren't building fortunes either but at least had noble and somewhat prestigious jobs as environmental lawyers and climate scientists, had nodded with sympathy. Children were so difficult. You loved them more than life itself, but they had to find their own way.

In the email suggesting Mrs. Ban's ranch, which was empty at the moment, Mr. Levine told Helen that Mrs. Ban would probably want Helen to help her aspiring model daughter if things went well with Cartier. The thought made Helen blanch. *Please, no more unhappy children of the super-wealthy*. Then again, she adored her employers and would do almost anything for them.

"We've stocked up on all the supplies you requested yesterday," said Mabel, bringing Helen back to the present. Mabel was a tall, competent-looking Indigenous woman in her mid-twenties. She looked over Helen's shoulder at the Range Rover, in which Cartier Hightower still sat, staring at her phone.

"Ms. Hightower is taking care of some business," said Helen. "She'll be in shortly."

Mabel nodded. "Sure. I just have to let you to know that I don't work in the house. My cousin's the caretaker here. I look after the horses when the Bans are away, which is like ninety-nine percent of the time. But right now my cousin is visiting my sister in Williams Lake, who just had a baby. I can show you where everything is."

Helen told Nigel to wait by the door in case Cartier actually got out of the vehicle, and Mabel took her on a tour of the house, which was enormous and done up in a slightly overblown rustic style.

Almost every room had floor-to-ceiling windows that showcased the breathtaking vistas of fields, low, rolling hills, and endless skies. The main living room featured groupings of leather furniture and a fieldstone fireplace large enough to stand up in.

The kitchen was built on a similarly grand scale and included a top-of-the-line stovetop with eight burners, a bright-green Aga, clean expanses of stainless steel counters, and a walk-in cooler.

"I've turned up the heat for the pool," said Mabel, leading Helen into a glass-sided room dominated by a long turquoise pool and adjoining hot tub. Doors leading to a sauna, a steam room, and a fully equipped gym ran along the other side.

The entertainment room featured theatre-style reclining seating and a screen big enough for a commercial movie house.

The outdoor entertaining area had poured concrete floors and low river rock walls. Next to it were an outdoor pool, a brick oven, and a fireplace set into the wall between the inside and the outside of the house.

Helen marvelled at how good the ultra-wealthy were at taking care of themselves materially. There was no resentment or judgment about this in her heart. Only a certain wonder that had never gone away.

They toured seven bedrooms, nine lavishly appointed bathrooms with turquoise accents and engraved copper sinks and faucets, and a huge wine cellar before Mabel finally stopped and turned to Helen.

"So that's it," she said. "Weeping Creek Ranch House."

"It's beautiful," said Helen.

"The land is what's really beautiful here," said Mabel.

"I understand you also have some guest cabins?" said Helen.

"Sure. They're between the house and the barn. They're cute. But basic. Rich people basic, I mean."

They walked out of the house and toward a line of five small white-washed cabins, set in a straight line in front of the path that led to the vast red barn. Mabel explained that the barn contained twenty horse stalls with turnouts and an indoor arena. She led Helen along a small gravel path to the front of one of the cabins, which faced the hillside. A small window was set in the back of each cabin.

Mabel climbed the stairs to the first cabin and opened the door.

Inside was a red enamel woodstove the size of a large microwave, an upholstered easy chair and couch, a scarred table, and a tiny kitchenette, complete with stove and mini fridge, cupboards, and sink.

"Bedroom is through here. And the couch folds out," said Mabel. There was a modest double bed covered in a handmade quilt, and fabric curtains that fluttered in the breeze. A chair, a chest of drawers, and a rag rug sat on the plain wooden floors.

"The bathroom is in here." Mabel opened another door, revealing a small room equipped with a stand-up shower, a sink, toilet, and a little window with a view of the barn.

"Before the Bans bought this place and built the house and barn, these cabins were rented out to tourists. Now they're used by people who come here to work with the horses or to take a riding clinic or whatever. The ranch hands all stay at the staff barracks over on the other end of the ranch. I live in an apartment above the barn."

Everything about the little white cabin was pleasingly homey. Not luxurious, but functional and well-thought-out.

"Ms. Hightower and I will stay in these two cabins," said Helen. "But we'll take our meals in the house."

"What now?" said Mabel, looking mystified.

"Ms. Hightower and I will stay out here. She will take this cabin and I'll stay in the one next to her. Nigel will stay in the house, and so will the other staff I've asked to come and help. Ms. Hightower and I will work in the house during the day."

"I assumed you would be staying in the big house," said Mabel, suspiciously. "Reynolds said you were mega VIP, or your client is."

"We'll be fine out here," said Helen.

"Okay," said Mabel, sounding doubtful. "Does your girl in the Range Rover know this plan?"

Helen smiled back. The barn manager was perceptive. "Not yet," she said.

"You're a hard woman," said Mabel.

"No one has ever called me that before."

"You really want me to turn off the internet? We have satellite service out here. Dishes on the house and the barn. It can be a little glitchy when the weather's bad, but the service is pretty good overall."

"Yes, please. First thing tomorrow morning. Please also remove the modems and routers."

"What am I supposed to say if she asks why there's no service?"

"You can let her know that it's not available. If she asks more questions, she can speak to me about it."

"Well, duh. If the cowboys come around, they are going to be pissed," said Mabel. "But it'll probably be good for them, too."

"We'll all have an internet detox," said Helen, feeling pleased at the thought.

"If you say so," said Mabel.

They walked to the main house along the tidy gravel path. Mabel led the way through the massive wooden door at the front of the house and they stood in the light-filled living room surrounded by massive dark wooden beams and stonework and leather. The house was filled with earth tones, and the shiny stained concrete floors were heated, which made them feel alive underfoot.

Nigel appeared in the doorway to the living room with Cartier, the two of them surrounded by three overexcited Pekingese, who appeared as thrilled as Helen was to be out of the city.

Cartier didn't acknowledge Mabel. Instead, she continued to stare at what Helen presumed was the stream of abuse unfolding on the little screen in front of her.

"Ms. Hightower would like to go to her room now," said Nigel. He wore his mirrored sunglasses on his head and had the windswept look of a World War I–era valet who'd gone out for a joyride in his employer's biplane.

Cartier finally lowered the phone and looked around.

"Oh," she said. "This is okay, I guess. Good light. It will be fine to hang out here for a few days, I guess. Until everything blows over."

"Excellent," said Helen. "Follow me."

Nigel picked up two of Cartier's suitcases. There were another two trunks in the Range Rover.

Helen led the way out the front door and across the lavish patio area. They were nearly at the row of cabins when Cartier finally looked up and noticed that they were no longer in the house.

"Uh, where are we going?" she said.

"Right here," said Helen.

The look on Cartier's face when she saw the cabins was one of pure dismay.

"You'll be in cabin one and I'll be next door in cabin two," said Helen.

Cartier's mouth hung open.

Helen walked up the stairs and opened the door to the first little cabin, noting with approval the simple scent of woodsmoke and clean laundry and wood.

"Your bedroom is through here. Nigel, you will stay in the house."

He looked at her with almost as much alarm as Cartier had. "You sure it's not the other way around?" he asked.

"This is total bullshit," said Cartier, wheeling on Helen. "Why am I staying out *here*?"

Helen had been waiting for the question. "Your father asked me to help you, and that is what I'm going to do."

"Oh my god. So you're going to deprive me of, like, comfort? After all I've been through? I'm *literally mourning* here, Helen. This is not okay. I might have to call my dad. I bet this isn't what he meant."

"You are welcome to do that," said Helen.

It would be good to let Cartier sit with her own unhappiness and her insatiable desire for comfort, as well as the awareness that her father thought she was useless and that if she didn't become *less* useless, she would be forced to live on a mere two thousand a month.

The girl let out a sigh. She looked exhausted. But the shock of her accommodations had successfully distracted her from her phone for almost two minutes. Helen could hear the notifications going off. That seemed like a win.

"I guess I stayed in a place like this in Marfa once. I mean, we were in these little houses that were like modernist desert masterpieces? They had glass and steel doors that sort of pivoted. This isn't quite like that. Also, in Marfa the buildings had these little bathroom cubicles with these super-cool concrete bathtubs? The whole look was so dope. We got some incredible shots in there. I was literally in the bathtub. I was trying to channel Lucinda Williams, only like prettier? I got custom leopard skin cowboy boots in Marfa. Not real leopard, obviously. Trudee found the boot store."

Helen blinked at the barrage of words.

"I think you will find this cabin has everything you need. And as I noted, I'll be right next door. We will work in the house during the day."

"Work?" said Cartier.

"Work," said Helen.

"What kind of work?"

"We will discuss it tomorrow," said Helen.

"So fucking weird," muttered Cartier. She walked around the little cabin and then opened the door and stepped onto the porch. The three dogs ran through and began wrestling in the grass, panting and joyous at being outside.

"Well, at least *they* like it here," said Cartier. "I would be really mad if they didn't. This has already been the worst day . . ." She didn't finish the sentence and her face fell. Helen knew this day wasn't the most terrible day in her life. The worst had been the day her mother died. "During such a terrible time. You know, with everything that's going on."

"Can I make you a cup of tea or coffee while you settle in?" asked Helen. "Or I can unpack and put your things away while you rest."

"That's okay. You can leave everything. I just want to go to bed." Cartier rounded her shoulders as she stared down at her phone. She disappeared into the small bedroom and firmly closed the door behind her.

When Helen and Nigel left, the dogs followed. It didn't seem fair to coop them up with their depressed mistress when there was a whole ranch to discover.

CHAPTER 31

Helen put her own few things away in cabin two and then went back to the big house, where she found Nigel standing against the long kitchen island, staring down at his phone.

Helen was hit with a sudden desire to fling every phone on the planet into a volcano. Not only did the devices steal time and attention, but they were also the Wild West where etiquette was concerned.

"I think you need to see this," said Nigel.

Before they left Vancouver he'd shown her some of the videos taken at the club the night before. The stream of vitriol directed at Cartier had quickly grown into a river. Thousands upon thousands of comments and memes.

"Maybe you could just describe what's happening," she said.

"The internet has decided she tried to kill everyone in the club," he said.

"That's not true," said Helen. "I was there. Something happened, but it wasn't that." She thought of the reports from the security staff and the police that someone had managed to gum up the doors of the ReVibe Room so no one could get in or out. Someone had pulled the fire alarm and then tried to get everyone into the black box theatre room where the stage had been set up in front of the locked doors. Was that a coincidence? It didn't feel like one.

"Do we need to do something about this?" Nigel asked.

"I'm not sure. What people are saying online?"

"Nothing good," said Nigel. "Maybe we should issue a statement. Let people know that Cartier didn't do anything wrong."

"We've already spoken to the police. They know that Cartier was DJing when the stage was assembled. She didn't have anything to do with setting up the shoot. It was unwise to dance in front of the doors, but they were supposed to be closed off from the main room and the door to the outside should have been unlocked. Cartier didn't know the Deep State wasn't supposed to be in that room. The police were planning to talk to Keithen and Dixon, and they wanted to find out who let them into the little room."

"Someone should tell the internet that what happened wasn't Cartier's fault," said Nigel.

"The internet doesn't seem very good at listening."

"Also, I didn't get a chance to tell you what I found out about Trudee and Blossom last night." Something caught his eye. "Look. The Deep State just posted a video," said Nigel. He brought the phone up to watch.

Helen didn't get to hear what the remaining members of the Deep State had to say about anything because her phone buzzed. A Vancouver number.

She sighed and picked up.

"When Bunny and Benedict told me you were going to help, I believed them!" bellowed Archie Hightower.

Helen held the phone slightly away from her ear.

"AND LOOK AT WHAT YOU HAVE DONE!" he screamed. "She's a goddamned global pariah! You were supposed to get her out of there. Instead, she turned you into one of them! There you are, modelling that, that . . . hair. Then there was a riot! My girl was in a riot! She could have died. People hate her! She's enemy number one for anyone with an internet connection!"

Helen waited.

"How could you let this happen?" he continued, starting to wind down. "Those moron friends of hers could have killed every dipshit in that club with that stunt. I thought you were supposed to be a trained butler. Doesn't that mean that you have some basic common sense? How could you allow my daughter to act like such a complete idiot? Are you as much of a nitwit as the rest of them?"

Helen listened as though he wasn't talking to her.

Maybe, she thought distantly, he would get so angry he'd fire her. The idea was appealing. The level of chaos in the family and in the situation felt entirely untenable. *Unpleasant.* She breathed. *Unpleasant.* What was the remedy for chaos? The medicine for mayhem? It was calm. Peace, calm, and connection.

Nigel, who could hear everything because of Mr. Hightower's volume, stared at the ground, which made her feel bad for him. It was no fun to hear someone being abused.

Hightower was panting into the phone like an enraged bull getting ready for another charge.

"Mr. Hightower," said Helen. "I am going to have to ask you to stop there."

"What?"

"I understand that you feel upset. That's quite natural under the circumstances. But I cannot accept name calling. Not aimed at me or at your daughter."

He sputtered.

"If you cannot calm down and speak civilly to me, this conversation is over, I'm afraid."

"Oh really? Are you going to quit too?"

"If necessary, yes. You are welcome to come here and take over," said Helen.

"Oh, for Christ's sake. Where are you? At that bloody hotel? Goddammit, tell her to come home. I don't have any staff left. Not one person! Nobody wants to work anymore. Lazy. Everyone is lazy and useless and entitled. It's the fault of the communist bloody government in this country. You probably voted for them, didn't you?"

Helen decided not to respond. Butlers avoided political discussions at all costs. But, she reflected, if someone wanted to give Mr. Hightower a stroke, bringing up politics would probably be an effective method. "We're at Weeping Creek Ranch. Between Merritt and Kamloops."

Silence.

"So you're *not* in Vancouver."

"Cartier needs some time away from . . . everything. I arranged for us to stay here at the ranch. Let things calm down. We will work on some foundational skills she may need."

"So she's finally away from those mor— I mean, her internet friends."

"That's right," said Helen.

"Well, that's good, I guess," said Hightower. "This whole thing is a disaster. Did you know that another kid is dead? Another girl fell in the river doing god only knows what. And after that thing at the dance club, my daughter has all the fame she could have asked for, and she got it in the worst goddamned way. It's a nightmare."

"This must be stressful."

"Just stop it with that," he said.

Helen almost laughed.

"I like being furious. It's better than the alternatives, okay?"

"Okay."

"I'm going to contact a PR firm that specializes in crisis management. Nadine, our VP of finance, gave me a name. Her middle son sent a weenie pic to his law school magazine. By accident. Attached the wrong file to an email. There's no mention of it anywhere online now. That tells me the company does good work."

"Ah," said Helen. She considered telling him that his daughter might like to see him and that he should perhaps come to visit, but she didn't. Cartier needed calm.

"The police confirmed that Cartier is not a suspect in what has happened. Someone else locked the doors and pulled the alarm," said Helen. "That's why they let us leave."

"Thank fuck for that. But there's still a lot of cleanup to do on aisle twenty-two," he said. Then he took a long breath. "Okay. Well, that's better than I thought. Nobody tells me anything. The PR firm will be in touch. Tell Carty to keep her nose clean. I suggest you take that phone of hers and run over it with a tractor-trailer about twelve times."

"Thank you, sir," said Helen, but he had already hung up.

～～

At ten o'clock that night, Wallace and Lou Ellen arrived together in Lou Ellen's bright-blue Kia Soul. Perhaps to indicate that they still felt some resistance to coming out of their brand-new retirement, they both wore holiday-maker outfits. Wallace had on Bermuda shorts and a Hawaiian shirt. Lou Ellen was in a muumuu.

"Thank you so much for coming on such short notice," Helen said when she and Nigel went outside to greet them.

"We won't be staying," said Lou Ellen. "Right, Wall?"

"Don't call me Wall," said Wallace. "Unless you want me to serve you creamed kale for every meal."

"It might help my digestion," said Lou Ellen. "Too many mai tais since I retired." She patted her rounded stomach in a satisfied way.

Helen looked from one to the other. Had they gotten together as a couple since quitting the Hightower residence? If so, it would be a peculiar pairing. Wallace had something of the aesthete or at least the experimental-jazz appreciator about him. Lou Ellen was more like the aunt you have to keep away from the craps table when you go on your annual discount cruise line holiday. But perhaps the challenge of working for Archibald Hightower had cemented their bond. They were like soldiers who had gone to war and survived unthinkable conditions.

"So you need our help here for a few days?" said Wallace.

"No more than two weeks. And you will be paid for three. I've also arranged for you to get hazard pay," said Helen, feeling gratitude at the sight of them.

"Why?" asked Lou Ellen, darkly. "Are there hazards?"

"Not that I know of. I just want to make sure it's worth your while. And I think you'll be very helpful to the client. Full of information and insight."

192

"You said you're supposed to help her, but you didn't say with what or how," said Wallace.

"I've been asked to help prepare her for the life she will one day lead after her father passes and she inherits everything."

"Oh god," said Lou Ellen. "*I* could do that. I'd tell her to hire you, Helen, or someone exactly like you and then move to a spa."

"You know it's not that easy," said Wallace, gazing around at what he could see of the ranch house. "There aren't very many Helens out there."

"We're a little Helenish," said Lou Ellen. "But funnier, of course."

"And we're retired," said Wallace. "We're not available."

"Are you also supposed to intervene in her lifestyle?" asked Lou Ellen.

Helen didn't answer. She just gave them each another hug and invited them inside.

"Nice," said Lou Ellen, after she looked around the living room. "I especially like the lack of people."

"We have one client," said Helen. "But I think you'll find there is no shortage of things to do."

CHAPTER 32
CARTIER

It was nearly five o'clock in the morning and she was sure her dumpy little prison cell of a cabin was surrounded by cougars and bears and angry bald eagles. The wildlife here made a massive racket. The damned doors to these cabins didn't even lock, and so she'd been awake almost all night.

She'd thought that if she read *everything* she would get to the end of it. Or maybe someone would *defend* her and that would catch on and a lot of people would start defending her. Sort of like a Free Britney movement, but for her? A few people had tried to be nice in their comments. But they were the sort of people who always have something nice to say about everyone. Nobody listens to those kinds of people.

They wrote things like "walk a mile in her shoes" and "presumption of innocence" and "this kind of pile-on makes me feel kind of bad." Not exactly Free Britney energy.

It felt like the whole world had been waiting for their chance to attack her. People had all this pent-up hate they'd been waiting to dump somewhere, and she came along at the right time. There were multiple snark forums on Reddit devoted to crapping all over her. She had anti-fan websites and was a constant target on GOMIBlog, which stood for Get Off My Internets, and specialized in cyberbullying and harassing influencers. The incident in the club would throw gas on the various campaigns to destroy her. As far as she could tell, they hated her because she was privileged or whatever. But there was something else going on that had nothing to do with her. She could sense it, even if she didn't understand it. Someone was causing all of this. But before she could figure out anything else, she'd start scrolling again and soon she couldn't think or breathe. Or eat or sleep.

Did being trapped out in the sticks with boring Helen and her strange assistant make the experience worse? Probably. She'd had her fun, posting all the stuff about uptight Helen, but the assistant guy was borderline *unsightly*, even if he seemed nice. She was going to have to crop him out of every shot he wandered into. Oh right. No one wanted to see any posts by her anymore.

What were they even doing out here in the wilderness? What was the point? This was obviously part of her dad's plan to get her to act like a responsible daughter, like Ivanka Trump or someone like that. She missed Amina and Keithen. They were getting hammered by criticism too, but not like her. They were getting attacked with little hammers. She was getting sledgehammer treatment.

"Sledgehammer." That was a good song. Maybe she should use it in her next TikTok?

She googled it. Peter Gabriel. A golden oldie. Maybe there was a good remix somewhere. Maybe she could make one?

She should really speak up in her own defence! Post a response video. Let everyone know the police had confirmed that what happened at the club wasn't her fault, at least not completely. She hadn't known they weren't supposed to be in that room, although even if she had, she'd still have gone along with it, because that's what she did.

Probably the worst thing was that people were saying she didn't care about anyone but herself. That she didn't care about Blossom or Trudee. That wasn't true. Before Trudee came along, Cartier wasn't even sure she wanted to be alive. Trudee had been an amazing assistant. She'd introduced Cartier to the others, and she was the reason that Cartier had joined the Deep State, although now that she thought about it, why would they have gone along with what Trudee wanted? Trudee wasn't an influencer. She was just a . . . what was she? A facilitator. That was the word. She was good at setting things up. Organizing. Trudee had been the closest thing Cartier had to a real friend, other than her mother. She was good to talk to, easygoing, and she gave great advice, especially about content.

It was horrible when she died. Cartier could hardly even talk for like two days after. She stayed in her room for over a week, until the others reminded her that they had commitments to keep. She'd hung on to that idea. She'd never really had commitments before. The idea of having responsibilities and people who counted on her gave her a reason to get up.

It was different with Blossom. Cartier had seen the POV videos of Blossom mocking her. In one of them, Blossom even wore a knock-off of one of Cartier's most iconic outfits. Okay, maybe only Cartier thought the outfit was iconic, but so what? When Blossom wore the cherry-red track suit with the runners labelled *Museum Quality, for Display Only*, she was making fun of Cartier, who got called out for wearing '97 Nike x Eminem Airs in a video. The runners were collectibles and had cost her fifty thousand U.S. The seller had been very clear that they were too old to be worn, but it's not like she'd run a marathon in them! She'd just put them on and, you know, had Trudee film her walking around in them to go to that new vegan brunch place with Slim Shady playing in the background. So what? They were *her* shoes, although they were a men's seven and hadn't fit that well. It's not like she did a Kim Kardashian and ruined one of Marilyn Monroe's most famous dresses by squeezing herself into it. (There had been some damage to the runners, but no one needed to know that. After the controversy died down, she never wore them again.)

The worst thing was that Blossom got more views on the video she made that mocked Cartier than Cartier got for the video of herself wearing the shoes to brunch. There really was no justice. It had been hard to take when Bryan seemed more into promoting Blossom's career than Cartier's. Bryan had agreed to represent them individually and as a group, but Cartier hadn't even been sure he supported her being in the group at first, much less wanted to take her on as an independent client. She still felt like an afterthought around him. Luckily, she didn't need the money the way the rest of them did. Well, the way Blossom and Keithen did. As far as she could tell, Amina and Dixon had their own money.

Cartier had been doing some thinking about being a creator. The thing no one except other content creators seemed to get was that it felt amazing to make people happy. It was incredible when they liked you. It also made her feel like she existed, in some strange way.

I post, therefore I am, she thought. That would make a funny T-shirt. Or not. Cartier wasn't always actually sure what was funny. Sometimes she thought her sense of humour wasn't her best asset.

God, she missed her mother. Her mom had always been on her side. But maybe her mom should also have, like, expanded their social scene beyond just the two of them. But she definitely would have pushed back on some of the people who were attacking Cartier online.

There was that one poster called RUOkay who instigated a lot of the hate. He was everywhere: on her Instagram, on Twitter, on TikTok, on sad old-people Facebook, and all the hater sites. She blocked him, but he (she?) kept creating new accounts. RUOkay2. RUOkay3. And so on.

The things he (she was sure it was a he) said were vile.

I know you just kept filming to get attention

Poor little rich girl doesn't care who gets hurt

You're only pretty outside, or maybe you aren't

Did Daddy pay for those tits?

I heard Blossom was about to expose you as a fraud

That last one weirded her out. Cartier was a lot of things, but she definitely wasn't a fraud. She was nothing and she knew it. You can't fake that.

Why did he keep torturing her? She'd never done anything to him. Obviously she'd never answered him, because you weren't supposed to feed trolls, not even if they were framing or deframing her, or whatever it was called. The more she thought about it, the stranger that fraud accusation was. The whole point of the Deep State was to create illusions. There was the illusion that they had perfect lives. (HA! People should meet her dad.) There was the illusion that they always looked hot. (Well, Amina and Dixon always looked hot. Keithen, not so much. Cartier, rarely.) There was the illusion that they did rad stuff all the time. It was all a fraud, but a fun fraud. No one got hurt. Until they did.

She opened Twitter. She was still a top-trending topic. Hundreds of new posts. She started to scroll, but then her phone stopped working. No connection.

What the actual fuck.

She gave it a little shake. *Work, damn it.*

Cartier turned the connection to the satellite service off and on. No connection.

No connection.

No problem. She'd just use mobile data.

Still no bars.

It sent a shock through her body.

What. Was. Going. On?

This was such bullshit. She *needed* her phone. This was a crisis!

Her pathetic little room was covered in clothes and the uneaten plate of food the butler had brought her the night before. How had everything gotten so messy so fast?

She typed the butler a message.

can u please fix internet???

The message wouldn't send. Duh. Of course, it wouldn't.

Cartier looked around the room. She felt like she was leaving a movie theatre she'd been in for days. Or like she was coming down hard from a mega high. She got up, shoved aside the clothes on the floor, and peeked through the curtains. The sun wasn't up, but light had begun to glow over the hilltop horizon. Something filled her chest, and for a moment she felt . . . something.

Cartier took a deep breath, the first one she'd noticed taking since . . . since when? Since her mom died?

All at once, exhaustion hit her. She would go to bed now. Maybe it was good that the internet was out for a little while. They would still all hate her when she reconnected.

Cartier shuffled back to the messy bed. She'd just settled in when she heard the knock on the front door.

"Go away," she muttered into her blankets, which were pulled over her head.

Knock, knock, knock.

There was a pause, then the sound of the front door opening.

What the actual . . .

"Good morning," said the voice outside Cartier's bedroom door. The butler. The damned butler. What the hell did she want? It was dawn, for god's sake.

"Ms. Hightower? It's time to get dressed. We're starting in fifteen minutes."

CHAPTER 33

Cartier came out of her room ten minutes after Helen had knocked on her door. She wore a sweatshirt plastered all over with the Gucci logo all over her pyjamas.

"What's going on? It's not even daybreak hardly," she said.

"Our program starts this morning," said Helen. "Now, in fact."

"Our program will start after I've had some sleep. I'm going back to bed now. But first, I wanted to let you know that the internet isn't working. Can you please make sure it's fixed before I get up?"

"I'm afraid not," said Helen.

Cartier gave her the kind of look that only a person who has undergone an extended period of ferocious online bullying, sleeplessness, and extensive heedless privilege can give. It was also an expression common on the faces of tweens who are shocked at being told no.

"Uh, so if you can't fix it, can you get someone here to do it? Like, right away?"

"No, I can't."

"What do you mean you can't? The internet is like *my whole job*, Helen," Cartier said. "I really kind of *need it*."

"You don't," said Helen. "Not for what we're doing today. And tomorrow."

Now Cartier tried her Lady of the Manor impression. "It seems like you are confused about some things. I'm your *boss*. Your *employer*. I don't want to be rude or whatever, but you do what I want. Employer." She jabbed a thumb at her own chest. "Employee." A forefinger aimed at Helen.

Helen gave her a calm smile. "I understand this is unusual. But right now, our roles have shifted. Teacher." It was her turn to indicate herself with a thumb. "Student." She pointed at Cartier.

"Wow," said Cartier. "Just wow. I'm sorry, but this really isn't working for me. I agreed to stay in this little dump so you would tell my dad I'm a woman of the people. But this is too much. You, Helen, are fired. Prepare the vehicle. I would like to be driven back to Vancouver."

"As you wish," said Helen. "I will let your father know your decision."

Cartier stepped toward her, not in a threatening way, but as though she needed to whisper something, which she did. "Actually, I would appreciate it if you *didn't* mention this to him. Look, I get that you're very nice. That's sort of your brand, right? Well, it would be very nice and on brand to tell him we did the course. Because he'll cut me off if I don't do it."

"Yes, he will," said Helen.

"So you'll tell him I did the course."

"No," said Helen.

Cartier blinked her eyes dramatically several times. Her eyelash extensions were so long Helen thought she could feel a light breeze coming off them.

"Are you serious right now?"

Helen nodded. "I am."

"You're going to make me stay in a tiny cabin and take a course that starts at"—she pretended to look at an invisible watch on her wrist—"ridiculous o'clock?!"

"That's right. Please dress in something that you don't mind getting dirty, and let's head up to the house."

"Oh my god! This is a nightmare!" said Cartier, sounding on the verge of tears. The girl held her hands up to her head, the right one still clutching the useless cell phone.

"I hate my life," she moaned.

"Your life is precious," said Helen. "And so are you."

Cartier Hightower started to cry. Shoulders heaving, she shuffled into her room in her Jimmy Choo shearling and pearl slippers.

CHAPTER 34
NIGEL

At five minutes to six, Nigel and the two newcomers stood in the enormous, shining kitchen, drinking excellent coffee, talking about the menu for the next few days and discussing who would do what for the client.

Nigel already loved Wallace and Lou Ellen, who had arrived late the night before, loaded with enough groceries for at least a month. Wallace was a chef, and from the way he poked around the kitchen like a maestro assessing his new orchestra, Nigel thought he was probably a good one. Of course he was: Helen had invited him! Lou Ellen was one of those older babes who had a sore back and feet, which she mentioned right away. She was extremely salt of the earth and warm, and gave a person the feeling that she would be the perfect person to go on a cruise with because she knew her way around a buffet and would get too tan and drink too much and have hilarious things to say about the other passengers and would make at least fourteen new friends each night. Nigel had never been on a cruise, but if he were to go on one, he wanted to go with Lou Ellen or someone just like her.

He discovered that Wallace and Lou Ellen had just retired from working for Cartier's dad. They'd agreed to come to the ranch to help out Helen, whom they loved even though they barely knew her.

That was so Helen.

Nigel, who'd spent time with three different certified butlers, was getting used to being around hyper-competent people like Lou Ellen and

Wallace. Maybe after he finished his butler training, he, too, would make people feel at ease and in good hands and confident.

"Helen mentioned that Ms. Hightower is being given a bit of a fresh start," said Wallace. "A reset, of sorts?"

"That girl could sure use one," said Lou Ellen.

Nigel noticed that Lou Ellen had this ability to look like she was just chilling, but never lost an opportunity to put something away or straighten something or run a cloth over something else. She didn't seem fidgety. More like a smooth operator, household edition.

Nigel's own mother was not a smooth operator. All cleaning was accompanied by a semi-hysteria about how the tasks were too much for her, she never had enough help, he and his dad were incompetent, lazy, and messy. Only they weren't allowed to help because they "just made things worse." But when his dad broke down and hired a part-time housekeeper to come in once every two weeks for three hours, his mom went nuts cleaning everything so the cleaner wouldn't think they were slobs. Having a housekeeper ended up being way too much work for everyone and they went back to the old way.

Nigel was looking forward to learning from Lou Ellen and was not surprised to find out that she'd been head housekeeper at several fancy hotels and private estates.

He was pouring them all another cup of coffee and was about to ask for more details about their jobs when Helen walked into the kitchen. Shockingly, Cartier was trailing along behind her, looking miserable.

It was no surprise to see Helen. She got up super early to meditate and was almost always working by 6:00 a.m. But he had the impression that Cartier was up at that hour only when she was coming home from a rave.

Cartier wore a pale-yellow hoodie with a large glittery lizard on the front, matching yellow leggings, white running shoes, and a white ball cap that read: *C*nt*. For real. Nigel blinked. Helen must have nearly had a shit when she saw that hat.

Cartier had also taken the time to put on a full face of makeup.

"Good morning, Miss Cartier," said Lou Ellen.

"Ugh," said Cartier, showing no sign of whether she remembered them from their years of working at her house.

"Lou Ellen. Wallace. I'm so pleased you're here. I hope you had a restful sleep?" said Helen.

Cartier climbed listlessly onto one of the tall kitchen stools and sat there like a limp french fry.

"We did. Thank you. Glad to be here," said Wallace, who was keeping a wary eye on Cartier.

What *was* Cartier doing up at this hour? This was another Helen initiative. Nigel could feel it.

"Cartier? You remember Lou Ellen and Wallace?" said Helen.

"I guess," said Cartier, who'd pulled down her white ball cap so that her eyes were not visible. "I would love an espresso. And maybe later a bowl of pomegranate seeds with . . . what was that hangover recipe you made me, Hells? I could go for another glass of that. Room temperature, please."

Helen acted like she hadn't spoken. "Today, Cartier will be looking after you all, with my help," she said.

Every head in the room swivelled to look between her and Cartier.

Nigel found himself laughing nervously, which was inappropriate. But the look on everyone's faces! "Ha. Ha!"

"Cartier is going to learn the various aspects of household management from the inside," said Helen, who didn't seem to have noticed that she was the only one still breathing. "And she's going to learn it from the top professionals in the field."

Silence.

"We will start with breakfast," said Helen. "Actually, scratch that. We will start with appropriate attire."

Cartier looked on the verge of throwing up. "You are NOT serious right now. You want me to cook for, for . . . household help?"

"First, we are going to find you something to wear. But yes. After that, you'll be making breakfast for everyone."

"Uh, no," said Cartier. "I am not even that stoked to be in the kitchen with you . . . people. So no, I won't be doing that. You can tell me whatever you need to tell me about how to be responsible and manage my assets. But I'm not helping. Anyone." She seemed to hear how that sounded and quickly amended it. "Except through my art."

"That's fine," said Helen. "We will be happy to help you get the vehicles back to the city."

"Stop threatening me, Helen!" said Cartier. "It's not cool."

Another laugh leaked out of Nigel. "Ha. Ha ha," he said, in spite of himself.

"This is the program," said Helen. "And it is entirely optional."

"FUUUCK," said Cartier. "I hate this. It is abuse and I'm probably going to file a complaint."

Wallace and Lou Ellen had managed somehow to disappear into small tasks, and Nigel thought it was smart to give the client a bit of space while she acted like a complete d-bag. Rich people. How could anyone stand them? Maybe he *shouldn't* go to butler school. He couldn't think the super-rich were assholes *and* be a successful butler. Or could he?

The fight went out of Cartier as quickly as it had come.

She sniffed. "What do you want me to wear? I don't want to ruin this trackie. It's by Andersön. A Swedish boutique brand. I was on a waitlist for two months for this thing."

"Right," said Helen. "So when you run your own household, you will need to decide how you would like the staff to dress. The dress code should take into account each staff member's job description. Uniforms should be comfortable and adaptable. Today, you will be cooking and cleaning, so we will find you suitable clothes."

"This seriously has to be a nightmare," said Cartier. "Like a Saw movie."

It occurred to Nigel that Cartier wasn't quite right. She was like a child who had never in her life had to do anything she didn't like. He didn't know much about child development, but he thought it was probably pretty difficult to be a toddler when you were in your twenties.

"Let's ask Lou Ellen and Wallace and Nigel for advice," said Helen.

Another eye roll. "Fine. Whatever. What do my fellow servants think is a good look for forced labour?"

"Permission to speak freely?" asked Lou Ellen.

"Absolutely," said Helen. She smiled. She was enjoying this. Helen might be very calm, but she had a tough streak in her.

"Street clothes look sloppy. Traditional uniforms are usually ugly and uncomfortable. I appreciate high-quality, practical clothes. Basic colours. Staff should be easily identifiable. It's also critical that the clothing fit the staff member," said Lou Ellen.

"It also depends on the gig," said Wallace. "I trained in whites, so that's what I'm comfortable in. People who feel good do better work."

Lou Ellen took a sip of her coffee, relaxing into her role as a person with opinions on staff uniforms. "Our jobs are physical. Tight clothes, clothes that don't breathe, make everything harder."

"It's nice when the employer provides an allowance, especially for shoes," said Wallace.

"Good shoes," agreed Lou Ellen.

"And health care benefits!" said Wallace.

Lou Ellen sighed. "Dental!"

"Yeah, girl," said Wallace.

"Oh," said Cartier. "I guess I never thought about it."

"Helen always looks good. Neat, professional," said Wallace.

"Helen's got a great management look for household work," said Lou Ellen. "Also looks like she could leap a building in a single bound."

Helen beamed at them.

"You can't go wrong with a polo with a logo. Long sleeve or short, depending on the weather. Plain cotton pants. No skirts. It's not 1903 anymore," said Lou Ellen. "Preferably navy. Everyone looks good in navy."

Nigel found himself nodding. "At the Yatra Institute, we wear regular clothes and a long denim apron. We look like butchers, even though the place is almost completely vegetarian. It's a cool look."

"Hair needs to be up. No hats. And definitely no hats that say . . . no hats with logos," said Wallace.

"My hair is up," complained Cartier.

"He means your hair should be neat. You can't have it messy. Especially not in a kitchen. A simple ponytail. A braid. A bun. Not a messy bun, either."

"I'm not in the military," groused Cartier. "I don't want to be all heavy on my staff."

"If there's a hair in the food, the whole kitchen is basically on trial for war crimes," said Wallace.

"Come on," said Helen. "Let's go to the staff quarters. I'll show you where the staff uniforms are."

"Oh god, that's so gross," said Cartier, sounding near tears again, but she dragged herself after Helen.

CHAPTER 35

Thank god Cartier had posted from the ranch. The girl had the self-preservation instincts of a worm in a puddle. It had been easy to get one of the others to message her to find out where exactly she was and convince them that going to visit her was the right thing to do.

It had been an unpleasant shock when she'd gone completely offline. None of their messages were getting through. There had better not be a problem with the internet up there. Things were too hot right now to let the narrative unfold without some guidance. The wrong person could end up on the wrong side of the mob, and that would be bad for business.

Luckily, Cartier Hightower was the kind of girl who would stop her car on the middle of the freeway to check a notification. There was no way she'd stay off her phone for long.

Her addiction to social media was definitely going to lead to a tragic outcome. Tragic outcomes were very popular. This was all going to work out just fine. For the ones who remained, anyway.

CHAPTER 36

Helen was pleased with how Cartier, who had never cleaned anything in her life, took to the work. She seemed to find the experience of learning how to make her bed and properly wipe down a bathroom exotic. She brought to her efforts the fresh focus of someone learning to do science experiments. And although Cartier probably didn't realize it yet, it was almost certainly a relief for her to be away from the relentless online attacks.

Sayadaw U Nandisara had often instructed his senior monks to take students who brought an overheated, overwhelming intensity to their meditation practice and put them to work in the garden or the kitchen. In one instance, a particularly energetic student trimmed the entire labyrinth in the wildflower meadow using hand snips.

Predictably, Cartier began to fade early in the day. She'd had almost no sleep for at least two nights.

"It's only like five thirty?" said Cartier, stifling a huge yawn with a fist as she stood near the stovetop.

"Are you tired?"

"Well, yes," said Cartier.

"You are welcome to retire for the evening after you eat."

Cartier looked down at the fragrant vegetarian stew and gave the pot a stir. Wallace was removing the biscuits from the oven, and Lou Ellen was discussing something at the other end of the kitchen with Nigel, who was preparing dinner for the dogs.

"Would you let me go to bed if I wasn't me? I mean, if you were you and I was a regular employee?"

"You would most likely need to finish the work," said Helen. "It would also depend on your schedule. There are labour standards that need to be followed.

"I should sue me on my own behalf," said Cartier. "I've been grinding since six." She gave one of her little laughs. She'd had a number of long breaks during the day, but Helen didn't bring that up. The program was already a shock to Cartier's unregulated system. "It would suck so hard to have to keep going if you were really tired. I mean, I've done it. But it was always voluntary."

Helen nodded, grateful that the girl had come up with that insight. "Some household staff have multiple jobs. They work housekeeping during the day, for instance, and then take a shift in a restaurant at night."

Cartier looked at her. "I'm not dumb, you know. I know that people without money have to work a lot."

Helen said nothing.

"I work hard too. And my dad works, like, every minute of every day, practically."

Cartier gazed out the window at the evening light streaking down the hillside. "But he doesn't have to."

"We all have our path," said Helen. "But it's good to imagine how other people live, and act accordingly."

"It's actually sort of a bummer to think about how other people live, to be honest. Anyway, I'll serve everyone and then go to bed."

"Would you like to eat with us?" asked Helen.

At that, Cartier seemed to brighten and a smile flashed across her face. "Yes," she said. "But I'll still serve."

The meal started out somewhat stilted as the staff watched their trainee, who was actually their employer, awkwardly serve them. But after Cartier sat down, they all began to talk to each other like real people and soon the conversation was friendly.

After Wallace told a funny story about serving a famous and very drunk politician at a Michelin-star restaurant, Cartier held up a hand like a kid at school. "Is it always this nice?" she asked. "Like in the staff quarters? You know, with everybody talking and being friends?"

Lou Ellen, Nigel, Helen, and Wallace exchanged looks.

"Mostly I've had excellent co-workers," said Wallace. "Some of the chefs and owners have been a little . . ."

Lou Ellen gave the thumbs-down sign and Wallace nodded. "Yes, but the other kitchen staff, front-of-house people, we almost always feel like a team. I've met a lot of good people in hospitality. Made a lot of friends in the industry." He and Lou Ellen grinned at each other.

They were all sitting at a pretty table Cartier, Helen, and Nigel had set up in front of the massive window in the living room. A large fire burned in the enormous fireplace. There was an arrangement of fresh grasses on the table and the place settings were simple and pleasing to the eye. The stew was delicious.

"I love everyone I work with," said Nigel. "I'm sort of new to this. Helen hired me for a temporary position a few years ago and now I'm going to butler school in the fall. Probably."

"Probably?" said Cartier.

"I'm not a hundred percent sure it's the right thing for me. I'm not naturally fancy. Or ept."

"You're perfect," said Lou Ellen. "And what the hell is *ept*?"

"Opposite of *inept*," said Wallace. "At least, that's my best guess. We should look it up."

"You know," said Cartier. "I haven't had such a nice time at dinner in a long time."

"I'm glad," said Helen.

"My friends? I mean, my friends in the Deep State. Eating is never just eating. Or visiting."

Helen had noticed that. Either they ate in a highly restrictive way or it was more about showing off their meals to the internet than enjoying each other's company.

The mention of the Deep State seemed to remind Cartier that she hadn't been online all day.

"Is the internet working again?" she asked.

"Afraid not," said Helen.

"You turned it off, didn't you?" said Cartier.

"I had the modems and routers removed."

Silence greeted this announcement.

"That's really not cool," said Cartier, finally. Some of the petulance and addiction had crept back into her face, which had been so open and curious a moment before. "Look, things are very intense for me right now. Maybe I could just go back on the internet tonight? After I go back to my cabin."

"I'm afraid not. The equipment has been stored away."

"So you can unstore it."

Helen didn't answer.

"Oh my god. Fine. When are you plugging them back in?"

"After we leave," said Helen.

Cartier let her head loll back on her shoulders as though she couldn't quite believe what she was hearing. "People are probably calling me a mass murderer by now."

"Are you?" asked Helen.

Cartier's head snapped up. "No. Obviously not."

"Then it doesn't matter what people say."

"Clearly millions of people don't think *you* are a psycho, or you wouldn't be so cavalry."

"Cavalier," said Wallace, who caught himself as he said it. "Apologies."

"Look, I need to monitor the situation. Make sure it doesn't get out of control."

Helen looked at her carefully before speaking. "Has your time on the internet kept anything under control?"

"Well, no. But . . . that's not . . . Look, you're sort of old and religious and a butler, so it's hard for you to understand. But most of us live there now."

"Live there?"

"Online. It's social. It's our work. It's like *very important*."

Wallace, Lou Ellen, and Nigel listened to the exchange like a small crowd at a not-very-good tennis match.

"I've decided that it's best for us all to stay offline until we leave," said Helen.

Cartier flung herself back in her chair. "Whatever. How long am I going to do chores and learn what it's like to hang out with poor people?"

Helen could sense the others pulling back from the girl's unkind words and made sure that she didn't react the same way. People had probably been pulling away from Cartier Hightower with her thoughtless privilege, her heedless words, and her bottomless need her whole life. "I have a wonderful program of study planned for you. I think you'll enjoy it. But it will be a surprise."

"You're very big on surprises," said Cartier.

That was true. Helen loved surprises. For others. She thought they were useful to people who needed help living in the moment.

"Should I clear up?" asked Cartier.

"No, hon. That's fine. You go get some sleep," said Lou Ellen.

Something about the word *hon* made Cartier's face soften. She looked on the verge of tears. "Thank you," she said. Then she got up and left the big house for her little cabin.

"What are the chances she hauls ass out of here in the middle of the night on the hunt for internet service?" asked Wallace in the silence after her departure.

"Low," said Helen. "Nigel has her keys."

"You are the strangest butler I've ever met," said Lou Ellen.

"But we approve," said Wallace.

CHAPTER 37

The next morning Helen once again knocked on Cartier's door at five thirty.

"What?" she replied in a voice that suggested she'd been awake.

"Good morning. This is your wake-up call."

There was a muffled reply and some noise inside the room. Helen turned to begin tidying the rest of Cartier's cabin and then stopped. It didn't need it. If there was a mess, it was all in Cartier's bedroom.

The girl emerged only a minute later, makeup-free and wearing the Weeping Creek household staff uniform of a navy polo shirt, khaki pants, and a grumpy attitude.

She did not say hello.

Helen felt a fresh wave of compassion for her client.

"What are you making me do today?" asked Cartier, after Helen let the silence stretch on.

"Today, we are going for a morning walk. A long one, so please wear comfortable shoes."

"Like now?" said Cartier.

"Yes," said Helen.

"Fine. Give me a minute."

Famous last words, thought Helen. She went to the porch to wait and was surprised when Cartier came out only ten minutes later wearing jeans, a plaid shirt, a fleece, and hiking shoes. Those trunks of hers were like Mary's Poppins's magic carpetbag when it came to clothes.

They walked down the porch and looked at the trail that led up and over the hill in front of the house.

"We're just going to . . . walk. Up there?" said Cartier.

"That's right. We're going to have a morning constitutional."

"If you say so."

They fell into step together.

The air was cold and damp, and Cartier, in spite of her thick fleece jacket, hugged herself. The birds carried on with their dawn chorus, untroubled by the doings of humans, and the early sky was dawning clear.

"How are you doing?" Helen asked.

"I'm out here freezing my ass off and have no idea how all this walking and cleaning and pretending to be poor is supposed to help or why my whole stupid life is falling apart," said Cartier. Then she added, "I don't know. And I don't want to know, you know?"

Helen understood and thought Cartier's answer was quite profound, in its way, and she told her so.

Cartier looked surprised at the compliment but didn't say any more.

They walked in silence until they reached the crest of the hill, where they stopped to admire the vista. Soft-blue mountains in the distance gave a sense of the vastness of the flatlands that stretched out beyond them. Scattered low clouds created shadows on the landscape. To the southwest a dark cloud threatened. All else was blue skies.

Helen looked at Cartier, half expecting that she would seem sleepy or bored. But she looked entranced. They walked for another fifteen minutes before Cartier spoke again.

"How long will we be here?"

"I believe that the Bans are in Brazil for the next month at least. We will probably be here for a week or two. There is a lot to cover."

"Well, at least it's really pretty here," said Cartier.

Helen nodded.

"Before you were a butler, you used to be a . . . What was it? Like a minister or something?"

Helen smiled at her. "I was a nun for a time. In my twenties. Then I worked as a meditation teacher and a manager at a retreat centre until I went to butler school."

Cartier looked at her, showing more interest and curiosity than Helen had thus far seen her direct at another person.

"What was that like? I guess you prayed all the time? Did you worry you were never going to get to do the—" Here, she widened her big eyes. "You know, do the do again?"

That made Helen laugh. "I was a Buddhist nun. And no, that wasn't a major consideration for me."

"Can Buddhist nuns get it on?"

"Those who have taken the robes are celibate," said Helen.

"Bummer. I couldn't be a nun, then."

The conversation struck Helen as strange because Cartier had never mentioned any romantic interest. She seemed interested only in her own image and the attention it brought. She could be having a torrid affair with someone over the internet, but somehow Helen thought not. The girl didn't seem preoccupied with anyone other than fellow Deep Staters and her followers, at least how many she had.

"How does a person go from being a nun to being a butler?" asked Cartier.

"I left the monastery I lived in when my mother became ill and needed me. After she died, I went to work at the retreat centre, and my employer there sent me to butler school. I like looking after people. Making things go smoothly."

"I'm sorry about your mother," said Cartier. "I miss mine every day."

"Me too," said Helen.

"Can I be honest with you?"

Helen found the new, engaged Cartier quite enjoyable. Much better than the one who couldn't look away from her screen.

"You still seem sort of more like a nun than a butler."

"How so?"

"You're helpful and all that, but you're just soooo . . . calm."

"Have you met a lot of butlers?" asked Helen.

"A few," said Cartier. "They were all polite and helpful. And they seemed calm. But you're like *calm*, calm. It's like you're dead."

Helen let out a little laugh. "You equate being calm with death?"

"You sound like a shrink. But yeah. I like it when things are happening. Well, when good things are happening. Fun things."

"Most people agree with you," said Helen. Indeed, the desire to avoid boredom was almost as debilitating as chasing pleasure and being averse to pain.

Cartier stopped suddenly. They'd been walking for nearly forty minutes.

"Oh my god. Now I can't walk anymore," said Cartier. "These boots are killing me. And I think they're ruined. But they're so ugly I don't really care."

"I'll be happy to clean them for you when we get back."

"So you're butlering for me again?"

"I was always butlering for you."

"This whole thing is so confusing," said Cartier. "My dad gets the most insane ideas. I would like to know why he wants you to turn me into someone I'm not."

Helen looked at the clouds moving steadily across the ever-changing sky.

"No one can make you into someone you aren't," said Helen. "He wants you to be prepared for life."

"Next time you talk to him, could you remind him that I'm not an *infant*?"

Helen thought of Archibald Hightower's confession that he was sick and wondered when he planned to tell his daughter. She suspected that Cartier was no more prepared than the average infant for a world without her remaining parent.

She decided to take a chance and be honest. "What you have right now is more of a lifestyle than a life."

"Oh, thanks, Helen, for that awesomely deep observation. You are practically Deepak Chopra or that Gabe Maté guy. Life, lifestyle. What's the difference?"

In the distance, the morning grasslands looked silver.

Seeing, seeing, noted Helen. *Pleasant, pleasant.*

"What matters most to you?" asked Helen. "What would be left for you if your friends and your money went away?"

"I wish you wouldn't talk to me like I'm an idiot. Why would I worry about some having-no-money disaster scenario," said Cartier, showing a better sense of the underlying context of the conversation than Helen expected. "We have enough money to last generations. That's what Daddy calls it. Generational wealth."

"You haven't answered the question," said Helen.

"It's not a real question, because I'm always going to have money and so I'm always going to have friends. That's how it works."

Cartier's gaze was defiant, but her words made Helen profoundly sad.

"It seems to me that you are perilously close to having neither," said Helen.

"Obviously, it would suck not to have money," said Cartier. "Does that make you happy? It would suck to be a regular person. The problem with people like you, Helen, is that you don't get it. There's nothing *wrong* with what we do. We're not hurting anyone. Being online is how people connect now. It's, like, our *community*."

"Has your community helped you in your time of need?"

Cartier made an exasperated noise. "It's not that kind of community. Right now, everyone hates me. So I have to change how they see me. It's like we're creating a story." It was Cartier's turn to condescend to Helen, and Helen thought she probably deserved it.

Helen wanted to ask what kind of so-called community didn't help its members. Maybe one that was all too human and also one that was all too enthralled with its storylines.

"Who in your community really knows you?" she asked.

Cartier stared back the way they'd come, as though she wished she could be teleported back there. "No one. Not really. Not since my mom died. But Keithen and Dixon and Amina understand where I'm coming from, sort of. Any content creator gets it. Bryan gets it. He also sees our, like, humanity. The fans, well, they don't like me exactly, but they will. We curate our lives and show it to people so they have something to aspire to. That's what Bryan says, and he's right. We're using our lives to entertain people."

Helen nodded. All beings were constantly curating their lives in the sense that almost everyone was leaning toward what they liked and avoiding what they didn't. The only exceptions were those few fully enlightened beings who had moved beyond preference. Nobody at Weeping Creek Ranch was an enlightened being, including Helen.

"Your career is not my business. Your lifestyle is not my business. Your friendships are also not my business. Your father asked me to use my training as a butler to help you be more grounded and better prepared for the life you will inherit when he's gone. If I had to guess, he wants me to help you find meaning."

"You still haven't told me what the difference is between a life and a lifestyle."

"Maybe there is none," admitted Helen. "Either can go away in an instant."

"If making me depressed is grounding me, you're doing an awesome job," said Cartier. But she was smiling. With her face free of makeup and a genuine smile on her face, Helen thought she looked quite beautiful.

They turned and began walking back the way they'd come.

"My goal is to teach you by letting you experience things. Something tells me that is how you learn."

"You have that right. You could talk to me all day and it wouldn't sink in. But when I try something, I get it, practically instantly."

Changing the subject abruptly, Cartier said, "Keithen looked you up, you know. He told us that you solved a murder at your last job. He also said that, other than your bio on Butler.com, you barely even exist on the internet."

"Butlers are meant to be discreet."

"Sucks to be a butler," said Cartier, and this time they both laughed.

Now Cartier was in front on the narrow trail and Helen walked behind her.

"Do you ever want more attention?" Cartier asked.

Helen considered the question. Thought about the photos of herself with the awful hairdo posted to the internet. "No," she said. "I really don't."

She thought also of her teacher, Sayadaw U Nandisara. He had taught her that there were two main kinds of human suffering, one stemming from the desire to exist, which was often expressed as craving and clinging, and the other from the desire to not exist, which turned into avoidance and aversion. Helen had never been suicidal, but sometimes she imagined disappearing, and the thought was not upsetting to her. She never wanted to take to her bed, but she had sometimes wanted to disappear altogether.

"I think attention might be killing me," said Cartier. "And I can't stop trying to get it. I also think it killed Blossom and Trudee. I don't even know what I mean, exactly. But do you understand?"

Helen nodded slowly. "I think I do," she said.

They continued walking in silence and again stopped to appreciate the view when they reached the top of the hill and the low-slung house was in sight.

"Do you think someone is behind everything that's happened?" asked Cartier. "You know, Blossom's and Trudee's accidents. What happened at the club. Do you think someone is responsible?"

"I don't know," said Helen.

"Could you look into it? I mean, you caught a murderer before."

"What I did at the Institute was an accident," said Helen. "I was just following my late employer's wishes."

"You *solved* that crime. That's what Keithen told me," said Cartier.

"I'm a butler," said Helen. "If you want to look into these matters, I can help you find a qualified investigator." Doing that would fall neatly into the lessons on human resources that Helen had planned. Good. This would work out well, because Helen, too, wondered whether someone was trying to destroy the group. Nigel had told her that there was a person or people who relentlessly attacked Cartier online. What was that all about? And why had Dixon and Amina seemed to warn Helen that the fans didn't like Cartier? Did they want to get rid of her? It seemed they did. So why hadn't they done so? Whether she went willingly or not, being out of the Deep State would be a very good thing for Cartier Hightower. Of course, Helen couldn't tell her client that.

They walked down the gentle slope and Helen was, as always after a good morning walk, filled with a sense of accomplishment. *Pleasant. Pleasant*, she noted. The feeling of peace persisted until three figures came hurrying out of the barn, cell phones held aloft to film their arrival.

Helen's heart sank. They'd been found by the Deep State. *Unpleasant.*

CHAPTER 38
AMINA

The house was gorgeous. Even before they went inside, she knew that there wouldn't be a bad angle in the whole place.

The housekeeper who answered the door told them that Cartier had gone for a walk. If Cartier weren't the biggest pariah on the internet, Amina would have been sort of jealous. Not because she wanted to go for a walk. She literally couldn't think of anything worse. But she knew Cartier would get awesome pictures or at least have her butler or her butler's assistant take photos of her having a wholesome morning walk. Everyone liked to *imagine* themselves doing things like that, but hardly anybody did it—at least, not until they were very old.

They'd driven up to the ranch in Dixon's Expedition, which wasn't nearly as nice as Amina had thought a vehicle of his would be. It was strange that none of them had been in his ride before. They'd always driven around in her (not paid for) BMW and, later, Cartier's vehicles. Keithen had a Ford F-350, which was impossible to park and so he never took it anywhere. Maybe Dixon thought the Expedition had some retro cool vibe. It didn't. She'd have been embarrassed to take Bryan anywhere in a vehicle like that, so it was good Bryan had followed them in his own ride, which was a proper grown-up Lexus.

Overall, the way things were working out with Bryan was surprising. He'd turned out to be *so* nice and approachable and, most importantly, forgiving. She thought they were toast for sure after Blossom died, but he'd kept them on. Then the thing happened at the club. If she were

Bryan, she would have dropped all of them like poker chips after a losing hand. But they were getting more famous, thanks to the accident, which Amina knew might be very lucrative. She hoped they would be able to parlay that into bigger things, and Bryan said he thought the Deep State were being treated unfairly and that if they stuck together, he might find a way for them to come out of this as viable brand ambassadors. She thought that was a lot more likely if they got rid of Cartier, but didn't say so.

He'd used the word *redemption*. Easy for him to say. There would be no redemption if the truth about her and what she'd done came out. There are some things that don't get forgiven. Cartier definitely wouldn't be the scapegoat if the truth about Amina's past came out. But it never would. She'd made sure of that. At least, she thought she had.

After they got to the ranch, the housekeeper had invited them inside for coffee, but when they asked about the internet, she'd explained that it wasn't working. So they'd gone out to the barn to try to get a signal.

Keithen said he'd seen a satellite on the barn when they drove up, so there had to be some kind of internet available out there. Keithen and Dixon and Amina were walking up and down the aisles of the barn, looking in at the horses and getting exactly no bars of service, when Amina looked outside and spotted two people coming down the hill.

"There they are!" she called to the boys. "Get your phones." None of them wanted to miss anything. After all, this footage might be used in a documentary or at least a podcast one day. They had almost gotten famous enough for that.

A woman with dark hair came around the barn with a bucket in each hand. She looked cool AF. Like, very, very natural and casual and ranch-y.

"Hello?" she said.

"Hey there!" Keithen walked toward her with his phone held aloft, turning the video camera to her.

The woman, who was probably in her early twenties, gave him a hostile look. "Are you filming me?" she asked.

Amina lowered her phone so it was less conspicuous.

"I hope that's okay?" said Keithen. He was turning on the charm. Big smile. Alpha male energy. "You just look great, that's all."

"No. It's not fine."

That ranch girl was fire! So impolite! Amina liked her.

"What are you doing here?" asked the woman. Cartier reached them before they could answer, followed by the butler. They both looked wind-swept and almost as healthy as the woman with the buckets.

"You guys?" said Cartier, uncertainly.

There was something going on with her face. She looked calm, but not fresh-Botox-and-fillers calm, more like inner-peace calm. She looked really good. Cartier wasn't naturally photogenic. She took a lot of bad pictures. But in that moment, she looked like a girl who, like the ranch house behind them, had no bad angles. *It must*, thought Amina, *be sweet to be rich.*

Keithen did his gallant alpha male routine on Cartier, like Mr. Darcy, if Mr. Darcy wore a backwards ball cap and knew how to weld. "We couldn't let you go through this alone," he said, laying it on extra thick.

Cartier made a face and then looked at her butler, who was now a minor celebrity on the internet. All their fans had loved the pictures and videos of Helen. The shot Amina had posted of Helen standing outside the Rover holding all three of Cartier's Pekingese in her arms got over 22,000 likes. There were almost 24,000 likes on the one of Helen sitting in the hotel room with her eyes closed, waiting for everyone to decide where to go for dinner. The comments were all about how cool it was to have a butler with an off switch, how great it would be to be a butler who slept on the job. The #ThisButlerIsMe hashtag had trended.

Amina didn't really get the appeal. Yes, it would be nice to have a butler, but in person, Helen was underwhelming. She was unstylish, too quiet, and, when her eyes were open, she was way too watchful. Even with her eyes closed, she didn't seem to miss much. Keithen had researched her and found out what happened at her last job. She must be a snoopy but-ler if she'd caught the person who murdered her late boss and some other people besides. That alone made Amina nervous.

Helen and Cartier exchanged a look, and there was something wary in it, but then Bryan came around the corner of the barn and Cartier's mouth fell open. She really had a daddy complex about the agent, maybe because her own father was such a bitter asshole.

He approached, smiling in that nice dad way of his.

"Hello, Cartier," he said.

With his subtly retro sneakers, perfectly cut button-down shirt, and Earnest Sewn custom jeans, he looked good, but not like an older guy trying too hard. He struck the right balance. Nothing too trendy, but undeniably hip. He would make anyone in the fashion or entertainment business feel right at home. His face was so honest. Amina reflected again that if he knew the truth about her, he would freak TFO, at least.

"Oh," said Cartier. "You came." You could tell it meant everything to her. And all at once, she was back with them.

CHAPTER 39

H elen watched, dismayed, as Cartier was pulled back into her friends'
orbit of distraction and attention-seeking. She began gushing about
the opportunities for shoots at Weeping Creek Ranch, all the while
glancing at Bryan, who smiled reassuringly at her.

"Coming, Bryan?" asked Dixon. "Cart is going to give us a tour of
the house."

"I'll be along in a sec," said the older man.

He waited until Cartier and the others were gone and Mabel had
gone off to feed the horses. "I hope you don't mind us visiting," he said.
"We would have let you know, but we couldn't get through. Dixon and
Amina wanted to come here to show their support for Cartier. And they
seemed to think that she would find my presence reassuring. I'm a little
old and uncool, but maybe I can be a . . ." He considered his next words.
"A boring but calming presence. I talked it over with my daughter, and
she agreed, especially under the circumstances."

"Oh?" said Helen.

"Beth, my daughter, doesn't totally approve of my client base. She
thinks the internet is exploitative. Imagine hearing this from a seventeen-
year-old. She's always saying I'm feeding the evil machine. She keeps telling me about people, highly online people, who have had bad outcomes
after going through what Cartier is experiencing right now. You know,
online mobbings. Public shaming campaigns. To be honest, I feel somewhat responsible."

Helen didn't interrupt but listened intently.

"I encouraged them to expand their audience. I was the one who suggested Cartier try DJing after she told me how important music is to her."

"Don't get me wrong," he said, intuiting her train of thought. "Most of my advice for them is about things like brand incorporation, timing posts to coincide with marketing efforts, taking advantage of various synchronicities, if you will. They are the creatives here. The ones who come up with the ideas."

"I see," said Helen. She wondered whether they told Bryan about some of their more marginal ideas and she thought they probably didn't.

The surprisingly intense morning sun was prickling on her neck, and she could smell an unfamiliar but pleasant scent. Hay? There was also a faint tang from the manure pile neatly hidden out of sight on the other side of the barn.

The skies over Weeping Creek Ranch were moody and dramatic. Now there were visitors who seemed every bit as mercurial. The arrival of the Deep State was going to set back her plans for Cartier, and she couldn't tell whether this man would help or harm her efforts.

"Do you represent Ms. Hightower, or just the Deep State as a group?" she asked. The question was, like so many things she'd been doing recently, out of line. Butlers didn't question the business dealings of clients. They took orders. Anticipated needs and desires. But Helen wanted to understand the dynamics of Cartier's relationships with these people, business and otherwise.

The agent smiled ruefully. The hair at his temples was silvered, the rest dark brown. "I represent the Deep State as a group and as individual creators. It's just easier. But I care about all of them as people. And I worked in PR for years. I can probably help with some of what's going on."

Helen found herself wanting to tell Bryan that he need not worry, Mr. Hightower was hiring a top public relations firm to help Cartier deal with the crisis. She felt like telling this nice man that Mr. Hightower's main goal was to get his daughter away from the Deep State, and anyone associated with it. Including him. But she didn't. She would let Cartier decide what to do with her life and her lifestyle. Cartier seemed very pleased to have an agent, and Helen didn't want to take that accomplishment from her. She would stick to looking after the guests and teaching Cartier what Cartier allowed herself to be taught.

"You know," said Bryan, gazing at her. "Your content was really popular. You could do well online, I think."

"I'm sorry?"

"Your content. All those photos and videos of you that the kids posted when you were with them in Vancouver."

Helen remembered hearing tales, probably apocryphal, about traditional peoples who would not allow themselves to be photographed lest their souls be stolen. She felt a lot of sympathy with that stance and was momentarily overwhelmed with aversion to the notion that people could look at photos of her on the unreal plane of existence known as the internet.

"It is not my . . . no," she said. "I prefer to stay out of sight from now on."

Bryan laughed softly. "That hairdo was something. You might want to ask them to delete those photos. They didn't do you justice."

He was still looking at her keenly, which felt surprising. No one had looked at her like that for some time. She noted her warm response to his gaze and then let the feeling sail on by.

She had a lot to do and not much time to do it.

"Let's go in," she said.

CHAPTER 40

Helen and Bryan entered the house to find filming in progress. The reconstituted Deep State stood in front of the camera, and Keithen spoke directly to the unseen audience.

"Look, you guys. I know it seems like all we do is have fun. But it's not true. We are mourning our friends and colleagues. A lot of you feel like you know us. The feeling is mutual. But the truth is that you don't know us at all if you think we're not upset, really upset, at what has happened."

"And," Amina added, "you don't know Cartier if you think she's to blame for any of what has happened lately." She put a protective arm around Cartier's shoulders. Helen could see how moved Cartier was by the gesture and it made her feel a bit sad.

Amina and Keithen nodded. "We love making content for you all. But integrity matters. Friends matter," said Keithen.

"We aren't abandoning our friend just because the internet has turned on her and is blaming her for things that aren't her fault," said Amina.

Then it was Cartier's turn. "I would never hurt anyone. For any reason. I wasn't even there when the stage was set up at the club."

Amina nodded. "We love most of you guys, but if you're spreading rumours about Cartier, you need to remember that libel is a crime and Cartier is our friend. So knock it off."

"Let's stop with the conspiracy theories so we can all get back to mourning Trudee and Blossom," added Keithen. "We were given bad advice at the club about where to set up. No one was supposed to be able to get into that room except us. We have no idea how we got locked in from the outside or how the door to the other room was opened. What happened there wasn't our fault. The cops have confirmed that. Luckily, no one was killed. What happened was unfortunate but not intentional. We feel terrible for everyone who got hurt and scared when the fire alarm went off. But we have no idea what happened. We were also victims. Let's just focus on raising each other up instead of tearing each other down."

At this remark, they put their arms around each other to demonstrate that they were a cohesive unit.

Then Dixon stepped forward and turned off the camera. "Nice," he said, as he began to review the footage. The others gathered around him. "Great light in here. We look good. I'll give it a little edit and post it when the internet comes back on."

Keithen looked over at Helen. "When might that be?" he asked. "You've got satellite service here, right?"

Helen didn't answer. Nor did she voice her concern about the video they'd just shot. Would it really change anything or just sound like so much justification? She'd have liked Cartier to stay out of it, that much was certain.

Should she voice her concerns to Bryan? They seemed to listen to him. But he had gone back outside. Maybe he'd forgotten something in his vehicle.

"Looks like you might need another day or two to completely wean her off social media," whispered Nigel.

CHAPTER 41

When Helen had resettled into some semblance of emotional balance, it occurred to her that the forced absence of online distractions might have the same effect on the other members of the Deep State that it did on Cartier. Perhaps they, too, would become calm and focused and better able to connect with themselves and each other. Or maybe that was just another ridiculous thought by someone who didn't get modern life. *Unpleasant*, she noted, at the rather mean thought as it floated by.

Once she'd shown them to their rooms in the house, they all wanted to see Cartier's room and were equal parts horrified and excited to learn she was staying in one of the cabins.

"But WHY?" exclaimed Amina, looking around the modest living room. "Are you grounded or something?"

"I'm supposed to be getting less . . . how I am," said Cartier. "My dad and Helen are making me do it."

"Getting in touch with how the other ninety-nine percent live, eh?" said Keithen. "That must be a shock to the system."

As usual, Keithen seemed almost offended by Cartier's privilege. Odd, since he didn't seem bothered by Amina's and Dixon's wealth.

"Oh, I wonder if we should stay in cabins too?" said Amina. "That would be cool, right? And maybe you'd be less lonely?"

"I'm not lonely. I have the dogs, at least when they're not with Nigel. And Helen is right beside me."

"Nigel?" said Amina.

Cartier blushed. "Helen's assistant. He's really good with the dogs."

"I'll be in the house," said Dixon firmly.

"Same," said Keithen. "It's closer to the pool and the hot tubs. Plural."

"Only one hot tub," said Cartier. "The other is a cold plunge pool."

"Oh god, we're going to need to do that," said Amina. "It's so good for the immune system. After what happened at the club, my whole body has felt on the fritz."

"Not me, thanks," said Dixon. "I hate getting cold."

"And wet," said Amina.

There was a sharp silence as the remaining members of the Deep State seemed to feel a surge of genuine feeling about their lost friend and her death in the cold violence of the river.

"Poor Blossom," said Cartier quietly.

"I know," said Amina.

The two young women held hands briefly. Dixon's and Keithen's faces became older and more serious.

"I asked Helen to find out what happened," said Cartier.

"What?" said Amina sharply.

"Her?" said Dixon. Then he looked at Helen. "Sorry. No offence."

"It's fine," said Helen.

"She caught a murderer before," said Cartier.

"There has been no murdering, Cart," said Amina. "Just accidents. Bad luck."

They had moved outside and were lounging in the white painted Adirondack chairs on the small front porch of Cartier's cabin, while Helen waited off to the side.

"The only thing that got murdered," said Keithen, "was your reputation. And we're trying to fix that."

"Don't you feel like someone is trying to hurt us? Or at least, me?" said Cartier.

"No," said Dixon. "I think we've had a run of bad luck. And some people are getting blamed unfairly."

"I'm getting blamed," said Cartier.

"We're sorry," said Amina, taking her hand again. "It's very unfair."

The west edge of the afternoon sky had started to fill with layers of inky clouds that were slowly crowding out the blue sky. Where the sun could still pierce the cloud cover, biblical beams of light shone down on the grasslands before the shadows closed back over the landscape.

Helen needed to stop listening and focus on dinner.

"We will serve drinks at six," she told Cartier. "Dinner at seven."

"Thank you," said Cartier, who sounded remarkably gracious and comfortable in her role as hostess and chatelaine.

Her friends may have been distracting, but they hadn't taken away everything she'd gained in the short time she'd been at Weeping Creek Ranch.

~~~

By the time cocktail hour rolled around, the bored Deep Staters lay around on the various pieces of oversized living room furnishings. There'd been a number of discussions about "driving into town," to get internet, which would have been at least a two-hour return journey, but they hadn't done it. Yet.

"If you just show me the modem, I can fix it," Dixon had said, sidling up to Helen while she put the tablecloth on the table.

"I can troubleshoot your router," Keithen had offered while Helen and Lou Ellen set the table.

"It's really refreshing not to have the internet distracting us," said Amina, approaching ten minutes later. "But if you need help getting some tech support out here to get things fixed, I can probably hook you up." She smiled her big, perfect smile. "I think folks are getting sort of anxious."

Helen thanked each of them, but she was glad that she'd had Mabel hide the modems and routers in her apartment in the barn. If there was an emergency, there was the landline and a satellite phone. Right now, there was no emergency other than the internet detox the Deep State were undergoing.

Bryan was an easy, companionable presence while the others fretted. Helen even spotted him reading a book. She'd have bet that none of the others even owned any books.

At six o'clock, Nigel, trailed by the dogs, went around taking drink orders. Helen made the drinks and Nigel and Lou Ellen delivered them. That roused Cartier and her compadres from their stupor somewhat.

After the group had enjoyed a second drink, non-alcoholic for Bryan, and, surprisingly, Cartier, Helen invited everyone to sit down at the long wooden table decorated with wild roses and long grasses set among a collection of bleached antlers that were kept in the enormous pantry. The centrepiece was a full-sized silver deer skull out of which cascaded a spray of small white roses. Helen was impressed with Lou Ellen's floral arranging abilities and had told her about the course on floral design offered at her former place of employment and taught by Jenson Kiley, one of the best floral artists in the world. It turned out Lou Ellen had two of his books, *The Artist as Arranger* and *The Artist in Bloom*, and had devoted herself to mastering many of the arrangements shown in them.

Helen and Nigel welcomed Cartier and her guests to the table. They pulled out the oversized wooden chairs for each and placed massive gingham napkins in their laps. The guests took it as their due.

While Nigel poured wine, Helen and Lou Ellen delivered the first courses into the middle of the table so the influencers could serve themselves, family style. Wallace had prepared a simple salad of sliced green tomatoes in olive oil and red wine vinegar, covered with a crispy golden topping of oven-toasted sourdough crumbs mixed with Parmesan Reggiano, Castelvetrano olives, and fennel seeds, a salad he called All Green Goodness, which was, as the name indicated, entirely made up of green ingredients and tossed with a parsley-dill dressing.

"Ooooh, this is amazing!" said Amina.

"Is there bread on there?" asked Cartier.

"I have a plate for you," said Helen, who had suspected that, in the presence of her friends, Cartier would revert to avoiding carbs.

She set down a small plate of heirloom tomatoes topped with baby mozzarella and strips of fresh basil.

The next platter was another salad of julienned beets, pears, and green apples with mint and lemon and topped with feta. This was followed by tiny cups of salmon ceviche and a partitioned bowl with green pea pureed with mint, broccoli pureed with walnut, and Wallace's special yogurt dip. The bright dips were served with toasted fingers of homemade bread and seedy crackers.

"Oh my god," said Amina, after learning that Wallace had been Cartier's dad's personal chef. "It must have been non-stop feasting at your place."

"Nope," said Cartier. "My dad doesn't like fancy food."

"Then why would he have a chef who can do this?" asked Keithen, marvelling over the broccoli-walnut puree.

"Because someone told my dad all successful people have a Michelin chef at home, so he had to have one."

"At least *we* won't waste his talents," said Keithen.

Helen noticed that Bryan was gracious, but he still didn't say much. Mostly, he laughed softly when others made jokes and agreed with whatever the dominant opinion seemed to be. He was an extremely diplomatic individual. Perhaps all agents were?

"This truly is excellent," he said when Helen cleared his salad plate.

Helen smiled and noted how happy Cartier seemed to be with how her guests were responding to what was essentially a dinner party.

Cartier sat at the head of the table, smiling as each new dish that arrived was greeted with enthusiasm by her guests. "Isn't it so fun having a home-cooked meal?" she said.

"Why do we never do this together?" wondered Amina.

"Because we only eat in restaurants," said Dixon. "I'm not even sure I *have* a kitchen at home."

"Do you have a cook?" asked Amina.

Dixon frowned. "No," he said. "Why would I?"

"Oh, it's just that I thought your family . . . never mind."

"I don't live with my parents," he said stiffly.

"Sure. That's cool. Having a chef at home would totally cramp your style," said Cartier, showing a tact Helen hadn't seen from her before. Perhaps Bryan's calm approach was rubbing off on her. "Even if you have a huge apartment."

"I just don't eat at home," said Dixon, looking down at his watch as though for reassurance.

"None of us do," said Keithen. "Although I probably should. It would work with my whole"—he waved his hand around—"thing."

"Public shaming and cooking. Makes sense," said Amina, rolling her eyes.

Helen stood back as Nigel and Lou Ellen set down the platter of pan-fried gnocchi and roasted asparagus with browned butter and a hint of lemon zest.

"It does, actually," said Bryan. "I see the connection. There's something about fighting on behalf of the underdog that is satisfying to people on a visceral level. That's why what you do works so well, Keithen. And cooking is nurturing. Do you know how to cook?"

Keithen gave Bryan a curious look. "Yeah, I guess. Mostly basic stuff."

"You are a fabulous cook," said Amina. "Remember when you made us that vegan mapo tofu and the dan dan noodles in Costa Rica that time? I was shocked."

"You'd have to figure out where to film your cooking," said Dixon. "From your videos, your apartment looks like it's sort of a dump."

Amina turned to him. "Don't be mean. It's just a normal apartment. You wouldn't relate."

It was Keithen's turn to roll his eyes. "Not all of us were born rich. You wouldn't understand, Dix." He turned to Bryan. "And weren't you pushing me to start gaming instead of shaming?"

"I want my clients to be double, triple, and quadruple threats," said Bryan.

When Helen and Nigel returned with a pot of mint tea and coffee a few minutes later, the topic of conversation had changed.

"How did we get together? As a group? That's a good question," said Amina. "First it was me and Dixon."

"Where did you two meet?" said Keithen.

Helen noticed that both Amina and Dixon seemed to freeze.

"I don't know," said Dixon. "It was just one of those things that happens."

"How does any group of artists form?" said Amina. "Shared values and aesthetics, probably. We were both in Vancouver."

"And you're both gorgeous," said Cartier.

"Then you came along," said Dixon, looking at Keithen.

"Trudee told me I should check you guys out. She was always everywhere. You know, all the industry events. Clubs. Restaurants. I think she might have helped out on a shoot we did for a magazine? Was that it?"

"I can't remember," said Dixon, staring at his cup.

"Blossom came in right around the same time as me," added Keithen. "I think Trudee knew her from somewhere."

"And after Trudee came to work for me and saw that I was interested in making content, she put me in touch with you guys," said Cartier, sounding shy. "I couldn't believe it when you all invited me in."

Helen caught the look the others exchanged. What was going on here?

"Right," said Dixon. "Well, obviously, Cart. You're great. And since you started DJing, you're really developing your brand."

"And you pay for a lot of stuff," said Keithen.

Amina shot him an angry glance.

"I hope I do more than that."

"Of course you do," said Amina. "We all contribute. We're an odd mix and that's part of our charm. It makes us funnier."

"Trudee knew everyone," said Dixon. "It was crazy."

Cartier nodded. "That's why I hired her, initially. She loved social media so much. She was like an encyclopedia of content creators."

"Too bad she was about as photogenic as an old potato," said Keithen.

"Keithen." Amina gave him a tap on his shoulder. "Stop being so awful. She was sweet. And she looked fine in person."

"Who cares how anyone looks in person?" said Dixon.

"Well, Blossom definitely thought Trudee looked all right," said Keithen. "I'm ninety percent sure they were boning."

"Boning?" said Amina. "Seriously, Keithen? What would your fans who think you're a feminist ally say if they could hear you?"

"It's true. I saw some very shady doings that weekend at the resort in Costa Rica. I saw Trudee coming out of Blossom's hut one morning. Very racy. Older woman and all that."

"How old was Trudee?" asked Bryan, speaking up for the first time.

"Thirty?" said Keithen. "I think she was around five years older than us."

"I miss her," said Cartier.

When Helen returned to the table to drop off dessert, they were still talking about Trudee.

"I met her at an event at Holt Renfrew. For makeup influencers. Ion Mintner was launching their Twice Shy campaign," said Cartier. "Trudee came right up to me and introduced herself. She said she liked my feed, and I should have a higher profile. She asked if I needed an assistant. I hired her on the spot." Cartier looked pleased at the memory.

"What's dessert?" asked Keithen.

"A mango crème brûlée with ginger and pear," said Helen. "It's very light."

Amina looked down at her flat belly and made a face. "I'd like to."

"No," said Dixon flatly. "Out of the question for me."

"Yes, please," said Cartier. "I love mango."

"And something else to drink?" asked Helen.

"Water," said Dixon. "This place is drying out my skin."

"It's funny," said Keithen, "and sort of depressing to think that such a"—he snuck a glance at Bryan and amended his words before they came out—"that a person who was so, like, behind the scenes basically created us."

"Seems like she was a girl with good instincts," said Bryan.

When Helen left the table, she found herself thinking about Trudee gathering all the members of the group together. Why, she wondered, had Trudee thought the different members of the Deep State would work together? Helen knew from listening to Cartier that there were dozens of high-profile influencers in Vancouver and perhaps hundreds of lesser-known ones. Maybe Trudee had introduced everyone she knew? But it sounded as though she'd been deliberate about connecting these particular people, and about cultivating Cartier in particular.

The group's activities had led to two deaths, and Helen hoped they would allow Bryan to guide them in a more professional direction. She also hoped that they would all have a good sleep and a healthy breakfast, and then the boredom of living without the internet would encourage them to leave so Helen could get back to working with Cartier.

CHAPTER 42
NIGEL

It was like waking up in an arcade. Pings and beeps and bells sounded all around the house, followed a minute or two later by yells and slams. More yells. The dogs, who were having a sleepover in Nigel's room, began barking.

The sounds of footsteps running up and down the hallways.

Nigel put on his dressing gown and picked up Clarice, who hated being woken up suddenly.

He opened the door to the hallway and found all the members of the Deep State, except Cartier, gathered in the living room. The agent was there too. They all held phones buzzing with notifications.

"Oh my god. This is unbelievable," said Amina, staring horrified at her screen. She wore a satin pyjama set with a metallic cheetah print that looked like liquid gold as she moved. They were the fanciest pyjamas Nigel had ever seen.

Keithen, who was shirtless and in briefs, held his hand to his head and stared down at his own phone, muttering "Holy shit, holy shit" to himself.

Dixon wore a royal-blue bathrobe and a deathly grim expression as he looked at his screen.

Even unflappable Bryan, in pyjama pants and a white T-shirt, appeared pale and shaken by whatever he was seeing.

Nigel didn't know what to do, so he did the only sensible thing. He went to get Helen. As soon as he stepped outside, followed by the dogs, he heard a scream from the direction of the cabins. Lights appeared in the windows. Cartier and Helen were up. One of them sounded hysterical, and he was pretty sure which one it was.

"Come on," Nigel said, and he ran toward the noise.

Helen met him outside. She'd somehow managed to get dressed and was zipping up her sweater against the night chill.

"Someone turned on the internet," he told her.

"So it would seem," said Helen.

They climbed onto the neat porch of cabin one and knocked on the front door.

"Can we come in?" asked Helen.

There was another howl of pain in response.

The dogs began barking and Nigel held Clarice a little closer.

Helen opened the door. Cartier was in her bathroom and she was in a frenzy.

"Cartier?" said Helen. "Are you okay?"

Cartier rushed out of the bathroom and began walking in circles, flapping her free hand while she stared at her phone.

"It's not true!" she cried. "It's not me!"

Helen went to her, and something about the solidity of her presence seemed to bring Cartier back to herself.

"I didn't," wailed Cartier. "I didn't do it!" Tears poured down her face.

"Sit down," said Helen. "And give me the phone."

Cartier obeyed instantly. She sank onto the small, plain couch, and Helen took the phone from her hand, carefully avoiding her long, sharp nails.

"Give Ms. Hightower one of the dogs, please," Helen told Nigel.

After a moment's thought, Nigel handed her Miggs. Cartier held his small body against her chest and then settled him on her lap. Huge tears fell onto the dog, but he didn't seem to mind.

"What's happened?" asked Helen, turning Cartier's phone over so the screen was not visible.

"A video," said Cartier. "A video of Blossom. Falling into the river. Getting *pushed* into the river."

Nigel watched Helen take in the information. "May we look?" she asked.

Cartier drew her hand across her eyes and pointed at her phone. "It's right there," she said.

"Can Nigel see too?" asked Helen.

"The whole internet can see, Helen. It's been viewed millions of times already. It, it . . ."

Cartier started crying again, so hard she couldn't finish her sentence.

Helen gestured for Nigel to join her and handed him the phone. "You watch and tell me what you see. I'm going to get Ms. Hightower a glass of water."

Cartier stared, flabbergasted, at Helen through her tears. "You're not going to look at it?"

"No," said Helen simply.

Nigel thought it was the most baller move he'd ever seen anyone make. Helen was not going to stare at something on the internet just because everyone else was doing it. Instead, she was going to get a distressed person a glass of water.

That didn't stop *him* wanting to see what was causing a major freakout among Cartier and her friends.

He tapped the screen and it lit up but was locked.

"Here," said Cartier. She pressed her fingers to it and handed it back. A video was paused. It showed a dense, nearly black forest. Nigel hit play. He heard the rush of water.

Something rustled off-screen as the camera was angled down at a waterfall in the middle of the wide river.

A muttered "Oh damn" from off-screen and then a slim girl wearing a bikini walked into view. She tender-footed her way through the shallow water toward the waterfall, moving away from the camera. Spray surrounded the waterfall, which tumbled over a tall ledge of rock. Mist billowed around the cascade and created a dreamy effect. There had to be some serious volume happening at the top of the falls for there to be so much water in the air.

The camera watched impassively as she paused, then abruptly ducked under the curtain of water. A pair of birds swept low over the river and disappeared into the black forest. Pink and orange light had begun to pierce the treetops on the far bank.

After a moment, the drenched girl emerged from inside the waterfall like a water nymph. She stood on what looked like a rocky outcrop that jutted out in front. She lifted and smoothed her wet hair down her arched back and angled her body to show off her red and orange bikini.

Something in her body tensed, but she didn't look back at the camera, so it was impossible to see her expression.

She began to turn toward the camera, and he stared at the side of her face, wanting to see what was coming. But before she made it around, something seemed to shove her from behind and her body lurched forward. She struggled to stay upright, but her windmilling arms found nothing to hang on to, only the sheet of water coursing down behind her. When she toppled into whatever lay below, out of sight of the camera, the microphone didn't catch her scream. Her arms flew up. Then she was gone from sight. Gone from life. Pounded into the sides of the river as it narrowed into what Nigel imagined was a raging trough of water below.

Nigel hit pause, even though he could see that there was another ten seconds on the recording. He closed his eyes and felt sick. He hoped her final moments had been swift and that her panic hadn't lasted long.

When he opened his eyes, he was not just full of sadness but also questions. What had made her fall like that? He hit play to watch the rest of the video. As though in answer to his question, the video changed to a tight close-up of the moment when she had jerked forward. It showed a hand emerging from the curtain of water. A hand with distinctive long, pointy black and white nails.

"Holy shit," whispered Nigel. He looked at Cartier Hightower, at the hands that stroked the dog on her lap. She had nails like the ones on the video. Exactly like the ones on the video.

Cartier's face crumpled when she saw Nigel looking at her hands, and she made a fist to hide them.

Had Cartier really pushed Blossom into the chute below the waterfall? How was that even possible? Could someone even hide behind a waterfall? But someone or something seemed to have pushed her. Whose hand was that? Nigel had never in his life been in a waterfall. What lay behind the curtain of water? A rocky shelf? It was probably dark. Maybe there was a cave back there? Who would be crazy enough to do something like that? The person would have had to hide behind the waterfall *before* Blossom went into the river or the camera would have seen them. It all seemed totally impossible.

He stopped the video and looked at the stats. The video was on fire. The definition of viral.

The situation was completely beyond him. What would a good butler do when the client was revealed to the whole world as a murderer? Nigel waited to find out.

CHAPTER 43

Helen calmed Cartier as much as she could. She gave her a cup of valerian tea that Cartier said smelled like old boots and sat quietly near her.

When Cartier got up to use the small washroom in the cabin, taking her phone with her, Helen looked at Nigel, whose expression was stricken. He kept his voice to a whisper. "The video shows her, or at least someone with her exact nails, pushing Blossom into the chute. You should probably watch it."

Helen considered the advice. How would her watching the video change anything? It would only betray Cartier's privacy and make it harder for her to see the girl in front of her. The words of Bryan Stevenson, the lawyer who acted for death row inmates, came to her. "Each of us is more than the worst thing we've ever done." The compassion in that approach felt more useful than the small, meanly curious part of her that wanted to see what everyone else was seeing. The part that secretly enjoyed being shocked and outraged.

No. She wouldn't watch the video. She was Cartier's butler, and even if the young woman had done the unthinkable, Helen would behave with utmost professionalism and compassion.

It helped that no part of Helen believed that Cartier was capable of shoving someone to her death. Cartier was what Buddhists call the deluded type. She was a little greedy and a little aversive. But mostly she seemed not to entirely understand what was going on around her.

She was eager to get along at almost any cost. Killing Blossom would not have benefitted Cartier. Furthermore, Helen would have bet that even if Cartier had been jealous of Blossom's relative popularity and resentful that Blossom made fun of her, she had been only vaguely aware of her own feelings.

Cartier Hightower was a mystery to herself, but she did not feel like a mystery to Helen, who had met many, many people like her.

The mystery, to Helen's mind, was not whether Cartier had killed Blossom, it was the relationships between the members of the Deep State and all the misfortunes that continued to befall them.

Helen wanted nothing to do with life-and-death mysteries. But here she was.

At least this time the police could take charge. She would care for the client the best she could until Cartier was either arrested or exonerated, and then she, Helen, would go back to her regularly scheduled program of helping the wonderful Levines live gracious lives.

Helen gazed at Nigel. He looked worried and excited. Exactly the emotions the internet seemed to specialize in creating. All that was missing was the rage, and she imagined there was plenty of that going around in response to the video.

"I won't watch," she said.

"Wow," said Nigel, in the tone of someone who has had his mind blown. "Unreal. You're just . . . not going to watch it?"

"I'm not," said Helen.

"But it's really . . . well, murder-y. It looks like . . . you know . . . Cartier pushed that girl."

Helen's phone vibrated in her jacket pocket. "I'll take this call. Please stay with Ms. Hightower. She's in deep distress, so do what you can to support her. Try to get her to put down her phone."

Thus far the dogs seemed unconcerned with the drama swirling around them. Clarice and Jack were passed out in a lumpy puddle of hair at Nigel's feet. Miggs was on the couch.

"If she stays in there for too long, make sure to check on her."

Nigel nodded and Helen went outside to answer the phone, which had stopped vibrating only to start again.

"Tell her the cops know it's not real," growled Archibald Hightower into the receiver.

Helen took a deep breath of the sharp night air. It was cold enough to clear her head and almost bright enough to see clearly under the waxing gibbous moon. In the air was a hint of something grim and scorched.

"The internet just came on here," said Helen. "She's just seen it. She'll be relieved to know that people know the truth."

Hightower gave a dry laugh. "People don't know dick," he said. "I had my contact at the RCMP call the Vancouver PD. Apparently the video is a semi-deep fake. It's deep enough to convince all the conspiracists on the internet but not deep enough to get her arrested. What a fucking nightmare."

Helen agreed. It was a nightmare. She looked up at the moon for comfort and stopped. Was it getting redder? She could have sworn it was the colour of chalk dust earlier.

No comfort from above, she thought.

"How is she doing?" he asked.

"She is distraught." Helen wondered whether to tell him that Cartier had been joined at the ranch by the rest of the Deep State and that someone must have broken into Mabel's apartment to get the modems. He would not be happy. She steeled herself. Not all news could be good news.

"There have been some unexpected developments," she said.

"What now?"

"Some of Cartier's friends arrived this afternoon."

"She's only got those internet morons for so-called friends. Do you mean them?"

Helen thought the members of the Deep State were anything but morons, no matter how they first appeared.

"Yes."

"They're there? With Cartier."

"Yes. They're here. At the ranch."

"Jesus, Helen. What am I paying you for?"

Helen breathed deeply and looked up again. The moon was definitely changing colour. It was now an ominous shade of ochre. The sight disturbed her more than she'd have thought possible. If a moon was going to be red, it should start out that way as soon as it appeared on the horizon. This moon looked as though it were experiencing a medical emergency.

"You aren't paying me, sir."

"You know what I mean!"

"Cartier must have told her friends where she was. Where *we* are. They arrived without notice yesterday morning. She asked them to stay over. I work for her. I cannot override her wishes."

"But it seems that you'll override mine, no problem."

"They will not be staying long. Perhaps just tonight."

"And then you'll get rid of them?'"

Helen hoped they'd get rid of themselves but didn't say so.

"Why'd you turn on the internet? I thought you were shutting it down so my girl could . . . get right."

"That's the other thing," said Helen.

"What other thing? Why do you speak in riddles? If you were my butler, I would . . . I would make you talk normally."

Now that the moon had turned the colour of open heart surgery, the night had gotten much darker.

"Is this some weird Buddha thing? You can't just spit things out? Bunny told me I can't badger you, that you're a Buddhist or whatever, but for Christ's sake. The situation is serious."

"Someone took the modems and the routers from where they'd been stored, brought them into the house, and plugged them in."

"WHAT NOW!" screamed Archibald Hightower. "When?"

"A half hour ago."

"How's this okay?" he yelled.

"It's not okay, sir. But it happened." She didn't bother to tell him that she had no idea when the modems had been taken from Mabel's rooms. They needed to check on Mabel. Right now.

Helen walked down the side path beside the cabin and turned toward the barn but then stopped. Mabel stood in the now brightly lit doorway of the barn. Whoever had broken into her apartment hadn't hurt her.

Helen looked through the bathroom window of Cartier's cabin. Cartier's head and shoulders were visible and she was staring at her phone.

"Reynold, Mrs. Ban's butler, told me that the house has a guest safe as well as the main safe. I am going to put the modems and routers in there if Cartier agrees to go offline again."

"What if something happens? I know one of those influencers is behind all this. Trying to ruin my girl's reputation. Ruin her life."

"I don't know what's happening or who is behind it," said Helen. "If you like, we can leave or we can ask the guests to leave."

"Maybe I should send someone to you," he said. "But it will take time. I'm a little"—he gave a small cough—"understaffed at the moment. Give me a second."

He put her on hold and Helen stood under the bleeding moon, waiting.

"I've got an investigator looking into all of those Deep State nimrods. He's top notch and I know he's going to find something. You can let them know that if ONE MORE THING happens to my girl, they'll all be in jail and bankrupt. I will sue them from here to Sunday and then back around and up the ass of Monday. Little bastards."

Helen blinked and then her attention was caught by footsteps on the gravel. Multiple footsteps.

Here came the Deep State, Amina in the lead, followed by Dixon and Keithen. Bryan reluctantly brought up the rear.

"Is that you, Helen?" Amina said in a hushed voice.

"Yes," said Helen.

"Who's there?" demanded Archibald Hightower.

"Ms. Hightower's guests," she said.

"We want to check on Carty. See how she's holding up," said Amina.

"We also want to know why she pushed Blossom into the river," muttered Keithen.

"What are they saying?" asked Hightower.

"The police have determined that the video is a fake," said Helen, to all of them. "I am going to let Cartier know that as soon as I get off the phone."

"Have you seen it?" asked Keithen. "It's crazy. People think Cartier is—" He drew a hand across his neck.

His insensitivity was startling. "I've got Ms. Hightower's father on the phone. He's in touch with an investigator. The police and the investigator are in the process of tracking the source of this video."

She found herself watching their faces to see their reactions, but it was too dark to make out their individual expressions.

"Of course we knew she didn't do it," said Amina, unconvincingly.

"Exactly," said Bryan.

Helen had the impression that the agent wished he was anywhere else, doing anything else. He would probably not listen to his daughter the next time she told him to babysit his clients.

"Why is the moon like that?" asked Keithen, looking up.

Dixon was instantly distracted by the sight. "I need my Canon. Phone isn't going to pick this up."

"I have my S10," said Amina, digging her phone out of the pocket of her bathrobe.

Within seconds the three of them were photographing and filming the moon with whatever devices they had on hand. They appeared to have forgotten their deep concern for Cartier's well-being.

Only Bryan stared at the moon itself.

"Mr. Hightower?" said Helen. "I need to go. I'll call you back as soon as possible. I will also suggest Cartier call you as soon as she feels up to it. Then we'll make a plan."

Before he had time to protest, she clicked off her phone and looked at the Deep State. They were still milling around in their designer sleepwear trying to shoot the moon.

"Let me go and ask whether Ms. Hightower is accepting visitors," she said.

"Ooh la la," said Keithen, rolling his eyes, but the rest said nothing.

CHAPTER 44
CARTIER

It was hard to believe that only an hour before, she'd been doing good. Well. She'd been doing *well*. Her mother had told her to use proper grammar, even though her mother had so-so grammar at best. But who cared about grammar now that the entire world thought she was a murdering psycho?

When bossy Helen had turned off the internet, it had been terrible. Like someone turning off all the electricity. But it was also a little bit like getting unplugged from a chair in which she'd been slowly getting electrocuted. For months the fans had been blaming her for everything, including stuff that was *obviously* not her fault. And when the internet got turned off, all she had to deal with was the extreme boredom of being here alone with no one to talk to other than Helen and the rest of the help.

Helen had made her get up early, which was ridiculous from a looking-one's-best perspective. People with really good skin never got less than ten hours. Cartier didn't have good skin because she partied. But that wasn't as bad as doing hard labour, such as cleaning bathrooms and talking about *human resources*. Helen was such a nut. For a butler, she didn't seem to know very much about how people with money lived. Also, she was so low-key it was almost disturbing. Helen was borderline no-key, but at least she was very relaxing to be around, even though she was a brutal tastemaster or whatever they call it when someone makes you do a lot of work.

Strangely, Cartier had kind of liked learning how to clean a bathroom and do regular things. It had been interesting to find out how to hire staff and fun to pretend to be a staff person. Of course, she wouldn't want to actually *be* a staff person, but now she understood what they did, and yikes! That shit was no joke. The best part was when the employees, Lou Ellen and Wallace and Nigel, had started talking to her like she was a normal person and not the spoiled daughter of a man who couldn't stop screaming at everyone. Getting talked to like a regular person had been powerful. It was the first time she hadn't felt lonely in her bones since her mother died.

Since the day she was born, Cartier had been told, directly and indirectly, that her family was wealthy, but she'd always known they weren't rich in the right way. They weren't political and rich. Or charitable and rich. Or famous and rich. They weren't rich of rich, which is what her mom called the old-money people. Her parents had grown up without money, and her mother never got used to having it, not really. Her dad didn't fit in with other wealthy people because he didn't fit in with people, period. Only Bunny and Benedict could stand him.

The other well-off kids in West Van had wanted nothing to do with her homeschooled self. That was fine, because she and her mom didn't need anyone else. She and her mom had shopped. Hung out. Cartier learned a few things from tutors, a few things from her mom, who had dropped out of school in eleventh grade. And that was it. So now she had terrible grammar, sus friends, and was the most hated person on the entire internet. Perfect. Oh, and she had mental health problems that were definitely not helped by the fact that the whole world hated her.

As soon as the internet came back on, Cartier had lost whatever it was she'd been feeling before. Scratch that. She'd lost it as soon as her friends turned up.

What *had* that feeling been when it was just her and the staff and the dogs out here in the ass end of nowhere? Calm? Or at least calm-ish? Incredibly, she'd started to like being outside. It felt good to stare at the sky. She'd kind of enjoyed being in this ridiculous little cabin. It had zero amenities. But it was neat and private and quiet. She'd felt good about herself for liking something like a quiet cabin.

For a while there, nothing else mattered. She felt like the internet wasn't real, at least not if it couldn't find her and she didn't have to hear it. She'd felt practically like Gwyneth Paltrow or one of those yoga and meditation babes. Mind-body connection. All that.

Then Amina, Dixon, and Keithen showed up, and they had Bryan with them. She'd tried to hang onto the feeling, onto the peace. She told herself that at least she wasn't back on her phone. She'd tried to take charge and be a good hostess, like Helen had taught her.

But then Dixon had given her an Adderall after dinner and Amina told her some stories about other influencers that made her feel jumpy and out of it, and they'd tried not to talk about how much everyone hated her, and she couldn't really maintain that calm she'd had. She'd gone to bed and at 3:00 a.m. she'd gotten up to go to the bathroom and out of habit, she'd turned her phone on and nearly dropped dead of surprise when it connected to the internet.

And now she was drowning in a flood of notifications. And it wasn't just about what had happened at the club anymore. It was the video of someone pushing Blossom into the river. Someone who had nails just like hers. Everyone was writing, writing, writing about her. Countless comments. Threats. Hot takes. They thought she was a murderer! How could anyone think that? She wasn't organized, like at all. Good murderers needed to have their shit together and be able to make a plan. She had harsh ADHD, like everyone else said they did, but she *actually* did. That was part of why her mom had pulled her out of school. She was too distracted to kill, unless she accidentally killed someone by forgetting to pick them up or something.

Cartier had watched the video four times already. Her chest went hot and cold and her face turned clammy with fear every time.

Poor Blossom. It was so horrible what had happened to her. The hand in the video was faked. She was sure of it. But someone *had* pushed

Blossom. Why else had she been shoved forward like that? And someone had locked them in the club.

Who had done all that?

What about Trudee? Had someone messed with her, too?

She needed to get her nails off. Cartier looked at Nigel, sitting across from her, clearly uncomfortable. Trying to respect her privacy. He obviously knew fuck-all about nail care or anything else to do with personal style.

"Can you get me Helen?" she croaked. Maybe Helen would be able to tell her what to do about her nails.

Nigel, who wasn't actually a bad guy and was kind of nice to talk to, nodded and opened the door. Helen stood in the doorway, about to knock. The rest of the Deep State were crowded behind her in the dark. Like bad omens.

Don't let them in, she thought. *Please don't let them in*. One of *them* had done this to her. Was doing this to her. She didn't know how or why, but she felt sure one of them was trying to destroy her.

Helen was speaking, but there was a crackling noise in Cartier's ears. A roaring. Was she about to faint?

She shook her head. Held up her hand. Showed Helen her long black and white nails. Tears poured down her face again. Was one of them filming her?

Helen seemed to sense what was happening. She turned around and blocked everyone's view of Cartier. Then she came inside the cabin and closed the door behind her.

"Please turn off the internet," said Cartier, surprising even herself.

Helen nodded, and in that moment, Cartier got the point of Helen. She'd been too distracted to see it before. But now that she felt like she was going to die, she got why people liked Helen. Why they loved her.

Helen was the kind of person who made you feel like even if you were about to die, it would all be okay.

CHAPTER 45

The next morning was strange. After talking to Cartier, Helen had taken the modems and routers and locked them in the large guest safe, but she felt acutely aware of the precariousness of their situation. Archibald Hightower had promised to call the landline if his investigator learned anything about the members of the Deep State.

In the meantime, what was she supposed to do with these people? They were like all addicts whose drugs had been removed. Irritable. Discontent. She wanted them gone, but they didn't seem eager to leave and Helen couldn't ask them to do so.

"Are you sure it's safe to *not* have internet access?" said Bryan doubtfully. He was the only one who was ready to go, but seemed to feel it would be disloyal to do so without the others.

"It feels necessary to me," said Dixon, who had changed into his velour cow print track suit, perhaps in an effort to get into the spirit of ranch life.

"We could play board games?" said Amina.

"Can you give it a rest for five seconds?" said Keithen. "I know you're making a play for the board game crowd."

"Like you're loving it here," muttered Amina.

Keithen gave her a searching look. "What I love might surprise you. You're into secrets, right, Mina?"

"What do you mean by that?" Amina narrowed her eyes. She wore a low-cut midi-dress with an empire waist. The dress fabric was patterned with tiny red and pink pastel roses against a soft grey. She'd topped the dress with an undersized cardigan that served no actual function and a floppy straw hat. She looked ready to scandalize everyone in a Jane Austen novel. She'd informed Helen that the outfit was "peak cottagecore."

"Nothing," he said. He'd made no effort to adjust his outfit to suit the setting. He turned to Cartier. "You must be relieved that the cops have already let you off the hook. Your dad must have some serious pull with the department."

Cartier didn't respond. She still seemed dazed.

Normally Helen wouldn't argue with a guest, but this was not a normal circumstance. "Mr. Hightower was informed by the authorities that the video is quite clearly a fake. There are, apparently, telltale signs that they recognized immediately."

"Why would someone do that?" asked Amina, taking a nibble of toast.

"Someone obviously wants to stir up some shit," said Dixon.

"It couldn't have been any of us. We were here when the video was released," said Amina. "The post appeared last night. We had no service until . . . someone plugged in the modem and router in the house."

Now they were all paying close attention.

Amina, Dixon, Cartier, and Keithen sat facing each other in one of the furniture groupings near the huge front window. Bryan sat to the side.

"Who did that?" asked Keithen.

"I was just outside taking a few pictures and I saw that girl who deals with the horses, and she said she didn't know what happened. The equipment was in her apartment over the barn and someone took it. They didn't wake her up. It was just gone. She doesn't know when it was taken," said Amina.

Helen had just come over to offer them fresh coffee, and she couldn't help but listen while she waited for a break in the conversation. She'd planned to go and speak to Mabel, so she was interested to hear Amina's report.

"You can preprogram things to post," said Keithen. "That video could have come from anyone."

"Obviously not," said Amina. "It must have been backed up automatically to Blossom's cloud storage. Someone needed her password to retrieve it."

"I don't have her passwords," said Dixon.

"Me neither," added Keithen.

"Cartier?" asked Amina.

Cartier, who wore a soft-yellow track suit, shook her head. "Trudee had my passwords because she worked on my accounts," she said. "And sometimes she stored her bigger files to my cloud. But Blossom didn't have my passwords and I didn't have hers."

The members of the Deep State stared at each other.

"Maybe Trudee gave Blossom access to your accounts?" said Amina.

"What are you even talking about?" said Dixon. "This came from Blossom's cloud storage. Only the cops have the original footage from the camera the hiker found. It didn't show her getting pushed or Cartier would be arrested right now."

"Someone hacked into Blossom's computer for her passwords and that's how they got the video," said Bryan. "Then they faked some of it so it looked like Cartier did it."

"Who would do that? It's crazy," said Amina. "And what would be the point?"

"Who would lock us in at the club?" said Dixon. "Who pulled the fire alarm? Why did Blossom go into a sketchy waterfall?"

"Could this video be from Blossom's family, trying to get revenge? They blame us, you know," said Amina. "Maybe they got her passwords."

"We probably should have gone to the funeral in person," grumbled Dixon.

"Then we wouldn't have had time to go shopping and do *Flashdance* videos," said Keithen.

"Oh yeah, you really protested that. You were just dying to go to Whateverville for her funeral," said Dixon. "At least I'm honest about how I feel."

"You're honest, all right," said Keithen.

"Can we not fight, you guys?" Amina put an arm around Cartier, who was starting to wilt on the couch beside her. "Look, let's just agree that none of us did this. We are being targeted from outside."

"Two dead people is more than bad luck," said Keithen. "And a faked murder video is . . . insane."

"Okay. We've had some tragedies. We're not the first people that's happened to."

"You could film an investigation into all of this," said Bryan. "That would be compelling."

"I would rather forget all of it," said Dixon. "Maybe we should talk about going our separate ways?"

"Don't talk like that," said Amina. "We have something good here. And Bryan is right. Everyone loves true crime."

Silence for a moment. Then Keithen spoke up. "I've been looking into it." His voice was quiet. Serious.

"And?" said Dixon.

"I'll let you know when I figure it out." Then he looked at each of them in turn.

"If you figure it out," said Dixon.

Helen watched, fascinated by the exchange. Then her mind moved to the day ahead. Four agitated influencers. One agent. Overwhelming paranoia. No internet. The situation felt like an Agatha Christie set-up, only with more track suits. She needed to keep them busy until they finally decided to leave.

"How would you all like to go for a trail ride today?" she said.

CHAPTER 46

Helen found Mabel in the barn. The young woman had a stocky horse with thick legs in the cross ties. She wore heavy leather chaps and was fitting a metal shoe onto one of the horse's pie plate hooves.

"You're a farrier, too," said Helen, who had made sure to make some noise on her way in so she wouldn't frighten Mabel or the horse.

"Went to school for it. I took the horse husbandry program at Olds College. My mom says I could be making good money at some fancy show-jumping barn in Ontario or someplace. But I like it here. They pay me good and I get to ride all the time. And usually, there's no guests." At this, she smiled at Helen, who nodded. She could appreciate the sentiment.

"Plus, most of the horses here go barefoot. So I just do trims. Nice to know some horses still have healthy feet." Holding the horse's foot propped on top of her thigh, she used her free arm to wipe her forehead of sweat. "But this girly keeps getting cracks, so we need to keep her shod."

Helen thought that Mrs. Ban was exceedingly fortunate to have this young woman in her employ.

Mabel ran something that looked like a large nail file around the edge of the hoof and then gently let down the mare's leg. When she straightened up, her lean face broke into a big smile.

"I heard from one of my aunties that you are a good woman to know," Mabel said.

"Oh?" said Helen.

"Yeah. One of my cousins is Tla'amin. Lives over on the Sunshine

260

Coast. He started going out with a guy named Leon when they were going to Vancouver Island University for cooking."

Helen felt her heart gladden at the memory of Leon, who'd been working as a gardener at the Yatra Institute when she went back to take care of her late employer's affairs. She remembered him saying he was heading off to university in the fall to take the culinary arts program. How wonderful to find out that he'd met someone there. Helen thought the day was coming when she would want to hire Leon as a personal chef or perhaps encourage him to go to butler school. She thought he'd make a fantastic, if slightly sardonic, major-domo for some lucky family. Or not. Leon might end up with his own restaurant or running a hotel.

"Anyway," said Mabel. "His mom was talking to my mom and your name came up. The band up there appreciated your work. Making sure there were Elders on the board of that yoga place when the new person took over."

Helen had been grateful when the Elders had accepted the invitation to sit on the board at the Yatra Institute.

"Please say hello to Leon for me," said Helen. "I miss him."

"Will do. Anyway, the word is that you can get things done. And you don't talk too much, which is rare now."

It was one of the best compliments Helen had ever received.

"I would like to take Ms. Hightower and her party riding this morning," she said.

Mabel's eyebrows signalled deep skepticism. "Do they know this plan?"

"They do and are quite enthusiastic. They seem to think they will get good pictures."

Mabel's doubt was obvious by her expression, but she was game. "If you say so."

She laid one strong hand on the back of her neck and another on the shining brown neck of the horse at her side. "This gal here? She's a good horse. But her feet are lousy. Needs a lot of extra support to go out on the range. You know what I'm saying?"

Helen did know.

"She got rescued off a meat truck. I saw her and I knew she was going to be a good horse. And she is. But she's a real softie. Needs little boots that cover the bottoms of her feet. Most of our horses were born to this life. But she came from Saskatchewan. Long story. Anyway, if we don't put some protection on her, sure as shit—sorry, Helen—sure as heck she'll get a bruise and be hobbling around for a month."

"I see," said Helen.

"A lot of the people who visit here are like that too. Most of 'em, actually."

"But when you put the proper footwear on this horse, she can have an adventure?" said Helen.

"Well, yes."

"Let's get Ms. Hightower and her friends the right shoes, then."

Mabel tilted her head back as though searching for answers in the rafters of the huge barn. "How far do you want to take them?"

"I'd like everyone tired by the time we get back."

"Tired I can do," said Mabel.

~~~

An hour and a half later, seven horses were tacked up in front of the barn.

Helen was not an experienced horse person, but she knew enough to ask Mabel whether the horses they would be riding on the trail were calm.

"Bombproof," said Mabel. "That's what we call real calm horses. Even the worst riders should be able to stay on them." She rubbed the forelock of a sturdy bay mare with a dark mane and tail. "Right, Grindylow? No killing the clients."

In response, Grindylow flicked an ear at a fly and leaned into the scratch.

The horses were tacked up in Western gear and tied to a long hitching post.

"These are the ponies the Bans ride when they're here," said Mabel, who looked as though she'd been born in jeans, a cowboy hat, and boots. "They LOVE riding, the boys especially, but they aren't going to win any equitation competitions. They might, though, after I'm done with them."

While they waited for Cartier and the others, Mabel told Helen all the horses' names.

She indicated the black horse with Rorschach-style white splotches who was tied a little way away from the others. "Black Dahlia. She's mine. She's definitely *not* bombproof. But she's fast and she's smart."

Helen found being near the horses calming. At the Levines', she hadn't spent much time around the rescued-off-the-track thoroughbreds. She was too busy working in the house. Maybe she would start visiting them. The longer she was near the horses, the calmer she felt.

"Here she comes. Oh, wow," said Mabel.

Cartier strode toward them from her cabin. She wore fuchsia jeans, a white satin Western-style shirt, a pair of extremely fancy white snakeskin boots, and a brilliant white hat. Nigel followed behind her with a camera, clearly filming her. Cartier stopped and turned every so often to say something into the camera.

"Okay!" she instructed him. "When I go up to the horses, try to frame the shot so we don't see that there's anyone else around. I want it to look like I'm alone and I know what I'm doing. Let the camera linger on my butt. Just a tasteful amount, please. And if I go over a jump and it looks cute, make sure to get that, too."

Nigel, apparently fully immersed in his role of videographer, nodded intently.

Helen watched as Cartier strode up to the black and white mare, who pinned back her ears. Helen didn't know much about horses, but she could tell the horse wasn't happy.

"Uh, miss, you might not—" Mabel started to say, but it was too late.

Cartier, who had been staring winsomely back at the camera as she reached out to pat the horse, didn't see when Black Dahlia snaked her head around to bite. The mare moved faster than Helen would have thought possible.

Cartier screamed and leaped away from the horse, who faced front again with a sour, mulish look on her face. The sudden movements caused the other horses to skitter to the side, which startled Cartier further. She staggered backwards and ended up falling on her behind, white hat spilling over her eyes.

"—want to touch her," finished Mabel.

Mabel was trying to hide her smile, and Helen couldn't fault her for it.

"You said the horses were safe?" Helen whispered, wondering whether she should call a halt to the plan.

"I said *your* horses are safe. BD's my old barrel racer. She's kinda mean."

Nigel had stopped filming and was helping Cartier get up. She dusted herself off. "These jeans are Givenchy," she complained.

There was slow hand-clapping from Amina and Dixon, who'd joined them.

"Smooth," said Dixon.

Mabel approached. "I'm sorry Ms. Hightower. BD is, uh, tricky. We'll have you ride Bella."

Cartier had pushed her hat back on her head, but it was still crooked. There was dirt all over one side. "Which one is Bella?" she said.

"That one." Mabel pointed at a sturdy little roan horse who had gone right back to sleep after the commotion.

"She doesn't really go with my outfit," complained Cartier. Then she snuck a glance at Helen. "Kidding! Only kidding."

"And you will all need to put on helmets," said Mabel.

Cartier looked disappointed but she patted her white hat, ran her fingers through the long blond hair that tumbled down from underneath, and then took a helmet.

Soon they were all mounted. Helen was on Honey, a tidy bay mare with a long mane, and felt instantly in love.

They rode out in front of the house along a track that led through the grass. The horses walked steadily, and at the sound of their hooves hitting the earth, the sway of their bodies, and the squeak of the leather saddle, Helen feel a near-instant state of transcendent peace.

The seven of them rode out single file along the narrow track. Keithen had chosen to stay at the house. He said he had a back problem that precluded him from riding. Helen had quietly asked Lou Ellen and Wallace to keep an eye on him.

To Mabel's dismay, Cartier had insisted that all the dogs come along, and Nigel had been put in change of carrying them.

Mabel kept looking over at Nigel, who was speaking in soothing words to the dogs, who seemed to have accepted their fate with their usual good grace. "It's crazy that we are bringing all these dogs. These kinds of dogs are what the coyotes and bears and cougars around here like to call appetizers," she said.

Helen couldn't argue. Cartier had said she needed the dogs because she was so upset, but it seemed very unfair to the dogs. The internet would probably have something to say if they saw three Pekes in carriers on a horse. Then again, people brought their dogs on motorcycles. Maybe this wasn't so different.

The air was full of the scent of smoke from a fire burning somewhere in the distance. Helen had asked Mabel if it was safe to be outside with the smoke and had been assured that if people and animals in these parts didn't go outside during fire season, they would be stuck inside for about five months a year.

Other than the vague yellowish haze in the air, the day was mild and fine, with barely enough breeze to move the clouds or ruffle the grasses.

There wasn't a lot of talk. Cartier had seemed shell-shocked after the latest assault on her reputation, but grew more composed after the internet was shut off again.

Amina had changed from her flowered dress into jeans and a perfectly weathered checked shirt. Bryan was in Blundstone boots and his usual smart casual wear. Dixon, like Amina, wore an outfit that would have worked on the set of any Western movie over the past hundred years.

All of the influencers were equipped with phones and cameras and were taking extensive footage of each other and the landscape, presumably so they could post it later.

"I wish we could livestream this," said Amina. "It's just so real out here, you know?"

Helen thought that all the phones and cameras interfered with the realness in some fundamental way, but didn't say so.

After about two hours, the influencers' initial enthusiasm had been dampened considerably by the discomfort, but they all perked up when three riders appeared, heading toward them.

When the groups met, the three men were revealed to be weathered, mid-sized, and obviously related.

"Hey, Scott," said Mabel.

Scott, a white guy in a battered hat, nodded and grinned.

"Aaron," added Mabel.

Aaron likewise nodded.

"Trev," she said.

Trevor's hat was even more battered than the ones on the heads of the other two.

"We're riding up to the old Foreguard Cabin," said Mabel.

"Yeah?" said Scott.

"Going to have a picnic."

Aaron and Scott and Trevor said that sounded like a fine idea.

Then Aaron tilted his head at Nigel. "Whatcha got there?" he asked, pointing at one of the packs on the back of Nigel's saddle.

Nigel, attempting to be as laconic as the cowboys, said simply, "Dogs."

"And what's going on in that one?" asked Scott, pointing at another bag with his hand loosely holding his horse's reins.

"More dogs," said Mabel.

"They're Pekingese," said Cartier.

The three cowboys grinned. "You got more than one Pekingese out here?" asked Trevor.

"That's right," said Mabel.

"Jeez, Mabel, how many dogs that can't walk by themselves did you bring?"

"Three," said Mabel, her face not giving anything away.

"Holy," said Trevor.

Touché, thought Helen.

"You shoulda brought a proper dog to make sure nothing eats all the portable ones," said Scott.

"We'll remember that next time," said Mabel.

The influencers had by this point come out of their discomfort-induced funk and had their Instagrammer eyes trained on the three cowboys. Cartier slipped her camera out of her Moschino belt bag with the cartoon teddy bear motif.

"Do you like Pekingese?" Amina asked the three men.

"I don't know 'em," said the one called Aaron, who rode a raw-boned buckskin horse.

"Would you like to get to know some?" asked Amina, who had straightened up and was beginning to pour on the flirtatious charm.

"I think she's trying to give you her dogs, bro," said Scott, who slouched easily on a red and white Appaloosa.

"They're great dogs," said Cartier. "Like you said, they're super portable, so they can go anywhere. Nigel? Would you please show the dogs to these gentlemen?"

Nigel grimaced. "Okay. Just let me get off this thing."

"This thing!" said Trevor, delighted. His horse was so dark brown it was nearly black. "He means his horse!"

Nigel made sure Miggs, Clarice, and Jack were secure in their cases before he slowly, and painfully, swung his leg over the horse. His mount was short, but it was too tall for him to keep one foot in the stirrup and the other on the ground without giving his legs a far bigger stretch than they could comfortably accommodate.

He gave a cry of pain before the stirrup finally released his trapped foot.

"Good dismount," said Aaron.

"You all right, there?" asked Scott. "Looked like you might have pulled something."

Nigel's face was a study in embarrassed discomfort, but he hobbled closer to his horse, which had fallen asleep again.

"I'll just get Clarice out of the carrier," he said stiffly.

"Its name is Clarice!" crowed Trevor, who was clearly having the time of his life.

The three cowboys watched as Nigel gently extracted Clarice and brought her over to Scott.

"Awww," said Scott. "She looks like a country singer's head."

"Don't drop her, please," said Nigel.

"Please tell me the other one's called Hannibal," said Aaron.

"In fact, he's called Miggs," said Cartier, who, along with the others, was surreptitiously snapping photos of the cowboy cradling her dog. "I've got Clarice, Jack, Miggs."

"Better let me see one," said Trevor.

"And me," said Aaron.

Soon the three men were fussing in their few-words way over the Pekingese, who in turn seemed unfazed to find themselves in the hands of genuine cowboys.

Cartier, who'd completely perked up, said, "May I take your photos?" As though she hadn't been photographing and videoing them the whole time.

"Well, sure," said Scott. "They're probably going to put us on the cover of *Pekingese World.*"

"The dog for all seasons," said Aaron.

Trevor didn't speak because he was holding Miggs up and gazing into his eyes. "He says he needs to go to the can," he said, finally.

"Okay. I'll take them potty," said Nigel, struggling to maintain his dignity. "I mean, to the john or whatever." He pulled a tangle of rhinestone-studded leashes out of his fanny pack and stiffly collected the dogs from the cowboys. Then he set about letting the dogs relieve themselves.

"You don't need to pick that up," said Aaron, when he saw Nigel trying to open a small mint-scented poop bag to collect something Clarice had left on the ground.

"Bylaw hardly ever gets out here to check for dog shit," said Scott.

Nigel looked to Helen, who nodded. It was probably best that they not carry several tiny bags of dog poo for the rest of their journey.

Finally, the cowboys dragged their eyes away from the spectacle of the young man cleaning up after the herd of Pekingese.

"You going back to the ranch?" Mabel asked them.

"Probably. We're looking for a mare we think foaled out here in the last few days. If we don't find her here, we'll head for the Cut. See if she's in there. Trev says he feels a storm coming. I'd like to get her and a few of the other horses in before it hits."

Trevor nodded.

"There was nothing on the weather service about a storm," said Mabel. "I checked before we left."

"You know how Trev is about weather," said Scott.

"If you've broken almost every bone you have falling off horses, you can feel rain coming," said Aaron, speaking for his brother.

"Well, I hope it waits till we're back."

Nigel was putting the dogs back into the panniers.

"You folks guests of the Bans?" asked Scott.

"Yup," said Mabel. "Ms. Hightower is, and she is being visited by her colleagues, Amina, Dixon, and Bryan. And Helen and Nigel here are"—she paused for dramatic effect—"her butlers."

"Sheeeiiit," said Trevor, before he tossed back his head and laughed along with his brothers.

"Honest to god butlers?" said Aaron.

Helen nodded. "I am, yes. Nigel is my assistant."

"You and them *Silence of the Lambs* dogs must be pretty important to need two butlers," said Scott to Cartier, who was scrolling through her photos.

"Hmmm?" she said. "Oh, yes. My daddy got them for me."

The three brothers exchanged glances. "The dogs?"

"No. The butlers," said Cartier.

"Our dad never got us anyone," said Scott. "No staff whatsoever."

"I'm going to put your pictures on my Instagram feed when I get reception again. Is that okay?" asked Cartier, suddenly conscientious about consent.

"You going to make us famous?" said Aaron.

"Maybe," said Bryan, looking at them with a professional eye.

Helen thought being posted to Cartier's Instagram might just make the three brothers more famous than they wanted, and not in a good way, but she would speak to Cartier about it later.

They all waved goodbye and the picnicking party continued riding toward the destination Mabel had in mind.

CHAPTER 47
NIGEL

The whole rest of the way, Nigel thought about those cowboy guys and how cool they were. Genuine outdoorsmen. The kind of guys who could start fires using only willpower and a stick, survive on beans, and ride horses that buck and be happy about it. For about ten minutes after the group ran into them, he wanted to give up the whole domestic service thing and become a cowboy. But then his ass started to kill again and his inner legs were rubbed raw and it was taking forever to get to wherever they were all supposed to go and he decided against becoming a ranch hand. He'd rather be the kind of guy who was put in charge of handling someone's fancy dogs than a cowboy. But still, those guys had been incredibly cool. No one had ever wanted to put *him* on their Instagram, except close friends who didn't care how their feeds looked from a visual perspective. Well, there had been that one girl who had an anti-fashion blog who posted one of his outfits in a condescending way, even though she was no hell herself in the looks department, so it hadn't bothered him too much.

He'd been hoping the Foreguard Cabin would be kind of like the ranch house, just smaller, but it turned out to be just an old log cabin with a caved-in roof and most of one wall missing. What was left standing was falling in on itself. Very picturesque but not great from a hospitality perspective.

He pulled his horse up beside Helen's. Or rather, his horse fell asleep when they pulled up beside her.

"Are we supposed to stay in there?" he asked. "It looks a little death-trappy."

"It's just a landmark," said Mabel. "We'll have our picnic beside it."

"I've brought some drawing stuff if any of you want to do a sketch," said Helen.

Amina stared at the falling-down cabin. "It's very . . . rustic," she said. "I mean, I'd like some photos of me near it, but . . ."

But what, she never said.

"Nigel, you want to give me Sleepy?" asked Mabel.

"You can help me set out lunch," said Helen, who was already off her horse.

Cartier looked like she'd been expecting something very different from a dilapidated pile of logs surrounded by grass and rocks and scrubby trees. And sky. Major quantities of sky.

"Would you like to help?" Helen asked Cartier. "Or would you prefer to look after the dogs and rest?"

"Rest where?" asked Cartier. She didn't sound bitchy about it, just extremely confused.

"Let's see what Mabel has planned for us."

Mabel put the horses in hobbles and unpacked the bags. She put out seven chairs whose frames clicked together like tent poles.

"Camping coffee, coming right up!" she said. Nigel helped Helen organize the food Wallace had packed for them.

"I'm going to move the horses to the creek over there while people eat," said Mabel, while Helen handed out tin cups of the extremely strong-smelling coffee Mabel had made.

The lambs were waddling around, sniffing everything.

"Will the dogs stay close?" Mabel asked.

"I think so," Nigel answered. "But they don't get off the leash much, so I'm not sure."

"Well, if one of them heads for the hills, the nearest hill is about ten miles thataway," she said.

"Noted," said Nigel. "I'll let them know not to bother."

CHAPTER 48

"Okay, everyone," said Mabel, standing up to survey the guests. "I should mention a couple of things before we eat."

Cartier rejoined them from where she'd been taking photos of the horses with the Foreguard Cabin in the background and a dark mountain in the hazy far distance.

"This is bear country," Mabel announced.

Helen felt herself go still. Of course it was. Helen was a practical person, but she was not a wilderness guide.

"That's hilarious," said Nigel. "You've got an awesome sense of humour."

Mabel looked at him the way a person might look at a piece of undercooked chicken.

"What kind of bears?" asked Cartier.

"We have grizz and black bears up here. Mostly grizzlies. They won't let black bears live in their territory."

"I've seen bears in Whistler," said Cartier. "From the car."

At that, Mabel gave her the same look she'd just given Nigel.

"We are very far away from help," she said. "So it's best if we don't need any. I've got a shotgun and bear bangers. There are a lot of us, so I don't think we'll have any problems. There's sometimes a big sow around here, but at this time of year, she's probably foraging with cubs. If we do get a visitor, we'll make lots of noise. Keep the dogs close."

Nigel and the Deep State had gone pale. Even uber-steady Bryan looked concerned. Helen wondered about her own skin pallor.

Cartier turned to Helen. "If I get killed by a rampaging grizzly bear, I guess that'll solve my online problems." Then she gave a braying laugh.

"You aren't going to get killed," said Mabel. "Probably."

"Maybe we should eat quickly?" said Dixon. "Or eat while we ride?"

"The horses need a break," said Mabel. "Don't worry. There aren't that many bears in this area, because the province has done a terrible job of protecting them. We're in their house here and we need to respect that." She sounded angry for the first time since they'd arrived. "At least the Bans don't allow trophy hunting. Not like the last ass—I mean, the last guy who owned this land." The air quotes around "owned" were nearly audible. "For real. If we don't get it together, there won't be any grizz left in this region."

Her ferocity seemed to impress everyone, and they stopped complaining. "We're at more risk from fire than bears," said Mabel, finally. "I'm going to start taking the horses to the water."

When she was out of earshot, Amina leaned into Cartier. "If a bear comes, she's definitely going to feed us to it."

Cartier nodded.

"Mabel knows this land," said Helen. "We'll be safe with her." She hoped that was true.

Soon they were eating the tabouleh salad and rainbow sandwiches full of grated carrot, beet, cucumber, sprouts, rutabaga, and fresh herbs between thick slices of seedy bread, cups of steaming coffee by their sides.

"God, it's beautiful out here," said Amina, looking relaxed in spite of the bear threat.

"Smile," said Dixon. He held a camera up and snapped a picture of her.

"Delete that right now. I've got stuff in my teeth. You need to tell me before you take pictures. I don't want any photos of me eating. We agreed about that."

Dixon ignored her and looked at the shot on his camera's LCD screen. "You look good with a grill full of sprouts," he said.

"Seriously, Dixon. Can you just quit for five minutes? We don't have to document everything always. There's no internet out here. Let's just have lunch. Take a picture of yourself eating if you want to."

Instead, Dixon put the camera down low and took a photo of his enormous, colourful sandwich, perched messily on the bright-red tin plate.

"Consent," continued Amina. "It's a thing. Look it up."

At that, Dixon raised his gaze to her. "Oh really? You're the queen of consent now?"

"What do you mean by that?" she asked. She'd lowered her plate and was glaring at him.

"Would anyone like any candied salmon?" said Nigel. "We should eat it before the smell draws all the bears in a hundred-and-fifty-mile radius." He wafted his hand over the container.

But Amina and Dixon weren't listening.

"You're such a . . . a . . . you're an awful person sometimes," said Amina. "Also, you should talk." She got to her feet. "I'm going to help Mabel with the horses."

"Sure you are," said Dixon.

"You really want to do this now?" asked Amina, her hands bunched at her sides. "We can both make little comments."

Dixon stopped talking.

"I thought so," she said and stalked off behind the falling-down cabin in the direction Mabel had led the horses.

Helen went to the small stove and busied herself making more coffee and heating up water for anyone who wanted tea.

"What was that all about?" whispered Nigel.

Helen just shook her head.

"What did they mean by *consent*?" asked Nigel.

"It's a real thing with creators," said Bryan, coming up behind them with his empty coffee cup. "Especially ones who shoot in public. You really don't want to involve people who don't want to be in a shoot. It can get very complicated."

He looked back at where Dixon now sat on his own, picking bits of sprouts out of his sandwich. "Dixon is a little more fastidious than the others on that front. I think he worries about liability."

"Right," said Nigel.

To Helen, that explanation made almost no sense.

"I'd love some more of that coffee," said Bryan. "Something about being out here makes it taste incredible."

"Of course," said Helen. She filled his cup. When Bryan was back at his seat, she turned to Nigel. "I'm going to go and check on Amina."

"Don't get attacked by a bear," he said. "Or anything else."

CHAPTER 49

Helen found Amina sitting on a rock behind the cabin, out of sight of the group. She seemed to be watching Mabel and the horses, who were gathered at the edge of a stream a short distance away.

Helen made sure to clear her throat as she approached so she wouldn't scare the young woman.

Amina turned and looked at her. "Oh, hey," she said, and looked back toward the tableau of Mabel and the little herd of horses grazing and leaning forward to drink from the stream. "They look like a painting, don't they?"

"Yes," said Helen. "They would make a lovely picture."

"Are you suggesting I photograph them?" Amina laughed. "I thought your whole thing was that we shouldn't be on our devices all the time. We should be raw-dogging life. Sorry. That was crude. I mean, more present for life."

Helen had zero idea what Amina's words meant and would not be looking it up. "I think the artistic impulse is a noble one. There is nothing wrong with trying to capture something beautiful or noteworthy."

"You think we're idiots who create pointless content that has the shelf life of a British prime minister."

"No," said Helen. "I can see that what you do takes a lot of work and creativity."

"Try telling my parents that. They hate me being a creator almost as much as Cartier's dad does. My mom is the one who said the thing about the British prime minister and our content."

Helen didn't say anything. She could sense that Amina had something she wanted to get off her chest.

"Can I tell you something?" said Amina. Her face was tilted up to the sun, which was obscured by the fine haze in the air.

"Of course," said Helen.

"Will you tell anyone? I mean, you're a nun, right? As well as a butler?"

"A former nun. Many years ago. I'm just a butler now."

"But you're trustworthy. People tell you things. Ever since I met you, I've wanted to confess everything to you. I bet that happens to you all the time."

It did, actually, but Helen didn't say that. It would have undermined this moment. Every time someone told her something that mattered to them was an important moment. A special moment.

"I'm trustworthy," said Helen.

"Before the Deep State, like way before, I did some cam work."

Helen was sitting on a rock near Amina's and had turned so that she, too, was watching Mabel and the horses, who did indeed look worthy of a painting. Or a photo on Instagram.

"Do you know what cam work is?" asked Amina.

"No."

"It's where you film yourself. In intimate ways. I sort of fell into it. I begged my parents to let me have social media in middle school. They said absolutely not. My mom is an academic. A hardcore feminist. She'd read the research about kids and the internet. The anxiety. The predators. The distractions. My dad is a composer. He works with orchestras all over the world. They're busy people. They're serious people."

Helen waited.

"I was allowed to play some educational games, though. So I figured out how to create secret accounts. My parents weren't around much. Big careers. I was too old to need a nanny by then. Anyway, it was easy to get around the rules."

"I expect that's common," said Helen.

"Totally. A lot of parents would drop dead if they knew what their kids were doing online. Some would, anyway. Mine definitely would have." She took a deep breath. "So I started to post. I was thirteen or so. I hadn't really . . . grown up, you know? I still had braces. I hadn't worked out my style. I attended a private school where everyone had a laser focus on academics. But I'm not academically inclined. I was actually sort of worried I wasn't anything. But I realized that I looked good in pictures. Like, much better than I looked in person, especially back then. I figured out how to make the most of how I look. You know, clothes and angles and filters. All that stuff."

Helen didn't like where this was going, but she stayed very still.

"My parents had no idea. I used another name. I almost never showed my face, and when I did, I wore so much makeup no one would ever know it was me. Or so I thought. And the more, you know, provocative the pictures were, the more people liked them. Men. Men liked them. And I liked the attention."

Helen had heard of young people being exploited on the internet. Asked to send revealing photos and then blackmailed. Her heart ached for the woman in front of her, who was still so young, but who seemed to be mourning her teenaged self.

"I started chatting with this guy. You know, the internet is full of terrible guys. The kind of dudes who always want pictures of your body. I usually blocked them. But this one guy, he told me that I was stunning, and he thought I was so smart to hide my face. He told me about this platform he ran. Subscription only. I'd get paid to do what I was doing. Only I had to do a little more."

"I see," said Helen.

"I could still keep my identity private. He showed me the site. Let me check it out. I was so flattered. The girls on there were beautiful—at least, their bodies were. They were women, not girls. He put me in touch with some of them. One I talked to made thousands of dollars a week. She said she felt like a star. And it was all private. The site was called Sweet Connections." She gave a bitter little laugh. "If you think it sounds sketchy, that's because it was. But I was a kid. Not very worldly. He got me to sign something that said I was eighteen, but he knew I wasn't. We never met or anything, but I know he could tell. I figured it would all be okay. He didn't know who I was. No one did. I was just this person on the internet that everyone thought was very beautiful. And what could be better than that?"

Helen waited.

"Right away, the work was more intense than I could handle. My 'connections,' the guys who paid to subscribe to my channel, they wanted me to do things I didn't want to do. Things I'd never even heard of. You would not believe the things they said to me in chats. It was so awful. I didn't feel special anymore. I felt sick and tainted by them. So I quit."

Helen let out a long breath, full of relief.

"But the guy who ran the site, he called himself Randy, he wouldn't let me quit. He said he knew who I was. Who my parents were. He'd somehow hacked into my webcam and recorded me. All of me. My face, too. No mask. I know a lot of women who aren't ashamed of being cam girls or whatever. But I cared. My parents would have died. I mean, my mom's whole thing is about not letting men take advantage of you. And I'd been doing it for months. She would have been devastated. Ashamed of me."

"That sounds very painful," said Helen.

"It was like a nightmare. I was trapped. Either I had to keep doing cam work for these subscribers I found disgusting or Randy was going to send videos to my parents. My school. The university where my mom works. The orchestras where my dad's work is performed. Newspapers, even. I thought about killing myself, but maybe he'd still send the videos around. My parents would still be destroyed."

Amina was speaking as though she couldn't stop. She had to get it all out as soon as possible. Helen wondered how long she'd been holding all of this in.

"Then he gave me an out. He said if I got him another girl to take my place, he'd let me quit. So I did it."

Helen's heart broke a little bit at these words. She'd heard enough people talk about being victimized and then turning around to victimize others to know that the pattern was uniquely crushing to the spirit.

"There was this white girl at my school. Kind of a try-hard, you know? She moved to our school from somewhere in the States and she didn't have any friends. I was awkward, but by that time, I'd grown up a lot. I wasn't super close with anyone, but no one thought I was a loser. You know how girls can be."

Helen knew how people could be, girls and boys and everyone in between.

"This girl's dad was like some right-wing politician. Her mom was religious and a little downtrodden, at least according to this girl, who used to try to be hard and say shocking things to make people pay attention to her. She was a severe oversharer, but totally full of shit, you know?"

Helen nodded.

"I started talking to her. Paying attention to her. I needed to make sure she wouldn't rat me out to the school if I made my pitch and she didn't go for it. But she was so grateful for any scrap of friendship that she would never have done that. Anyway, eventually I told her about my gig when she asked how I could afford such expensive clothes and buy anything I wanted. And just like that, she wanted in. I introduced her to Randy and then he let me shut down my account. A month later she was dead."

Helen started at the suddenness, the terribleness of it.

"She probably tried to back out when she realized what it was. How awful the clients were. But it was too late. She tried to call me, you know. But it was summer holidays by then and I didn't take her calls or return her messages. We'd gone to France to visit my grandparents. I tried to forget about all of it. By the time I got back, she was gone. I don't think her parents ever found out why she did it. But I know. She did it because of me."

Now Amina was crying silently.

Helen let out a breath she'd been holding. Finally, she said, "I'm sorry that this man, the men on that website, took advantage of you and your friend. What was her name?"

"Harlow," said Amina. "Her name was Harlow."

Helen thought of Dixon's comments, the ones that had led Amina to walk away from the picnic. "Does this have anything to do with what is happening now? To the Deep State?"

Amina swept her fingers along her cheekbones.

"It has everything to do with the Deep State. Dixon also worked for Sweet Connections. So did Trudee."

CHAPTER 50

When they arrived back at Weeping Creek Ranch, everyone but Mabel and Helen seemed exhausted. The group had ridden back in near silence. Dixon cast many curious glances at Amina and Helen but didn't say anything. Helen hadn't gotten the chance to ask Amina any more questions because Mabel had approached leading two of the horses.

Helen debated whether she ought to talk to Dixon. Should she tell Mr. Hightower's investigator what she'd learned? How many people in the group had been part of . . . what was a site like Sweet Connections called? She didn't know. A site for predators to target young people? How could something like that be allowed to operate? Easily, she suspected.

Helen had taken part in hundreds of interviews with retreat participants over the years, and she'd heard people speak about all manner of traumas, small and large. She had no illusions about what people driven by greed, hatred, and delusion did to one another, and about the damage that resulted.

Had Cartier also been on Sweet Connections? If so, Helen wasn't sure Archibald Hightower could cope with the knowledge.

While the riders limped off to their rooms after thanking Mabel in subdued voices, Helen stayed at the hitching post with Honey. She inexpertly untacked and brushed the mare in the time that it took Mabel to untack and brush all the others before she led them into their stalls to be fed. Helen reluctantly said goodbye to the horse and fed her a last carrot. And she thought about what Amina had just told her.

It was five thirty and Helen knew she should go in to check on preparations for dinner, but she also knew Lou Ellen and Wallace would have everything well in hand.

What was her role here? She was not investigating the history of the Deep State. Her job was to help Cartier navigate the minefield that surrounded the group. She would keep doing that, which meant she would make sure the internet stayed off and the group was sent graciously on its way. That was it. It wasn't up to her to untangle the web of lies and secret connections between them. Her job was to move the mess along and help Cartier, just as her father had asked.

The group was subdued throughout dinner. Keithen, who Lou Ellen reported had spent the morning reading on the couch and the rest of the day sleeping in his room, tried to ask questions about the ride, but got only curt answers, and he soon stopped asking. Amina and Dixon separately checked some of the footage they'd shot on the trail ride and asked Bryan advice on when they should post it. They declined dessert, citing exhaustion, and went to their rooms. Bryan was the exception. He took a slice of key lime pie and talked happily about getting home to his daughter.

"I'm going to head out really early, if you don't mind," he said. "I should have gone this morning, but with all the drama, it felt wrong to leave them. But it sounds like things are sorted. Tomorrow I'm going to leave before anyone else is up. Beth is probably wondering where I am."

Helen let him know that there would be a bagged lunch waiting for him in the fridge when he got up.

By eight o'clock all the guests had gone back to their rooms and Nigel, Helen, Mabel, Wallace, and Lou Ellen sat around the island in the kitchen, eating a late meal of vegetarian pad Thai, coconut rice, fried tofu, and mango and cucumber salad.

"That must have been some trail ride," said Wallace. "They all seem thrashed."

Helen agreed that they were far more tired than even a long day on horseback could account for. But then again, they'd all been woken up in the middle of the night when the internet connection was restored. She saw Nigel nodding off over his plate and suggested he go to bed.

Soon all of them were heading for their rooms and the house was silent. Helen stopped outside on her way to the cabin. The fading edge of light at the horizon was a ghastly orange and the night seemed to be moving in from all directions. She took a deep breath. Let it out.

Helen noted the questions that kept floating through her mind. Trudee, Amina, and Dixon had all been on the Sweet Connections website. Had they all been coerced? Blackmailed? She wasn't going to find out tonight. Maybe she would never find out and would be able to sidestep all of this. With that comforting thought in mind, she headed for bed.

CHAPTER 51
NIGEL

When Amina came into the kitchen the next morning at six thirty and said she couldn't find Keithen, Nigel told her he'd help her look.

"You're sure he's not in his room?" he asked as he followed her into the living room.

"Yes. I knocked. We were going to do some yoga this morning. I mean, he was going to film me doing yoga."

He went with her to check all over the house and didn't find the red-haired man. Lou Ellen and Wallace said they hadn't seen him.

"Maybe we should try his room again," said Nigel. Did he dare disturb a guest at this time of the morning? He looked at Amina's worried face. Yes, he did dare.

He knocked, waited, then pushed open the door. Keithen's bed wasn't made and his stuff was still scattered around the room. Nigel tiptoed into the ensuite bathroom. Shaving stuff on the counter. Keithen had a lot of toiletries for a guy who pretended like he was still a welder. But he wasn't in there.

"Could he have left with Bryan? He said he was leaving before 6:00," said Nigel.

"He wouldn't have done that," said Amina.

Nigel decided it was time to get Helen involved. On that note, where *was* Helen? She was almost always working by this time.

"Let me check something outside," he said.

Amina waited in the house while he put his shoes on and headed for cabin two, walking softly as he passed cabin one so he wouldn't wake Cartier.

Helen didn't answer his knock. He looked through the front window. Her cabin was neat. No lights on. No shoes on the front mat. She was gone.

She must have gone for a walk. It looked like it was going to rain, so maybe she'd wanted to get some steps in.

Maybe she and Keithen were walking together? Maybe it was his turn to spill his guts to the best listener in the world? It happened eventually to everyone who spent enough time around Helen.

Before he could be sure of that, there was one last place to look. Maybe Keithen was out in the barn, trying to get some pictures of horses or something.

Nigel headed to the big barn and slid open one of the big double doors and walked inside. It was quiet and smelled like hay and horse, a very nice scent. He flipped the switches to turn on the overhead lights.

The guy just went for a walk, he repeated to himself. He was walking with Helen. That would be a good thing for anyone to do. No need to send out a search party. No need to freak out.

The horses in the first few stalls looked out over their stall doors. When he peered into the seventh stall, Mabel's mean horse stood with her butt to him.

No Keithen in there.

Some instinct made him decide to peer through the rest of the stall doors on the other side of the barn. They were empty. They didn't even have shavings on the floor. Just heavy rubber mats and an empty automatic water bowl on the wall. Then, at the final stall in the row, something caught his eye. He peered in and his brain struggled to process what his eyes were seeing. A foot with a flip-flop on it. Attached to the white leg of someone sprawled on the ground.

"Oh shit," Nigel whispered as he fumbled to open the latch so he could roll the door open. *He's just resting*, he told himself. It was a bizarre place to take a break, but whatever. Cartier and her friends were full of strange ideas. Sitting in the dark in an empty stall was probably some new trend on TikTok.

Why, Nigel asked himself, with mounting panic, had he even come outside? Why had he left the Yatra Institute? He didn't like this job or this place. This place was overrun with influencers.

With these thoughts whirling through his brain, he stepped into the stall. Keithen lay with his back resting against one wall. His long red hair had come out of its usual ponytail and lay across his shoulders, like a shampoo advertisement. The guy really had nice hair. But he was a shade of white Nigel had never seen in a person before, not even a person who was naturally pale. Keithen was almost blue, except for the marks around his neck. They were red and purplish black. His eyes were open and the whites were blood red.

Nigel was no doctor and had never played one on TV, but he knew dead when he saw it.

"Holy shit, holy shit, holy shit," he said, and backed right out of the stall and into Mabel, who stood behind him, her arms full of hay.

CHAPTER 52

Helen came back from her long walk filled with a sense of dread. The sky, which had at first hinted a royal-blue day, was now a discontented purplish. Black and steel clouds roiled in from the north. Light glanced down from the heavens through the lingering smoke, giving the whole landscape a wrathful, end-times appearance.

A storm was coming.

Of course a storm was coming, she thought. A storm was always coming. Clear, fine days were coming, as were drizzly days and days filled with slanting rain, days where every living thing gasped for water and days when the snow lay suffocating a frozen landscape.

She had been taught to pay attention to her experiences, to note how sensations moved through her body and mind, and to be alert to the feeling tones that came with them: pleasant, unpleasant, neutral. Her feelings now were definitely on the unpleasant side, though she wasn't sure why.

The act of noting her discomfort brought ease.

She was halfway down the hill when she paused to look at the house. There seemed to be a lot of lights on, but it was hard to tell with all the windows reflecting the landscape. Maybe the light was just a reflection from outside.

Anxiety still thrummed in her chest.

What was it one of her favourite teachers, Michele McDonald, liked to say? "If the word *still* is happening, aversion is present." Helen had always found that to be true. Normally by this hour, unless she was taking the client for a walk, she'd have been well into her workday in the house, but for some reason she hadn't wanted to turn around and come back this morning. So she'd kept walking.

A movement off to the west caught her eye. Figures on horseback moved a small herd of horses toward the fenced pastures on the far side of the house. Tiny foals moved in among the loose horses.

It was a sight to gladden the heart. "Cowboys," she whispered to herself, and enjoyed saying the word. Everything was okay if there were cowboys around.

She was still some distance from the house when Nigel came running out of the massive barn. He was probably nervous about the storm. The last storm they'd been through together at the Yatra Institute had been truly terrifying.

She took a deep breath, which was cut short when a loud crack sounded overhead. Nigel lurched sideways, and at first she had the surreal idea that he'd been shot, but that wasn't it. There was a boom, followed by an echo.

Thunder and lightning. Coming from the inky clouds roiling overhead. This had been happening in the distance since late the night before. Now the thunderclaps were right overhead.

She wanted to watch the cowboys, but Nigel was yelling something and she thought she should probably get inside before she got hit with a bolt of lightning.

Crack! Boom!

The cowboys were hurrying the panicked horses through a gate and into a pasture that had a number of open sheds where the horses could take shelter from the storm. A wobbly-legged foal, head high, drifted away from its mother, and one of the cowboys turned his horse and gently shooed it back. Then the cowboys were back in among the animals, taking halters off the horses they'd been leading.

Rain began to fall as though the world had sprung a leak.

Near the barn, Nigel, who'd gone into a crouch, straightened up, held a hand ineffectually over his head, and hurried toward her again.

"Helen!" he shouted.

"Let's get inside," she said when he reached her. But he wasn't listening.

"You have to come," he said. "In the barn. It's—" But Helen couldn't hear him over the driving rain and the cascading thunderclaps that seemed to cartwheel across the land, chasing the lighting.

They were both instantly soaked, and he pulled her toward the barn. His forcefulness came as a surprise because Nigel usually treated her with such respect.

Once they were inside, she gave her head a shake and wiped the water from her eyes, flicking it away as it continued to course down from her hair. When she was able to focus again under the bright lights, she saw Mabel and Nigel looking at her, both with stricken faces, and she knew something had gone very wrong.

"What is it?" she asked. "What's happened?"

Nigel spoke up, his normally cheerful ruddy face drawn. "We found Keithen. In here. He was missing."

Helen waited for him to say the rest, even though part of her knew what was coming, had been sensing it all morning.

"He's dead. It looks like . . ." Nigel's eyes were huge as his hands moved up to his neck to indicate what had happened to Keithen.

Helen went very still for a beat. Took a slow breath and closed her eyes. *Unpleasant. Unpleasant.* A feeling of panic, connected by a thread of memory to the last body she'd found, rose in her. She felt it and then let it go. This was another situation. Another person. It deserved to be treated as the new tragedy it was.

"May I see?" she asked gently.

Mabel nodded and led the way to a stall door. There was nothing remarkable about it, other than the small pile of hay that had been dropped outside, unusual in the spotless confines of the barn.

Mabel moved as though to open the door and Helen put up a hand. She used her handkerchief to cover her hand and slid the door open.

Keithen lay against the wall, his fair skin ghostly. She didn't need to get any closer to know that he was dead. But still, she had to ask. "Did you check for a pulse?"

Mabel, standing at her right side, nodded. "I did. He's cold. And he's . . . you know. Kind of stiff."

"Did you both go inside?" she asked. This was information the police would want when they arrived.

"I opened the door and stepped inside. I didn't go any closer," said Nigel.

"You remember everything you touched?" Helen asked Mabel. "The police will want to know."

"I just went in and touched him here." Mabel indicated the side of her neck. "And here." She held up the inside of her wrist. "Then I got out of there."

Tears glistened at the corner of Mabel's eyes and Helen wanted to give her a hug. "You did well," she said. And when Mabel's face crumpled, Helen did give her a hug, and then she put her arm protectively around Nigel. They were strong people, but they were also young.

More thunder boomed, right overhead it sounded like, and the lights flickered on and off. There was a scuffling and clopping noise of people and horses entering the barn.

"Mabel!" called a man's voice.

"We're messing up your barn!" called another voice.

"You got any coffee on in that fancy tack room?"

"This storm is bullshit!"

The men they'd met out on the range swaggered down the walkway like actors in a heist movie. They seemed completely unconcerned that they were drenched and so were their horses.

Helen went to meet them, and something in her face made them stop. Looks of concern dawned over their faces.

"I'm sorry, but we need to stay out of this part of the barn," she said.

"Everything all right?" asked the one Helen recognized as Trevor.

"No. Someone has been . . . a man is dead. He's in one of the stalls," said Mabel. "It's one of the guests. He's in there."

"Oh shit," said Scott. "You want to go have a look, Aar? You got first aid."

His brother shrugged. "I can look if you want. But I'm guessing you know how to tell if a person is dead or not." He gave Helen and Mabel a sympathetic look that Helen appreciated.

Helen nodded. "Yes. He's gone."

"Okay, then. We don't need to see," said Scott. "I guess we should all clear out of this area. We'll use the stalls on the far side, if that's okay. We left a bunch of horses in the side pasture."

The men turned their mounts around and led them back down the aisle and around to the other side of the building. Helen, Nigel, and Mabel walked silently behind them but stopped in front of the massive sliding doors, which were open. The storm was already easing—at least, the rain was slowing. The pounding of water against the high metal roof had turned to a patter. The short downpour was barely enough to tamp down the dust.

"I need to finish feeding the horses," said Mabel.

"Can you feed them from outside their stalls?"

Mabel nodded.

"Nigel? Can you please ask one of the brothers to come and help Mabel with the horses? And then I'd like everyone to come to the house."

"Okay, boss," he said and hurried off, his shoulders hunched.

Helen had no idea who was responsible, and part of her didn't want to know. It was all unpleasant. Deeply unpleasant. That poor young man. So white and lifeless, so ineffably sad.

"I'll go in the house and use the landline to call the police. Then we can just wait together until they tell us what to do," she said.

She quickly left the barn, followed by the silence of the dead man in the stall.

CHAPTER 53

In the house, Wallace, Lou Ellen, and Amina were gathered in front of Dixon's room. He stood in the doorway and seemed to be explaining something.

When Helen got closer, she realized that he didn't look right. His left eye was bruised and swollen nearly shut. His lip was cut. In spite of herself, Helen looked down at his hands. The knuckles were cut.

He'd obviously been in a serious fight.

Lou Ellen looked to Helen. "He doesn't want to come out of his room. And he won't tell us what happened to him. We found him in the hallway with his bags packed. But no one can leave."

Helen tried to take the information in. "No one can leave?"

Lou Ellen clutched at a towel. "We just got a call saying that the road out of here is closed. They just figured out how to contact us. I guess lightning strikes started a fire. The guy said we should be safe here for now. They want to see how the fire reacts. He said something about there not being much fuel around here. They think more rain is coming. I don't know. It was all a little confusing. I don't understand why there are fires if it's been raining."

"The first guy said there have been lightning strikes all over the area, starting last night," said Wallace. "Things were already dry. I guess there wasn't enough rain to put the fires out."

"Okay," said Helen. She looked at Dixon until he met her eyes.

"You were leaving," she said. "Alone."

For once Dixon Cho didn't look as though he could get caught in a tornado and emerge without a hair out of place. For once he didn't look slightly removed from the rough and tumble of human concerns. He looked thoroughly messed up.

He nodded, curtly, and moved to touch his eye, and then he took his hand away quickly as though he didn't want to call attention to his battered face.

"What happened to your face?" asked Helen gently. He was trapped here. Outnumbered and obviously guilty. There was no telling how he would react if she pushed too hard. But something about the way he looked at her made her think he wanted her to ask him directly.

"Keithen and I had a fight. Last night," he said. "He hit me. A couple of times. And I put him down."

Amina's hand flew to her mouth. "Oh," she said, in a small voice.

Dixon looked at her. "Not like that. I hit him and he went down. I've boxed for years. He shouldn't have come at me. I had to get him to . . . stop."

"Stop what?" asked Helen.

"Never mind. I don't want to talk about it."

"Keithen is our friend," said Amina.

Dixon gave a bleak laugh. "No, Mina. He isn't. Let's just drop it, okay. Let's just say that we're down a member."

"He's quitting?"

"Either he goes or I do," said Dixon.

Dixon Cho's comments made no sense, not if he'd killed Keithen. He was far too casual about it. Or was this a ploy to conceal his guilt?

Should she tell everyone that Keithen was dead? Or would that make Dixon run? Would he attack the rest of them?

Behind her, she heard the front door open and footsteps entering the great room. She looked to make sure it was Nigel. He was accompanied by the cowboys and Mabel, who still looked stricken.

She waited until they were nearby, and then she looked to make sure Dixon had nothing in his hands that he could use as a weapon. He wore a tight T-shirt and spotless black track pants. She was almost sure he didn't have a gun and could only hope he didn't have a knife.

"Dixon," she said. "Keithen is dead. We found his body in the barn."

Dixon gaped. "No, he's not. He was fine when I left. I knocked him down and he was getting up. He came at me again and I . . . I hit him again. But not that hard. He was on his knees. His mouth was bleeding. But he wasn't . . . he was just shook up. Not hurt. Not dead."

"Well, he's dead now," said Scott. "Someone strangled him."

Now Dixon's mouth hung open. He looked at his hands. Turned them over to show the battered knuckles. "No," he said. "That's not right. I didn't . . ."

"Dixon," said Helen. "I'm going to ask you to wait in the living room. I need to call the . . . call for help."

"But I didn't do it," he said again, his voice rising with panic.

"If you didn't have anything to do with his death, that will be clear soon enough."

She hoped that was true. There was something going on here that she didn't understand. Several somethings, actually.

Give this matter to the police. That was her only job. Keep everyone safe and hand the situation over. She was a butler, not an investigator.

What kind of karma did she have that kept landing her in the middle of murders? She shook her head at the self-centred thought.

"I saw you," said a hoarse voice. "Last night. I was in the bathroom. I had my phone and I was trying to see if I could get a signal, which was dumb. It's just like a habit, you know? Anyway, I heard a noise outside and I saw you walking past my cabin. You looked like you were coming out of the barn, heading to the house. I saw you walk by. Right behind my cabin. You were holding a rope, Dixon."

It was Cartier and she was staring, white-faced, at Dixon.

"It wasn't me. Someone else must have gone in there after me," he said.

"I watched for a long time. Seeing you out there, wandering out of the barn like that, in the dark, kind of freaked me out. Plus, I couldn't sleep. I only saw you."

CHAPTER 54

The police told Helen that they were doing the right thing in detaining Dixon. She explained everything that had happened thus far. That morning and before.

They told her to reconnect the internet in case the phone lines went down and have someone stay on the phone with an officer. They were going to see about getting through the road closure. Maybe they would take a helicopter, but it would be tricky with all the smoke and water bomber planes coming in and out of the area.

"Just hang tight," said the detective. "Don't let anyone out of your sight."

She handed over the landline to Wallace and went to the safe to extract the modems and the routers.

When Helen got back to the living room, she found all three cowboys sitting near Dixon, who had his elbows on his knees and was staring at the floor. Cartier, Amina, Nigel, and Lou Ellen sat on their own, not speaking. Even the dogs seemed afraid to move.

Helen held up a hand to indicate that she wanted everyone's attention.

"I'm going to have Nigel turn the internet back on," she said. "But I don't want anyone to post anything about what has happened here this morning. No photos. No videos. We need to wait for the police."

"Well, hurry up," said Amina. "Turn it on. I don't feel safe with the internet off. I mean, look at what happened."

Helen felt an urge to say that she was almost certain the internet

297

was the *cause* of everything that befallen them, but she held her tongue. However, Amina's desperation to get reconnected told Helen that asking them not to post would be insufficient.

"I need all of your devices," she said. "You can have them back after the police have talked to you. There's a good chance the police will want to see what you've got on your phones and cameras. We'll leave everything on the big table so you can see that no one else has touched it."

Helen spoke in such a way that no one argued. In fact, everyone seemed relieved to be told what to do.

"But what about you?" said Amina. "And your phone?"

"Helen doesn't even have social media," said Cartier. "She's not about to start posting shit now."

One by one the assembled people got up and put their cell phones and cameras, some of which they had to retrieve from their rooms, on the table until there was a small stack of them. Helen doubted she had everything. It was like trying to disarm a militia.

"If you need to use the washroom, please do so one at a time."

"Well, thanks, Miss Marple," muttered Dixon.

Everyone stared at him and he lapsed back into silence.

He wasn't wrong. Helen felt like Miss Marple attempting to take control of a completely out-of-control situation. She was in her mid-thirties but had felt ancient since the day she went to work with Cartier.

Nigel got up and turned the satellite internet back on, and Helen used her cellphone to call Mr. Hightower and fill him in on what was happening.

She was surprised when he did not react with volcanic anger. He sounded, more than anything else, afraid.

"But Cartier's okay?" he asked. "She's not hurt?"

"No, sir. The police are on their way. And Cartier's fine."

"Can I speak with her?"

"Yes, sir," said Helen. "I'll get her for you."

Cartier went to a corner of the room to speak to her father, which she did in whispers, and the rest of them continued sitting around, trying not to stare at Dixon.

After Cartier came back, wiping her eyes, she sat down and Helen had an idea.

"Excuse me," she said. "Can I ask for a moment with just Amina and Dixon? If the rest of you could move to the other end of the room, I would like to have a private conversation."

"Of course," said Wallace. He and Lou Ellen, Cartier and Mabel, and the cowboys and Nigel went to the far end of the room and sat in the nook at the side of the fireplace.

Helen thought about what Amina had told her the day before about her time on the website when she was a teenager. She'd said Dixon and Trudee had been on the same site. What did that mean? Did it have anything to do with Keithen's death? It might not be her place to get involved, but she felt she had to know.

The three of them stayed silent for an endless minute.

Finally, Amina spoke. "Why did you do it?" she asked Dixon.

"I didn't."

"That's pretty hard to believe. Look at your face. Cartier *saw* you."

"All I can tell you is the truth," said Dixon. "After everybody went to bed last night, he knocked on my door. Asked me to go for a walk. He said he needed to talk to me. We went into the barn. I kind of like being near the horses and I didn't want anyone to overhear us. I had a feeling he was going to . . . I don't know. Talk about private stuff. And I was right.

"He told me he found out about you and me, Amina—at least, he was pretty sure it was us. And he asked me if the two of us were doing all of this. Meaning, like, did we kill Trudee and Blossom. He asked if we did the thing at the club. And I told him no. Absolutely not. But I don't think he believed me. He'd found out about that girl at your school. He'd found out that I stole from my parents."

"Oh my god," said Amina, her face ashen. She pulled her sweatshirt over her hands more tightly.

"When did you all meet?" Helen asked. "Did you know you'd all been involved with Sweet Connections before you formed the Deep State?"

"No. It was weird. We were all at this big influencer party. We had some drinks. And Trudee said something to us. Right out of the blue. She said something like 'Sweet Connections ruined a lot of lives. It sure wrecked mine.' And she gave us this look. And so we knew."

"Did you ask her about it?"

"No!" said Dixon. "We were trying to leave the whole thing behind. Start fresh. Reinvent something for ourselves."

"I still don't understand how you all ended up in this group," said Helen.

"Lots of creators were forming content groups then. It was this trendy thing. And after we met Trudee, I guess we felt connected or something because we shared . . . you know. That sense of shame. That need to start again. We started doing work together, and then Trudee introduced us to Keithen."

"We knew who he was," said Dixon. "He was one of the biggest guys in town. And we mentioned the Deep State project to him and he was down. It was surprising."

"Why would you invite a guy who specialized in investigating people if you all had a secret background?" asked Helen.

They looked at her.

"He wasn't about to investigate us," said Amina. "There was no reason. We'd have been crazy not to work with him. He had tons of followers. And anyway, he wasn't like Sherlock Holmes or some CIA agent or anything. He just used a good facial recognition app and the usual internet tools to find people's names and addresses. And he sicced his fans on people. I think his followers did a lot of the work. Ratted people out."

"For a while, I wondered if *he* was the one picking on Cart," said Dixon. "You know, that account called RUOkay or some version of that name?"

"Why would he do that her?" Amina asked.

"Who knows? He wasn't that opposed to people having meltdowns on camera, and Cart"—Dixon shot a glance over at Cartier, who was

sitting with her knees up against her chest, wiping tears from her eyes—
"always seems pretty close to a crack-up."

"We didn't think he could find us out, even with his techniques," said Amina. "We never showed our faces on that site. Only the guy who ran it, Ryan, knew what we looked like, because he recorded us secretly."

Like everything else to do with the Deep State, this account of their pasts was confusing and chaotic. Nothing made any sense.

"So Trudee was behind your whole group," said Helen.

"All she did was make introductions. We formed ourselves. We met Blossom through her. Then Cartier. It just happened to work out. At least for a while. Until people started dying." Amina leaned over and took a deep breath.

There was another painful silence.

"What happened in the barn?" Helen asked.

"Keithen said he was going to have to tell the audience about us."

Dixon spoke as though he still couldn't believe it.

"I asked him why. I told him it would ruin everything. Make us look bad. We already look terrible enough. We'd get dropped by our agent. The fans would turn on all of us, not just Cartier. We might even be liable. And we'd definitely be all over the news. People would think we are monsters. People who don't understand what we do already think influencers are a waste of space." He gave Helen a significant look, which was hard since his face was swollen.

"He said he was sick of working with the Deep State, which, yeah, I get that. Doing the group stuff is pretty lucrative, but it's exhausting. He was the most popular one of us. Everyone loves a vigilante. He was going to tell everyone about us just for the drama of it. The internet would have eaten it up. Eaten us up. Me and Amina. He was going to use what happened to us for *clout*. He was the only one who'd have survived it. Maybe Cartier, but I doubt it. She's never connected with the fans."

Dixon touched a thumb to his injured lip. "We argued. It got a little heated. He punched me. A couple times. Then I hit him and then left him there, in the barn. Told him he was a selfish asshole. 'Backatcha,' he said. And that was it. I went back to the house."

Helen considered his words and her response.

"I'm sorry," she said. "For all of it."

He gave her a searching look. A suspicious look.

"It is terrible to feel afraid," she said.

Dixon huffed out a little laugh. "I was going to say I'm not afraid, but that would be untrue. You know what scares me most?"

"What?"

"Getting turned into Cartier. Having that much hate directed at me. Brutal, man." He shook his head in wonder. "I couldn't handle it." He looked over at Cartier, huddled in her seat. "I honestly don't know how she does it."

Helen thought he'd probably survive it, if he had to. Life, on the internet or off, was often overwhelming if you got too caught up in the web of your own story or other people's. Mental constructs, as stories were sometimes referred to in the teachings, were ever-tightening prisons that prevented people from seeing the truth of how things really were.

Helen didn't say any of this to Dixon. He lived in a world built on dreams and reproductions of dreams. He seemed to mostly like it there.

"So you walked back to the house after your argument with Keithen?"

"Fight. My fight with Keithen. My face and hands are messed up because we fought. I'm not denying that. But I didn't kill him. And I never went anywhere with a rope."

CHAPTER 55

They waited together awkwardly in the enormous living room for an hour, and then Miggs started whining.

"He needs to go out," said Nigel. "They all do. They haven't had a walk yet."

Keeping in mind what the police had said, Helen said she'd take them out. And she wanted to think. She was trying to put the pieces of the story together. Was Dixon lying? Cartier had seen only him. Why didn't he just confess? He had every reason to kill Keithen.

But there was something off here. Something missing.

Helen stood and waited as the Pekes sniffed around, waddling here and there to find the right place to relieve themselves.

Somehow, she thought, they were going to have to prepare brunch for the suspect and everyone else. What did you serve a person who had killed someone? Helen gave her head a little shake.

The police would be here soon and they would take over. She looked and saw that the sky was thick with smoke. She couldn't even see the hill from here. Her throat felt scratchy from the particles in the air.

Miggs had been sniffing a little farther than Clarice and Jack, and suddenly the little dog began to run toward the barn.

Helen called after him, but he didn't turn around. She should have put leashes on them. "Come on," she told the others as she hurried after him. The last thing they needed was one of the dogs being trod upon by a horse. Or worse, interfering with Keithen's body in the barn.

Cartier really should have spent more time training her little pack. They had almost no recall.

Helen and the other two dogs reached the barn, and she peered down the aisle where the cowboys had stabled their horses. It was on the opposite side of the barn from the other horses and the body. No Miggs. The grain room? Or was that the tack room back there? Either way, she had to get the dog out of the barn before he ate something that upset his tummy. They'd done so well avoiding accidents, even with all the upheaval.

She checked the dark room and saw the dog sniffing at the desk. Sniffing at a foot that belonged to a man sitting at the desk.

"Hello, Helen," he said.

It was Bryan Ulrich. The agent.

Helen felt sick and afraid and not at all surprised.

"You're back," she said.

"Never left." He grinned at her. There was something different about his hair. He'd combed it so it was slicked close at the sides and stood up from his head. Like a tall fade. Like the kind of tall fade worn by Dixon. He wore a sweater she'd seen Dixon in. It was that odd pink colour that Dixon used in his clothing line. Mountbatten pink.

The questions piled up in her head. He was dressed like Dixon. He was the one Cartier had seen leaving the barn. Which meant that he'd killed Keithen. But why? And if he'd killed Keithen and framed Dixon, then . . .

"You faked the video of Cartier," said Helen. She felt herself get very calm. Very still. Every breath was an event. Every heartbeat worth celebrating.

"Why would I?" he said. Still with that charming, easy smile.

"You are responsible for all of it," she said.

"Helen, for a seemingly well-adjusted person, you sure do jump to a lot of conclusions. False conclusions."

His eyes, which had seemed warm and friendly, were now empty of human feeling. Still with that eerie smile in place, he got to his feet. He had on a pair of Dixon's strange white leather high-tops. He looked like a grown man dressed like a kid. He looked ridiculous and also very dangerous.

Helen began to back up.

"Come," she said to the dogs. She took another step back.

"Where are you going?" he asked.

Helen didn't answer.

He took a step toward her, and the Pekes, who were arrayed around his feet, began to growl.

"Kindly fuck off," he said and aimed a vicious kick at Clarice. The little dog tried to back up but wasn't fast enough, and he sent her flying with a yelp. Miggs and Jack went for him. Jack sank his teeth into his ankle and Bryan Ulrich swore and kicked out again in the strange white shoes.

"Stop," said Helen. "Leave the dogs alone. They're just afraid."

And that makes four of us, she thought.

"I'm going to stomp them into hamburger meat if you don't get them away from me," he said. His voice stayed exactly the same.

"Come on," she said. "Leave it." And Jack and Miggs came over to her. She moved to pick up Clarice, who lay still in the corner of the office, which was filled with bins of grain on the floor and shelves with vitamins and hoof lotions and medicines, as well as the desk and chair.

"Don't touch her," said the agent. "We've got things to do, Helen."

CHAPTER 56
NIGEL

When Helen didn't bring the dogs inside after several minutes, Nigel announced that he needed to check on them.

"Not by yourself, you're not," said Lou Ellen. "You heard what Helen said. We stick together."

"Except Helen," muttered Dixon.

"Helen is exempt," said Wallace. "Because Helen is the law here."

Lou Ellen and Cartier nodded, and Nigel felt himself nodding along. Maybe Helen had taken the dogs for a short walk. She was very diligent about their care. But something didn't feel right.

"So what's the plan?" asked Nigel. "Do we all go?"

"That would be ridiculous. Our friend here is a murder suspect. We can't let him go traipsing around the place. What if he cuts and runs?" said Wallace.

"We'll stay with him," said Scott.

"What if you did it?" asked Dixon.

The brothers didn't respond. They just sat very still, the way they'd been doing since they got to the house.

"I'm going. Cartier? Anyone else want to come?" Nigel asked.

"I'll go," said Cartier. "They're my dogs. And they aren't that, you know, obedient? Maybe one of them ran off."

"The rest of us can wait for the police. They've got to have the road open soon," said Mabel.

Trevor, the oldest, toughest-looking brother, looked out the window.

"I don't know. That smoke's pretty thick. Might be having some trouble knocking the fire back."

Nigel shuddered. He'd had a bad experience with a big windstorm. Now he was learning to be terrified of fire. Pretty soon he was going to have to live in a . . . what? Place without weather?

"You ready?" he asked Cartier.

She nodded.

They walked outside and looked around. Helen and the dogs were nowhere to be seen.

They looked behind the house and then on the far side.

"Let's try the barn," he said.

Cartier nodded.

They walked in silence to the huge barn. Several of the horses were outside in their narrow turnout paddocks, and they seemed agitated. Maybe it was the smoke. Their heads were up and they paced back and forth, snorting, tails flying as they moved.

"I don't like this," said Cartier.

"Me neither," said Nigel.

She took his hand and they walked into the barn.

CHAPTER 57

Helen was having some trouble believing what was happening to her. After making her get on Honey, the little mare she'd ridden the day before, the agent had tied her hands in front. It was like something out of a spaghetti Western.

"Come on," he said, either to her or to the horse.

He opened the gate out of the turnout connected to the stall at the farthest end of the barn and led Helen and her mount outside.

"Hope you don't mind riding double?" he said.

She didn't answer. This entire scenario was insane. Did he know that? What would be gained by running away on horseback? For all they knew, the ranch was surrounded by fire. They weren't going to be able to ride to a country without an extradition treaty with Canada. She imagined the two of them trotting along the Coquihalla Highway heading for Mexico and nearly laughed.

But it would be best not to laugh at Bryan Ulrich. He was not a well man.

He pulled a kerchief over his face, presumably to keep some of the smoke out of his lungs, but maybe also because he thought it made him look cool. Then he swung up onto the saddle with more agility than she'd expected. She'd noticed the day before that he seemed comfortable on his horse. More so than anyone other than Mabel.

She strongly disliked the feel of his body behind hers. *Unpleasant*, she thought. *Unpleasant*.

The thought of the young man lying dead in the barn behind them. *Unpleasant.* The injured dog lying in the grain room. *Unpleasant.* The other dogs had been locked in there too when Bryan led her out.

"Now, don't you worry," he said into her hair, far too close to her ear. "We're not going far."

Instead of going up and over the hill, they rode into the treeline at the back of the property, parallel to the long driveway.

The situation was absurd but that didn't mean it wasn't happening.

"What are you doing?" she asked.

"Oh, I think the question is what are *you* doing?"

"I don't understand."

"Those kids back there. The other staff. They like you a lot, don't they?"

Helen didn't answer.

"They are definitely going to look for you. All over the place. In the house. In the barn. Everywhere."

Helen waited, her mind as quiet as the aftermath of a ringing bell.

He sighed and his breath was a warm ruffle against her ear.

"I've been busy, Helen. Very busy."

She looked around her. They were riding along a trail through a narrow band of woods. The smoke didn't seem as thick in here, maybe because the trees took some of the pollution from the air.

"Not sure whether you know this, but the road is closed," he said. "I nearly drove right into the roadblock. But I saw the lights just in time to shut mine off before I turned the corner. I threw my car in reverse. It's a miracle they didn't see me."

"I see," said Helen.

He jabbed a thumb into her ribs. "Don't sass me, Helen."

Unpleasant, she thought.

"There was a little pullout onto the trail a ways back. I drove the car off the road and left it in there."

Helen knew better than to make any response.

"So I'll tell you what's going to happen, Helen. I'm going to tie you and this horse up not too far from my car. Then I'm going to light you both on fire. And that fire is going to spread along the line of gasoline I poured all the way from that site to the house and the barn. You're all going to burn. Major, major tragedy. Tremendously sad. People will be telling the story for years. I imagine there will be a movie. Not Hollywood. You're not interesting enough for that. More like movie of the week."

Helen couldn't turn back to look at him, but she could tell that nothing in his expression had changed.

"Won't you burn too?" she said.

He laughed and then, to her horror, he kissed her ear.

"I'll be driving to get help. The wind is heading south. Away from the roadblock. Toward the house."

"Why the horse?" she asked.

"You really seemed to like this horse." He patted Helen's leg. "Isn't that right? But to be honest, I was expecting to be dealing with the girl who looks after the horses. I was going to get her to ride out here with me. Doesn't really matter."

She realized that he did smell like gasoline. She hadn't noticed it at first because the air was choked with wildfire smoke.

"You're the guy, aren't you," she said. "The one from that website. The one who blackmailed Amina and Dixon and Trudee."

"Helen!" he said. "I can't tell you that! Industry secrets." He patted her thigh again and laughed. "But I can tell you that Trudee was no innocent. She was my first employee. She was a cam girl and then my admin. She brought in her fair share of little cammers for our clients. So when I decided to shift into more, what's the word? Forward-facing work? When I decided to make the change, I was just following all my little cammers into the creator economy. They were all getting into influencing. You need a certain . . . shamelessness to succeed online. And they all had that. Trudee was already deep in that scene. I knew she could get me in with them. Trudee knew who'd worked for Sweet Connections. She'd done my paperwork. Arranged to get them their money. Cash or whatever. She had everybody's names."

As he spoke, Helen could feel his hot breath against the side of her face. He kept running a hand up her leg. She noted, *Unpleasant, unpleasant,* to stop herself from reacting. To stop herself from panicking. *Keep him talking,* she thought. Isn't that what people did in these situations?

"So you started the Deep State?" she asked.

"Nothing so direct as that. I knew Amina and Dixon had gotten into making non-adult content after they left Sweet Connections. I asked Trudee to introduce them to each other and put a bug in their ear about working together. They did the rest. Then Trudee brought in Keithen. He wasn't one of mine, and he definitely wasn't someone I'd have chosen. For obvious reasons. The whole internet detecting thing was a problem with him. I think she did it to warn me. Then she brought in Blossom on her own. Blossom wasn't one of mine, either. To be honest, most former Sweet Connections cammers wouldn't make it as mainstream performers. They developed a number of problems that no one wants to look at. It happens. You never know how young people will turn out. Anyway, then Trudee got herself a job with Cartier, and I couldn't let that beautiful opportunity go to waste. I was Bryan Ulrich by then. Not Bryan Union. Isn't that name the best? Anyway, I'd already gotten some bottom-feeder clients. Strictly D-listers, but it was a start. You have no idea how easy it is to sign influencers. These are not savvy people, for the most part. They're like preteens, most of them.

"Anyway, I primed the Deep State to want to work with me. Told them a few fibs about big clients. I think Keithen suspected it was bullshit, but it was too late. Things were already in a tailspin."

Helen noticed that Honey's neck was wet with sweat and the mare's head was up. She was obviously picking up on the tension. Helen tried to pet her, to reassure her, but it was hard with her hands tied.

"Trudee knew who I was, obviously. I used to babysit her. You would not believe what she grew up with. Her mother was an addict. God, it's a wonder that girl survived—as long as she did. Anyway, when she and Blossom got together, I thought for sure she was going to start talking. And Trudee was too fond of her new boss by half. I couldn't trust my girl T anymore, and I needed the legit gig to work out. Sweet

Connection had a reputation by then. I had to shut it down before the cops found me."

Bryan was chatting happily into Helen's ear as though they were two friends on a stroll.

Honey's steps had gotten shorter. Helen could feel the tension in the mare's body.

"So I decided to take Trudee out. Not permanently. I just wanted her to back off for a while. There were some things I wanted to do with the group and I was worried she'd get in the way."

They'd been riding for what felt like forever, and her aversion to him—his words and his body—was threatening to overwhelm her. But she kept asking questions. "Some things?" she said.

This time, Bryan didn't just pat her leg. He grabbed her thigh, and it hurt.

"The idea was to get some attention for my little collective. Good, bad. It's all the same. You see, Helen, the internet loves scandal and so does everyone else. You have to shape it, though. Get people fascinated. Hooked on every new development. That's when you can start signing deals. Delve further into the scandals. At least, that's my theory. I was already getting them some good contracts. And they were getting sweeter all the time. Fame, baby. People are fascinated."

Helen nodded, not wanting to provoke him again.

He pulled back on the reins and Honey stopped.

"Here we are," he said. They were near a tree. At the base was a thick pad of dried grasses and tiny sticks. A pyre. A red jerry can of gas stood nearby.

"Where's your car?" asked Helen.

"Wouldn't you like to know? Don't worry. I can get to it before the flames really get going."

Helen looked at the tree. She tried to understand his reasoning. How had he known someone would find him in the feed room? What was the point of all this? Why burn them? Why was the plan so baroque?

"Back to Trudee. I did a little tinkering with Trudee's kiteboarding set-up. We're both from the Jordan River area. Both good on a board. I hoped she'd get the message and get lost. Realize that she shouldn't interfere with me and my clients. I was the most surprised one when she hit that boat. It was sad, but so beautifully final. But then I got to worrying that she and Blossom had been talking. Blossom's attitude had been going to shit for a while. So when we were on Vancouver Island for the shoot at the potholes, I got her out of bed, early, early. And I took her to the waterfall and helped her over the fence. Said I'd film her coming out of there like some river goddess. Told her about the ledge at the front. My timing was impeccable, if I do say so."

Helen turned her head to hear him better. Honey shuffled her feet.

"The dam let out that morning at five thirty. Just that extra bit of water pressure on those slick rocks, and boom. Down she went. Good thing I didn't have to shoot her, or there'd have been some 'splaining to do about her body. Amiright?" He chuckled. "I left the camera there for someone to find, so everyone knew it was an accident."

He ran his hand along her side, which made her stomach turn.

"I bet you want to know about the club, too. For a butler, you're very curious. I bet that gets you into trouble." His hand moved up farther, and she took a deep breath and forced herself to stay present. To wait.

"The club thing was all about scandal, Helen. I wanted them to be responsible for a fucking gong show. Maybe even a mass casualty event. What could be more exciting than influencers causing mayhem? I knew Keithen was getting a key to that little room from the bartender. I guess he'd been in there before for a poetry reading or something. Knew it would be perfect for the *Flashdance* recreation. All I had to do was get the key from an actor I know who uses that room for rehearsals for his godawful play. I told him I needed it for my daughter's youth theatre group. Ha." Bryan laughed happily. "I have no daughter, Helen. But if you say you're a dad and you talk about your daughter the right way, like you care, people think you're a good person. Anyway, I bet there are dozens of keys to that room floating around. I had no trouble fitting in with the crowd in the ReVibe Room after I locked the door to the black box theatre room from the outside. I was dressed like a Beastie Boy." Bryan's hand had made it up Helen's rib cage and she continued to breathe slowly. *Stay present*, she told herself again. *Listen and get ready.*

"Isn't this the craziest story you ever heard?" Bryan continued. "It's too bad no one else will ever hear the truth. But the lie should be good enough. Anyway, I had cans of spray paint for my costume, but one of the bottles was actually adhesive. I sprayed the doors to the main room shut, propped open the door to the little room so people could get in there. Hit the fire alarm and watched everyone freak out."

He sighed.

"Good footage, but it could have been more dramatic. Still, it was a big story for at least a full news cycle. I could go on, but it's time to finish this narrative. What should we call it? This fire in the bush. This conflagration in the . . . where do conflagrations go?" he mused.

And that's when Helen leaned forward quickly and then slammed her head back with every ounce of strength she had. She felt his nose break and his teeth cut into her scalp and his body slip sideways.

"Go!" she yelled to Honey. And the little mare leaped forward like the fire had already been lit. Bryan Ulrich slid off behind her and lay in a heap as Helen crouched low, her tied hands holding onto the pommel for all she was worth.

They'd made it a few yards when Helen saw a trail that led, she hoped, to the road. How far to the roadblock? How far back to the house? Which was closer? She closed her eyes, said a prayer, and willed Honey in the direction she'd chosen, praying that Bryan Ulrich wouldn't wake up and light the fire, sending it racing after them.

CHAPTER 58

Helen, on Honey, hit the driveway at high speed and found that Bryan's prediction had come true. People were going in all directions, looking for her.

First she saw two of the cowboys, Aaron and Scott, about to ride down beside the road. "Help!" she cried, and they wheeled their horses around.

"She's here!" yelled another voice.

It was Lou Ellen, who was getting into the Kia with Wallace, who had a cell phone clapped to his ear.

"You've got to get him. He's in the woods, along the trail, and he's planning to start a fire," said Helen.

At her words, Aaron and Scott wheeled their horses back around and disappeared into the trees at a run.

"Take the car to the roadblock and tell them there's a man about to start a fire. He's part way down the trail that runs parallel to the road," said Helen. "I think he's poured fuel along the path."

Seconds later, Wallace and Lou Ellen were racing down the road in the Kia.

Nigel and Cartier ran up to Helen and Honey, whose neck was white with lather.

"Where is Mabel?" Helen asked.

"Went looking for you. She's gone out on her horse in front of the house," said Nigel.

"Can you get her back?"

"Trevor could, but he's watching Dixon."

"He doesn't need to do that. Can you untie my hands? I'll see if Honey and I can catch her."

Nigel was staring at Helen like he thought she'd been body-snatched. She held up her hands. "I need my hands."

"Oh my god!" said Cartier, and then, in spite of everything, she giggled.

"Mabel said there was a good fire suppression system in place here. It needs to be activated," said Helen.

"Okay," said Nigel, and he sprinted for the house. He came back followed by two of the dogs, who were frantic at all the activity, and cut the ties using kitchen scissors.

"Trevor says to wait here. He'll get the sprinklers ready and start watering down the house and barn and the grounds. Then he'll go get Mabel."

Helen slid off Honey and felt her legs give way. Shock.

She patted the mare. "We all need to help him. Make sure everything is soaked. There's a line of gasoline around the property. At least, there might be."

"What?" yelped Nigel.

Before Helen could explain, they heard a helicopter coming in fast. Helen, Nigel, and Cartier strained to see it through the yellow haze.

A black helicopter appeared like something out of a movie about the Vietnam War, hovering over them. Helen held tight to Honey's reins and walked her quickly away as the helicopter descended and the wind from its rotors made dust fly in every direction.

They all stopped to watch after the engine shut off. The doors flew open and out came a short, red-faced, wild-eyed man in his fifties, a tall man in a black T-shirt and pants, with a gun in a holster, and two men in uniforms.

"Daddy?" said Cartier.

CHAPTER 59

Archibald Hightower took his daughter in his arms, gave her brief hug, then looked at her.

"You look good," he said. "Thank Christ."

He looked around. "It's okay, everyone. I've brought backup. Junior and Tao. They're firefighters from South Africa. I had them flown in this morning."

The two men smiled and looked sheepishly around them. "Good money," said one.

"And Boris. He's former Ukrainian military. Currently doing private security here in Canada."

"Boryslav," corrected the granite-jawed man.

Before anyone else could speak, Aaron emerged from the trail behind the house, moving fast. "We got him," he yelled as he approached. "The police have him. They were just coming up the road when we got to him. The fire is contained and the roadblock is over. Lou Ellen and Wallace are on their way back with the police." He pulled his horse up short and stared at the helicopter.

"Got who? What?" blustered Mr. Hightower.

"We've had a situation here. But . . ." Helen had been about to say it was under control. But it wasn't, not really. Keithen was dead. Perhaps the threat was gone, but that didn't mean the situation was under control. She could still feel Bryan behind her and knew it would be some time before she felt like herself again.

"He's arrested?" said Cartier. "Bryan?"

"What?" barked Mr. Hightower. "Your supposed agent? Arrested? Why?"

They were interrupted by a line of police cars moving up the driveway, lights on but sirens off.

"Let's go in the house," said Helen. "And I'll tell you what I know."

"Before we do that, there's something in the helicopter," Mr. Hightower said. "What did you call this thing, Boris? A bird?"

"What?" said Boryslav. "No, I didn't call it a bird."

"He means the helicopter," said the one called Junior, in a lilting accent. "The pilot called it a bird."

"Oh," said Boryslav. "Okay, then."

"Can someone get it?" said Archie Hightower.

No one moved.

"Oh, Daddy," said Cartier.

"Fine. I'll get it myself," he said, and he stomped off toward the chopper. They watched him climb in. The pilot waved through the window. Moments later Archie was back, carrying a small case.

He walked stiffly back to his daughter and handed the case to her. "There. Now you have a complete set," he said.

Cartier held the case up by the handle. A squeak sounded. "A puppy?" she said.

"Yes. I ordered it from New York. The parents are champions. It's fine if you call it Hannibal. I won't mind."

"Oh my god, Daddy. This is so sweet."

Nigel moved over and whispered something into her ear and Cartier clapped a hand over her mouth.

"The helicopter!" she said. "We need it. We need it now."

"Another fire?" said Tao, sounding hopeful.

"One of my dogs is hurt," said Cartier. "Can you take her to the emergency vet?"

"Yes!" said Archie Hightower. "Get me the dog and let's get this done. Come on, Boris."

And just like that, Cartier's father headed back to the helicopter with his team, one of the firefighters carrying Clarice's tiny body on a large cutting board.

"I'll be back," Archie Hightower called over his shoulder, obviously having the time of his life and also completely overwhelmed.

Then the police ushered Helen and everyone else into the living room to tell their stories.

CHAPTER 60

It took hours for the police to finish interviewing everyone and to process the crime scene. People left as soon as they were able. Dixon and Amina went back to the city as soon as they were allowed, barely stopping to say goodbye. They both seemed eager to get away.

After Mr. Hightower returned in his helicopter, he and Cartier walked around the property for an hour and talked. When they were done, she was drying her eyes.

He informed them that he needed to get back. Helen, Nigel, Lou Ellen, and Wallace walked outside to see him off.

He stopped, hands behind his back, and looked at Wallace and Lou Ellen. "Would you like your jobs back?" he asked.

"No thank you, sir," said Wallace.

"We're retired," added Lou Ellen.

"Fine, fine," said Mr. Hightower grimly. "I've added a bonus to your final pay periods. Thank you for your service."

"Thank you," said Lou Ellen, her face softening.

"Cartier, would you like to come home now?"

"Soon, Daddy. I'm going to finish this thing with Helen. I promised."

"That's fine, then. I will have your dog collected from the vet when she's better. They said about a week to make sure there are no internal injuries. The vet is taking her with him at night. He's going to keep her in his room. In fact, he's promised she will not be out of his sight."

"Thank you."

"Good work, everyone!" said Archibald Hightower, who seemed to have turned into a major general somewhere along the line.

Then he and his increasingly bemused-looking team got back into the helicopter and it rose into the air and flew away through the clearing smoke.

"Now can you tell us what happened?" said Cartier.

"Yes. After the police have gone, I'll tell you everything he told me."

———

Two hours later, she finished the story. Of course, everyone had questions.

"What kind of a stupid plan was that?" asked Nigel. "What was the point of doing all those things?"

"Money and attention, I think," said Helen.

"Yeah, but surely there are easier ways to get those things."

"Scandal is by far the easiest and fastest way to get famous on the internet," said Cartier. She cradled the sleeping Hannibal in her arms.

"I still don't understand how that's lucrative," said Nigel.

"He thought he'd make money selling your stories after it was all over and the blame had been placed on Dixon," Helen said.

"So why did he keep picking on me online?" asked Cartier.

Nigel slid a glance at Helen. She wasn't sure how to interpret it. Did he feel protective?

"I think you were useful because you have a high profile and are a person of privilege. Watching you struggle was compelling for some part of the audience."

"Ninety percent of the audience, you mean," said Cartier. She kissed the top of the puppy's head. He looked like a small red squirrel. "I make a good punching bag."

"And he dressed like Dixon? That's why Cartier thought he was Dixon?" said Mabel.

"The police think he followed Dixon and Keithen into the barn. Saw them fight. After Dixon left, he took a lead rope and strangled Keithen. Then he got into clothes that he'd bought at Dixon's shop and made a bunch of noise when he went past Cartier's window so she would wake up and see him. He put the rope in Dixon's car. Then he got into his car and left. But the roadblock was up by then and so he had to hide and wait for the road to reopen. While he was waiting he got the idea to set this place on fire. From there, things get very murky. He wanted to have one of us die while trying to reach the roadblock and the rest of us would go in the fire that spread from that ignition spot behind the fire line. He seemed to think the only thing more exciting than three dead influencers would be seven dead influencers, along with a few bystanders," said Helen.

"That's horrific," said Wallace. "And bizarre. Wouldn't he have perished in the fire, too?"

"He didn't seem to have considered that possibility," said Helen. "He was very swept up in his storyline."

Lou Ellen nodded in appalled wonder.

"He seemed proud of his thinking and his planning," said Helen. "He was proud of his storylines."

"People on the internet will understand," said Cartier. "They don't care if things make sense or they're true, as long as the story is exciting."

That, thought Helen, was absolutely true.

EPILOGUE

Two weeks later, Mabel loaded Honey into the trailer. The mare wore a special Weeping Creek Ranch blanket in blue and gold and matching travel boots. Her halter was padded, and the trailer, also branded with the Weeping Creek Ranch colours, glistened in the sun.

"She'll be okay for the trip?" asked Helen.

"We could put her in an egg carton if you like?" said Mabel.

Helen sighed. "If I could, I would."

"Your first horse. How does it feel?"

"Scary. What if she gets hurt?"

"W.C. Honey is a ranch horse. You're essentially moving her into a spa for retired horses."

"I do plan to ride her," said Helen. "After I learn to ride properly."

"Yes, and you'll do fine. So will she. I've seen where you're going. You have the name of a good riding teacher. Your little Honey just won the lottery," said Mabel.

"Thank you for selling her to me."

"You and that horse have something special. You took down a killer together."

"We all did."

"You and a pack of Pekingese and a ranch pony did that. The rest of us just flapped around."

Cartier and Nigel stood to the side. Cartier was all packed up, and Nigel and she were going to drive to the hotel in the pink Mercedes.

Helen would follow in the Range Rover. Mabel was driving Honey to the Levines', where the little mare would take up residence among the retired racehorses and the rescued greyhounds.

Cartier and Nigel had begun spending quite a bit of time together, playing canasta and hanging out with the dogs, and Helen knew Cartier had asked him to come and work for her after he finished butler school. Helen thought perhaps Cartier liked Nigel as more than a butler, and she was worried about him, but she didn't say anything. He was a grown man. A Pekingese whisperer, as Cartier liked to call him.

Trevor and Aaron and Scott had gone back out onto the land to do cowboy things, and Wallace and Lou Ellen had left that morning. They were heading out on a two-week luxury cruise that evening, paid for in part by the enormous bonus Archibald Hightower had given them.

Back in Vancouver, Amina and Dixon had given interviews to every news outlet in the world. They were in talks to make a Netflix documentary about their experiences with the agent, tentatively titled *Killer Representation*, which Cartier thought was too hard to say. They had abandoned the Deep State and now ran their social media accounts under their first names: Amina and Dixon. The duo's new focus was on telling true crime stories from the point of view of the survivors, "preferably with a celebrity angle," according to their bio. They'd been signed as models for a luxury fashion company's new Redemption campaign. Amina had texted Cartier several times to say that she and Dixon were in counselling and to suggest the same therapist for Cartier when she got home. Dixon had not been in touch.

Overall, the two of them seemed to be recovering well, in a very modern and online sort of way, thought Helen. She was less sure about Cartier.

"How do you feel?" she asked Cartier for what seemed like the hundredth time since they met.

"Kind of lost, to be honest," said Cartier. "But also okay."

"Are you going to stay off the internet?"

"Highly doubtful," said Cartier. "I mean, it's sort of where I live."

"Fair enough."

"Thanks for everything," said Cartier Hightower, and she gave Helen a big hug.

Helen watched Cartier and Nigel get in the car, which was also packed full of Pekingese. Soon they had disappeared down the road. Then Helen got in the Range Rover. After she dropped it off in Vancouver, she would return to the Levines in West Vancouver, where she would get better acquainted with her new horse. She'd be back to living the life she loved, at least for a time. *Pleasant*, she thought. *Pleasant*.

ACKNOWLEDGEMENTS

To begin, thanks to everyone who wrote to me about *Mindful of Murder*. Did I seriously start an acknowledgments list by thanking *fan* mail? Yes, yes, I did, because those letters meant the world to me. Hearing from those of you who connected deeply with the book meant a great deal, and your enthusiasm for ultra-calm Helen is surely what encouraged my marvellous editor, Iris Tupholme, to ask me to write two more books in the series. It has been a lifelong dream of mine to write a mystery series and good lord, it's happening! So thank you, readers, and thank you to all the booksellers who put the book in people's hands.

As always, I am grateful for the support of my agent, Hilary McMahon at Westwood Creative Artists and everyone at HarperCollins Canada for helping me to get things right and for making beautiful books. I am particularly grateful for Canaan Chu, production editor; Catherine Dorton, copy editor; Sue Sumeraj, proofreader; my publicist, Shayla Leung; Lisa Rundle, who organizes and produces the audiobook recordings; and everyone else whose hard work, thoughtful attention, and skill goes into making a manuscript a finished book.

My test readers are always on the mark and their feedback once again saved the day. Thank you to Susin Nielsen, Andrew Gray, Anicka Quin, Bill Juby, Sandra Thomson, and John Hill. You are all top-notch brains and you are miraculously able to deliver hard truths so diplomatically that a person barely feels the magnitude of what is needed until at least an hour later.

Thanks to Grant MacPherson, elite windsurfer and an ace on boards of all kinds, for the advice on kitesurfing. All mistakes in that regard are mine. Sigh.

The character of Helen would not exist but for the teachings and example of my spiritual teachers and mentors. *I'm* not particularly spiritual, though I try. Anyone who has ever seen me drive knows there is plenty of work to be done on that front. I continue to learn about the dhamma from Mia Tremblay who steadfastly leads our Nanaimo sangha, and from the amazing teachers at Vipassana Hawaii: Michele McDonald, Steven Smith, Jesse Maceo Vega Frey, and Darine Monroy. Jesse, in particular, has been endlessly patient and generous in answering my questions about Buddhism. He may not know this, but I consider him Helen's personal advisor. Another special thanks to Jake Davis, who helped me navigate the suttas and who is another powerful dhamma teacher.

I must also take a moment to acknowledge my most excellent husband, James, who doesn't complain that I spend half my time with people who do not exist, and my niece, Emily, who is generally excellent, effervescent, and inspiring. I appreciate her insistence that I join the world of people who do exist. Thanks also to the rest of my family, and my students, who are endlessly entertaining and inspiring.

And finally, thanks to all the influencers, TikTok, and YouTube stars who provided such a wealth of creative material for others to enjoy, as well as my friends on social media. I had a fantastic time researching this book. For once, I wasn't just wasting time when I got on the endless scroll.